MAIL ORDER BRIDE SERIES
NO. 5
1855
USA
AL & JOANNA LACY

RANSOM OF LOVE

Ransom
of
Love

MAIL ORDER 5

AL & JOANNA LACY

Multnomah®Publishers *Sisters, Oregon*

This is a work of fiction. The characters, incidents, and dialogues are products of the authors' imagination and are not to be construed as real. Any resemblance to actual events or persons, living or dead, is entirely coincidental.

RANSOM OF LOVE
Mail Order Bride Series #5
Published by Multnomah Publishers, Inc.

© 2000 by ALJO PRODUCTIONS, INC.
International Standard Book Number: 0-7394-0946-8

Cover illustration by Vittorio Dangelico
Design by Kirk DouPonce/David Uttley Design

Scriptures are from: *The Holy Bible,* King James Version

Multnomah is a trademark of Multnomah Publishers, Inc., and is registered in the U.S. Patent and Trademark Office. The colophon is a trademark of Multnomah Publishers, Inc.

Printed in the United States of America

For information:
MULTNOMAH PUBLISHERS, INC.
POST OFFICE BOX 1720
SISTERS, OREGON 97759

This book is lovingly dedicated to our special friend and authors representative,

Penny Whipps.

Without your help, our job would be much more difficult. Thank you, Penny, for always being there for us. We love you.

3 JOHN 2

For there is one God,
and one mediator between God and men,
the man Christ Jesus;
Who gave himself a ransom for all,
to be testified in due time.

1 TIMOTHY 2:5–6

Prologue

The Encyclopaedia Britannica reports that the mail order business, also called direct mail marketing, "is a method of merchandising in which the seller's offer is made through mass mailing of a circular or catalog, an advertisement in a newspaper or magazine, and in which the buyer places his order by mail."

Britannica goes on to say that "mail order operations have been known in the United States in one form or another since Colonial days, but not until the latter half of the nineteenth century did they assume a significant role in domestic trade."

Thus the mail order market was known when the big gold rush took place in this country in the late 1840s and 1850s. At that time, prospectors, merchants, and adventurers raced from the East to the newly discovered goldfields in the West. One of the most famous was the California gold rush in 1848–49, when discovery of gold at Sutter's Mill, near Sacramento, brought more than forty thousand men to California. Though few struck it rich, their presence stimulated economic growth and lured even more men to the West.

The married men who had come looking for gold sent for their wives and children, desiring to stay and make their home in the West. Most of the gold rush men were single and also desired to stay in the West, but there were about two hundred men for every single woman. By applying the mail order concept to their personal lives, they began advertising in Eastern newspapers for women to come West and marry them. Thus was born the "mail order bride."

Women by the hundreds began answering the ads. Often when men and their prospective brides corresponded, they agreed to send no photographs. They would accept each other by the spirit of the letters rather than on a physical basis. Others, of course, did exchange photographs.

The mail order bride movement accelerated after the Civil War ended in April 1865. This was a time when men went West by the thousands to make their fortune on the frontier. Many of the marriages turned out well, while others ended in desertion or divorce.

As we write this series, we will tell stories that grip the heart, bring some smiles, and maybe wring out some tears. As always, we will weave in the gospel of Jesus Christ and run threads of timeless Bible truths into the stories to apply to our lives today.

Introduction

SLAVERY—THE KIDNAPPING AND SELLING of human beings to the wealthy for low-cost labor—goes back to early human history. We read about it in the early Bible days. Slavery thrived in ancient times among the Jews and, as time passed, found its way into Africa, Greece, Italy, Germany, Spain, and throughout the Roman Empire, especially around the Mediterranean Sea.

The word "slave" is derived from "Slav." The Slavs were victims for centuries in Europe, having been captured from the eastern Adriatic shores and trade routes along the Black Sea. In central Europe, the use of slaves began to fade toward the end of the eighth century and was extinct by the middle of the fourteenth century. It was revived after 1492, at the start of the American empire. By this time, all slaves in Europe, Great Britain, and America were Negroes who had been captured in Africa by the Spanish and Portuguese.

When the supply of Slavs began to fail because of the fall of Constantinople to the Turks in the late fifteenth century, the wealthy all over Europe turned their full attention to the blacks in Africa. In 1508, shiploads of African Negroes were being sent to America and the Caribbean by the Spaniards. By 1540, King Charles V of Spain tried to halt the practice, decreeing the end of African slavery and the beginning of freedom for the Negroes. The decree failed. At the same time, the British decided to get into the slave business.

In 1556, Sir John Hawkins sailed from England to the West African coast and sent some eighty soldiers to kidnap Negroes, load them on ships, and sail to America where they would sell them to the wealthy rice and cotton plantation owners in the deep South.

In 1652, Dutch explorers discovered the wealth of the land in South Africa and reported it to their government leaders. Soon, Dutchmen swarmed the state, pushed the native South Africans off their land, and established cattle and sheep ranches, as well as grain farms and vineyards. They soon began to capture the South African Negroes and force them to work on the ranches and farms and in the vineyards. Thus, South Africa had become a slave state.

In 1795, Great Britain and Holland were in a heavy dispute. In the course of the Napoleonic Wars, South Africa was captured by British forces, and the English government prevailed in the state. Slavery continued full force in South Africa until General Harry Smith became British high commissioner in 1845. As the years passed, Harry Smith had a growing desire to rid the state of slavery and establish a more respectable economy.

In 1854, Smith began to encourage the ranchers, farmers, and vineyard owners to sell their slaves to the American slave traders, then hire help at a low rate and not have the expense of feeding, clothing, and housing slaves. The American slave traders were thrilled to purchase the slaves at a very low price and take them to America where they would sell at a huge profit.

ON A HOT, HUMID DAY in February 1855, thirteen British soldiers rode northeastward through the rugged, mountainous area of Great Karroo in Cape Province, South Africa. Behind the mounted men were four military wagons that rattled along the rough and dusty road.

Captain Charles Jameson, who was every inch a soldier, led the party. On either side were Lieutenants Deighton Ross and Peter Waldman. They sat their saddles straight backed, military style, emulating their leader.

The setting sun was at their backs, heating them with its blazing rays and streaking the mountains and forests around them with a golden hue. The men were looking forward to the sun's disappearance, even though the night air would be extremely warm and humid. But at least they would get a reprieve from the fiery heat of the sun.

As they climbed a steep hill, Lieutenant Waldman said, "Captain, do you still plan to pick up the slaves from the Rhodes ranch tonight?"

"Yes," Captain Jameson said. "That way we can move back toward Cape Town and be there about midnight. I estimate our arrival at the ranch to be eight o'clock. It won't take long to load our cargo in the wagons, and we can start back by nine o'clock.

"When we stop, we'll have a good start on tomorrow's ride, and we'll have them housed with the rest of Thomas Green's slaves when the ship docks in Table Bay five days from now. It's supposed to be in about eight o'clock that night. With two hundred miles to go, I want to be sure we're back before that ship docks."

At that moment, the column reached the summit of the steep hill. A deep misty valley spread out below them and sloped up the other side in little ridges like waves of the sea. The ridges were dotted with clumps of brush and trees, and to the right and left rose tree-fringed, craggy mountain peaks.

Lieutenant Waldman had recently been assigned to the South African British army. He had never seen Africa before. He fixed his gaze on the peaks that were quickly losing their golden color and clicked his tongue. "Captain, those mountains sure are beautiful. Do they get snow caps in the winter?"

"Most certainly. The snow will start in late May. During June, July, and August it will blanket the high country and last until October."

Waldman chuckled. "It's still hard for me to get used to being below the equator, sir. It sure seems backwards to have summer in December, January, and February. Right now, the folks back home in good old England are wearing heavy coats, mufflers, and gloves."

"It took me about two years to get used to it, Lieutenant," Deighton Ross said.

The captain laughed. "Well, gentlemen, I've been here for almost four years, and I haven't even begun to get used to it!"

One of the men behind them called out, "I've been here for ten years, Captain, and I still think it should be snowing up there on those peaks right now."

A rumble of laughter moved through the ranks along the column.

There were a few moments of silence, then Lieutenant Waldman said, "As you know, sir, this is my first time to pick up slaves for shipment to America. Are there other wealthy men like this Thomas Green buying slaves?"

"Oh, yes. I know of eight men. And they're getting richer with each shipload of slaves they take to the United States. There's plenty of work on the rice and cotton plantations in what is known as the Deep South."

"So Thomas Green has already paid rancher Kent Rhodes for the sixty-two slaves we're picking up?"

"No. Mr. Green's Cape Town representative, Arthur Pendleton, gave me the money to pass on. Pendleton made the deal with Rhodes back in December, just after Green was here to take a shipload of slaves back with him. The ship holds six hundred slaves, and I'm sure it will be full again this time. At the rate Thomas Green and the other slave traders are taking Negroes out of South Africa, we'll soon see the fulfillment of the plan to rid this state of slavery."

As the last light faded, a full moon began lifting its round rim above the mountain peaks to the east.

Lieutenant Peter Waldman pondered the captain's words, then said, "Sir, refresh my memory, please. The newspapers have carried reports for some time that British high commissioner Harry Smith has been working hard to end slavery in South Africa, and that Queen Victoria backs him enthusiastically, as does Parliament. Was the idea of encouraging South African ranchers, farmers, and the like to sell their slaves to American slave traders the high commissioner's idea, or did it come from the queen herself?"

"As far as I know, the idea was totally Mr. Smith's, Lieutenant. However, it certainly sounds like our queen, doesn't it?"

"Yes, sir."

"I agree," said Lieutenant Ross. "When I read about it, I thought her Majesty just might be behind it. The wording, 'rid South Africa of slavery and give it a more respectable economy' sure sounds like her, doesn't it?"

"Aye, that it does," said the captain. "Either way, I'm glad to be doing my part to rid this state and its provinces of slavery. Of course, Transvaal Province hasn't had slavery in decades, so we haven't had to go there."

"Too bad the Americans are willing to purchase the slaves," said Waldman. "If there were no market for them, it seems to me the ranchers, farmers, and vineyard owners here would have to free their slaves, then hire them as workers and pay them wages."

Jameson sighed. "I think the Americans will have to learn the hard way, like pharaoh in the Bible days, that God doesn't look with favor on people who make chattel of other human beings."

The rising moon cast deep shadows over the hills and mountains. Lieutenant Waldman squinted as he ran his gaze over the moonlit hills ahead of them and said, "Captain, sir, what are those dark spots up there?"

"Small patches of forest."

"Indeed? They certainly are beautiful in the moonlight." He stared at the dark blots, which seemed almost to float in the atmosphere above the hills and mountainsides. They had no clearly defined margins, and the pale silver light gave them the sensation of wavering and shimmering. As the column moved along the winding road, some of the dark blots faded and vanished from view. "What a sight!" Waldman said. "This is wonderful country . . . except for the humidity."

"Comes from being relatively close to the equator," Captain Jameson said. "Even on the mountaintops you can feel the oppressive dampness in the air. England has dampness, too, but it isn't suffocating like this."

"Not at all like this," Ross said. "What I'd give to feel some good, cool, wet British air right now!"

Darkness had fallen over the Kent Rhodes ranch, and all of the slaves were in their cabins as the moon began its majestic climb into the night sky.

In one cabin, a nineteen-year-old slave stood at the window without glass and looked out at the moonlit hills. He could see the cattle milling about in the fields. Calves were bawling for their mothers, and the deeper bawl of the mothers rode the air.

He turned to look at his parents. A single candle burned on the small table.

"Father, shouldn't we make an attempt at getting away?"

Robert, who was barely forty years old, said, "No, Benjamin. Like Master Rhodes said when he told us of our bein' sold to the American slave trader, if we run, the soldiers will hunt us down. When they catch us, they will be angry and no doubt beat us severely for running away. It is best that we go to America with the other slaves."

Nannie looked at her tall, handsome, muscular son as he jutted his jaw. "Benjamin, you must not fight this. The British soldiers are told to deliver us to the ship in Cape Town, no matter what. Do you want to be crippled for the rest of your life? You remember what we heard about those slaves who tried to run away down by Laingsburg, don't you?"

"Yes, Mother. But—"

"There is no need to argue, son," said Robert. "It is too dangerous to try to escape. We have no choice but to be transported with the other slaves who have been sold to the American slave traders. Better to do this than to end up crippled or dead because we resisted them."

Benjamin rubbed a hand across his forehead. "But, Father, we can escape them if we go now. We can go to Transvaal and obtain jobs from whites and live like them. They don't have slavery in Transvaal anymore."

Robert sighed. "Benjamin, Transvaal is seven hundred miles from here.

We would never make it. We would be caught and punished severely, and still be put on a ship to America."

"But, Father, there are only so many British soldiers. South Africa is a huge state. We are natives here. We know the land. I know we can—"

Benjamin's words were cut off by the sound of men's voices. They heard the rattle of harness, the creak of wheels, and the dull thump of hooves on the soft ground inside the circle of cabins.

Robert hurried to the window and peered out. "It is them," he said. "They are here to take us to Cape Town."

Nannie rushed up beside him and looked out. By the light of the several lanterns in the soldiers' hands, she saw Kent Rhodes and his foreman, Richard Lawford, walk toward the three British officers.

Benjamin moved up close to his parents. "It is too late now to escape from here. But it is a long way to Cape Town. We will be on the road for days. We will find a way to escape."

Robert laid a hand on his son's muscular shoulder. "Benjamin, we must not attempt an escape. As I have already said, we could never get away from the soldiers."

Benjamin started to argue once more but then held his words. When he had figured out a way to escape the soldiers on the journey, he would inform his parents.

The soldiers were already guiding slaves toward the wagons. A few small children were crying.

When they saw Richard Lawford coming toward their cabin, Nannie took hold of her husband's hand and said, "Let us go. It is best that he does not have to tell us to come out."

Soon Benjamin and his parents were climbing into one of the army wagons. Rancher Kent Rhodes stood close by, stuffing money into his shirt pocket. Suddenly Rhodes looked up and met Benjamin's eyes. Benjamin held his gaze a few seconds, then looked away.

When all the slaves were in the wagons, Rhodes stood beside the captain so that all could see him. He frowned at the sound of crying children and said, "Mothers, make your children stop crying now. This is Captain Charles Jameson of her Majesty's royal army. He has a few words for you before the journey begins."

As a couple of babies continued to wail, Jameson explained that they would travel until midnight, then make camp. There was enough food and water to take care of them on the journey to Cape Town. He spoke crisply, telling them there would be severe punishment for anyone who tried to get away. In fact, the hard labor required by their new owners in the United States would be pleasurable compared to the punishment they would take if they attempted an escape.

The army officers shook hands with Rhodes and his foreman, then mounted their horses and led the procession southwestward.

As the wagon Benjamin rode in rocked and bumped along the rough road, he sat on the floor in a corner, his knees pulled up close to his chest, and stared out into the hot, humid night. The moon was a brilliant silver disk, clear edged and beautiful. Beyond the moon, the night sky was a black velvet canopy with countless stars twinkling in their spheres.

Fixing his gaze on the stars, Benjamin moved his lips silently and said, *It must be wonderful to be free to ride your chosen trails through the endless sky. Never to be locked up. Only to have your freedom forever. I wish I could be free like you.*

As the wagon rolled on, dipping into valleys and rising to the next crest, Robert and Nannie held hands. They rode silently, looking at their son from time to time.

At midnight, Captain Jameson called for the wagons to halt and make a circle in a shallow valley. Since the wagons were well loaded, he suggested that some of the slaves sleep on the ground, and he warned them once more of the penalty for trying to escape. His men built a fire in the center of the circle.

As everyone else was settling down to sleep, the soldiers assigned to the first shift began to pace the perimeter of the circle, their eyes alert and muskets ready.

Benjamin lay next to his parents on the soft grass.

The flickering firelight allowed Nannie to see her son's wakefulness. "Son, you must not lie awake all night. Please go to sleep."

"I will try, Mother. Good night . . . I love you."

Nannie smiled. "I love you, too."

Sleep, however, eluded the young slave. He watched the flames of the fire dance in the light wind. From time to time he saw the soldiers move into his line of sight as they patrolled the circle.

Benjamin pondered what it would be like to be free to choose his own destiny. He had been well educated by British teachers who had been hired by rancher Kent Rhodes. He knew English better than he knew the language of his tribe. If he could have the chance to make it on his own in

Transvaal, he knew he would make his mark in the world. He would give his parents reason to be proud of him.

But what could he ever become as a slave? He would spend his life using the strength in his body to make some American plantation owner rich. Then he would die and be forgotten as soon as they placed his body in the ground. Wasn't there more to life than this? Had he only been born to be a slave for some white man, then die and pass out of existence?

He had heard white folks talk about a place above the sky called heaven. It was supposed to be much better than earth with all of its sickness, pain, and sorrow. He had heard one white man say there weren't any graveyards in heaven. And nobody ever got sick.

Do rich people have slaves in heaven? Benjamin wondered. *This God they talk about . . . if He really exists, does He want people to be slaves? Or does He want everybody to be free?*

Everyone else seemed to be sleeping around him, but the night passed slowly for Benjamin. It wasn't yet dawn, but it had been some time since the soldiers had added any logs to the fire. Now there was only a great heap of red coals with small flames flickering around the edges. The wind picked up and fanned the embers, whipping flakes of white ashes upward.

Soon there was gray light over the mountain peaks to the east. Benjamin's eyes finally closed in sleep. He was just drifting off when a soldier moved about the circle and shouted for everyone to get up.

It was another hot, humid day in Cape Town when the column of mounted soldiers and creaking wagons pulled into the compound of the Old Supreme Court buildings. The slaves were ushered into a log structure where hundreds of other Negro men, women, and children were crammed.

When Benjamin saw the other slaves, he felt his stomach tighten.

Captain Charles Jameson collected his group of slaves just inside the door of the large building and said, "You will all stay here until the ship comes in tonight. Mr. Green, your new owner, will come and talk to you. There are two floors of rooms in this building, so there will be enough space to sleep. But until Mr. Green has come, you will remain here with the other slaves."

Inside the temporary prison, the incessant wailing of babies and the crying of children filled the air. Their cries were mixed with the laughter of older children who had found space to play.

17

Benjamin and his parents sat on the floor and talked to a slave family from a sheep ranch near Port Elizabeth. Benjamin found them as resigned to becoming slaves in America as were his parents.

The man seemed to read Benjamin's mind as he said, "It's no use to even think of trying to escape anywhere on this journey to Cape Town. I know two slaves who tried it on the way here. Don't you know, they were caught by the British soldiers and punished severely. One of them died a few hours later, and the other one suffered a broken leg. The soldiers did nothing to relieve his pain."

When the man and his wife left to wander about the building under the watchful eyes of the dozen or so British military guards, Benjamin said, "Father . . . Mother . . . there has to be a way out of this. Perhaps after we are in our room overhead?"

Robert shook his head. "Benjamin, did you not listen to what we were just told about one slave being killed and the other one maimed? Is this what you want for us?"

"No, Father. I want us to escape, to go to Transvaal and live as free people. If we do not do something, we will be slaves for the rest of our lives."

"But if we make this attempt, son," said Nannie, "and we fail, we could end up dead like the one slave . . . or even with broken limbs. We must not try it."

Benjamin fought the volcano-like emotion rising within him. He quietly nodded and told himself he would have to wait until he had a workable plan—a plan that his parents could see would work.

At nightfall, after dinner, the soldiers lit lanterns in the slave lodge, and the British officer in charge of the guards called for all of the slaves to gather in one place near the main door and sit on the floor. When they were seated, he went to the door and said something to someone outside. In a few moments, two men appeared. The larger man stood at the front of the crowd and said, "I know that most of you understand English, but if you have some friends who speak only your native language, make sure they understand what I say. My name is Thomas Green. I am your temporary owner. Tomorrow morning at dawn, you will be put aboard the American slave ship *Berkeley,* which is docked in Table Bay.

"You will be taken across the Atlantic Ocean to the United States of America. You will dock and leave the ship in the coastal city of Charleston, South Carolina, where some of you will be sold to plantation owners

whom I choose. The rest of you will be auctioned off to whatever plantation owners are willing to pay the highest price for you."

Green went on to explain that he had a crew of men who would be
aboard ship to make sure they were fed well and obeyed all rules, which
would be explained when they were on the ship. Then he nodded to the
man with him and they moved outside together.

When the door closed behind them, Green said to Arthur Pendleton,
"As usual, Arthur, you keep an eye on things here. I'll be back in the
morning when it's time to move them to the ship."

"Will do," said the younger man.

Green started to walk away, then stopped. "Oh, Arthur. That slave
with the broken leg . . ."

"Yes, sir?"

"See if you can get a couple of the soldiers to put some kind of a splint
on it. If he's mobile at all when we get to Charleston, he'll still bring a few
dollars."

"I'll see to it, sir."

That evening, after the slaves had been fed, they were allowed to go to the
second and third floors of the slave lodge. The rooms were small, but there
were enough of them to allow individual families to occupy a room privately if they chose to do so.

As soon as Robert, Nannie, and Benjamin were in a room on the
second floor, Benjamin went to the window, which was nailed shut. He
peered through dirty glass at the space between the slave lodge and the next
building in the compound. There were kerosene lanterns at both ends of
the building.

"Benjamin, what are you thinking?" Robert asked.

"I was thinking that it is not very far down to the ground from this
window."

Nannie glanced at her husband and sighed.

"But there will be soldiers guarding this building all night," said Robert. "And haven't you noticed the window is nailed shut?"

"Yes, Father, but the nails are driven in at an angle, and they are not
driven deep. With a little work, I can loosen them and have the window
open. We can drop down to the roof over the back door of the building,
then drop to the ground."

"But, son, what about the soldiers?" Nannie said.

"They are few in number, Mother. They will have to walk patrols. This will no doubt mean there are spaces of time when they are not on this side of the building. We will make our move when we can run into the shadows of the building behind this one. The fence around the compound is only chest high to Father and me. We can get over it easily and escape. We will go to Transvaal."

"But Transvaal is so far away, son," said Robert. "It will be a long journey, and we will have to avoid the soldiers who will be on our trail."

"It is worth it to me to try," said the nineteen-year-old. "Do you not feel the same way, Father?"

Robert looked at Nannie and sighed.

She smiled grimly. "We do, don't we?"

"Yes," said Robert. "We do."

It was nearly three o'clock in the morning when Benjamin watched the guard make his round along the rear of the building, then turn the corner at the far end. He had counted the seconds before the guard would reappear on their side. It was a short space of time, but it was sufficient for someone who was desperate.

When Benjamin was on the ground, his father lifted his mother down and Benjamin assisted her to the ground. When Nannie's feet touched earth, Robert scrambled down. The three of them made a dash into the deep shadows of the next building. When the guard vanished around the corner again, they darted to the other side of the compound and soon were over the fence and outside the compound.

They kept to the shadows and made their way along the streets that were dimly lit with kerosene lanterns. Finally, they reached the wall that surrounded the Castle of Good Hope, the city's oldest monument. They huddled in the shadows to catch their breath, then hurried on.

Soon they were running along the shore of Table Bay in the pale light of a moon partially covered by clouds. When they reached a small hut along the shore, they paused for another breather, then dashed around the steep slopes of Table Mountain. After a few moments' rest at the tip of Table Mountain, they pressed on toward Devil's Peak, then headed northeast toward the rolling hill country.

At sunrise the next morning, Thomas Green was standing near the front door of the slave lodge, observing the armed guards ushering the slaves along the street toward the docks at Table Bay. He was in conversation with Captain John Orr, the officer in charge of the army guard, but kept his eyes on Arthur Pendleton as he checked off the slave families and individuals from his list when they passed by him and gave their names.

When the last of the slaves had left the building, Pendleton turned to his employer and frowned. Green excused himself to Captain Orr and said, "What's wrong?"

The younger man shook his head as he studied the list. "Sir, three slaves are missing. One named Robert, his wife, Nannie, and their son, Benjamin."

"Are you sure?"

"Positive."

Green motioned to Captain Orr and told him of the three slaves who were unaccounted for. Two guards were sent to the room the trio had occupied. When they found that the window frame had been removed, they reported it to Green and their commander.

A short time later, Orr had dispatched a dozen mounted soldiers from army headquarters across town to search for the runaway slaves.

2

IT WAS ALMOST NOON when Benjamin and his parents stumbled down a grassy embankment toward a river near the town of Worcester.

The sky was clear, and the oppressive heat seemed to have weight and substance. Perspiration plastered their clothing to their bodies. The sight of cool water in the heat-blasted hills made them hasten to it.

"We cannot stay here very long," Robert cautioned them. "Just enough time to cool us a bit. If the soldiers are close behind, they will find our tracks in the grass on the embankment. We must swim downstream and leave the river on the other bank."

"I need to cool off here," said Nannie. "The water will help my strength to return. You two go down where you want to cross the river. I will join you when it is time to climb out on the opposite bank."

Benjamin followed his parents into the waist-deep water, looking back up the long embankment for any sign of pursuit. When he turned his head back again, he saw his father beneath the surface, paddling downstream. His mother was in the river up to her chin, which accentuated the fear in her dark eyes.

"We will call for you soon, Mother," said Benjamin, and plunged in, swimming toward his father. The coolness of the water rejuvenated him.

Nannie watched her two men for a few moments, then dipped herself all the way down, holding her breath and enjoying the cool river. She let the air out of her lungs slowly, sending tiny bubbles upward. When her lungs were almost empty, she stood up, raising her head out of the water and drew in a fresh breath of air.

She repeated the dipping several times, staying down as long as she could. When she had expelled nearly all the air in her lungs once more, she

23

raised up and broke the surface, enjoying the refreshingly cool water while drawing in the hot, humid air into her lungs.

Some fifty yards downstream she saw her two men going under the surface again. She decided to go beneath the surface one last time. When she came up seconds later, she shook her head, throwing water from her long, black hair. Little beads glistened in her hair and on her bronze face. Her eyes were closed as she sought to absorb the last vestige of the fortifying coolness that clung to her skin.

A sudden strange sound brought her eyes open, and a gasp escaped her lips when she saw British soldiers standing on the bank. Her chest felt like it was being crushed in a vise as the fact that she was caught penetrated her mind.

"Where are the men?" demanded the lieutenant in charge.

Nannie could see downstream from the corner of her eye. Robert and Benjamin evidently were still submerged. Without replying, she looked up at the lieutenant, fearfully meeting his gaze.

"Come up here, woman!" he commanded, motioning to her.

When she didn't move, he shouted to his soldiers, "Two of you get her out of the river! The rest of you find the men. They're somewhere close by."

Nannie backtracked, shaking her head, as the two soldiers came after her. She felt a scream tear upward in her throat as they seized her arms and dragged her toward the bank. She screamed again and one of them backhanded her across the mouth.

"Shut up, woman! Scream again and I'll break your jaw!"

When they neared the bank, the soldiers lifted Nannie out of the water none too gently and tossed her through the air. She let out a short, piercing cry of pain when her hip struck a rock and she rolled on the rough, hard surface of the bank. Her momentum caused the sharp rocks to scrape her bare arms and face.

As soon as Robert and Benjamin heard her cry they turned their heads and found themselves facing a half dozen black muzzles.

They were forced up the bank at gunpoint, but when they saw Nannie sitting on the ground with blood on her arms and face, they ran to her. Robert knelt down beside her and mutely looked into her eyes, then folded her in his arms.

When the lieutenant came toward them, Benjamin stood up to meet him.

"She didn't obey me when I told her to come out of the river," the lieutenant said.

"Let my mother tell us about it," said Benjamin.

"She's not to speak to you, and neither you nor your father are to talk to her or to each other until you are aboard the ship. Mr. Green is holding the ship because of you, and he's very angry."

Benjamin stiffened. "My mother is bleeding. We need to wash her wounds."

"Not now. The three of you will ride aboard the horses of my men. Let's go."

When the soldiers and the runaway slaves arrived at the dock, Thomas Green met them at the gangplank.

The cuts on Nannie's face and arms had stopped bleeding and were beginning to scab. But Robert and Benjamin held her up between them because of the injury to her hip.

Green's words were almost a roar. "How dare you try to escape! I paid good money to Kent Rhodes for you, and you had no right to run away!"

The soldiers stood around Green and the slaves in a tight circle.

The slavemaster stepped closer. "I should have all three of you whipped for this! But I won't. Consider yourselves very fortunate. I need all three of you in good condition when we arrive in South Carolina, or I can't get top dollar for you."

Green ran his gaze over the physique of young Benjamin and grinned stonily. "You will bring a very good price, boy. I'll put you on the auction block for sure."

Benjamin frowned. "Mr. Green," he said, attempting to hold his voice low and level, "will whoever buys me allow me to bring my parents along? They will buy them, too, will they not?"

Green laughed hollowly. "I doubt that, boy."

"But I do not want to be separated from my parents."

"What you want and what you'll get will be two different things."

Green turned to the soldiers and barked out the words, "Take them aboard."

"I will have to carry my wife," said Robert.

Green nodded curtly. "All right, all right. Hurry up. I need to get this ship on the ocean."

Robert lifted Nannie into his arms and said to his son in a hushed voice, "Please, Benjamin, do not rebel against Mr. Green. It will only cause you pain. If he chooses to separate us in America, there is nothing we can do about it. Your mother and I do not want that to happen, but we have discussed it between us. If you fight Mr. Green on it, you will be beaten and still he will have his way. Please do not resist him."

Benjamin hesitated for a few seconds, then nodded.

As Robert held Nannie in his arms and walked up the gangplank, his head was bent low. The run for freedom had failed. They were doomed to a life of slavery in a strange land and probably would be separated from their son forever.

Benjamin, however, followed his parents up the gangplank with his proud, handsome head held high, realizing that for a few hours he had been a free man. He promised himself that someday . . . somehow . . . he would again be free.

A crewman with a whip in his hand stepped up to Robert and said, "Follow me." Glancing at Benjamin, he tossed his head in the direction of the ship's bow. "You, too, boy."

Benjamin did not like the term "boy," but he held his peace and followed. Slaves all along the deck watched as the small family walked past. Benjamin nodded when he saw two families from the Rhodes ranch. They afforded him grim smiles.

As they neared the bow, the crewman led them through a metal door at deck level and along a narrow passageway that led to a series of smaller metal doors. When they came to a room where the door stood open, the crewman stopped and gestured into its cramped interior.

"This is your room for the trip," he said. "There are two cots. One of you will have to sleep on the floor."

"I will sleep on the floor, Father," said Benjamin.

Robert did not comment as he laid Nannie on the nearest cot.

Soon the ship's big steam engines were rumbling beneath the deck, the screw propeller at the stern began churning water, and the ship pulled out of the harbor under the direction of the ship's captain, Spencer Kimball.

The sun bore down from a cloudless sky, reflecting its brilliant glare off the deep blue water.

On the second day out, the sky was still clear, and even though there was water in every direction, the sun's heat punished the slaves who were swabbing the deck and the narrow walkways on the upper levels. They worked under the watchful eyes of the crewmen.

Nannie was allowed to sit and observe as her husband and son wielded mops and perspired heavily in the sultry air. There were water barrels positioned along both sides of the deck, each one well guarded by two of Green's men. When the sweating slaves asked for water, they were given only minimal amounts and sent back to work.

Thomas Green and Spencer Kimball looked on from the shade of the ship's bridge on the third level.

By midafternoon, some of the women and older Negro men were feeling ill from the combination of exertion, stifling heat, and lack of water. An elderly woman passed out and fell to the deck. Seconds later, an old man who was working near Benjamin and his father collapsed.

Robert immediately knelt beside him and called for water.

A crewman named Gerald Rapp stepped close and said, "The water's rationed. He had half a cup an hour ago. That's all he gets for another hour."

"That isn't enough!" Benjamin cried. "You can't expect any of us to—"

Rapp's face contorted with rage. "You're in no position to tell us what to do, boy! And if you want to address me, you call me *Mister* Rapp, understand?"

Robert laid a hand on his son's arm. "Calm down, son."

Hearing his father's soft-spoken words, Benjamin said, "Mr. Rapp, sir, I don't understand why the water is rationed to us. You can't expect us to work like this without plenty of water to drink."

Crewman Evan Cropper edged up beside Rapp and said, "Gerald, you don't have to explain anything to this low-down slave." He turned to Benjamin with a scowl and said, "Get back to work, boy!"

"It won't hurt these slaves to know the situation, Evan," said Rapp. Then he said to Benjamin, "We can only give you slaves a certain amount of water because we only carry a certain number of barrels aboard ship. We have to make sure we don't run out before we reach South Carolina."

Benjamin swallowed hard. "I don't see any crewmen passing out. How much water do *you* get?"

Evan Cropper moved up to stand nose to nose with Benjamin. "I told you to get back to work. Do it or you'll feel this whip."

Benjamin met his gaze but said nothing.

"Come on, son," said Robert. "Let us get back to work."

Cropper moved back a couple of feet. "Good advice, Dad. Do it, boy!"

The old man on the deck was coming around. As Benjamin started to bend over him again, Cropper laid a hand on his shoulder. "We'll tend to him. You pick up your mop."

As they moved side by side, Benjamin whispered to his father, "These crewmen are lying. They ration the water to us in such small amounts because they like to see us suffer."

"You are probably right, son, but there is nothing we can do about it. We have a long journey ahead of us. We must make the best of it. Let us do what we are told."

Benjamin glanced up at the bridge and saw Thomas Green and Captain Kimball watching him. Looking back at his father, he said, "I am going to talk to Mr. Green. They must give us more water. Especially the older people. If they do not, some are going to die. Mr. Green has paid money for them. Why would he want them to die?"

Robert bent down to pick up his mop and said, "Benjamin, it will do no good to talk to Mr. Green. He must do it this way on all of his voyages as he carries slaves to the United States."

"But it isn't always this hot, Father."

"I know. But you will only make Mr. Green angry if you take it upon yourself to talk to him."

"I must, Father. I have to do what I can to—"

His words were cut off by the sound of an elderly woman collapsing on the deck near the bow. Two crewmen harshly commanded the slave kneeling over her to get back to work. When the silver-haired old man looked up at them and said he was her husband, they threatened punishment if he disobeyed. There were tears in the old slave's eyes as he backed away and picked up his mop.

"That is enough, Father," said Benjamin. "I am going to talk to Mr. Green."

Before Robert could say another word, Benjamin was threading his way among the slaves swabbing the decks. He reached the metal stairs that went to the other two levels and soon was on the third level, approaching the bridge. Both Green and Kimball saw him coming.

Green scowled at Benjamin and said, "You're supposed to be down there working."

"I know, but I wish to talk to you, Mr. Green."

"About what?"

"This water rationing. Our people need more water in order to work in this heat. Especially the older ones. They must have more. Why do the crew not give them enough?"

A wicked sneer twisted Green's features. "They're acting under my orders. There is a limited supply of water for everyone on board, boy. We must not run out before we reach America. The older slaves will just have to make do with the amount of water allowed."

"Why, then, do you not carry more water on the ship? Starting out with a short supply does not make sense."

"You get back to work!" Green snapped.

Benjamin's muscular body seemed to swell as a hint of fire flashed in his dark eyes.

Green leaned over the railing and called for crewmen Lester Winters and Jack Hensley to come up and escort Benjamin down to the deck.

As the two men raced up the stairs, Benjamin stared intently at Thomas Green and said, "Are my questions so difficult to answer, Mr. Green? I only want my people to be treated as human beings."

Winters and Hensley reached the bridge. Benjamin noticed that Winters was very tall and quite slender. He towered over Benjamin by at least four inches.

Green looked past Benjamin at his two men. "See that he is back to work immediately."

Benjamin gave the slavemaster a quizzical look, then turned and descended the stairs ahead of the two crewmen. When they reached the deck, one of the crewmen at the bow of the ship called out to Thomas Green that the old woman who had collapsed was dead. Benjamin's eyes flicked that direction. He saw the body lying on the deck, next to the railing.

As a moan went up from the slaves, and some began to weep, both Winters and Hensley hurried toward the bow to fortify the other two crewmen who stood over the body.

"Jack . . . Lester . . ." Green called out, "toss the body overboard!"

Winters and Hensley were about to pick up the dead woman when her bent and silver-haired husband began to wave his arms and wail.

"No-o-o!" he cried. "No-o-o! I want to have a service over her body!"

The two crewmen paused and waited for their employer to instruct them.

"Please, Mr. Green," pleaded the old man. "It is not right to just throw my wife's body overboard! We must mourn her death in our way."

"The body has to be buried," said Green. "It will turn bad in a hurry in this heat. We have no choice but to drop it in the ocean. Throw it overboard, men."

A hard, brittle anger flared up within Benjamin. He dashed toward the spot where Green stood and yelled, "No!"

Every eye swung to the broad-shouldered young slave.

Nannie rose from her chair, ignoring the pain in her injured hip, and stared in terrified silence as she saw the look on Thomas Green's face. Her dark luminous eyes were huge in her face, and her lips made a perfect *O* while her mind tried to convey a message to her son.

She took two faltering steps toward the spot where Benjamin was about to confront Thomas Green, then stopped suddenly when she felt a gentle hand on her shoulder. Tilting her head, she looked up to see Robert's eyes on her. A frown creased his brow, and a slight shake of his head kept her from going to her son.

Robert and Nannie watched in dismay as the scene unfolded before them.

Green pointed a stiff finger at Benjamin and said, "Stop right where you are, boy!"

As Benjamin came to a halt, he opened his mouth to speak, but Green was already looking at Winters and Hensley, telling them to throw the body into the sea. The two men obediently bent down to grasp the corpse.

"No!" cried Benjamin, and bolted toward them. The closest to him was Winters, who stood to his full height, bracing himself and doubling up his fists.

Thomas Green's voice cut the air as he called for other crewmen to come and help take the slave below and lock him up.

Jack Hensley leaped in front of Winters and swung a fist at Benjamin's jaw. Benjamin dodged it and shoved the crewman to one side. His strength was enough to send Hensley rolling across the deck.

Lester Winters yelled something at Benjamin and cocked his fists for combat.

"Please, Mr. Green," Benjamin said, "let the old man have the service over his wife's body."

"Take him!" Green shouted at his crewmen. "Lock him up!"

Benjamin felt Lester Winters move up behind him and start to wrap his arms around him. Benjamin's natural reaction was to send an elbow into the man's stomach. The impact sent Winters backpedaling, the breath whooshing out of him. His momentum sent him hard into the railing and over it.

"Lester can't swim!" Hensley cried. "He can't swim!"

Ryan Cropper gripped the rail and looked over, shouting, "Mr. Green, Lester's too close to the ship! The propeller will suck him into its blades!"

While Thomas Green stood frozen to the spot, Benjamin took off his shoes and dived over the side.

Nannie gripped Robert's arm and let out a high-pitched squeal. He quickly hugged her close to his pounding heart.

When Benjamin plunged into the water, Lester Winters was bobbing up and down, gasping and choking. When he saw Benjamin, he let out a wordless wail, waving his arms helplessly.

Benjamin swam toward him with powerful strokes. "Let me get hold of you!" he yelled.

Winters wailed again in abject terror and lunged for Benjamin, wrapping his arms around his neck in a death grip. At the same time, Benjamin saw that the ship was moving past them and the stern was coming up. With it would be the pull of the propeller.

Benjamin rolled over in the water and used all of his strength to swim away from the powerful vortex threatening to pull them toward certain death.

Captain Spencer Kimball pushed and shoved his way through the crowd of slaves to the bridge and shouted through his communication pipe to the engine room, commanding the men down there to cut the steam engines.

Robert and Nannie watched their son swim with all his might and remove Lester Winters and himself from the pull of the propeller, even before the engines were cut. A loud cheer went up from crewmen and slaves alike as they saw Winters and his rescuer bobbing up and down in the water behind the ship.

The ship's crew lowered a lifeboat into the water, and four of Kimball's men rode the boat down. When the lifeboat was back at deck level and the slave and slave crewman stepped from it, the crowd pressed close around them.

Robert and Nannie pushed their way forward until they could throw their arms around Benjamin's soaking wet body. As Robert hugged his son's neck, he whispered, "Son, if Mr. Green shows anger toward you for sending his man over the rail, please do nothing to anger him more."

Benjamin nodded.

A young male slave about Benjamin's age said, "You are a brave one, my friend. I do not think I could have brought myself to dive in and save the man."

Gerald Rapp's eyes flashed fire as he said to the young slave, "Why shouldn't he go in after him? It was Benjamin who knocked Lester overboard!"

One of Captain Kimball's crew frowned at Rapp. "Hey, pal, it wouldn't have happened if your boss would have granted the old man the privilege of having a service over his wife's body. It would have been the decent thing to do."

Green heard his words and said, "What's your name, fella?"

The sailor's face lost color. "Mack Langford, sir."

"Well, Mack, you're right. It *was* the decent thing to do. I was wrong. I should have allowed the old slave to have his service. He can go ahead with the service right now. We'll bury the body at sea when they are finished."

The steam engines were started up again, and the ship went on its way across the vast expanse of blue water. Green said nothing to Benjamin.

The body of the dead slave woman was carried to the wide space on the deck near the stern. While all the slaves partook in the wailing and chanting, Captain Kimball and Thomas Green returned to the bridge.

When they were out of earshot from all others, Kimball said, "Mr. Green, I'm a little puzzled."

"About what?"

"Well . . . why do you purchase elderly slaves and take them to the States? Wouldn't you be better off to leave them in Africa?"

Green smiled. "I don't purchase the old ones, Captain. You see, since the slave owners in South Africa are converting their system to paid help, they don't want the responsibility of the old slaves, so they give them to me free of charge, just to take them off their hands."

Kimball grinned. "So you're able to sell them to the plantation owners?"

"Sure. And I make 100 percent profit off them. Their price to the plantation owners is, of course, lower than the younger ones. But as long as they can do any work at all, the plantation owners will buy them. So . . . if an old slave dies while crossing the Atlantic, I don't lose much."

Kimball grinned again. "I see your point. That's good thinking."

The chanting sounds and the heartrending wails went on for over an hour while the slaves mourned the loss of one of their own. When it was over, Green's crewmen gently lifted the body over the railing and dropped it into the sea.

As the crowd dispersed and Robert was walking his limping wife back to their room, Benjamin picked up his mop and went back to work. Moments later, Lester Winters approached him. "Benjamin, I want to thank you for saving my life."

The young slave dipped the mop into a soapy bucket of seawater. "I'm glad I was able to get to you before the propeller did."

Winters licked his lips nervously. "Well, it amazes me that you would risk your own life to save mine."

"Why?"

Winters cleared his throat. "Well, I . . . ah . . . I'm a white man, and you're a black man."

Benjamin shook his head. "So, is a white man's life not supposed to be important to a black man?"

Winters cleared his throat again. "Well, I thought—"

"Negro people have hearts, too, Mr. Winters. We have feelings just like you white folks do. Why shouldn't I care if you drown or are cut to pieces by a propeller?"

Emotion flooded Lester's face. "I'm sorry. I guess I've just had my brain filled with the wrong ideas. Please forgive me . . . and thank you for saving my life."

When the ship had been on the Atlantic for six days, two of the slaves were feverish and unable to work. Thomas Green called for the captain to look at the slaves and see if he knew what was ailing them.

It took Kimball only minutes to pronounce that the slaves had dysentery. He explained that there was no treatment for it. All they could do was give them plenty of water and hope they lived through it. When Green brought up that they were carrying a limited supply of water, Kimball told him he should still give them plenty. He would put in at Bermuda and replenish the water supply.

By the seventh day, three more slaves had come down with the sickness, including Robert and Nannie.

By the ninth day, some twenty-one slaves were down with dysentery and the water supply was getting seriously low.

The next day, three slaves died and were buried at sea. On the eleventh day, Robert and Nannie were at the point of death. Benjamin labored over them to relieve their suffering and gave them his meager share of water, trying to keep them alive until they reached Bermuda.

As he stood between their cots, he said, "Mother . . . Father . . . you would not have this sickness if we had not been forced at gunpoint to board this ship. If we could live free in Transvaal, as we wanted, you would not be lying here at the point of death. Slavery is a wicked and vile thing. If there *is* a God that lives above the sky and cares about people here on earth, why does He allow this?"

Nannie looked up at him with dull eyes and said weakly, "Please, my son . . . do not become bitter. It will only dry up your heart and take away the goodness in you. Some questions cannot be answered. Just go on being the good son you have always been since you were born to us."

"Yes," said Robert, hardly able to speak. "If we do not live to see America, please remain our kind and generous Benjamin."

That day, more slaves died, and the water supply was now depleted.

On the thirteenth day, Nannie died, and Benjamin wept inconsolably. His father was so sick that he was unaware when Nannie's body was carried out of the room. Neither did he know how Benjamin wept when he saw his mother dropped into the ocean.

The next day, Robert died only moments before the Bermuda islands came into view. Benjamin's heart felt like stone as he watched his father's body sink into the sea just ten miles from Bermuda's main island.

Thomas Green brought two doctors aboard to examine his slaves. When the doctors had completed their examinations, they told Green there were one or two slaves who probably would die yet, but now that he had plenty of water, the others would have a good chance of pulling through.

As the ship steamed away from Bermuda and headed southwest toward South Carolina—still eight hundred miles away—Benjamin and a small group of young slaves sat on the deck and discussed their future in America.

A slave named Wasson told the group he had learned from one of the ship's crew that most of the rice and cotton plantation owners treated their slaves well, and they fed, clothed, and housed them decently. But there were also those who beat their slaves for various reasons, fed them poorly, and made them live like animals in cheap and run-down quarters.

Benjamin ran his gaze over the faces of his fellow Africans and said, "I . . . I believe that if there is a God up there above the sky, someday this loathsome treatment of human beings will surely be brought to an end."

3

THE WINTER OF 1855 was a mild one in South Carolina, and by the second week of March, spring had come with its balmy days and summery nights.

On the Finn Colvin plantation, a few miles inland from Charleston, the wealthy plantation owner stood between two of his barns, glowering at the twenty-nine-year-old slave who was being dragged toward him by Colvin's two sons. A group of slaves stood looking on, fear evident in their widened eyes. Two of the younger women held small babies.

Twenty-three-year-old George and twenty-one-year-old Edward Colvin held the cowering slave as their father said, "Nathaniel, George told me you refused to work in the fields today! Don't you realize we've got to get the spring planting done? What's this stomach problem stuff?"

Nathaniel had been beaten several times during his years at the Colvin plantation. His lips quivered as he said, "Massa Finn, it's true. My stomach is a-hurtin' me bad today. I tol' Massa George this when he come to the shack an' asked why I wasn't in the fields."

Finn set cool eyes on George and said, "Give me the details."

"Well, Pa, like I told you, when the slaves showed up to work their assigned places in the fields this morning, Matilda was there, ready to do her work, but she said her husband wasn't feeling well . . . that his stomach was hurting him, so he stayed in the shack."

"Go on."

"I got the rest of them started to work, then went immediately to the shack and found Nathaniel, here, washing clothes. I asked him how he could do the wash if his stomach was hurting him. He told me he was doing it for Matilda to help relieve her work load. He said that doing the

37

wash wasn't as hard as working in the fields, so he could do it. That's when I came and told you about it."

Finn glared at Nathaniel with cruel eyes. His voice shook as he said, "If you could wash clothes, Nathaniel, you could plow ground. You need to be punished so this kind of thing doesn't happen again. Take him to the barn, boys!"

At the same time Finn Colvin was dealing with Nathaniel, Martha Colvin was on the front porch of the stately mansion, watching the carriage from the Moore plantation wind its way down the lane toward her.

Her heart leapt with joy at the thought of the weekly visit with her friends Evelyn Moore and Catherine Johnson. The Moores were the Colvins' nearest neighbors to the north, and the Johnsons were their nearest neighbors to the south. Today the ladies would spend their time at the Johnson plantation. Although Martha would have loved to entertain Evelyn and Catherine in her own home, Finn objected because the women were Christians.

Martha recognized Evelyn Moore's favorite male slave at the reins of the carriage as it pulled to a halt. "Good morning, Malcolm," she called.

Malcolm flashed his white teeth in a smile and said, "Mornin', Miz Colvin." Immediately, he was out of the carriage and opening the door for Martha.

Inside were Evelyn's seventeen-year-old daughter, Priscilla, with Priscilla's personal slave, sixteen-year-old Dorena. In the seat just ahead of them, Evelyn sat beside a middle-aged woman who was a stranger to Martha.

"Good morning, everybody," Martha said.

"Good morning," echoed a chorus of greetings.

The ladies and young Priscilla were prettily dressed in spring pastels, and each held a dainty parasol. White lace gloves adorned their hands. Martha was dressed in like manner.

"Martha," Evelyn said, "I want you to meet my cousin from Delaware, Earline Faulkner."

Martha smiled amiably. "I'm so glad to meet you, Earline. Evelyn has mentioned you to me several times."

"Earline is leaving tomorrow," Evelyn said. "She could only stay three days."

"Well, then, I'm glad she could be here today."

"My husband is in New York on business," Earline said, "so I took a train down to Charleston."

Martha nodded, then looked behind her. "So how are you girls doing?"

"Just fine," said Priscilla.

Setting her eyes on Dorena, who was strikingly beautiful, Martha said, "Dorena, that's a pretty dress you are wearing."

Dorena looked down at the dress that had been given to her by Priscilla. "Thank you, ma'am."

As the carriage rolled along the lane toward the road, Evelyn and Martha chatted about the visit they were going to have with Catherine Johnson and her seventeen-year-old daughter, Angeline.

Although Martha Colvin was not a Christian, she loved to spend time with Evelyn and Catherine. The ladies had caused her to think much about her need to know the Lord, but they spoke in a kind and tender manner, never trying to push salvation on her.

The Moores had one heavy heartache in their lives—their twenty-two-year-old son, Lewis, who was not a Christian and was somewhat of a rebel. Talk in the community was that Lewis was living for the day when he would inherit the plantation and run it the way he wanted to. Lewis, Martha told herself, was much like her own husband and two sons. He thought slaves should be kept in fear by frequent beatings, whereas Charles Moore treated his slaves kindly.

The carriage was turning onto the road when Evelyn said, "Earline, I haven't told you this, but Martha and her husband are the most wealthy plantation owners in Charleston County. They are very successful in the cotton business."

"Now, Evelyn . . ." Martha said, shaking her head.

"Well, it's true. Earline, they have the largest plantation . . . eighty-five hundred acres, and they have the most slaves. How many now, Martha? Three hundred and fifty?"

A bit embarrassed, Martha said, "No. Right now, we have three hundred and thirty-one."

Evelyn chuckled again. "So I missed it by a few." Turning to her cousin, she said, "The second most wealthy plantation owners in the county are the Johnsons. Zack and Catherine have eight thousand acres and just under three hundred slaves. No other plantation owners in Charleston County can come close to their wealth."

"Well, now, Evelyn," said Martha, "you and Charles aren't doing so bad. After all, you haven't been in the cotton plantation business near as long as the Colvins and the Johnsons. One day you will pass us up."

"I doubt that, Martha. Both Finn and Zack are hardworking men. They will continue to prosper."

Even as Evelyn spoke, Malcolm turned the carriage off the road and headed toward the Johnson mansion, which could barely be seen from the road. They found themselves driving through a canopy of trees laden with Spanish moss. The sun was lifting higher in the eastern sky, and they were beginning to feel its warmth and the humidity it emphasized.

Soon the Johnson plantation came into view as they passed through a heavy stand of trees. The house stood on a small knoll, glistening white in the bright morning sun. Huge white columns supported the balcony off the second-floor rooms, and each sparkling window was open to catch what errant breeze might come along.

Wide steps led to the wraparound porch adorned with colorful pots of budding flowers and green ferns. Comfortable padded chairs and white linen-covered tables extended their invitation to family and visitors to sit and rest a while.

The grounds were manicured to a fair-thee-well and dotted here and there with magnificent rose gardens, lush shade trees, stone benches, and a pair of stone lions that guarded the wide porch at the base of the steps. Over all, the breath of spring was on the massive Johnson yard. It was a grand scene and a treat to the eye.

When Malcolm drew the carriage to a halt in front of the porch steps, a male slave came through the ornate doors and descended the steps to help the ladies and Priscilla down. Dorena alighted without help.

As they ascended the porch steps, the Johnsons' youngest son, Alexander, came through the door. At sixteen, the youth was tall and handsome.

Alexander greeted them with a smile. "Please come in, ladies. Big brother Dan took Mother and Angeline into town quite early this morning. I know they expected to be back before you arrived. I'm sure they will be here soon."

Evelyn introduced Alexander to her cousin Earline, and the young man welcomed her, saying that he was glad she could come along with Mrs. Moore.

Earline was all eyes as Alexander guided his mother's guests inside the mansion. An atmosphere of serenity greeted them. When they were ushered into the lush sitting room, Alexander told them he was to meet his father at one of the fields quite soon and politely excused himself, saying that he would send his mother's personal slave, Daisy, to take care of any needs they might have.

The ladies made themselves comfortable on richly upholstered couches and chairs. It was a lovely room, full of treasured pieces collected over many years and placed carefully on mantel, small tables, and coffee table. The tapestried walls were adorned with exquisite paintings of outdoor scenes and eye-catching still-life paintings.

As Earline was commenting on a particular painting, Daisy entered the room with a warm smile. "May I bring you ladies coffee and cookies?"

"No, thank you, Daisy," said Evelyn. "We will wait until Miss Catherine and Miss Angeline arrive."

Daisy curtsied politely and left the room.

Less than ten minutes had passed when above their light conversation they heard a carriage draw up in front of the mansion. Dorena hurried to the front window and peeked through the lace curtains. "It is them, Miss Evelyn."

"Thank you, Dorena."

The young slave girl returned to the small couch where she sat beside her mistress. Priscilla smiled at her and patted her hand affectionately. The love Dorena felt for her mistress shone from her dark eyes.

Seconds later, they heard the mansion's front door open, and Daisy's voice telling Catherine that her guests were in the sitting room. Footsteps echoed in the hallway, and presently Catherine Johnson entered the room with Angeline at her side. Dan Johnson followed close behind, and Daisy brought up the rear.

Dan was in his midtwenties, just over six feet tall, with dark brown hair and eyes to match. Like his younger brother, he was quite handsome. Blond Angeline showed a close resemblance to her mother . . . tall, slender, and pretty.

Greetings were offered and introductions made, then Dan excused himself and left the room.

"Ladies, I'm sorry to be late," Catherine said as she removed her hat and handed it to Daisy, "but we were detained on the road in front of your place, Martha."

"What was it?"

Catherine's voice was a bit shaky as she said, "Just as we were passing your plantation, we came upon your slaves, Henry and Trevor. They were repairing fence near the gate, right by the road. They were weeping."

Martha's brow furrowed. "Weeping?"

"Yes. I had Dan stop and ask them what was wrong. Martha, they told us that one of their fellow slaves died this morning, just minutes before we came along. They said you couldn't have known about it . . . that it happened after you left to come over here."

"Did . . . did they say who it was?"

"Yes. Nathaniel."

"Oh, no!" Martha began to wring her hands. "Did Henry and Trevor say what happened?"

"I asked them, but they seemed frightened. Trevor said that Nathaniel wasn't feeling well this morning, and one of the other slaves had come to tell them he had died."

Martha put trembling fingers to her face and tears filled her eyes. "If whatever was ailing Nathaniel took his life, that would be no reason for Henry and Trevor to be frightened."

Catherine moved to where Martha was sitting and eased down beside her. She looked toward Evelyn and gave her a meaningful look.

Immediately Catherine turned to Priscilla and Angeline and said, "Why don't you girls go up to Angeline's room for a while? We'll let you know when coffee time is on."

Dorena sprang to her feet and offered her hand to Priscilla. When her mistress was up, she offered her hand to Angeline. All three girls left the room quietly. Daisy followed them and headed down the hall toward the kitchen.

When they were gone, Catherine took hold of Martha's hand. "You're afraid it's happened again, aren't you?"

Martha closed her eyes and nodded.

Evelyn left her chair and knelt in front of Martha. "Honey, we know about your strong aversion to the way Finn and your sons treat the slaves."

Martha looked into Evelyn's eyes and said, "The only thing you don't know is *how* strong my aversion is. Every time this happens I feel like something has died inside of me."

Earline rose from her chair, pale of face. "Maybe I should go elsewhere."

"There's no need for that, Earline," said Martha. "It won't make any difference if you know that my husband and my two sons have beaten slaves to death in the past. The slaves are afraid to tell it to anyone. Case in point . . . Henry and Trevor. Catherine says they would only say that Nathaniel was not feeling well and now is dead. They know what killed him, but they were too frightened of Finn, George, and Edward to tell her. They probably know *who* did the beating, too."

Earline's shocked face grew even paler. "I . . . I've heard about plantations here in the South where this kind of thing happens, but I've never been this close to it. Do people in the community suspect what's going on?"

"Not that I know of," said Martha. "It's no secret in the community that Finn beats on his slaves and often works them too hard, but I've never heard it said that they think Finn and my sons have killed any slaves.

"Neighbors around usually know when a slave has died. We all have special burial grounds for the slaves, and some neighbors can see them from the roads or from their own places. Most slaves die before they're fifty, so there are many burials. Anyone observing services on our plantation wouldn't know the difference between a slave being worked to death or beaten to death.

"It wouldn't do any good to report my husband and my sons to the law, either. Neither the county sheriff nor the town constables would do anything about it. Like so many white people here in the South, they look at the Negroes as no different than animals. For a plantation owner to kill a slave is no worse than if he decided to kill one of his horses. The cotton growers own their horses and they own their slaves. So, in the eyes of the law and in the eyes of so many people, it's nobody's business what they do with them."

Earline pressed a hand over her eyes and shook her head. "Oh, Martha, how do you stand it?"

"It's horrible, Earline. I was raised on a rice plantation in North Carolina, but my father, his foreman, and his overseers always treated our slaves well. When I married Finn, I didn't know he had a cruel side. And now my sons are the same way. It's almost more than I can bear. But I love my husband and my boys. I can't just up and leave them."

"I understand that," said Catherine. "But I don't know how you can take it when those poor slaves die unnecessarily."

Martha squeezed her friends' hands. "Sometimes I think that if another slave dies from a beating or overwork, I'll lose my mind. Evelyn . . . Catherine . . . what will it take to change Finn and my boys?"

Catherine glanced at Evelyn, then bent close to Martha and said, "Honey, if they were to open their hearts to Jesus, He would change them so they wouldn't want to be that way with the slaves. Only Jesus can do a work within us that will make us different."

Evelyn nodded and said, "Just this past Sunday, Martha, our pastor preached a wonderful sermon about the change that takes place in a lost sinner when he or she is born again. He used Saul of Tarsus as an example."

"Who is Saul of Tarsus?" Martha asked.

"He's the man who became the apostle Paul. You see, Saul of Tarsus had a burning hatred toward the Lord Jesus Christ and against Christians. He led others who felt as he did in putting Christians to death. He is quoted in the book of Acts as saying that he was a killer of God's people. But when he became a Christian, he did a complete turnaround and became one of the mightiest preachers this world has ever seen. It took the hand of the Lord to give him a new heart and a new outlook, just as it does for all of us sinners."

"That's right," Earline said. "If your husband and your sons would let the Lord save them, He would also change them like He did Saul of Tarsus."

"And the rest of us, too," said Catherine. "All of us are not like Finn and your sons, but we *are* guilty sinners before a holy God, and we need our wicked hearts cleansed and made new through the blood of Christ. This can only come when we are willing to admit we're depraved hell-deserving sinners in need of salvation, and we ask the Lord Jesus to save us."

Martha nodded. "You've talked to me about this several times before."

"Have you given it more thought, honey?" Evelyn asked.

"Yes, I have. But there is a problem. I . . . I just can't do it."

"Don't you want to be saved?"

Martha took a deep, shuddering breath. "Evelyn, I'm afraid."

"Of what?"

"Of Finn. I'm afraid of what he would do if I became a Christian."

"I understand your fear, honey," said Evelyn, "but if you die lost, you will spend eternity in hell. You mustn't let your fear of Finn's reaction keep you from being saved."

"That's right," said Catherine, "Proverbs 29:25 says, 'The fear of man

44

bringeth a snare.' Martha, please don't let the devil snare you into hell by using your fear of Finn to keep you from the Lord."

Martha passed a shaky hand over her face. "I . . . I'll seriously consider what you two are telling me."

"You do that, honey," said Evelyn. "And don't put it off."

"Martha," Catherine said, "I know my family will want to attend the burial service. We met both Nathaniel and Matilda when you had them working around the house serving guests."

"Yes," said Evelyn. "Will you let us know when the service will be held, so we can come too?"

"I certainly will. And I appreciate your willingness to come."

"I'm sure other neighbors who knew Nathaniel will want to attend too," said Catherine.

"I'll see that all the neighbors are advised," Martha said, wiping a tear from her cheek. "I feel so terrible about this. I'm so ashamed of the way Finn and my sons treat our slaves. Not only are they overworked and underfed, but they have to live in broken-down huts."

"I don't want to be overbearing about this, honey," said Catherine, "but one reason there's a difference in the way we treat our slaves is because we're Christians. We give them Sundays off to attend church services morning and evening on the plantation grounds, and they're only worked ten hours a day the rest of the week."

Martha nodded. "Finn allows our slaves to hold their church services only because all the plantation owners do it, but they pay for it during the rest of the week by working twelve hours a day to make up for not working on Sunday."

Silence followed Martha's words, and Catherine said, "Well, ladies, let's call the girls down from Angeline's room and have some coffee together."

When everyone was seated around the beautiful marble-topped table in the center of the sitting room, Daisy carried in an ornate silver coffee server. She placed it on the table along with a silver tray of sweet delicacies.

Catherine poured the steaming, pungent brew and handed the cups and saucers around, inviting her guests to help themselves to the sweets. The women settled back into their comfortable chairs and talked of happier things.

Angeline and Priscilla listened quietly as they had been taught to do.

Dorena sat next to her mistress and listened to the ladies talk. From time to time, she found Priscilla's eye and gave her a smile.

Martha spoke periodically, but most of the time, what the other ladies were saying seemed to be coming from a distance. Her thoughts were on Nathaniel's death. A deep horror filled her heart. She knew there had been times when one of the overseers had beaten a slave to death, but most of the time, it was Finn, George, or Edward.

She prayed it was one of the overseers this time.

When Martha Colvin returned home late that afternoon, Mammy was at the door to meet her. "Did you have a nice day, ma'am?"

"Yes, I did." Martha removed her hat and handed it and her parasol to Mammy. "Is Master Finn in the house?"

"Yes'm. He's in the library."

Martha thanked her and made her way down the long, broad hallway to the library. She found the door closed but tapped on it, saying, "Finn, are you in there?"

"Yes," came the response.

When Martha stepped inside, she saw her husband sitting at his large Mediterranean-style desk. She closed the door behind her and crossed the room to stand before him.

Finn looked up from the paperwork spread before him and gave her a tight smile. "Have an enjoyable day?"

"I did until I found out that Nathaniel died this morning."

"Oh. Mammy tell you?"

"No. Catherine did. She heard from a couple of our slaves who were working on the fence by the gate."

Finn's face hardened. "Who were they? Did they give her any details?"

"No. Only that Nathaniel had died. It was Henry and Trevor. Apparently Catherine and Dan stopped to talk to them because they saw them weeping."

"Mm-hmm."

Martha's delicate features paled slightly and her throat tightened as she said, "What happened?"

Finn eased back in his chair and squared his jaw. "Nathaniel became very insubordinate this morning. Instead of showing up at the field where he and Matilda were to work, he stayed at the shack. When George went to see him, he was doing the wash. George told him to get to the field, but he refused, saying he had a stomachache."

"Well, if he said he had a stomachache, he most certainly did," said Martha. "Nathaniel wouldn't lie about it."

"Well, he *did* lie! If he could do the wash, he could work in the field!"

"So he was beaten for it, I assume?" said Martha.

"He was. I administered the punishment myself, inside one of the barns. None of the slaves saw it."

Martha's eyes misted and her lower lip trembled. "Did you have to beat him to death?"

Finn bristled and stood up. "He tried to resist me while I was lashing him, Martha! He had it coming! No more questions."

Martha turned silently and left the room. She wiped tears as she climbed the broad, curving staircase. Mammy was at the top of the stairs, waiting for her. Frowning, she said, "Are you all right, Miz Martha?"

"I just want to be alone," Martha said, choking on her tears. "Thank you."

Martha was sniffling as she entered her room that she had not shared with Finn for over ten years. Her head was pounding, and her heart was sore as she stepped to a small table near the dresser.

With shaking hand, she poured water from the pitcher into the wash bowl. Using a soft cloth, she began washing her face, wishing she could wash the filth of her fragmented world away as easily.

After dabbing at her face with a towel, she went to the comfortable lounge by the window and looked down into the yard. She saw a trio of sad-faced male slaves working in one of the flower gardens. All of the slaves loved Nathaniel, and they would mourn his death for a long time to come.

Martha lowered herself slowly onto the lounge and leaned her head back, closing her troubled eyes. Her mind immediately returned to the conversation that afternoon when her friends had spoken about salvation and Catherine had quoted the Scripture from Proverbs about the fear of man. As she mulled it over in her mind, the picture of Finn's angry face flashed before her. She shuddered and turned her thoughts to other things.

IT WAS MIDMORNING ON the second day after Nathaniel's death. At the Charles Moore mansion, lovely Dorena left her small room on the second floor and tapped on the door next to hers.

"That you, Dorena?" came Priscilla Moore's soft voice.

"Uh-huh."

"Come in."

Priscilla was seated on her bed, clad in a black dress. She was bent over, tying the laces of her black shoes. She looked up to see Dorena in her Sunday-best checked gingham dress.

"You look very nice, Dorena."

"Thank you, Miss Priscilla."

"You look more than very nice."

Priscilla pulled the bowknot tight on her shoe and left the bed, taking hold of Dorena's shoulders. Keeping her voice low, she said, "I've told you . . . when we're alone you don't have to put the 'Miss' in front of my name. We're best friends, aren't we?"

"Oh, yes," said Dorena, her eyes shining.

Priscilla embraced her and whispered into her ear, "Then best friends call each other by their first names. I call you Dorena, and when no one else is around, you just call me Priscilla."

Dorena kissed her mistress's cheek and said, "I love you, Priscilla."

"I love you, too."

"Should I take my Bible to the burial service?"

"No, honey. Ol' Mose will have his Bible when he preaches, but this isn't like church services."

Dorena nodded. "I just didn't want to—"

49

Her words were cut off by the booming voice of Lewis Moore thundering down the hall. They couldn't tell for sure what he was saying, but his tone was sharp and filled with anger.

Priscilla crossed the room and opened the door. Dorena eased up beside her. They saw Charles and Evelyn Moore standing at their son's door. Lewis was partially visible as he said, "I'm amazed that you would even ask me! No! I am not going to that stupid burial service! I hate those black beasts, and I wouldn't waste my time watching one of them buried!"

Priscilla felt Dorena stiffen. She put an arm around her and whispered, "Don't pay any attention to Lewis, honey. You know how the rest of this family feels about Negroes."

Dorena nodded as they heard Charles say, "Son, it is more for the Colvins' sake that we'd like to have our whole family there. We've been trying to win their confidence so we can get them to come to church and—"

"So why should I be there, Dad? If you ever get the Colvins to church—which I seriously doubt—they won't see me taking up space on a pew!"

Evelyn broke the silence by saying, "Lewis, you're a part of this family. You know how it hurts us that you won't go to church with us. But couldn't you at least give in a little and come with us to the burial service? Is that asking too much?"

"Yes, it is, Mother. This conversation has become a bore. You two go on and watch them drop that slave's corpse in the ground if you want to, but I've got better things to do."

Charles's voice was tight as he said, "You watch your mouth, young man. You have no right to talk to your mother like that. You apologize to her right now!"

There was a brief pause, then Lewis said, "I'm sorry, Mother. Can I go back in my room now?"

Charles said something the girls couldn't make out, then they heard Lewis's door close.

"Come on, Dorena," Priscilla said. "I'm sure Mother and Daddy are ready to go."

When the girls stepped into the hall, they saw Charles and Evelyn heading toward the winding staircase. Dorena's mother, Liza, met them at the top of the stairs, and Evelyn said to her, "Will you go tell Priscilla and Dorena we're ready to go, please, Liza?"

"Yes'm." She took only a couple of steps, then said, "They's comin', now, Miz Evelyn."

Both Charles and Evelyn turned to watch the girls. When they drew up, Charles said, "Liza, did you hear Lewis's comment about Negroes?"

"No, suh."

"Good."

"Dorena did, Daddy." Priscilla touched the blond curls that dangled over her ear.

Charles's brow furrowed as he looked at Dorena and said, "I'm sorry, dear. Lewis sometimes uses his mouth before he engages his brain. You know he doesn't speak for the rest of this family."

"Yes, sir. I do know that." As she spoke, Dorena put an arm around her mother. "My parents know that, too, Master Charles."

Liza set soft eyes on Charles and Evelyn. "You have been so good to us. My Caleb says almos' every day how good Massa Charles and Miz Evelyn have been to us. We's sorry that Massa Lewis feels toward us black folks like he does."

"Maybe someday he will see how wrong he is," Priscilla said.

Charles gusted a sigh. "We'd best be going, ladies, or we'll be late for the burial service."

Dan Johnson guided the family carriage into the lane of the Addington plantation and headed for the large brick mansion nestled in a grove of pines. Douglas and Jane Addington were the newest plantation owners in the area and had expressed to the Johnsons and the Moores that they would like to attend the burial service for Nathaniel.

Alexander, who rode in the front seat between his father and his big brother, said, "Pa, do Mr. and Mrs. Addington know that Nathaniel was beaten to death by Finn Colvin?"

"I don't know, son. Probably," Zack said. "Most everyone has learned of it like we did."

"You mean when George Colvin told it yesterday in town when he was drunk?"

"Yes. But now that George has sobered up, he would just say he was drunk and didn't know what he was saying. There's no proof that Finn did it."

"And even if somebody had proof," put in Dan, "everybody around here knows it wouldn't do any good to go to the law about it. Finn has the sheriff and the constables in his hip pocket."

"Sad, but true," Catherine said.

Angeline spoke up. "Daddy, do you know what the Colvins are telling people about the cause of Nathaniel's death?"

"Well, honey, Martha is totally mum about it, as she was to us and the Moores when she let us know when the burial service would be held. But from what I've picked up, Finn and his sons are telling people that Nathaniel had sudden pains in his stomach. After a few minutes of agony, he died."

"That's awful," said Angeline. "And, of course, the slaves are afraid to tell anybody."

"That's right. If they did, they would suffer severely for it."

Dan shook his head. "Something's got to be done, Pa."

"I don't know what that would be, son."

"But Finn and his no-good sons shouldn't be able to get away with this kind of thing!"

"I agree. But I don't know what we can do about it."

"All we can do is let God handle it," Catherine said.

As the carriage drew near the mansion, the Addingtons were waiting on the porch. Douglas was in conversation with two of his male slaves. Jane Addington smiled at the Johnsons and gave a tiny wave.

Moments later, when the Addingtons were settled in the carriage, Dan put the horses to a trot as they headed back to the road. Douglas and Jane rode in the back, facing Catherine and Angeline.

Douglas spoke up so all could hear. "We've been told by some folks at church about this dear old preacher on the Colvin plantation called Ol' Mose. They say he'll be doing the service today."

"He sure will," Zack said.

"They say that in spite of his age, he can still put out a good sermon."

"That he can," said Dan, guiding the carriage up the winding lane. "We've heard him preach burial services on several occasions. If he does that well in the slaves' church services, I know they're hearing good preaching."

"Do you know how old he is?" Jane asked.

"He turned ninety-one last December," said Catherine. "Ol' Mose's birthday is on Christmas Day."

Douglas gasped in surprise. "Ninety-one! Bless his heart."

"He's getting somewhat feeble," Zack said, "but he will preach till he simply can't stand up."

"And then he will probably try to do it sitting down, Daddy," said Angeline.

Zack chuckled. "That wouldn't surprise me, honey."

"I assume his name is actually Moses?" Douglas said.

Catherine nodded. "Mm-hmm. But I guess he's been called 'Mose' since he was a child. And, of course, the last forty years or so, it's been Ol' Mose."

"With a Bible name like Moses," Jane said, "he must have been born here in the South."

"You would think so, but he was born in West Africa."

"Well, there must have been some kind of Christian influence that would cause his parents to give him a Bible name."

"There was," Catherine replied. "British missionaries went into that part of West Africa about 110 years ago. From what Ol' Mose has told us, the chief of his tribe was led to the Lord by the missionaries, and hundreds in the tribe eventually were saved, including Mose's parents. Because of the British influence in the tribe, they were taught about the calendar, and this is why Mose's parents knew he was born on Christmas Day.

"Mose was saved as a child and educated by the British missionaries. He can read and write English as well as anybody. When he grew up, he married a young lady in the tribe named Jasmine. Mose and Jasmine were captured by white slave traders in 1834 and brought here. They were sold to Finn Colvin, who had his plantation running well by that time and was adding slaves. Jasmine died, I believe, about fifteen years ago. That dear old man has been the preacher on the plantation ever since he first arrived and he has led a great number of the Colvin slaves to the Lord over the years."

When the few local plantation neighbors had gathered with the Colvin family on one side of the open grave, all the Colvin slaves gathered on the opposite side. Two elderly slave women stood beside the young widow, Matilda, whose features showed the anguish of mind and heart she had suffered since her husband's death.

The slave cemetery was at the extreme back side of the plantation in a grove of tall white oaks and hickories. A soft spring breeze ruffled the limbs, and the South Carolina sun sent its rays earthward as if to somehow brighten Matilda's day, as well as that of the others who mourned Nathaniel's death.

The only slave on the white side of the open grave was Dorena, who stood next to her mistress.

Nathaniel's body lay inside a thin wooden coffin that rested on the ground next to the grave. The lid was nailed shut, and a crude wreath of willow limbs lay on top.

At the head of the coffin stood Ol' Mose, holding a well-worn Bible in his gnarled hands. His wrinkled skin was a deep black, with the gleam of graphite. He had a flat nose and full lips, but his face was thin and worn. His back was bent and his slender shoulders stooped, yet his eyes had the luster of a much younger man.

When all were assembled, Ol' Mose began to sing a hymn about heaven in his cracked and broken voice. The slaves immediately joined him, as did most of the plantation neighbors. Finn Colvin and his wife and sons stood in silence.

Tears flowed freely down the cheeks of the slaves as they sang.

Martha Colvin wiped her own tears with a hanky, her heart broken over Nathaniel's unnecessary death. She felt strong emotion for Nathaniel's wife, Matilda, who couldn't sing for the sobs that broke from her.

When the hymn was finished, Ol' Mose ran his gaze over all the faces in the semicircle. The sun glistened in his silver hair as he gave a heart-touching eulogy about Nathaniel, telling what a fine man he was, and told of the day he had the privilege of leading both Nathaniel and Matilda to the Lord Jesus Christ some six years previously.

Matilda was leaning on the elderly women flanking her, trying to maintain control of herself and avoiding any glance at Massa Finn for fear he would read the scorn in her eyes.

Ol' Mose put on a pair of cracked spectacles that were barely intact. Although he could hardly see the print on the pages of his Bible, he preached a straightforward gospel message, quoting most of the passages by memory as he reminded all within the sound of his voice that one day their time to die would come.

He warned of the danger of dying without Christ and without hope. For those who were saved, he gave comfort that no matter when their time came to leave this world, the Great Shepherd would be there to take their hand and lead them through the valley of the shadow of death.

He closed off by showing from the Scripture that Nathaniel was now in heaven with Jesus, and waiting for his dear wife and his Christian brothers and sisters to meet him on the golden streets of the New Jerusalem.

The old man's voice was gravelly as he looked at the faces around him and said, "An' folks, listen to Ol' Mose. If Nathaniel's voice could be heard from those heavenly portals this mornin', he would plead with those of you who are not saved to turn to Jesus before it is too late."

Letting those words sink in, Mose closed the service with prayer, asking God to comfort Matilda and the others who mourned Nathaniel.

Edward Colvin told the slaves who had dug the grave to lower the coffin into it and cover it up. When the burial was completed, plantation foreman George Colvin ordered the slaves back to work.

All eyes were on Ol' Mose as he shambled toward Matilda and embraced her, speaking words of consolation. The rest of the slaves wept as they turned and headed toward the fields, their heads bowed low and their bare feet shuffling in the red dust. Only the very aged slaves remained in a tight-knit group. They waited to speak to Matilda before slowly making their way back to their shacks.

The Colvins began talking to some of their plantation neighbors. But when George Colvin noticed that Ol' Mose was still talking to the young widow, he frowned and excused himself to the neighbors, then walked over to the pair and said, "Mose, you have chores to do at the house, and Matilda, you've got a field to help prepare for planting. Get to it."

Matilda's lips began to quiver, and she drew in a shaky breath.

Mose looked at George, his mouth hanging open in undisguised astonishment. Risking discipline on himself, he said, "Does Massa George have no heart? Matilda's husban' was just put in the ground. She is in no condition to work. She should be allowed to go to her shack and rest."

George stared at the old man, angered that he would dare speak in such a manner. A red flush crept along his cheekbones, and there was a wicked rasp in his voice as he said, "You get back to your chores, old man! I'm the foreman here, and I told this woman to get to her field and go to work! You stay out of it!"

"Excuse me, George," Dan Johnson said.

George turned toward the voice to find that Dan was standing only inches from him.

While George was still blinking at this intrusion, Dan said, "Ol' Mose is right. This dear lady just saw her husband buried. Surely you can't expect her to walk away from this grave and work in the fields the rest of the day.

You should let a couple of the women take her to her shack, keep her company, and do what they can to comfort her."

Ol' Mose was smiling on the inside.

By now the small crowd of plantation neighbors were looking on, waiting for George's response.

There was a hard edge to his voice as he said, "You're sticking your nose in where it doesn't belong, Dan Johnson! If I say Matilda is to go to the field, that's exactly what she is going to d—"

"George!" cut in Finn, hastening to him. "Dan is right, son. This dear woman has just been through a dreadful ordeal. Let's send a couple of the older women with her and let them attend to her in her shack."

George looked at his father as if he had lost his good sense, but then turned and called to the two aged women who had stood beside Matilda at the graveside service. He told them to take her to her shack and stay with her till sundown.

"Now, that's better, George," said Dan. "A man's got to have some compassion and understanding."

Finn laid a hand on George's shoulder, smiled at Dan, and said, "You'll have to excuse George. Losing Nathaniel has hit him hard. As foreman, he's concerned that we will have to buy another slave to take Nathaniel's place. And that won't be easy. He was an exceptionally strong man and a hard worker."

"Sure, Finn," Dan said. "I understand."

Ol' Mose took a couple of shuffling steps toward Finn Colvin and said, "Thank you, Massa Finn, fo' helpin' Massa George to see that Matilda needs some time to rest."

Finn nodded, then said, "Well, George, we have some more neighbors to speak to."

When the Colvins had walked away, Ol' Mose moved up to Dan and said, "Massa Dan, I've got to head back to the mansion, but I just wanted to say that I 'preciate you talkin' to Massa George like that."

Dan winked at the old man. "Anytime, Ol' Mose. Anytime."

Douglas and Jane Addington, who had ridden to the funeral service with the Johnsons had made arrangements to ride back with the Moores. They had seen Dorena at church since coming to Charleston, but had not yet met her. After Priscilla Moore introduced them to her, the Addingtons boarded the Moore carriage for the ride home. They were charmed by Dorena's beauty and sweet personality.

As Charles drove the carriage across the fields, Jane looked at Evelyn and said, "It's so nice that Priscilla can have such a lovely companion. I assume she lives in the house with you."

"Yes, she does. She has her own room right next to Priscilla's."

"How nice," said Jane, smiling at Dorena. "And you're how old, dear?"

"I am sixteen years old, Mrs. Addington."

Jane ran her gaze to Priscilla. "And you're just about the same age, aren't you?"

"I'm seventeen, ma'am. And Dorena will be seventeen very soon."

"You see, Jane," said Evelyn, "Dorena's father is one of our field slaves, and her mother, Liza, is a house slave. Liza has been one of our house slaves since Dorena was very small and she brought her to the house while she worked. Soon these two girls—being so close to the same age—became fast friends."

"I see."

"When Priscilla turned fifteen, she asked her father if Dorena could be her personal slave, and Charles granted her wish."

"And I'm sure glad," said Priscilla.

"Me too," put in Dorena.

Charles looked over his shoulder and said, "Dorena's father, Caleb, is my favorite field slave. He's the hardest working man on the plantation."

"Sounds like they're a fine family, Charles," said Douglas.

"The very best."

"I think it's so nice that you two girls are such close friends," Jane said.

Priscilla put an arm around Dorena and hugged her close. "I love her like a sister, Mrs. Addington."

When the Johnson carriage swung off the Colvin property onto the road, young Alexander said, "I'm proud of you, big brother. You really nailed George's hide."

"Yes," said Angeline. "I think Mr. Colvin only sided with you because it would look good to the neighbors."

"That was it exactly, honey," Zack said.

"This whole thing disgusts me, Pa," Dan said. "Finn Colvin murdered

Nathaniel, and he's getting away with it. Something has just got to be done."

"But what, son? We already agreed there's nothing we can do about it. We'll have to let the Lord handle it."

"But Pa, don't you think sometimes the Lord expects us to do what we can about bad situations, before He will go to work on them?"

"I'm sure that's true. But in this bad situation our hands are tied."

"You mean because the chief constable and the sheriff are in Finn Colvin's hip pocket?"

"Exactly. Hugh Mulvey likes the money Finn slips him now and then, and so does Sheriff Washburn. Sure, nobody believes such a thing is happening, but you and I know it is."

Dan sighed. "Yeah. But we can't prove it. Still, I think we need to give it a try. At least put some pressure on Mulvey and Washburn. I know you've got your hands full of business matters today, so I'll go to Mulvey's office and tell him I have reason to suspect that Finn beat Nathaniel to death. When Mulvey asks what my reason is, I'll tell him about George bragging at the Three Lanterns that his father had flogged Nathaniel to death for insubordination. Then I'll go to Washburn's office and lay it on him, too. Maybe a little pressure in the right spots will produce something."

Zack shrugged. "Well, it sure can't hurt anything. Go ahead. But I'm sure it'll turn out that you were wasting your time."

"Probably. But I still have to try, Pa. No man should get away with murder."

The carriage was moving past the Colvin mansion. Dan eyed the grandiose structure and said, "Pa, they've got to be stopped before another slave is beaten to death."

"Well, you do what you feel you have to, and from that point, leave it in the Lord's hands."

"All right."

"And remember, Dan," Catherine said, "the Lord's wheels of justice sometimes turn very slowly. Let Him handle it in His own time."

"Yes, ma'am." Dan squared his shoulders, then added, "Of course, I would like to see justice done before I leave these parts."

The subject of Dan's big dream to go out West and become a cattle rancher was a touchy one in the Johnson household. No one liked the idea of him living more than a thousand miles away.

"Well, that will be quite a while yet, son," said Catherine. "This is something you want to move very slowly on."

"Sure, Mama, but I'm twenty-one years old. A man can't put his big dream off too long. I found an article in the *South Carolina Gazette* yesterday about ranching in the West, and it was fascinating. People are going out there by the hundreds to build new lives on the frontier, and new cattle ranches are springing up all over the West. I mean, from Dakota, Nebraska, and Kansas all the way to the Pacific Coast. Cattle ranching is really big business in Texas, according to the article. The market for beef is growing rapidly in the East and here in the South, and they're looking to the ranchers in the West to produce it. And, of course, as the population enlarges in the West and towns grow into large cities, the demand for beef will become greater out there."

"Son," Zack said, "I hope one day it will work out for you, if it's God's will for your life. But like your mother said, move slowly. Don't rush into it and make a big mistake. The most miserable Christian is one who gets out of God's will."

"I understand that, Pa. I assure you, I'll go slow and put a lot of prayer into it."

IT WAS EARLY AFTERNOON in Charleston when Chief Constable Hugh Mulvey, who was standing behind his desk talking to one of his officers, heard the door open.

He saw the stalwart form of Dan Johnson silhouetted against the brilliant sun. "Hello, Dan," he said, an amiable smile forming on his lips.

Dan nodded as he held the door open. "I need to see you, Chief. Am I here at a bad time?"

"Not at all. I was just sending Officer Morehead on an assignment." Then he said to the officer, "Let me know what kind of reception you get."

"Will do, Chief," the deputy said and hurried toward the door. Dan left it open for him, and Morehead closed it behind him as he went out.

Mulvey sat down behind his desk and gestured toward a chair. "Sit down, Dan. Now, what did you need to see me about?"

"Sir, did you hear about one of the slaves dying at the Finn Colvin plantation?"

Mulvey frowned. "No. I have no reason to know when slaves die. Is there some reason I should know about this one?"

"Yes there is, sir."

"Male or female?"

"Male."

"What was his name?"

"Nathaniel."

"Young? Old?"

"Young, sir. Twenty-nine."

"But why should I know about his death?"

"Because he was murdered, sir."

Mulvey's head bobbed. "Murdered?"

"Yes, sir. He was beaten to death."

"By whom?"

"Finn."

Mulvey smiled and shook his head. "C'mon, now. Why would Finn beat a man to death who cost him good money?"

"To instill fear in the rest of the slaves, lest they forget the power Finn and his sons have over them."

"Kill the slave simply to instill fear in the others?"

"Well, the beating Finn administered was supposed to be for insubordination on Nathaniel's part. I knew Nathaniel, Chief. Not intimately, of course, but I knew him well enough to tell you that he wouldn't rebel against the authority of Finn and his sons. Or any of the Colvin overseers, for that matter."

"So what makes you think he was beaten to death? And how do you know it was Finn?"

"Because yesterday at the Three Lanterns tavern, George Colvin was bragging to some of his pals that his father had beaten Nathaniel to death for insubordination. He said that only he and Edward were allowed inside the barn where Finn did it. None of the slaves actually witnessed the beating, but you can be sure they heard it. Of course, I realize no slave's word is any good to the law, but there were enough men in the tavern that if you did a little investigating you would find plenty of witnesses who heard what George said."

Mulvey pulled at an ear, cocking his head to one side. "Was George drunk?"

"Word is that he had certainly put down a sufficient amount of whiskey to make a man slur his words."

"And what exactly do you want from me?"

Dan leaned forward. "Chief, I want you to arrest Finn Colvin and see that he is tried for murder."

Mulvey showed no emotion, but only said, "Was Nathaniel married?"

"Yes. He left a widow named Matilda. They had no children."

"All right, Dan. I'll investigate it. Come back tomorrow morning and I'll let you know what my investigation has revealed."

Rising from the chair, Dan said, "See you tomorrow, Chief."

Mulvey quickly rounded his desk and walked Dan toward the door. "Have you talked to Sheriff Washburn about this?"

"Not yet, but I'm going over there right now. I want to get both of you on it."

"Well, with a charge like this, I would go to the sheriff anyway, Dan. I'll go over there right now and give him the information you've given me. He and I can work together on it."

"All right. I'll head on home then. See you tomorrow."

Hugh Mulvey stood on the boardwalk and watched Dan Johnson ride away. Turning back to the door, he stepped inside, hung a sign on the door that he would be back later, and hurried down the street toward the sheriff's office.

Edward Colvin was in the front yard of the mansion, giving instructions to two male slaves about trimming the shrubbery, when he saw a buggy racing down the lane from the road.

Looking back at the slaves, he said, "Any questions about how I want it done?"

Both shook their heads, saying they understood his instructions. Leaving them, Edward looked back to the oncoming buggy and saw that it was Chief Constable Hugh Mulvey. He angled across the yard toward the hitching posts near the porch.

Seconds later, Mulvey skidded the horse to a halt near where Edward stood and said, "Is your father on the place?"

"Yes, sir. He is administering discipline to a slave in one of the barns at the moment. I'll escort you into the sitting room, then go tell Pa that you're here."

While Mulvey waited, he admired the expensive paintings on the sitting room walls. In a couple of minutes he heard soft footsteps, then saw Martha Colvin come through the door.

"Oh! Chief Mulvey! I didn't know you were here."

He rose quickly to his feet. "Sorry, ma'am. I didn't mean to startle you."

"Are you here to see Finn?"

"Yes. Edward brought me in here, saying he would go after his father."

"May I have one of the maids get you some tea?"

"No, thank you, ma'am. I just need to see Finn for a few minutes and be on my way."

When footsteps came from the rear of the house, Martha glanced

63

toward the hall. "This must be Finn and Edward now. You're sure I can't have some tea brought to you? I know it's hot."

Mulvey managed a weak smile. "No. Really. Thank you."

Finn came through the door. Edward quickly disappeared as Finn said, "Let's go to my den, Hugh. We can talk in private there."

Martha stepped aside, allowing the chief constable to move past her, and watched as the two men hurried down the hall.

When they were seated in overstuffed chairs that faced each other, Finn said, "All right, Hugh. What's got you looking so worried?"

"Dan Johnson."

Finn's features hardened. "What's he done?"

"Asked me to arrest you and send you to trial for murdering Nathaniel. He was going to go to Jake, too, but I told him I'd talk to Jake about it."

Finn laughed. "See there, Hugh? Didn't I tell you somebody would try to make something of my drunken son shooting off his mouth?"

"You sure did."

"Did Dan bring up that George was drinking when he filled everybody's ears with it at the tavern?"

"No. He didn't say a thing about it until I asked him if George was drunk at the time."

"And what did he say then?"

"He said word is that George had put down enough whiskey to at least make a man slur his words."

"Well, Mr. Dan Johnson will have to learn that George was so stinking drunk he hardly knew what he was saying. In fact, when word first came to us what was being said by men who heard him in the tavern, I told George that when anybody brought it up to him, to tell them he was so drunk he doesn't even remember saying it."

"Hey, that's quick thinking. That'll make it look even more like there's nothing to it."

"So what about Jake?"

"I went to his office right after Dan left. Told him about Dan coming to me. Our good sheriff is still holding fast to what we both told you we'd do—take the position that since George was drunk, it wouldn't offer substantial proof of your guilt."

"That's good, Chief!"

"Jake said to tell you he'd have come with me today, but he had some papers to serve for Judge Weatherby, and he had to do it immediately. Last thing he said was to tell you that as long as he wears the sheriff's badge, Finn Colvin has nothing to worry about from the Charleston County sheriff's office."

Finn chuckled. "Good for him," he said as he left his chair and went to his desk. Taking out a key, he opened a drawer and picked up a thick envelope stuffed with currency.

"So, what story are you telling about Nathaniel's death?" Mulvey asked.

"Well, Nathaniel had been having problems with stomach pain for quite some time. That day, my boys and I took him into the barn to examine him, and while we were in there, poor Nathaniel died in my arms."

Nodding, Mulvey said, "All right. Who knows what could have gone wrong inside him? Good enough."

Finn took a wad of currency out of the envelope and peeled off several bills. Handing them to Mulvey, he said, "Here's a special bonus for you above your usual monthly amount."

The chief constable's eyes widened. "Thanks, Finn."

Peeling off a like amount, Colvin handed the wad to Mulvey and said, "Give this to Jake for me, and tell him the same thing."

"Sure will. Jake will appreciate it as much as I do. We're both glad to be of service to a generous man like you."

Finn laughed. "Well, being rich does have its advantages. I know you and Jake are being paid by a few other plantation owners. But since lawmen don't make much pay, this ought to be helping both of you to live a little better."

"It sure is. We're both putting some money aside for a rainy day."

"Good. Well, you probably need to get back to your office."

"Right," said Mulvey, rising from the chair and stuffing Jake Washburn's bonus into one of his pockets. "You tell George to stick to his story."

"He'll stick to it, all right."

Colvin walked outside with the chief constable. Edward was with a second pair of slaves, giving directions as they planted flowers in front of the wide, sweeping porch.

When Mulvey drove away, Finn walked to where Edward stood.

"Everything all right, Pa?"

"Just fine."

"So what did he want?"

"To tell me that Dan Johnson wanted him and the sheriff to arrest me and put me on trial for murdering Nathaniel."

A sour look settled in Edward's eyes. "Dan Johnson, eh? So what're Mulvey and Washburn going to do?"

"Nothing. They will stick by the fact that George was drunk when he blabbed about my beating Nathaniel. We'll be fine, son. But I do need to talk to George. Will you find him and tell him I'll be in my den?"

"Sure," said Edward, and headed toward the rear of the mansion.

Finn was seated in his favorite overstuffed chair, browsing through the latest edition of the *South Carolina Gazette,* when George entered the den.

"Little brother said Hugh Mulvey was here and you wanted to talk to me."

Laying the paper down, Finn said, "Yes. Did Edward tell you what Mulvey was here about?"

"Dan Johnson. He told me what the fool is saying."

"Everything's fine, son. With Jake Washburn, too."

"So is there a problem, or did you just want to fill me in on Hugh's visit?"

"The problem, George, is your getting drunk. You've got to learn to take a couple of drinks and leave it alone. When you're in public and you drink too much, your tongue comes loose, and you can't seem to control it. If you'd kept your mouth shut at the Three Lanterns the other day, I wouldn't be having to ask for help from Mulvey and Washburn to make sure I don't get charged with murder. Dan Johnson will ride this thing as far as he can, and I'm sure his father will, too."

George's jaw clenched and there was cold fire in his eyes as he said, "Dan Johnson. Maybe he needs his mouth shut. I'd like to—"

"Forget it. We don't need that kind of trouble. Just don't get drunk and shoot your mouth off anymore. Understood?"

The flame left George's eyes as he met his father's gaze. "Yeah. I understand, Pa. I'm sorry. I'll be more careful from now on."

Finn laid a hand on George's shoulder and squeezed it. "Good. I'll take your word for it. You can go back to whatever you were doing."

It was just before nine o'clock the next morning when Chief Constable Mulvey looked up from his desk to see Sheriff Washburn come through the open door. The air was warm, and Mulvey even had a couple of windows open.

Washburn pushed his hat to the back of his head as he approached the desk. "Guess Dan's not here yet?"

"Nope. Sit down."

Washburn eased onto the chair in front of the desk. "Your officers around?"

"Not at the moment. But if they should be here when Dan comes, they won't hear anything they shouldn't. We'll just lay it on the line to Dan and tell him there's nothing we can do."

"Good," said the beefy sheriff, glancing out the front window. "Here he comes now."

Both men stayed seated as Dan entered the office. There was a second chair in front of the desk.

"Morning, Dan," Mulvey said warmly. "Come sit down."

When Dan was seated, he looked at Mulvey and said, "So, how did the investigation go, Chief?"

Easing back in his chair, Mulvey said, "I went to Sheriff Washburn after you left, as I said I would."

"Mm-hmm."

"Told him what you told me. He had important business, so he couldn't go to the Colvin place with me. Anyway, I went to the Colvin place and talked to Finn. I told him what you said. He laughed about it. Said there wasn't a word of truth in it . . . that George just goes way out of his mind when he gets drunk. I talked to George and he admitted he was drunk but said he doesn't remember saying anything about his father beating Nathaniel."

"You didn't swallow that, did you?"

Mulvey leaned forward, putting his elbows on the desk. "No, I didn't. I probed further. I asked Finn exactly what did happen with Nathaniel. He told me Nathaniel had been having problems with his stomach for quite some time."

"Oh?"

"Mm-hmm. Said Nathaniel told George his stomach was hurting him so bad that he just couldn't work in the fields."

"Yeah? So how did that sound to you?"

"Well, I wanted to be sure this story was true, so I told Finn I'd like to talk to some of the slaves."

"And?"

"Well, I talked to probably two dozen of them. They all confirmed that, indeed, Nathaniel had been having stomach trouble for quite a while. And those who were right there when Nathaniel was taken into the barn said that Finn was kind and gentle to him. They didn't hear any flogging going on. After a while, Finn and his sons came carrying Nathaniel's dead body and saying he had died in Finn's arms."

Dan shifted his position on the chair and glanced at the sheriff, then said to Mulvey, "Finn, no doubt, put the fear in his slaves, forcing them to lie to cover his crime."

Mulvey shook his head. "I don't know about that, but let's say you're right. How do I prove they lied?"

"You can't," put in Washburn. "And besides, if you could find some slaves who would say they were lying—that they knew Finn beat Nathaniel to death inside the barn—no Negro's testimony counts for anything here in the South."

"Too bad that's true," said Dan. "So are you men going to find the Three Lanterns patrons who heard George say his father beat Nathaniel to death? Must've been a pretty good number of them, from what I've heard. Their testimonies would bear weight in court."

Mulvey shook his head. "Not so, Dan. Even if those who heard George say it were willing to testify, it wouldn't hold up in court because George was drunk at the time and not responsible for what he said. In fact, he doesn't remember saying such a thing."

Dan looked at Mulvey for a moment, then said, "Because he was drunk and doesn't remember—or says he doesn't—that's it? Matilda is a widow because her husband was murdered, but the murderer walks away a free man?"

Mulvey shrugged. "I'm sorry, Dan, but there's nothing that Sheriff Washburn and I can do. You have to look at it this way. Maybe George really was just shooting off at the mouth, and whether he remembers what he said or not, maybe Nathaniel did die with stomach problems as Finn says."

Dan set his jaw. "You could open the grave and take a look at the body. If there are bruises, you'll know Finn is lying."

Mulvey looked at Washburn, who was already shaking his head.

"Can't do it, Dan," said the sheriff. "Nathaniel is buried on private property. We can't open the grave. I feel like Chief Mulvey does. I'm sorry, but there's nothing more we can do."

Zack Johnson was at the small barn where the buggies and the buggy teams were kept when he saw Dan drive around the mansion and head his direction.

"How'd it go, son?"

"Let me put the buggy and the horses away first, Pa."

When Dan emerged from the barn, he told his father about his talk with Mulvey and Washburn at Mulvey's office. "I don't care what they say, Pa, Finn is guilty of murder."

"Of course he is. But as you and I know, Finn has both of those men in his pocket, and they aren't going to bring him to trial. I appreciate that you were willing to try, but to pursue it further would do no good."

Dan sighed and removed his hat, running splayed fingers through his thick mop of dark brown hair. "I did what I could. It's in the Lord's hands now."

"He can handle it, son."

The next day, Ol' Mose was working in a flower garden at the rear of the Colvin mansion with a slave named James, who was in his seventies. As they planted seeds together, James said, "Ol' Mose, you is still carryin' a burden 'bout Nathaniel. I c'n see it in yo' eyes."

"Well, I guess I'm not tryin' to hide it from anybody but the Colvins an' the overseers, James. It bothers me no end that Massa Finn and his boys have beat other people to death, and it bothers me that they mistreat us so."

"Guess dat ain't gonna change unless those men die," said James, his wrinkled face reflecting the sunlight.

"The only other answer would be that they get saved," said Mose. "If Massa Finn would become a Christian, he wouldn't mistreat his slaves anymore. The same with Massa George and Massa Edward. My heart has been heavy for the whole family for a long time. I want to see Miss Martha saved, too."

"Wouldn' dat be wonderful!" James said.

"I feel I have to work with Massa Finn, first," said Mose. "If he would get saved, he would be a real help in gettin' the rest of the family saved. I've talked to him many times over the years about bein' saved, but he just won't listen. I have to keep praying for him, and keep tryin'."

"Well, if he was gonna listen to anybody on this plantation, Ol' Mose, it would be you. But I'll sure be a-prayin' the Lawd will give you wisdom and power as you keep talkin' to him."

The next day, when Mose was working inside the Colvin mansion, Martha set him to work using a feather duster in each room where two of the maids had swept the floors and cleaned furniture ahead of him.

When Mose entered the library, Finn was there sitting in an overstuffed chair, reading a book. He looked up and said, "The maids told me you would be coming in to dust."

"I'll hurry, Massa Finn."

"No need to hurry, Ol' Mose. Just do your job thoroughly."

"I will, suh." Mose started with one of the paintings on the wall. Soon the old slave preacher was at the bookshelves, working the feather duster to rid dust from the spines of books on the long rows. When he came to the old Bible that lay on its side, he smiled at it. He had dusted it many times in days gone by but had never opened it.

He glanced at Finn Colvin and noted that the man was engrossed in the book he was reading. Ol' Mose picked up the Bible, pulled a soft cloth from his hip pocket, and began wiping dust from its cover. He looked back at Colvin, and this time found the man's eyes on him.

Mose held the Bible a little higher and said, "My, my, Massa Finn. This Bible has gathered a lot of dust. Do you ever read it?"

Finn laughed dryly. "Naw. I have many more important books to read than that outdated Bible. My grandmother gave it to me when I was in my teens, but I've never looked between the covers."

"Outdated, Massa?" Mose flipped the pages of the Bible. "Oh, it isn't outdated, suh. It is the Word of God, and it never goes out of date. With God there is no past or future, just eternal now. This is why the Lord was able to give His Word as He did, and all of its prophecies are true."

Finn chuckled hollowly. "They are?"

"Yes, suh. For sure. Many of the prophecies, written thousands of years ago, have already come true. I mean, to the letter. And all the other prophecies will come true in God's time, even those about judgment to come against sinners who have rejected God's precious Son, the Lord Jesus Christ."

Finn didn't respond, though his eyes were still on the old man. He gave a slight shake to his head and went back to reading his book.

Mose flipped page after page in the New Testament, noticing that salvation passages and those about heaven and hell had been underlined.

"I see yo' grandmother marked lots of verses in here, Massa."

Finn looked up. "Oh? Well, like I said, Mose, I've never looked inside."

"You really should." The old man was praying in his heart for God to use him at that moment. "Listen to this place that she underlined. John the third chapter. The Lord Jesus is talkin' to one of the rulers in Israel. Verse 3: 'Jesus answered and said unto him, Verily, verily, I say unto thee, Except a man be born again, he cannot see the kingdom of God.' "

"Mm-hmm."

"Massa Finn . . ."

"Yeah?"

"I talked to you 'bout this before. You need to be born again or you can't go to heaven."

Finn laughed mockingly. "Being born once is enough for me, Mose."

"But it's not enough for the Lord, Massa. Your grandmother underlined verse 7 here. Jesus said, 'Marvel not that I said unto thee, Ye must be born again.' To be a child of God, you have to admit to the Lord that you are a lost sinner and receive the Lord Jesus into your heart. Only God's children go to heaven when they die, Massa. Lost people go to hell."

"So says that old outdated Book, Mose. I'm not worried about hell. Go ahead and get your dusting done."

Mose swallowed hard, determined to press harder since Finn Colvin had not become angry up to this point.

"MASSA FINN, IN THE BOOK OF ROMANS, God says that all have sinned and come short of the glory of God. That includes you and me, does it not?"

Finn, who was looking down at the book in his lap, lifted his eyes and said, "Nobody's perfect, Mose."

"True, suh, but we are sinners before God. We sin on purpose, and this makes us guilty before Him. As sinners, we need to be forgiven, and we need to be saved."

Mose's eyes settled on a page he had purposely found. He was pleased to see that Finn's grandmother had underlined the verse he planned to read. Though his vision was hindered, like the other verses he had shared with Colvin, he followed it with his eyes but was actually quoting from memory.

"Massa, the apostle Paul wrote in 1 Timothy, 'This is a faithful saying, and worthy of all acceptation, that Christ Jesus came into the world to save sinners. . . .' Jesus is the only one who can save us and forgive our sins, Massa Finn. Ol' Mose repented of his wicked ol' sin many years ago and took Jesus into his heart. John 1:12 says about Jesus, that 'as many as received him, to them gave he power to become the sons of God, even to them that believe on his name.'

"Ol' Mose is goin' to heaven because he has received Jesus and been born again, Massa . . . born into God's family. God's only begotten Son went to the cross of Calvary and paid the price to save sinners. But He will only save those who will put their faith in Him. Those who do are heaven-bound. Those who don't are hell-bound. Jesus said hell is everlasting fire, Massa."

"Look, Mose," Finn said, "we've had this conversation many times before and I've heard you preach the slave burials and tell the same thing. I'm simply not interested."

"But, Massa, one day you will die. If you die without Jesus, you—"

"That's enough, Mose! I have different beliefs about life, death, and eternity, as does the rest of my family. I don't care what the Bible says. I don't believe it."

Heavy of heart, the old man said, "Massa Finn, I simply care about you and your family. I don't want any of you to go to hell when you die."

The plantation owner wiped a hand over his mouth. "Mose, we aren't going to hell. I don't believe in hell. My family and I are good people, and good people go to heaven."

"Massa Finn, how do you know there is a heaven? The only way mankind has ever heard that there is a heaven is from the Word of God— the Bible."

For a few seconds, Finn Colvin's mouth was stopped. Then he cleared his throat and said, "I do believe that part of the Bible, Mose."

"But, Massa, the same Bible that says there is a heaven says there is a hell."

Again, Finn was speechless.

Mose took advantage of the silence to say, "Massa, the existence of heaven demands the existence of hell."

Finn Colvin drummed the book in his lap with his fingertips. "And why is that?"

"You said that good people go to heaven. Are there bad people, Massa?"

"Well, of course."

"Then, where do the bad people go?"

"Look, Mose. Let's just say that I believe part of the Bible. It can't all be true. I don't believe I need to be saved. I don't believe that part of the Bible, nor the part about an eternal burning hell for people who don't get saved . . . or born again, as you call it."

Tears filmed Mose's eyes. "But Massa Finn, what if you are wrong and the Bible is right? That means without Jesus in your heart, you will die and spend eternity in hell. Please don't reject Him any more. Please open your heart—"

"That's enough, Mose! I want to get back to my book. You get your dusting done."

Mose nodded. "Yes, Massa."

He put the Bible back on the shelf and went back to his work.

Colvin did not look up from his book until the old man had left the library, closing the door behind him. Seconds after the door went shut, Finn Colvin pulled a handkerchief from his pocket and mopped his sweaty brow.

Mose's words reverberated through his mind: *Massa Finn, what if you are wrong and the Bible is right? That means without Jesus in your heart, you will die and spend eternity in hell.*

Finn laid down his book and went to the bookshelves. With dry mouth and trembling hand, he picked up the Bible and opened it to the New Testament, noting verses his grandmother had underlined. He took a few minutes to read the underlined passages on several pages, then closed the Bible and returned it to the shelf.

When he sat down in the chair again and picked up his book, he found it difficult to concentrate. The Scriptures he had just read, and those read and quoted to him by Ol' Mose kept pressing themselves into his mind.

Dan Johnson opened the door to Charleston's post office and greeted a man and woman who were just leaving, then went to the counter.

"Hello, Dan," said the clerk.

"Hello, Eugene. I'm just here to pick up the mail."

The clerk pivoted and disappeared behind a partition.

Seconds later, he returned, bearing a small stack of envelopes. "Here you are, Dan."

"Thanks, Eugene. See you later." As he spoke, Dan's eyes fell to the envelope on top. "Oh! Good!"

Eugene cocked his head. "Somebody you've been wanting to hear from, I take it?"

"Yes. You remember the Wickburgs?"

"Oh, sure. Sold their plantation a couple of years ago and moved out West."

"Right. Their oldest son, Bill, was one of my closest friends in school and at church."

"I remember that."

"This letter is from Bill. We've been corresponding some."

"I see. Where are they living out there?"

"Texas. They've got a large cattle ranch about ten miles south of Austin and are doing well."

"I'm glad for them. Nice people."

Dan nodded and headed for the door. "See you later."

At the Johnson plantation, Zack entered the kitchen, sniffed the pleasant aroma, and smiled at their cook, saying, "Sure smells good, Samantha."

The silver-haired cook gave him a big smile. "Thank you, Massa Zack. Cornbread and beans. Yo' favorite."

Zack headed for the table, where Catherine, Alexander, and Angeline were already seated. He looked at Dan's empty chair. "He's not back from town?"

"No," Catherine said. "We'll have to go ahead and eat lunch without him."

Zack looked at his youngest son. "It's your turn to pray, isn't it, Alexander?"

"Yes, sir."

During Alexander's prayer, there were footsteps on the back porch, and just as he said the amen, the door opened.

"Sorry to be late," Dan said. "I ran into Jed Farnham and Foster Wiggins when I came out of the post office. I told them I had a letter from Bill Wickburg, and they wanted to know all about how the Wickburgs are doing in Texas. Took a few minutes to tell them what I know without opening the letter and reading it right there. I did read it after I was in the buggy."

"Well, get your hands washed, son," said Catherine.

"Okay." Dan laid the mail on the cupboard and sniffed the pleasant aroma. He grinned at the cook. "Ah-h-h, Samantha. Cornbread and beans. You are the best cook in Charleston County."

Samantha giggled. "How does you know that, Massa Dan? You ain't eaten all the other cooks' food in the county."

He went to the washstand then looked over his shoulder and said, "Don't have to. When you have the best, you know it."

Samantha giggled again. "Well, if I's that good, why haven't you said anythin' about takin' me to the West with you when you go out there to become a cattle rancher? Somebody's gotta cook fo' you."

Dipping his hands into the soapy water in the basin, he said, "Sh-h-h! Don't tell that bunch at the table, but I am planning to take you with me!"

Zack laughed. "No way, son. You'd have to buy her from me, and Samantha's not for sale. Not at any price."

"Then I guess I'll just have to kidnap her!"

"We'll talk about it later, Massa Dan," said the cook. "Now, all of you enjoy yo' cornbread and beans. I'll be back to clean up in a little while."

As the Johnson family started to eat, Zack said, "So what did Bill say in his letter, Dan?"

"Well, Pa, it's full of how great the cattle ranching business is in Texas, and how happy he and his parents are to be there."

"That's wonderful," said Catherine. "Certainly it was God's will for them to sell their plantation and go West."

"I would say so," said Zack. "When a Christian is in God's will, he is content."

Alexander looked at his brother and said, "Is this why you aren't content to be here anymore, Dan . . . because the Lord wants you in the West?"

"I'm really beginning to feel strongly that way, little brother. Bill's encouraging me to come to Texas, since he knows I feel I should be in the West. He says Texas is the place to be out there if a man wants to get into cattle ranching."

"Texas is God's place for Bill and his family," Zack said. "But that might not mean that's where God wants you, Dan."

"Maybe not, Pa, but I'm sure going to be praying about it."

"Please put a lot of prayer into it, son," Catherine said. "Your father and I are. As we have cautioned you . . . don't rush it."

"I won't, sweet mother. Oh! And something else Bill told me in his letter. He's getting married!"

Angeline gasped. "Really? Found him a nice Christian girl out in Texas, huh?"

"No."

"What do you mean?" Catherine said. "He's not marrying a Christian girl?"

"Oh, yes. But he didn't find her in Texas. As he explained in his letter, young, single, unattached Christian girls are scarce out there. In fact, young, single, unattached girls of any kind are scarce out there. So you know what he did? He advertised for a mail order bride in several Eastern newspapers, and at this very moment, she's on her way to Austin from Indianapolis, Indiana."

"Dan, you're joking!" Catherine said.

"No, Mama, I'm not. Her name is Betty Rhodes. She's a farm girl . . . born and raised on a farm about ten miles east of Indianapolis."

Zack swallowed a mouthful of mashed potatoes, then said, "Mail order bride, eh? Seems scary to me."

"It would be for me," said Catherine. "I can't imagine leaving my home, wherever it was, and going out West to marry some man I had never met."

"I sure couldn't do it," Angeline said.

"I remember when the mail order bride system started back in 1849," said Catherine, "when the big gold rush hit California. I've really never heard how successful it has been."

Zack had some hot coffee and set the cup in its saucer. "I'm wondering about this situation with Bill and the girl from Indiana. How could the mail order bride system possibly work for Christians?"

"I heard some Christian girls at school talking about it just last week, Pa," said Angeline. "One of them knows of a Christian young woman in Augusta, Georgia, who answered one of those mail order bride ads from a Christian man in Wyoming, and he had stipulated in the ad that he wanted a born-again woman. After she sent her reply, she got a letter from him. He explained in detail what he meant by born-again, using Scripture. He asked for her testimony, and when he received it, he wrote back and asked her to come to Wyoming with the prospect of becoming his wife. She went to him, they married, and have been happy ever since."

"Knowing Bill," said Dan, "I'm sure he put something like that in his ads. You know how close he walks to the Lord."

Angeline set adoring eyes on her big brother. "Dan, if you go to Texas, I'll miss you something terrible."

"We all will, honey," Zack said. "But your mother and I want him to go out West only if it is God's will. And the way he's feeling about it . . . it just may be exactly what the Lord wants him to do."

"That's how I'm thinking, Pa," Dan said.

Zack smiled at his eldest son. "If the Lord leads you to do it, your mother and I will dip into your share of your inheritance and give you the

money so you will have the proper start in the cattle business out there
. . . in Texas, or wherever. We want you to be a real success in it."

"Thank you, Dad. I'm so glad both of you feel that way."

That same afternoon at the Moore plantation, Priscilla and Dorena were
sitting on the back porch of the mansion. For some months Priscilla had
been teaching Dorena how to read and write. The lessons were an hour
long, five days a week.

During this time the girls' hearts became knit together in a special way,
for it was Priscilla who had led Dorena to the Lord a week after Dorena
became her slave. Shortly thereafter, Dorena's parents had come to know
the Lord. Priscilla and Dorena enjoyed each other's company immensely,
whether Dorena was doing her work for Priscilla or they were just doing
things together.

This day was an especially warm one. The porch was shaded by huge
oak trees, and once in a while a gentle breeze wafted over them. They
sipped lemonade periodically to quench their thirst.

Priscilla had placed an English textbook in Dorena's hands, and after
the one-hour grammar lesson was over, Dorena closed the book and said,
"Thank you so much for doing this for me, Miss—" She looked around to
make sure they were alone. "I mean . . . Priscilla. Because of your tutor-
ing me, I'm doing better and better at reading the Bible you gave me."

"I'm glad, honey." Priscilla picked up her pleated fan. She plied it
briskly, stirring air to cool her warm face, and looked at Dorena with envy.
Dorena was clad in a light cotton frock and was barefooted. Priscilla let her
eyes trail down to her own dress with the many petticoats she was required
to wear, along with cotton stockings and lace-up shoes.

Dorena's cheeks dimpled in a grin, and she said teasingly, "There are
some advantages to being a slave."

Both girls broke into a giggle, then Priscilla said in a serious tone, "You
are doing well in your studies. It won't be long before you'll be able to read
and write as well as anybody, Dorena."

As she spoke, Priscilla saw her brother moving past the porch.

When he laid eyes on them, he stopped and glared at Priscilla, waggled
his head, and echoed in a mocking tone, "It won't be long and you'll be
able to read and write as well as anybody, Dorena."

Dorena felt her stomach muscles tighten.

"Leave us alone, Lewis," Priscilla said.

Lewis scowled at her tone of voice and clamped his teeth together, then bounded up the porch steps, and said, "You're wrong to be teachin' her to read and write, Priscilla! If certain people found out, you'd be in real trouble! You know it's against the law in South Carolina to teach Darkies to read and write! If the authorities found out, you'd be punished severely . . . maybe jailed! And for certain, they would take Dorena away from you!"

Lewis's demeanor frightened Dorena. She trembled and ejected a tiny whimper.

Priscilla jutted her jaw stubbornly, fixing her brother with flashing eyes. "That law you're referring to, Lewis, is a stupid one! Dorena is my slave, and I can help her become literate if I want to! It's nobody else's business! Dorena has the right to be able to read her Bible as much as any white person does!"

A dark flush moved swiftly up Lewis's face. "You shouldn't be so friendly with Dorena! You're puttin' yourself on a low level to fraternize with a slave like you do! Darkies are nothin' but animals!"

Hot tears surfaced in Dorena's eyes.

Priscilla shoved back her chair and took a step toward her brother and swung an open palm at his face.

Lewis deftly seized her wrist and squeezed down hard as he said, "Don't you ever try that again!"

"Let go of me!" Priscilla leaned toward him in an attempt to ease the pain.

"What's going on here?" Evelyn's strained voice came from the back door of the mansion.

Releasing his grip on Priscilla's wrist, Lewis met his mother's gaze and said, "We were just havin' a little disagreement."

"About what?"

"He's being his usual repugnant self, Mother," Priscilla said. "He just called Negroes animals."

Evelyn's gaze ran to a teary-eyed Dorena, who was slumped and cowering in her chair. Turning back to Lewis, she said, "Lewis, you apologize to Dorena right now!"

Lewis gave his mother a defiant look, wheeled about, and stomped off the porch.

"Lewis! Don't you turn your back on me!"

He ignored his mother and set fiery eyes on his sister. "You shouldn't be teachin' that black animal to read and write, Priscilla! I've got a good mind to report you to the authorities!" With that, he pivoted and stomped away.

"Lewis!" Evelyn screamed. "You leave it alone, do you hear me? Don't you dare go to the law! Your sister has a right to teach her own slave anything she wants! Do you hear me?"

Lewis did not break his stride. Seconds later, he disappeared around the corner of the house.

Priscilla rushed to Dorena and wrapped her arms around her. Dorena sucked in a sob, feeling a hot drift of tears on her cheeks.

"I love you," Priscilla said, squeezing her tight.

"I love you too . . . Miss Priscilla. I don't want to be taken away from you!"

"I'm not going to let that happen. Nobody is going to take you away from me."

"That's right, honey," Evelyn said, patting Dorena's shoulder. "Don't you worry. Master Charles will keep Lewis in line."

Looking up at Evelyn through her tears, Dorena said, "Why does Master Lewis hate me and my people?"

"I don't know. But don't let him frighten you. Everything will be fine."

Brushing tears from Dorena's cheeks with her fingertips, Priscilla said, "I'm so sorry for Lewis's cutting, untrue words. I don't know what's the matter with him, but don't let what he said bother you."

Dorena drew a shuddering breath and nodded. "I'll be fine as long as you two and Master Charles love me."

Evelyn bent over her and said, "Well, then, you'll be fine. Because we do." With that, she went back into the house.

Priscilla sat down at the table again, facing Dorena. "I'm so glad we have each other," she said.

"I am, too. I . . . I hope we can still be close, even when we are adults."

"I'm sure the day will come when we will have to part. I mean, when the young man God has for me comes along and I get married. For sure, we won't live here on the plantation. We'll have to live in our own home and live our own lives. But whether we live in Charleston or many miles away, you and I will still be together in our hearts."

"But you will come and see your parents now and then, won't you? Even if you live many miles from here?"

"Of course."

"So we can see each other then."

"Yes. And when the Lord brings His chosen young man into your life, you will marry him and be very happy. Of course, that young man will have to be a slave here on our plantation, and you will live in one of the cabins."

"As long as it is on this plantation, I will be happy," Dorena said. "Even if your brother does hate me."

"Forget him, honey. Just think about the future and the happy life the Lord has planned for you with the man He has picked for you."

Dorena smiled. "Isn't it wonderful to know that as God's children, He does plan our lives?"

"It sure is," said Priscilla with a soft sigh.

Both girls grew quiet, and a faraway look captured their eyes as they thought about their futures. After a few minutes, Priscilla took hold of Dorena's hand.

"Even though we both know that we will be separated by our cultures, and maybe by miles . . . let us both vow in our hearts that we will always have our special friendship."

"Oh yes," Dorena said. "Always."

"Always," Priscilla echoed. "Because we are true friends, time and circumstance cannot change our love for each other."

"Never," Dorena said softly.

Priscilla squeezed her best friend's hand. "Never."

There was silence between them for another brief moment, then Priscilla said, "I've thought about it a lot. The Lord will probably bring His chosen young man to me by putting him in our church."

"I would think so," said Dorena. "And the only way I can see the Lord bring His chosen young man for me into my life is for your father to purchase him as a slave."

Priscilla smiled. "Unless he's already here."

Dorena shook her head. "Not from what I have to choose from at the moment. As you know, there are some boys my age, but only a few are Christians, and even then, they don't interest me. They're nice boys, but . . ."

"But not husband material?"

"For sure."

"Well, then, the Lord will have to guide my father in his slave purchases and put that right young man on his heart. And He can certainly do that."

"I know He can," said Dorena, her eyes shining.

"Oh, honey! It will be wonderful to watch the Lord work in His marvelous way to accomplish His will in both of our lives."

"Yes, it will. Dear Priscilla, I'm so glad you brought me to Jesus!"

"I'm glad I had that privilege," Priscilla said. She rose from her chair and Dorena stood up too.

As the girls embraced, Priscilla said, "We'll make every minute count before we grow up and get married."

It was a bright, sunny Sunday in Charleston as the church services let out and the people emerged from the white frame building. They were rejoicing in the good number of people who walked the aisles to open their hearts to Jesus.

Charles Moore and Zack Johnson stood together talking, squinting against the harsh rays of the sun. Both Evelyn and Catherine held their lacy parasols to block the sun from their faces.

Zack Johnson noticed a middle-aged couple come out the door. He waved to them. To the Moores, he said, "Charles and Evelyn . . . have you met Darrell and Roberta Brown? They're new in town."

"We were in the line that greeted them when they joined the church a couple of weeks ago," Charles said, "but other than that, we haven't gotten to know them."

Zack motioned to the Browns. When they stepped up, he formally introduced them to the Moores, explaining to Charles and Evelyn that the Browns had moved to Charleston from way up in Maine and were New Englanders by birth. They now owned and operated the Main Street Clothiers in downtown Charleston.

After a few comments about the contrast between Maine and South Carolina, the Moores excused themselves and headed for their carriage.

"Nice folks," said Darrell Brown, watching Charles and Evelyn walk away.

"The best," Zack said.

Catherine ran her gaze over their faces and said, "Darrell, Roberta, our cook has plenty of food on the stove at home. Would you honor us by having Sunday dinner with us?"

"We'd be delighted!" Darrell said. "We've never been on a plantation before. They don't have them in Maine."

The Johnsons laughed.

"We would love to see your plantation," said Roberta.

"Tell you what," Catherine said. "After dinner we can sit out on our shaded back porch and maybe catch a stray breeze."

Roberta chuckled. "That will be better than being cooped up in our living quarters above the store!"

"Right, Mama," Darrell said. Then to the Johnsons he said, "We'll follow in our carriage."

When they reached the parking lot, the Browns saw Dan, Angeline, and Alexander waiting in the Johnson carriage. Dan was already in the driver's seat.

The Browns invited Angeline and Alexander to ride with them, then both vehicles pulled out of the parking lot with the Johnson carriage in the lead.

WHEN THE TWO CARRIAGES ROLLED TO A HALT on the back side of the Johnson mansion, the slave church had just let out. The slaves, in small groups, passed by from the enclosed pavilion where they held their services. When Zack Johnson saw the last group, he smiled and waved at them, calling out, "Zebulun! Come over here and bring the others."

As the older man led the rest of the group toward the two carriages, Zack got out and said to the Browns, "Zebulun is the preacher of our slave people. I want you to meet him and the others with him."

The Johnsons and the Browns were out of the carriages as the group of black people drew up. "Yassuh, Massa Zack?" said the silver-haired man who was in his late seventies.

"Zebulun, I want our new friends to meet you. They are Christians and new members of our church."

While the introductions were being made, Zebulun noticed a quizzical look on the Browns' faces.

Smiling at them, Zebulun said, "Mr. and Mrs. Brown, you look amazed that Massa Zack would care to have you meet some of his slaves. Am I right?"

Darrell's features crimsoned. "Well . . . ah . . . yes, Zebulun. We've always heard that slave owners treat their slaves as exactly that . . . slaves. But I can assure you that both Mrs. Brown and I are delighted to see the Johnsons care enough for you to introduce you to their friends. We expected that as Christians they would be kind to you, but this goes beyond that."

Tears filled Zebulun's eyes as he said, "Mr. Brown, Massa Zack and his family are fine Christians and always deal with us slaves in a Christlike

85

spirit. One thing we appreciate so much is that Massa Zack uses the Task System with us."

"That's right, Zeb," spoke up one of the slave men in the group. "Lots of the plantation owners don't use it, but we are so glad he does." He turned to Zack and said, "Thank you, Massa Zack, fo' bein' so kind to us."

Zack grinned. "Oswald, I wouldn't have it any other way. I want all of you to have some time to rest and to have as much happiness as possible in your lives."

Speaking for the rest of the group, Zebulun told the Browns it was a pleasure to meet them; then he led the other slaves away.

Darrell turned to Zack. "What is the Task System?"

"I'll explain it to you while we eat dinner."

Upon entering the mansion, Catherine and Angeline left the men in the sitting room and showed Roberta to a small powder room on the ground floor where she could remove her hat and freshen up.

While Roberta used the water to wash road dust from her face, Catherine left Angeline with her, saying she would let Samantha and the servants know they needed two more places set at the dining room table.

When Catherine returned to the powder room, and both she and Angeline had freshened up, the three women returned to the sitting room.

"All right, everybody," Catherine said. "The cook tells me she will have the meal on the table by the time we get there."

Catherine led her family and guests down the hall and into the lovely, well-appointed dining room. The long windows were open, and a cool draft floated through the room, fluttering the lace curtains. A white damask cloth covered the spacious table set with blue willow china and a large bouquet of fragrant roses in the center.

Mouthwatering aromas drifted from the sideboard as the servants stood ready to serve the meal.

Roberta Brown's eyes grew wide as she took in the loveliness of the room. In her heart, she was not at all envious. She was thankful for the way the Lord had blessed Darrell and herself in the clothing business, but she did stand amazed at the opulence that surrounded her in the Johnson home. She smiled in appreciation and said, "Catherine, you have a beautiful home."

"Thank you, dear," Catherine said, placing an arm around her shoulder. "The Lord has blessed us beyond our fondest dreams."

When everyone was seated, Zack asked Dan to give their prayer of thanks for the food. When the prayer had been offered, the servants were quick to see that the Browns were served first.

As the Johnsons and their guests began eating, Darrell Brown said, "I want that Task System explained, Zack; but first let me say that I am so pleased to learn that all slave owners do not mistreat their slaves. Up North, that's the impression everybody has. I couldn't picture Christian plantation owners being that way, but what you've shown me is better than anything I could even imagine. I commend you for it."

Zack set his fork down. "Darrell, I can't understand how any plantation owner could be mean and brutal to his slaves, but many of them are. I could tell you and Roberta some awful stories about slave mistreatment in this Charleston area, but it would ruin your dinner."

"That's for sure, Daddy," Angeline said.

Darrell smiled at the girl, then looked at Zack and said, "Now . . . tell me about this Task System."

"It's fairly new, Darrell. About five years ago, a slave owner in Mississippi named Stephen Walsh became concerned about the way slaves all over the South were being worked so hard that great numbers of them were dying from exhaustion. Many of the plantation owners work their slaves fifteen, sixteen hours a day."

"Mercy!" Roberta said, her eyes wide.

"That's especially bad in the heat of the summer," put in Dan.

Zack nodded. "Stephen Walsh had seen enough of this horror, and it stirred him to do something about it. He was also upset that slaves were being robbed of their dignity, and like all human beings, needed something in life other than hard labor."

"Well, God bless him," Roberta said.

Zack smiled at her. "Amen. Of course Walsh couldn't force the Task System upon the plantation owners, but when he came up with it, he asked all slave owners to give it serious consideration and to subscribe to the system for the sake of their slaves. The system provides a decent life for them. It regulates the amount of labor each slave is assigned. A task is a specific measure of work that can be reasonably completed in a ten-hour day. And this means reasonable according to their age and whether they are male or female."

He took a sip of hot coffee, then went on. "After the 'task' is finished, the slave has the rest of the day off. If he or she chooses to do additional work that day, he or she is paid for it."

"I've never heard of this!" Darrell said.

"Like I said, it's only been around for five years. But this income, no matter how small, provides a way for the slaves to have some dignity and to have a bit of comfort in their lives."

"That's wonderful," said Darrell.

"You should point out, darling," Catherine said, "that you were almost using the principles of the Task System before Stephen Walsh came up with it."

Zack nodded. "Almost. I was working my slaves only eight hours a day, six days a week, which I still do. But I had never thought of paying them wages when the unavoidable times came that I had to work them more than eight hours. Of course, I do that now."

"Well, I'm glad you use the system," Darrell said.

Alexander spoke up for the first time. "So are all our slaves, sir."

"I can see why, now that I understand it," Roberta said. "I really do commend you for it."

"Me, too," said Darrell. "Now, could you explain something else? Up North they say that in the South there are two kinds of slaves. One is the 'chattel' slave, and I can't remember what they said the other kind is called. Neither do I know the difference."

"The other kind is the 'freehold' slave," Zack said. "The difference is that the freehold slave is bound to a piece of land and cannot be transferred or sold away from the estate. The master of a freehold slave owns the slave's labor but not his or her person. The chattel slave is the equivalent of movable property and can be sold away, even as horses and cattle are sold.

"Our slaves are all the chattel kind, but as you and Roberta can see, they are not treated like animals. I feel that the chattel system is far better for the slaves. If we should sell this plantation, go elsewhere and buy another one, all of my slaves could go with me."

"So who establishes whether the slaves are freehold or chattel?" Darrell asked.

"The plantation owner has that choice when he has his property licensed to own slaves. Many owners like the freehold system better, so if they sell out, they are paid a good price for their slaves, who have to stay with the plantation. As I said, I like the chattel system better."

"Thanks for explaining it," Darrell said.

Dan chuckled. "Now, you take me, for instance. I'm the 'chattel' kind. It looks like I may be leaving the land here and going to Texas. I can do it, since as a chattel slave I am movable property."

The Browns laughed, then Darrell said, "Are you really going to Texas, Dan?"

"It's in the 'praying about it' stage right now, sir, but every day I feel more confident that it's what the Lord wants me to do."

"What will you do there?" Roberta asked.

"Become a cattle rancher."

"That sounds interesting. Tell us about it."

Dan told the Browns about Bill Wickburg and what he had learned from him, and of Bill's desire to have him come to the Austin area.

"Well, this kind of move does warrant a great deal of prayer," Darrell said. "Roberta and I prayed hard for quite some time before we left Maine to come to South Carolina. We are superbly happy with our decision because we know we're in God's will. We have perfect peace about it."

"That's right," Roberta said. "We love it here."

"Just as much as you'll love it in Texas, Dan," Darrell said, "if it's God's will for you to go there."

It was late in the afternoon the next day when Angeline Johnson left her room and headed toward the winding staircase. As she drew near Dan's room, she noticed that his door was standing open. He was sitting on his bed engrossed in a newspaper spread before him.

Angeline leaned against the doorjamb and studied him silently. Tears filmed her eyes. It was when she sniffed that Dan looked up and realized she had been there for a while. Smiling, he said, "Hello, favorite sister."

She palmed away the moisture on her cheeks. "I'm your only sister, silly," she replied, walking toward him.

"True, but you're still my favorite." When she came closer he frowned at her countenance. "What are you crying about? What's wrong?"

"I was just thinking about how much I'm going to miss you when you go to Texas. You are going to Texas, aren't you?"

"I really believe I am, sis."

Angeline nodded. "Mm-hmm. I really believe you are, too." As she spoke, her eyes fell to the open newspaper on the bed. She saw that it was that day's edition of the *Columbia Daily Sentinel*. "Are you reading something about the West?"

"Yes," he said, leaning over to pick up the paper. Folding it so she could see the article he had been reading, he moved beside her and pointed with his forefinger. "Right here, little sis. This article tells abo'it how the gold rush that started in California in 1849 is beginning to wane, but not the migration of people to all parts of the West. It says here that cattle ranching is now big business in Texas and is swiftly becoming so in all of the western territories."

Angeline laid her head against her big brother's shoulder and stared at the paper in his hand. "Dan, I know you aren't going to be happy until you're ranching in Texas. I want you to be happy . . . but I sure am going to miss you."

He pressed her tighter against his shoulder. "I'm going to miss you, too, baby sister. But a man has to do what he has to do. When I get my ranch established, you can come and visit me."

Angeline chuckled. "I'll be there with bells on."

"I'm sure the whole family will come. They'll want to see my ranch."

"We sure will." Angeline let a few seconds pass, then said, "Dan, what about Sophie Lanham and Edna Hamilton? They both have romantic ideas about you."

"Well, sweetie, Sophie and Edna are nice Christian girls, and I've enjoyed taking them to some of the church functions. But I'm not interested in either of them for a wife. I'm in no rush to get married yet. I'll no doubt wait till I get to Texas to find the right young woman and marry her. Since the Lord is leading me that direction, I'm sure the one He has picked out is waiting there for me."

Angeline turned so she could hug him, and as she squeezed hard, she said, "It sure won't be the same around here without you. I really am going to miss you terribly."

On Thursday, March 22, Dan Johnson came to the supper table with a newspaper folded under his arm. He laid the paper on his lap, but not before his father noted that it was that day's edition of the *South Carolina Gazette*.

Zack gave him a curious glance. "Are you going to read today's *Gazette* to us while we eat, son?"

"Not exactly, Pa. Have you seen it?"

"No. Haven't had time. What is it you want to show us?"

"Let's go ahead and get started, then I'll tell you."

"Yes," said Catherine, smiling. "If we don't get started, the food is going to get cold."

After prayer had been offered and the family had started eating, Zack said, "All right, son. What is it?"

"Well, Pa, lately you've been talking about buying a few more slaves."

"Mm-hmm."

"This edition has a full-page advertisement about a slave auction to take place at the outdoor auction arena this coming Monday."

"Oh, really? Let me see it."

Dan lifted the paper from his lap and handed it to his father. "I have it folded so you can see the whole page when you open it up."

As his eyes ran down the page, Zack said, "It's Thomas Green again."

"Yes, sir."

"Hmm. Says he's bringing a shipload of slaves from South Africa again. If I remember correctly, this makes his third load from there. He used to bring them all from West and East Africa."

"Why do you suppose he changed locations, Pa?" Alexander asked.

"I'm sure it's because South Africa is under British rule and the Negroes there all speak English." Zack's eyes roamed the page. "Yes, it says right here that all the slaves Green is bringing with him know English, and some of them can read and write. He's using the slave ship *Berkeley* this time. It's supposed to dock in Charleston Harbor sometime Saturday evening. It says here that, as usual, Green has already sold many of the slaves to plantation owners who ordered them in advance, but most of them will be sold at the auction on Monday. Green says he will have a good number of choice slaves on the block."

"How many do you think you'll buy, Zack?" Catherine asked.

"Don't know for sure, honey." Zack folded the paper and handed it back to his oldest son. "We'll see how it looks and what kind of prices they're going for."

On Saturday evening, March 24, the *Berkeley* swung off the Atlantic Ocean in the last moments of sunset's afterglow and steamed toward Charleston.

As the ship edged into port, it was obliged to move slowly because of the sandbars and oyster shoals lining the channel. All of the slaves stood on the deck and set their gaze on the view around them. They took in the lush coastline with reedy marshes edging the waterfront and green grass rising waist-high out of soft gray mud. Beyond the marshes stood firm soil with a curtain of trees and thickets so dense that light could barely penetrate it at midday.

The harbor at Charleston was shaped by the confluence of the Ashley and the Cooper Rivers. Flowing south, the wide rivers formed a peninsula and met at a place called Oyster Point, a protruding piece of land colored white with shells. The Cooper ran around the eastern edge of the point and the Ashley around the west.

Charleston stood on the east side of the peninsula, facing the Cooper River. At the entrance of the harbor stood Fort Sumter on Sullivan's Island. Uniformed men could be seen at the flag pole, bringing the red, white, and blue flag down for the night.

Benjamin stood at the railing between two male slaves. Soon the docks came into view, and by the light of many large kerosene lanterns that lined them, he watched the dock workers preparing the big thick ropes to secure the ship to the dock. A dark feeling descended over him like a suffocating blanket. With everything that was in him, Benjamin wanted to be free.

Soon the *Berkeley*'s propeller was churning in reverse, bringing the vessel to a halt. Captain Spencer Kimball's crewmen dropped the anchor, and the dock crew went to work to secure the ship. When the gangplank was lowered into place, Benjamin watched Thomas Green walk down it. As he reached the dock, a man hurried up to meet him.

Thomas Green smiled at the approach of his assistant, Jim Lynch. The man ran his gaze over the crowd of slaves standing on the deck and said, "Well, boss, it looks like you got yourself a pretty big load."

"Would have been bigger, Jim, but quite a number of the darkies came down with dysentery on the way over. Twenty-four of them died by the time we were a hundred miles from the Carolina coast. Forty-two others are getting over it. We buried the dead ones at sea. But we've still got a pretty good bunch to sell."

"Well, I'm sorry for the ones you lost, but I guess it could have been worse."

"Yeah. It could've been much worse. Is the big barn at the auction arena ready to house the slaves until the auction on Monday?"

"Yes, sir. It sure is. The food is ready, too."

"Good. We'll have to put the sick ones in the barn, too. When they get well, we'll have to figure out a way to sell them."

Lynch nodded. "I have it all set, sir. The slaves you have already sold will be picked up Monday morning before the auction starts at ten o'clock."

"All right. I assume the ad I left for you to put in the *Gazette* was placed as planned?"

"Yes, sir."

"Good. And you have the men ready to escort the slaves across town to the barn?"

"Sure do. Fourteen of them. If you'll look over there in the shadows at the back side of the dock, you'll see them."

Green glanced that way and could make out the men who waited with rifles in their hands. "Okay. Let's get the slaves off the ship."

Benjamin and his two friends watched Thomas Green as he stood on the dock, talking to his assistant.

Benjamin's breathing turned ragged as he said, "I can't do it. I just can't do it. I've got to escape."

"There is no way to escape," Jarod said, who was just a year older than Benjamin. "If you try it, those men down there with the rifles will shoot you."

"Jarod is right, Benjamin," said Stamus, who was in his thirties. "If you try to escape, they will kill you. And what possible way is there? Jump overboard and swim back to Cape Town?"

Benjamin's eyes were riveted on the armed men in the shadows as he said, "You jest, Stamus. Of course I cannot swim back to Cape Town. But the only possible way of escape is to jump overboard and swim until I find a place to come out where I can run and get away. If I could do it without being seen, by the time they missed me, I could be somewhere inland where they cannot find me."

"But they would track you down," Jarod said. "If Mr. Green let you live, you no doubt would be beaten severely. Or they might just shoot you on the spot when they find you."

"You are very strong physically, Benjamin," said Stamus, "and you are a good swimmer. But Jarod is right. Mr. Green would be very angry if you escaped, and he would have his men track you down. You must not try it. They will kill you."

Benjamin's eyes followed Thomas Green and his assistant as they walked toward the gangplank. "Better to be dead than a slave for the rest of my life," he said through clenched teeth. "Both of you have wives to be concerned about. I have no family. My father and mother are dead. I have nothing to lose. I am going to jump overboard."

Both men kept their eyes on Benjamin as he made his way through the crowd of slaves as if he were merely positioning himself to walk down the gangplank when the orders came to do so.

"He will not make it," Stamus said.

"I fear not," said Jarod. "But I hope he does."

Down on the dock, Thomas Green and Jim Lynch started up the gangplank with half of the armed men following them. The others formed a semicircle where the slaves would come down on the dock.

When Green and Lynch reached the deck, Captain Spencer Kimball was there to greet Lynch.

Kimball handed Lynch a clipboard with papers on it and said, "Jim, all of the Negroes who were put aboard the ship in Cape Town are listed here. Those who were buried at sea have a line drawn through their names, and those who are in their cabins sick are marked as such."

"All right, Captain. Thank you."

"We'll come back for the sick ones shortly, Captain," Green said. Then, running his gaze over the crowd of black faces, he called loudly, "Everybody line up at the gangplank. Families stay together. You will go down the gangplank one at a time so you can be checked off the list as you leave the ship."

Keeping himself at the edge of the crowd, Benjamin felt his mouth go dry. His heart was pounding. He had to make his move now.

MAIL ORDER BRIDE SERIES

NO. 5
1855
USA

AL & JOANNA LACY

BABIES AND SMALL CHILDREN FUSSED and cried as preparations were made to take them off the ship. There was a hubbub of voices and the sound of parents trying to hush their frightened, unhappy children.

Before the slaves started down the gangplank, Thomas Green stood at the opening in the railing and raised his hands. "Get those children quiet! I mean it! Right now!"

There was a hurried effort to obey his command, and within a moment, the noise volume lowered.

"Now listen to me!" said Green. "When you are taken from the harbor, you will be escorted through the streets to the place where you will stay until Monday morning. The men who will escort you are armed. They have orders from me to shoot any slave who attempts to escape. Those of you with children, make sure they stay in your grasp at all times. If one of them should decide to run from you and you go after him, you will be shot as one who is trying to escape. No one is going to escape! Now, let's get lined up and move off the ship."

While the slaves moved as one body toward the gangplank, the front of the crowd began to form a single line to pass by Jim Lynch while Thomas Green looked on.

Benjamin ran his gaze to the dark waters of Charleston Harbor that lapped against the dock. How was he going to get overboard? The armed men would see him move toward the edge of the deck.

There was an ever-tightening knot in the pit of Benjamin's stomach. His tongue felt thick and dry and clung to the roof of his mouth. He stayed at the edge of the slow-moving crowd and saw Jarod and Stamus with their wives. Both men were looking at him covertly, deep concern showing on their faces.

Benjamin avoided their eyes, running his gaze once again past the edge of the deck to the murky water below. His heart thudded against his ribs.

The name checking began, and one by one the slaves started down the gangplank. Infants and small children were in their parents' arms, and others were being held by the hand. Many of the children were crying again.

Tension mounted in Benjamin as he inched his way closer with the crowd toward the gangplank. In just a few minutes, his opportunity to slip away and go into the harbor waters would be gone.

Suddenly, a small boy three or four years old got loose from his mother and ran across the deck toward the bow of the ship. The father was holding an infant in his arms as he dashed after the child, calling him by name. The mother was on his heels, crying for her little son to stop.

With the attention of the crowd on the pursuing parents, another child broke loose and ran the same direction. There was instant confusion as two more parents, both holding smaller children, ran after him. Thomas Green shouted for the men to grab the child, and there was a loud hubbub on the deck.

When Benjamin saw that everyone's attention was fixed on the excitement happening on the starboard side, he went to the port side. When he was in the shadows, he turned and ran. Just before he reached the edge of the deck, he turned to look behind him, a pulse pounding in his ears. No one had noticed him, for there were no pursuers.

He swung a leg over the rail and eased himself down, using the horizontal rungs to lower himself until his head was below deck level. His heart was pounding like a trip-hammer as he looked down at the inky water below. Taking a deep breath, he let go of the rung and felt himself plummeting downward. He stiffened his body straight as a board so he would make as small a splash as possible.

Suddenly Benjamin was in the water and felt as if he had been wrapped in ice. The water was still very cold from the recent winter months. When he surfaced, he swam as fast as he could toward the bow of the ship. His body was quivering, but he stayed close to the ship and listened for sounds above him.

All was quiet. Apparently the children had been caught and were moving back to the gangplank with their parents.

Benjamin knew he hadn't secured his escape yet. He still had to make it to dry ground, shake Thomas Green's armed men off his trail, then lose himself in a strange land where black men lived as slaves. How he would survive, he had no idea. But survive he would . . . as a free man.

In spite of the water's temperature, Benjamin went beneath the surface and swam away from the docks, surfacing periodically to take a breath of air. After a while, he made his way to dry ground and lay on the shore to catch his breath. By the light of lanterns burning along the town's edge, Benjamin could see that a dirt road ran along the shore, and from it, four or five streets cut inland.

His teeth chattered uncontrollably as he rose to his feet and glanced back at the docks, then looked at the *Berkeley*. The huge black ship seemed to him to be a floating prison from which he had just escaped. At the same time, it was a death boat that had taken his parents away from him forever. Grief filled his heart as he thought of his dead mother and father, then he took a deep breath and ran as fast as he could toward the town.

The first buildings Benjamin reached were simple clapboard structures with sharply pitched roofs, though a few brick buildings could be seen. Some had slightly pitched roofs, and others were flat.

When he came to an alley, he plunged into the pocket of darkness, leaned his back against a wall, and bent over to catch his breath. He wondered if Thomas Green knew by now that he was gone from the ship.

Once he was breathing almost normally again, Benjamin made his way toward the other end of the alley where he could see a patch of light that showed him a wide street. As he drew near the end of the alley, he heard the sound of horses' hooves on cobblestone and flattened himself against the wall of a frame building that reached all the way to the board sidewalk along the street. His heart lurched in his chest. Were they searching for him already?

His fear eased when he saw a carriage pass by with a lantern burning on each side of the cab. All was silent then, so he slowly inched his way toward the street.

Just as Benjamin reached the end of the large frame building, he heard male voices and the sound of footsteps on the board sidewalk. Suddenly two men appeared. Their conversation broke off as they set eyes on Benjamin's form in the pale light coming from the kerosene lanterns along the street.

"Hey, Ted. Do you see what I see?"

The other man let out an evil-sounding chuckle. "Yeah, Marv. It looks like we've got us a darkie prowlin' in the alley. What're you doin' here, boy?"

Benjamin tensed, every nerve in his body feeling like it was stretched to the limit.

"You know what we've got, here, don't you, Ted? We've got us a runaway slave from one of the plantations around here. Whoever owns him will give us a fat reward for bringin' him back. Which plantation you from, boy?"

Benjamin worked his tongue loose and said, "I am not from any plantation. I am not a slave."

Ted laughed. "You're not a slave? Well, black boy, what are you? President of a bank? If you're a free blackie, then you're carryin' papers to prove it. Let's see 'em."

Benjamin set his jaw. "Just go away and leave me alone. I was not bothering you."

"Of course not," said Marv. "But you are a runaway. You haven't shown us any emancipation papers. Now, just tell us which plantation you're from, and we'll take you safely back to your owner."

"I told you," Benjamin said, "I am not anybody's slave. I have no owner to whom you can return me."

"Then why haven't you produced your papers?"

A dog was barking somewhere a few blocks away.

A hard, brittle anger flared up within Benjamin. These men could cause him to be caught by Thomas Green and his men if he didn't get away from them. His breath was hot as he said, "You have no authority to demand that I produce papers. I am not a runaway from any plantation. You were on your way somewhere. Why don't you just keep going and forget you saw me?"

Ted chortled. "Guess we'll just have to take him to the constable's office, Marv. Let the law find out who he belongs to, then collect our reward."

"Okay. Let's take him."

As he spoke, Marv reached out and gripped Benjamin's left arm. "Let's go, boy."

Benjamin yanked his arm free. "Do not touch me!"

Marv looked at his friend. "C'mon, Ted. Let's wrap him up and deliver him to the law."

As both men stepped closer to him, Benjamin knew he had only one choice. Marv was closest to him and was opening his hands to grab him.

Benjamin planted his feet and unfolded like a coiled spring, driving a rock-hard fist into the man's face. The impact sounded like a flat rock falling into mud. Marv went down like a dead tree in a high wind, and Ted swung at the black man's jaw. All he found was thin air. Then he was greeted with a sledgehammer blow that exploded something inside his head like a million pinwheels of stars.

As Benjamin stood over the men, he could see they were out cold. The breath was sawing in and out of his lungs, more from anger than exertion. Suddenly he was aware of another carriage coming along the street.

He grabbed both men by their collars and dragged them into the deep shadows of the alley. He flattened himself against the wall of the building till the carriage had passed, then ran down the street the opposite direction and plunged into another alley.

After waiting there for a few minutes, he moved back to the street, looked both ways and crossed. He ran for two blocks and dashed into another alley as he saw a wagon approaching. He hid himself behind some large wooden crates and decided to stay there until the crack of dawn when he would make a run for it and get out of Charleston.

As he sat on the ground in deep shadow, Benjamin let his mind run back to the night he and his parents made an escape attempt from Cape Town, hoping to make it to Transvaal and live as free people. He told himself he would not fail this time. He would get away! And go where?

The thought tortured his weary mind. Where would he go? For sure, he would have to leave what he knew was the Deep South. Someone had told him that people in the north part of the United States were against slavery.

That is it! he thought. *I will go to the North and live as a free man.*

When the last slave had been checked off aboard the *Berkeley,* Jim Lynch frowned and looked at his boss. "Mr. Green, I think when you had the crewmen count the sick ones in their cabins, they must have made a mistake."

"What do you mean?"

"We're missing one person."

"Can't be," said Green. "I'm sure my men counted the sick ones correctly. They did a double check while the ship was docking. Their tally has to be right."

"Then how could we be missing one person? You stood right there and watched me check them off as they passed by. I know I didn't make a mistake."

"Who is missing?" Green asked.

"A nineteen-year-old slave named Benjamin."

Green's face stiffened. "Benjamin?"

"Yes, sir."

"Hmm. We had some problems with him on the way over. His parents died from the dysentery. Now that you mention it, I don't remember him passing the checkpoint."

"He sure didn't, sir, or I'd have him checked off here on the list."

Green rubbed his chin thoughtfully. "We're going to have to make a thorough search of the ship. He's got to be here somewhere. I want him found immediately."

Jim Lynch hurried to the bridge and told Captain Kimball that Benjamin was missing. Kimball assembled his ship crew with Thomas Green's crewmen, and they scattered throughout the ship. Almost a half hour had passed when they met on the deck. After covering every square inch of the vessel, they reported that Benjamin was not on board.

Thomas Green was furious. He ejected a string of profanity and said to his men, "He must be tracked down and caught immediately!"

"Mr. Green," said Kimball, "I can't let my men off the ship. We have to prepare to pull out by tomorrow afternoon."

"All right, all right." Then he said to Lynch, "Jim, we'll have to use every available man in our crew. That low-down blackie has got to be caught!"

"Tell you what, Mr. Green," said Kimball, "the best thing to do is go to the town constable's office and tell the man in charge about Benjamin. You'll catch him a lot faster if you have law officers after him who are familiar with the town and the area."

Green and Lynch hurried through the streets of Charleston to the constable's office. They found Lieutenant Howard Follett on duty, who was in charge of the office for the night. Green reported the runaway male slave and told the lieutenant he wanted law officers after him immediately.

"Now, calm down, Mr. Green," Follett said. "It would be futile for us to try to run the slave down in the darkness. We'll begin our search at dawn."

"All right," said Green, breathing hard. "My men will help you."

The lieutenant shook his head. "That won't be necessary, sir."

"But it could speed up catching him."

"You don't understand, sir," said Follett. "Chief Constable Mulvey would never allow your men to join us in the search. You have come here asking for our help. We will be glad to give it, but you must allow our officers to pursue the slave with no one to hinder us. If you would rather pursue him on your own, you are welcome to do it."

Thomas Green cleared his throat and said, "No. I'll let you do it. You will have your men begin searching for him at dawn, right?"

"Yes, sir. Now, I need a description of him. How old is he?"

"He's nineteen."

Follett wrote it down. "Approximate height?"

"He's a good six feet. Maybe six-one. Very muscular. Broad shoulders. Slender waist. His name is Benjamin. When he is placed on the auction block, any plantation owner will be able to see immediately that he can do a tremendous amount of work in a day."

As Follett was writing, Green said, "Lieutenant, it's very important that Benjamin be caught. With his physique and stature, he's my prime slave for the auction. Not only is he big and strong, but he speaks, reads, and writes English better than the average South African Negro by far. He will sell for top dollar. Do you understand what I'm saying? Slave trading is my business. It's my living. I need this man caught."

"Yes, sir," said Follett. "We'll catch him, sir. Now, where will we find you when we have him?"

"I'm staying at the Charleston Arms Hotel."

"All right, sir. Now, you go get yourself a good night's sleep and let us do our job."

As dawn broke over Charleston, Benjamin moved about the alleys, trying to find something to eat. He could find nothing.

He had resigned himself to the fact that returning to South Africa was impossible. His only hope was to get out of Charleston and head north where slavery was not allowed.

He checked the position of the rising sun and worked his way northward. As he dashed from alley to alley and street to street, he was becoming more confused. It seemed he was getting no closer to Charleston's north edge.

Benjamin was glad it was Sunday morning, for he had been told that all businesses were closed on Sundays in the United States. This would mean fewer people on the streets to see him.

When he reached an alley after darting a half block down a street, he saw two men in blue uniforms. They wore sidearms and carried long black sticks. They were standing at the mouth of an alley another half block away.

One of them spotted him and pointed him out to the other officer. Fear lanced through Benjamin's heart like a cold blade of steel. Already puffing, he dashed into the alley he had been about to enter. He heard a shrill whistle and men shouting.

When he saw two more uniformed men appear at the far end of the alley, he skidded to a stop. They were coming on the run, shouting at him to halt. With the breath sawing in and out of his lungs, Benjamin wheeled to run the other way but froze in his tracks. The first two officers were hurrying toward him, guns drawn. One of them commanded him to stand still.

Sweat beaded on Benjamin's brow as the four officers surrounded him. The first two made him place his hands behind his back and cuffed his wrists, then put shackles on his ankles.

"Now, blackie," said one of them, "you're going back to your owner."

As all four officers ushered Benjamin along the street, one of them said, "So how'd you get off that ship, blackie?"

Benjamin gave him a sullen look. "I went overboard and swam to shore."

"Took some courage to do that."

"Not courage, officer . . . desperation."

The officers looked at each other and shook their heads.

Moments later, the officers ushered their captive through the doors of the police station. Chief Constable Hugh Mulvey was in the office, talking to one of his men. When the men in blue came in with their prisoner, Mulvey smiled. "So you got him!"

"Yes, sir," said one man. "You want him in a cell, I assume, until Mr. Green can come and get him?"

"Yes. Lock him up. Good work, men. Walters and Manning, you go to the Charleston Arms Hotel and tell Thomas Green we've got his runaway slave."

As he was led to a cell with the chain clinking between his ankles, Benjamin clenched his jaws until they hurt.

In room 223 at the hotel, Jim Lynch was seated at a small table with his boss, giving him a report of the situation at the barn.

"Good work, Jim. I'm glad to know all is well."

"The slaves had a good breakfast, too, sir. Even all of the sick ones were able to at least eat a little."

Green smiled. "Very good! Maybe we'll have them well real soon and can get them sold in a hurry."

"I believe we will, sir."

Green's smile faded as he said, "Now my big concern is Benjamin. If they don't catch him—"

A loud knock at the door cut into Thomas Green's words.

"See who that is, Jim."

Lynch hurried to the door and opened it to find two uniformed officers.

"Good morning, sir," said one. "I'm Officer Reginald Manning, and this is Officer Henry Walters. Are you Mr. Green?"

"No, Officer. I'm his assistant. But Mr. Green is here. Please come in."

Green was on his feet as the officers stepped into the room.

"I'm Thomas Green," he said.

"Yes, sir. We have some good news for you, sir. We caught your runaway slave about a half hour ago. We have him in a cell at the station. Chief Mulvey sent us to let you know and to tell you that you can come and claim him anytime you wish."

Green chuckled merrily. "Well, Jim, let's go get him right now."

"Yes, sir!" said Lynch, glad to see his boss so happy.

A hungry, dejected Benjamin heard voices in the hallway that led from the cell block to the office. He looked up as the door opened and saw the chief constable leading Thomas Green and Jim Lynch toward his cell.

Benjamin looked up as Green stepped to the bars and gripped them. "So! You thought you could get away from me, eh, Benjamin?"

Giving the man a doleful glance, Benjamin said, "I tried."

Green's eyes flashed with anger. "Let me tell you something, boy! I would have you severely flogged as punishment for your deed, but I don't want any marks on your body. Tomorrow, you will bring me a good price at the auction."

Later that morning, at the slave church on the Finn Colvin plantation, Ol' Mose stood before his congregation and read them the words of the Lord Jesus Christ in John 8:36: "If the Son therefore shall make you free, ye shall be free indeed." He followed by reading them 1 Corinthians 3:13–14, explaining that it pointed to the judgment seat of Christ, where every Christian would one day stand:

> Every man's work shall be made manifest: for the day shall declare it, because it shall be revealed by fire; and the fire shall try every man's work of what sort it is. If any man's work abide which he hath built thereupon, he shall receive a reward.

"Brethren," said the old man in his cracked voice, "this mornin' I want to preach to you about the rewards that God's born-again children will receive at the judgment seat of Christ for their faithfulness to the Lord while they were here on earth."

Mose referred to John 8:36 first, pointing out that everyone within the sound of his voice who had received the Lord Jesus Christ as their personal Saviour had been set free. They were no longer slaves to sin and Satan, but were free because of the precious blood of God's dear Lamb.

Mose went on to explain that on earth, he and his hearers were slaves and had no riches; but by their faithfulness to serve the Lord while here, they would be rewarded generously at the Judgment Seat and would have eternal riches. During the rest of the sermon he tried to encourage every Christian to walk close to the Lord and serve Him faithfully all the days of their lives.

After the service, some of the slaves gathered around the old man, thanking him for the good sermon. One older woman said, "Ol' Mose, we 'preciate you preachin' straight to us. There's no question in my mind that fo' yo' faithfulness in preachin' the Word, and in bringin' many souls to Jesus as a personal soul winner, you have great riches laid up in heaven."

"That's right," spoke up one of the young men. "Lots o' riches!"

The old man bent his head downward a bit and said, "Whatever riches this Ol' Mose might have in heaven are only because of the grace of God."

At their usual Sunday morning late breakfast, the Colvin family was discussing the slave auction that would take place at the outdoor arena the next morning.

"Pa, how many slaves you planning on buying?" George asked.

Finn thought on it a moment while chewing a mouthful of pancake, then swallowed and said, "Well, we've had two women and one man die since the last auction, in addition to Nathaniel. So I want to pick up at least two women and two men. It will take a good one to fill Nathaniel's place. He put out a lot of work. I just wish he hadn't let his stomachache keep him from going to the field that day."

Martha looked at him levelly. "It wouldn't have hurt you to be more understanding, Finn."

"No lectures, dear," he said flatly. "I do want you to go with the boys and me to the auction tomorrow, since I've got to buy a couple of women. I need your sharp eye, as usual, to help me in that department."

Martha nodded her consent.

Just after noon, the Moores were heading home from church in the family carriage.

Evelyn, who sat in the driver's seat next to her husband, said, "Charles, are you still planning to buy a husband and wife tomorrow?"

"Yes. That's all we need right now. I'd like you to go along, honey, so you can give me advice on the woman."

"Sure. No doubt the Johnsons will be there. Catherine and I can sit together."

From the rear seat, Priscilla said, "Papa, may Dorena and I go to the auction with you? We have always enjoyed going."

"Sure, honey."

Priscilla looked at Dorena, then said to her parents, "I sure hope the

Johnsons bring Angeline. We three girls didn't get our time together last week. I really missed it."

Evelyn chuckled. "Well, girls, maybe things won't be so hectic around both plantations this week, and you girls can get together for your regular visit."

9

THE NEXT MORNING, after the slaves were fed, Thomas Green addressed them and explained that they would be taken from the barn into the arena about thirty minutes before time for the auction to begin. They would be placed in a fenced pen at one end of the arena and sent out to stand on the auction block as directed by Jim Lynch. Before the auction began, the prospective buyers would pass by and look at them. If any of the buyers asked questions of the slaves, they were to politely answer them.

Green set his eyes on Benjamin and motioned for him to come forward. Green took him aside and said, "Benjamin, this may mean nothing to you, but you are my prime slave in this sale. When all of you are taken into the arena and placed in the pen, I want you to stand right up close to the fence so you can be plainly seen . . . and stay there. You will be the last slave to go on the block. Do you understand?"

Benjamin nodded morosely.

"Get that sour look off your face, boy! I want a pleasant look on your face when you're in the pen and on the block. Got it?"

"Yes," said Benjamin, ridding his face of some of the gloom.

Green studied Benjamin's features for a few seconds and said, "Well, that's a little better. Now, before you go out there, clear it up completely."

Just after nine o'clock, the crowd of plantation owners and those who accompanied them began to enter the arena and take seats in the bleachers.

The Moores and the Johnsons had chosen seats together. Lewis Moore placed himself somewhat aloof from the rest of them.

When the Colvins entered the arena, Finn spotted the Moores and the

Johnsons and pointed to them, saying to Martha and his sons, "Let's go sit right in front of them."

"Why do you want to do that?" Martha asked.

"It'll make 'em nervous."

"Why do you have to be a thorn in their side?"

"Just because," Finn said.

When the Colvins were seating themselves in the row directly ahead of the Moores and the Johnsons, Finn greeted Charles and Zack. Both men returned the greeting in a pleasant manner.

Martha ran her gaze to Evelyn and Catherine and smiled, saying, "Hello, my dear friends."

"Nice to see you, Martha," said Catherine. "Glad you could come."

Martha chuckled. "Had to. Finn wants my advice if he sees a slave woman he thinks he might want."

"Well, at least he knows whose advice he needs," said Evelyn.

Martha shrugged and turned back around.

Suddenly someone in the crowd shouted, "Here come the slaves!"

All eyes in the bleachers went to the Negroes being herded through the big doors and into the fenced pen.

Thomas Green motioned to Benjamin and showed him the spot next to the fence where he wanted him to stand. Benjamin forced a pleasant look on his face and obeyed.

When the slaves were all in the pen, and Thomas Green and Jim Lynch were positioned at the gate, the owner of the arena and director of the auction, Lawrence Fowler, mounted the auctioneer's platform. Raising his hands to gain the crowd's attention, Fowler soon had the crowd quiet.

"Ladies and gentlemen," he said, "welcome to today's auction. Mr. Thomas Green, as you know, has just brought in a shipload of slaves. Our auctioneer, Clem Samson, is here and ready to begin. But first, Mr. Green has a few words to say to you."

There was light applause as Green took the central spot on the platform. "Good morning," he said in a cheerful tone. "I believe I have a choice load of slaves to offer to you. All of them were brought from South Africa, which you know is under British rule. This means that all of them speak English. Some of them can even read and write."

An approving murmur swept through the crowd.

"We will now give you fifteen minutes to go down to the pen and look them over," he said. "If you want to ask questions of any of them, feel free to do so."

Most of the viewers who left their seats in the bleachers were men. A small percentage were women. Soon they were collected at the pen and began to talk to some of the slaves. Some pointed to specific slaves, asking them to come to the fence so they could talk to them.

As the viewers scrutinized the slaves, not one person overlooked the stalwart, muscular Benjamin, who stood staring as if at some distant object. Only when spoken to did Benjamin look at those who addressed him.

Finn and Martha Colvin discussed two of the single slave women. Even as they talked, Finn's eyes drifted to Benjamin. Martha gave him her opinion about the two women, pointing out two others. They agreed on which two Finn would bid for, then he said, "Did you get a good look at this boy over here?"

Viewers were pressing close as Finn pushed his way up to the fence and waited while another plantation owner looked the muscular young man over. Charles and Evelyn Moore and Zack, Catherine, and Dan Johnson were right behind the Colvins.

Martha turned to them and said, "Isn't this one something?"

"That he is," said Zack, running his gaze over Benjamin.

As soon as the man ahead of him stepped away, Finn moved up, looked at Benjamin, and said, "What's your name, boy?"

The use of the word "boy" made Benjamin's blood heat up, but he did not show it. Barely moving his lips, he said, "My name is Benjamin, sir. And yours?"

Finn chuckled. "Did you hear that? The blackie wants to know my name!"

"Tell him," Charles said flatly.

Grinning at Benjamin, Finn said, "My name is Master Finn to you. Master Finn Colvin."

Benjamin had an immediate dislike for the man. Looking him square in the eye, he said, "I don't believe you are Master Finn to me unless you hold my papers, sir."

Finn's smile vanished. "Well, let me tell you what, Benjamin. I am going to buy you. With your physique, you'll put out enough work in a day to make up for two men. Then you will call me Master Finn, I guarantee you."

Benjamin did not reply, but inside a hope was born that some other plantation owner would outbid him.

Finn said, "You alone, or do you have a wife?"

"I am alone. I do not have a wife."

Finn looked back at Charles, Dan, and Zack. "Yep, I'm gonna buy this one."

"And make him do the work of two men?" Zack said.

"Sure. Look at him. He can handle it."

"Maybe for a while. But in time, you'll kill him off."

Finn laughed. "I doubt that. But even if I did, it wouldn't be any of your business, would it?"

Zack only stared at him.

Chuckling, Finn said, "Come on, Martha. Let's go sit down."

Finn glanced over his shoulder as they walked away and gave Benjamin a sly smile.

Benjamin heard someone in the crowd collected at the pen say, "Yeah. Finn will buy him, all right. He's the richest man in the county. What Finn Colvin wants, Finn Colvin gets."

Another man said, "You're right about that. And if he gets him, he'll work him to death."

"He sure will," said another voice. "Colvin isn't human. He's a beast. His poor slaves have to endure beatings, overwork, bad housing, and poor food."

Benjamin's mouth went dry. Why would this horrible thing fall on him? Wasn't life as someone else's property bad enough? Why would he have to be owned by a man like Finn Colvin?

Catherine Johnson whispered to Zack, "I fear what they're saying is right. If Finn buys this young man, he will work him to death."

Zack nodded solemnly.

"You're right, Mom," Dan said. "I sure hope someone besides Finn gets him."

Benjamin turned his gaze inward and stared into space.

Dan stepped up to him and said, "Hello, Benjamin. My name is Dan Johnson. I've studied much about Africa . . . especially South Africa. What part of South Africa are you from?"

Dan's soft voice and friendly manner caused the dread to ease within Benjamin. He looked at Dan and said, "I was a slave on a cattle ranch in the mountain country of Great Karroo, sir."

"Oh, sure. That's some two hundred miles northeast of Cape Town."

Benjamin was surprised at Dan Johnson's knowledge of his country. He smiled and said, "Yes, sir. That is correct."

Suddenly the voice of auctioneer Clem Samson called out, "All right, everybody, time to get started! Find your seats!"

Benjamin watched the Johnsons as they took their seats in the bleachers. He was sure the man and woman with Dan were his parents. He looked a little like both of them. Then his gaze fell on Finn Colvin, who was seated directly in front of the Johnsons. His blood ran cold at the thought of that man owning him.

Thomas Green mounted the platform and stood beside Clem Samson. "All right, folks," he said, "I'm going to give you a brief background on the slaves as my assistant, Jim Lynch, sends them to the auction block."

The auction began with the slaves who had children. With each family, Green read from information on a sheet of paper, pointing out their positive qualifications.

When the slaves with children had been auctioned off, the couples without children were brought to the block, two by two—the young ones first. Benjamin watched as his friend Jarod and his wife were sold, followed by Stamus and his wife. When all the young couples had been purchased, the older couples were brought to the block, some being so old they shuffled their way to the block and had to help each other climb up.

The younger male slaves had been sold for an average of 500 dollars apiece, and their wives for an average of 300 dollars. The older male slaves went for an average of 100 dollars, and their wives for 75 dollars.

Soon they were down to the younger individuals. The single women were put on the block first and sold quickly—two of them going to Finn Colvin.

At one point, Benjamin was looking at Dan Johnson when Dan happened to turn and set his eyes on him. Dan smiled, and Benjamin smiled in return.

Next were the single young men, who sold fast. One of them was an especially fine-looking man, and several plantation owners bid on him until Finn Colvin ran the price to 600 dollars and the others dropped out of the bidding. Benjamin watched the scene, knowing that the man was right who said what Finn Colvin wanted, Finn Colvin got.

The sun was at its zenith as the last man in front of Benjamin was taken from the pen by Jim Lynch and sent to the block while Thomas Green read his background and qualifications to the crowd.

Benjamin glanced Finn Colvin's way and saw the man turn and look at him. Colvin grinned wickedly and Benjamin felt his pulse quicken. He turned his eyes away.

The man on the block was sold quickly for 450 dollars, then Jim Lynch opened the gate and said, "Okay, Benjamin. Your turn."

Benjamin's mouth was dry as a sand pit as he passed the gate and headed toward the block.

On the platform, Thomas Green said, "Now, ladies and gentlemen, I present to you the young man I have been holding till last. Take a good look at him and you'll understand why. This is my choice slave."

There was an approving murmur from the crowd.

Benjamin climbed to the top of the block as Green said, "His name is Benjamin, folks. He was a slave on a cattle ranch in the mountains of Great Karroo. His owner wrote that Benjamin is a hard worker, and I think you can tell by looking at him that he could handle a good day's work."

There was light laughter and some words of agreement.

"Benjamin," Green said, "I want these folks to get a real good look at you. Remove your shirt."

Benjamin's backbone stiffened, but he knew he dare not disobey. As he was unbuttoning his shirt, Green said, "Something else about this choice young slave, folks—he speaks, reads, and writes English excellently. He was educated by the British owners of the cattle ranch where he was raised."

Voices oohed and ahhed as Benjamin removed his shirt and held it in his hand. His upper body glistened in the sun. He changed the shirt from one hand to the other, and even that slight movement caused his muscles to ripple and cord beneath his skin.

Thomas Green smiled and gestured toward Benjamin. "What do you think, folks? Look at those bulging, rock-hard muscles! Feast your eyes on those broad shoulders, the deep chest, and the slender waist! Don't you wish you had a plantation full of men like this? You wouldn't need so many, would you?"

There was laughter and a rumble of comments.

Suddenly Finn Colvin's voice called out, "Well, all you plantation owners might as well back off right now. I'm going to have this one!"

Thomas Green reveled in Finn Colvin's determination to purchase Benjamin. He smiled at Finn from the platform and said, "Well, Mr.

Colvin, we will see if you are willing to outbid all the men here today who would like to have Benjamin on their plantations!" He turned to the auctioneer. "All right, Clem. Let's see how badly Mr. Colvin wants this young man."

Before Clem Samson could speak up and ask what he was bid for Benjamin, Finn Colvin raised his hand and said, "I'll bid 700 dollars!"

A surprised oooh! swept over the crowd.

Finn looked around and grinned triumphantly, knowing he had started the bidding a hundred dollars higher than any male slave had gone for that morning.

Suddenly another plantation owner raised his hand and offered 725 dollars. Another raised it to 750 dollars. Colvin went to 775 dollars.

Clem Samson held the gavel in his hand at the podium, looked around, and said, "Do I hear 800?"

Another man shouted, "Eight hundred!"

Another raised it 25 dollars.

"Eight hundred twenty-five is the bid! Do I hear 850?"

Finn Colvin gave the signal, and Clem said, "Mr. Colvin raises it to 850 dollars! Do I hear 875?"

As another man offered 875 dollars, Catherine Johnson said to her husband, "Zack, you haven't bid. Wouldn't that young man be an asset to our plantation?"

"That he would, sweetheart. Without a doubt."

"I agree, Pa," Dan said. "He's a likable fellow, too."

"You haven't bought any other slaves, Zack," said Catherine. "Certainly you could give Finn a tussle."

"Yes, Papa," spoke up Angeline. "Wouldn't you like to have Benjamin? He's well educated, Mr. Green said. He could help educate our slaves."

Finn Colvin gave a signal that he would go to 900 dollars, then having heard the conversation going on behind him, he said, "C'mon, Zack. How about a tussle? Isn't that boy worth bidding for?"

Zack did not reply.

Finn turned around when he heard Clem Samson say that another had raised his bid to 925 dollars. Finn raised to 950 dollars.

Lowering his voice so the Colvins couldn't hear him, Zack huddled close to his family and said, "I've intended to bid on Benjamin all along. I'm just waiting till the plantation owners with less wealth drop out of the bidding." Then with a stubborn set to his jaw, he added, "I'm not going to let Finn have that fine young man. He would work him to death. I'm going to outbid Finn no matter how high the price."

Dan smiled and shook his fist in exultation, then whispered, "Good for you, Pa!"

Charles Moore leaned close and said, "Zack, you must be going to take Finn's challenge."

"You might say that, Charles."

"Good!" said Charles, then turned to his family and nodded with a smile.

As the bids by the other plantation owners kept going up 25 dollars at a time, Finn Colvin laughed as he kept raising his bid.

By the time the bid for Benjamin was 1,025 dollars, the last of the plantation owners except for Finn Colvin had dropped out. Colvin jabbed his elbow into Martha's ribs and said, "Well, I told 'em, didn't I? That pile of muscles is going to work on my plantation!"

Auctioneer Clem Samson was saying, "Going . . . going . . . for one thousand and twenty-five dollars—!"

Zack Johnson shouted, "Mr. Samson, I bid eleven hundred dollars!"

Applause broke out in the crowd.

Finn's smile died on his lips. He turned around and said, "Don't get cute with me, Zack."

"You want to pay more than eleven hundred, Finn? Raise the bid."

Colvin's cheeks flushed. Whipping his head around, he raised his hand and shouted, "Twelve hundred!"

"Mr. Colvin bids twelve hundred," said Samson. "Going for one thousand two hundred dollars . . . going . . . going . . ."

"Thirteen hundred!" called Zack Johnson.

There was more applause, punctuated with cheers.

Colvin's head whipped around. Fixing Zack with malevolent eyes, he said, "You won't be able to do it."

Zack gave him a bland look. "The bid is thirteen hundred. If you're going to raise it, you'd better hurry."

Clem Samson was already saying, "Going for thirteen hundred! Going . . . going . . ."

"Fourteen hundred!" shouted Colvin.

"Fifteen hundred!" Zack shouted.

Benjamin let a slight smile curve his lips when he saw Dan Johnson pat his father on the shoulder, then look toward him. When their eyes met,

Benjamin's smile broadened and Dan nodded, a look of confidence in his eyes.

"Sixteen hundred!" Finn yelled.

The disapproval of the crowd was loud and clear. Everyone waited with bated breath for Zack Johnson to top it.

Thomas Green could hardly believe the price for Benjamin. He put his gaze on Zack Johnson, as did everyone else.

Zack waited until Clem Samson said, "Going . . . going . . . for one thousand six hundred dollars . . ." then he raised his hand and shouted, "Seventeen hundred!"

Benjamin's heart started to pound.

Finn Colvin turned around and set fierce eyes on Zack. His cheeks were aflame. "Have you lost your mind?" he said.

"Have you lost yours?" came the crisp reply.

George and Edward Colvin stared at Zack in utter disbelief. Their father had never paid more than nine hundred dollars for a slave. And Zack Johnson was not backing off. How high would their father go to own the muscular young slave on the block?

Dan Johnson took hold of his mother's hand as both of them kept their eyes on Zack. Alexander took hold of his sister's hand. Angeline looked at him as if he was the one who had lost his mind. Alexander had not held her hand since they were small children.

Looking into his eyes, she said, "Are you all right?"

Alexander looked down at their clasped hands and grinned. "Uh-huh. I'm just nervous. I thought you might be, too."

Angeline grinned back. "You're right. I am."

Finn Colvin called loudly, "I bid seventeen hundred and fifty!"

Benjamin's mouth felt like a sandpit again. Sweat beaded his brow. How long would this go on? Already he liked Dan Johnson very much, and he was liking Dan's father better every minute.

WHILE FINN COLVIN'S ANTAGONISTS voiced their disapproval, Zack called out, "Clem, I bid eighteen hundred!"

The jeers and boos turned into cheers, whistles, and applause.

Finn Colvin turned around with teeth bared and eyes blazing. "What are you doin', Zack?"

"Bidding for a slave I want to buy. What are you doing?"

"Don't let him bother you, Pa!" George said.

"Yeah, Pa!" Edward piped up. "Go on and raise the bid!"

Finn held Zack's gaze for a few seconds, then heard Clem's voice calling out acceptance of the bid. He sighed once then shouted, "Eighteen-fifty!"

Zack stood up. "Clem, I bid twenty-five hundred!"

Gasps rippled throughout the crowd, followed by wordless sounds of approval that ended in more shouts, whistles, and applause.

"Twenty-five hundred is the bid!" Samson called above the noise. "Do I hear twenty-six?"

Thomas Green could not believe it. He had never known of a slave to sell for a price anywhere near that amount.

All eyes went to Finn Colvin, who had jumped to his feet. His sons stood beside him, watching his face.

Finn looked at Zack Johnson with hate-filled eyes and swore at him, saying, "No slave is worth that kind of money! You can have him!"

Clem Samson's voice was heard above the clamor as he slammed his gavel down with a bang and shouted, "Sold for two thousand five hundred dollars to Mr. Zack Johnson!"

A wild roar erupted from the crowd as they leaped to their feet and applauded.

Benjamin's knees were watery as he put his shirt on and began buttoning it up.

While the crowd's enthusiastic roar rocked the arena, Finn Colvin took Martha by the arm and said, "Let's go pay for the slaves we bought and take 'em home."

As they started down the steps of the bleachers, Finn looked back at Zack, who was talking to the Moores, and set fierce eyes on him.

Charles noticed him and said, "Zack, I think Finn wants to say something to you."

When Zack looked at him, Finn ejected a string of profanity, calling him several vile names, then turned and headed on down the stairs.

Zack bristled and started to move that way, but he felt Catherine's hand grip his arm. He paused to look at her.

"Don't do it, Zack," she said.

"He swore in front of you and my daughter! He needs his mouth smacked!"

"Honey, it would only make you look bad after all this hassle over Benjamin. It's all right. Angeline and I are fine."

Dan moved up beside his mother. "How about I smack his mouth, Pa? It won't make me look as bad."

"Please, Dan," said Catherine. "Just let it go."

"How about if a lowly sixteen-year-old belted his chops for him, Mom?" Alexander said.

"No. It would just make things worse than they are. I appreciate the men in this family looking out for the honor of their ladies, but please . . . no violence."

When the Colvins reached the ground, Martha paused and looked back at the Johnsons. Her face was crimson with emotion. Setting her eyes on Catherine, she mouthed the words, *I'm sorry.*

Catherine nodded and gave her a warm smile.

Just then, Zack took Catherine's hand and said, "Let's all go down and talk to Benjamin. It'll be a few minutes before we can get to one of the cashier's windows."

"Oh, let's do, Papa!" said Angeline. "I want to meet him!"

"Me too," said Alexander.

Before they could descend the bleachers, the Moores stepped up to them.

"Zack," Charles said, "we are so relieved that Finn didn't get that fine young man. You outsmarted him is what you did."

Dorena moved up close to Priscilla and whispered, "Would it be all right if I speak to Mr. Johnson?"

"Of course, honey." Priscilla addressed Zack by saying, "Mr. Johnson, Dorena asked for permission to speak to you. I told her it would be all right."

"Certainly, Dorena," Zack said, smiling at the lovely slave girl.

"Mr. Johnson, as a black girl and a slave, I want to thank you for caring enough to pay such a high price to keep Mr. Colvin from getting that young man. What you did means very much to me."

"Thank you for expressing your appreciation, Dorena. I'm glad I was able to do it."

She smiled sweetly and said, "I am sure he will work hard for you, sir. I could tell by the look in his eyes that he was scared Mr. Colvin was going to get him."

"I can understand that. Benjamin heard enough before he went on the block this morning to know what kind of man Colvin is. If I had been in Benjamin's place, I would have been frightened, too."

"I wish all slave owners were as nice as you and Master Charles, sir."

Charles Moore smiled at Dorena and said, "Well, little lady, if you will accompany this nice man and his family to a cashier's booth, I'll pay for the husband and wife that I made top bid on today and we can all go home."

Dorena curtsied. "Let us go, Master Charles."

When the Moores passed by, Benjamin's line of sight focused on lovely Dorena, and he instantly found himself fascinated by her beauty and the warmth of her smile.

As they moved away, Benjamin's attention was drawn to the Johnsons who had not yet reached the auction block. They were stopped by two other plantation owners and their wives who were lauding Zack Johnson for winning his bidding war.

When the two couples turned away, and the Johnsons stepped up to the block, Thomas Green was ushering Benjamin down the steps toward them.

"Mr. Johnson," Green said, smiling, "You've made an excellent purchase. I know Benjamin will work hard for you."

"He looks to be a fine young man," Zack said.

At that instant, Jim Lynch called to Green and hurried toward him. "Mr. Green, please excuse the intrusion, but one of the slaves who has been sick has gotten worse; I need you to come and take a look at him."

Green excused himself and hurried away with Lynch.

The rest of the Johnson family looked on as Zack said, "Well, Benjamin, by now you know who I am. You met my son Dan before the auction. Let me introduce you to the rest of the Johnsons. This is my wife, Catherine, our daughter, Angeline, and our youngest son Alexander."

Benjamin felt shock to be treated like he was on the same level with his new master and his family. He bowed first to Catherine and said, "I am very happy to make your acquaintance, Mrs. Johnson." He then bowed to Angeline and to Alexander, greeting them in the same manner. To Dan, he said, "I am honored, Master Dan, that you came to the pen and talked to me. You are very kind."

"It was my pleasure, Benjamin. And I am so glad my father outbid Finn Colvin for you."

Tears welled up in Benjamin's eyes as he turned to Zack and said, "Master Johnson, I am very thankful the other man did not get me. But sir, I am sorry you had to pay so much for me. I promise you, I will work extra hard and try to be worth it to you."

Zack smiled, then turned and looked toward the cashiers' booths. "Looks like the lines are getting shorter. Come, Benjamin and family. Let's go close this deal."

With Benjamin at his side, Zack stepped up to the cashier and said, "Hello, Bryan."

"Nice to see you, Mr. Johnson," said Bryan Arkin. "That was some contest in there. I'm sure glad you won out."

"Thank you."

"Those slaves you bought here a couple of months ago, Mr. Johnson . . . how are they doing?"

"Oh, you mean Elias and Georgianna?"

"Yes. That's them."

"They're doing quite well. Both are good workers. My wife has Georgianna working inside the house quite a bit."

Arkin set his eyes on Benjamin. "Looks like you've got yourself a fine one here."

"Sure do," Zack said, pulling out his checkbook. "Guess I'd better pay for him, huh?"

Bryan chuckled. "Yes, sir. That would be best."

"May I use your pen and inkwell, please?"

Arkin took the pen out of its holder and slid the inkwell toward him.

While Zack wrote out a check in the amount of 2,500 dollars, Arkin opened a drawer, pulled out a set of official looking papers, and held them in his hand. When Zack had blotted the check, he slid it across the counter to Arkin, who handed him the documents, saying, "Here are Benjamin's papers."

Zack scanned all three sheets, making sure the papers were in order. When he was satisfied, he said, "Bryan, may I borrow your pen again?"

The cashier's brow puckered as he looked at the papers. "But Mr. Johnson, there is nothing for you to sign on these papers. You ought to know that . . . as many slaves as you have bought."

Zack shook his head. "There is one place I need to put my signature."

By this time, Zack had his family's attention.

Arkin handed Zack the pen and pushed the inkwell toward him. "Whatever you say, Mr. Johnson."

"Mom," Dan whispered, "there's only one place for Pa's signature in those papers. That's on the last page. You know—"

Catherine's eyes widened.

Bryan Arkin frowned as he saw Zack flip to the last page, dip the pen in the inkwell, and put his signature on the bottom line. He could not believe what he was seeing.

When Zack blotted his signature, he handed the pen to Bryan and said, "Thank you."

The cashier blinked and nodded without speaking.

Catherine and Dan stepped closer, waiting for Zack to speak. They watched intently as he turned to the muscular Negro and said, "Benjamin, you are a bright-looking young man. I'm glad you can read and write English."

"Thank you, Master Johnson. I—"

"When I observed you and Dan talking at the pen, you impressed me."

"I did, sir?"

"Yes. In a very special way."

"In what way did I impress you, sir?"

"You have a very pleasing personality and you conduct yourself well with people."

Zack looked down at the papers in his hand, then met Benjamin's perplexed gaze and said, "Son, I see real potential in you."

"Yes, sir?"

"I believe you have it in you to make your mark in this world. I want to see your potential realized. Therefore, Benjamin, I have signed the bottom line on the last page of your papers. This means that I have set you free. You are no longer a slave owner's chattel."

Bryan Arkin listened dumbfounded.

Benjamin looked at the papers in Zack's hand, then raised his eyes to the man in utter disbelief. "M-Master J-Johnson. I . . . I m-must have heard you wrong. Would you repeat what you said, please, s-sir?"

Zack grinned as he laid his free hand on Benjamin's shoulder and said, "You didn't hear wrong, son. I have set you free. You are no longer a slave."

This time Benjamin was speechless. While he tried to find his voice, Zack said, "I couldn't let Finn Colvin buy you. I know the man well. He would have brutalized you if you hadn't been able to do the work of two men day after day. Eventually, he would have worked you to death."

Dan moved up close and squeezed his father's arm. "Pa knows what he's talking about, Benjamin. You're nineteen years old, aren't you?"

"Yes, sir."

"Believe me, if Finn Colvin had bought you, you wouldn't have lived to see your twenty-first birthday. And you would have had a miserable life until then, too. The first morning you woke up and your weary body was too weak to do a day's work, you would have been given a severe beating."

Tears streamed down Benjamin's cheeks as he shook his head. He had finally found his voice. "Master Johnson, this is all so overwhelming. How . . . how do I thank you?"

"By making a successful life for yourself. You are a bright young man. You can thank me by fulfilling the potential I know is there."

"I will do my best, sir, I just don't know where to go from here . . . what to do first."

Reaching into his pocket, Zack pulled out a wad of currency, laid it in Benjamin's hand, and said, "You will need this. There's enough here to take care of you until you find a job."

"No one will hire me, Master Johnson. I'm a black man. I will have to go up North, will I not?"

"Not necessarily. There are free black men in South Carolina—right here in Charleston—who have good jobs. The jobs are manual labor, but the pay is decent. A hardworking black man can make a good living."

Benjamin shook his head. "I did not know that, sir. I thought the only black people here were slaves."

"Well, now you know different," Zack said, smiling.

Dan chuckled at the young man's utter confusion. "Benjamin, I guess it would surprise you if I told you there are free Negroes in South Carolina who own slaves."

"You are jesting, Master Dan!"

"No, I'm not. There aren't any Negro-owned plantations this close to the coast, but farther inland, there are many."

"This surprises me, for sure," said Benjamin, wagging his head. "Nobody ever told me that before."

"As Pa said, Benjamin, a free Negro, even here in Charleston, can work and make a living for himself and his family. I sure would love to see you stay so we can get to know each other."

The black man grinned. "I would really like that, sir."

"Benjamin," said Zack, "on the north side of town they have boarding-houses where Negroes live. You need to get yourself a room there. They are owned by free blacks. They're all on Spruill Avenue close to the Cooper River. Just go straight north on Meeting Street, which is exactly one block east of where you are standing right now, and it runs into Spruill Avenue."

"Yes, sir," said Benjamin. "But . . ."

"Mm-hmm?"

"Well, Master Johnson, what do I do when some law officer, or just some citizen, stops me and wants proof that I am not a runaway slave?"

Zack lifted the papers in his hand. "You carry these with you at all times. They prove that you are a free man. And if anyone gives you a problem about it, the law will back you up." As he spoke, he placed the papers in Benjamin's hand.

"So these are called my em—eman—"

"Emancipation papers. They show that you were my slave, but that I set you free. That's what I meant when I said my signature on the bottom line made you a free man."

"I still can hardly believe this is happening to me, Master Johnson. I'm afraid I'm going to wake up and find out it really is only a dream!"

"It's real," Catherine said. "Your whole life will be different from now on, Benjamin."

"Yes, ma'am. Now . . . if I can only find a job."

"I have many friends in business here in town," Zack said. "If you wish, I can take you to some of them and see if I can help you find a job."

"That would be a real help, Master Johnson."

"Tell you what. You go on up to Spruill Avenue and rent yourself a room in one of the boardinghouses. You can't miss them. They are white frame buildings with lots of little Negro children playing in the yards. You will have no problem getting a room. You do know what a boardinghouse is?"

"A place where a man has a room to sleep in."

"More than that. They also have three meals a day for you, which is included in the price of the rent."

"I see. That's good, since a man has to eat."

"Tell you what, Pa," said Dan, "if you'll give me the time in the morning, I'll find Benjamin at whatever boardinghouse he's staying in and take him places where he might be able to find work."

"Fine with me, Dan." Then to Benjamin he said, "You go on now and find yourself a room. There aren't so many boardinghouses but what Dan will be able to find you with no trouble."

Benjamin nodded. Once again, tears filmed his eyes. "Master Johnson, I wish there was some way to thank you right now, even before I go to work on reaching the potential you see in me."

Zack patted his shoulder. "It's all right, son. Just seeing you this happy is really thanks enough."

Catherine moved to Benjamin and said, "I am so happy for you. I had no idea what my husband was going to do when he was bidding for you, but in my eyes, he most certainly did the right thing."

"Thank you, ma'am."

"Benjamin," Dan said, "I meant what I said. If you stay here in Charleston; I want to spend time with you so we can get to know each other."

"That sure sounds good to me, sir."

"Tell you what," said Zack, "we would love to have you come visit us at the plantation. Maybe tomorrow, after Dan takes you job hunting, he can drive you out to the place and we can show it to you."

"I would love that, sir."

"We'll have you out for an evening meal sometime soon," Catherine said.

Benjamin was overwhelmed at being treated like an ordinary human being. He wiped away tears from his cheeks. "I would be honored, ma'am."

"You'll like Samantha's cooking, Benjamin," spoke up Angeline. "She's the best."

"I'm sure I will, Miss Angeline. I will look forward to it."

"Well, dear wife of mine," Zack said, "we'd better be going. Benjamin is probably tired and would like to rest himself."

"I'm wondering, Benjamin," Dan said. "Did you leave family in South Africa when you were brought here by Mr. Green?"

"No, sir. Mr. Green bought my mother and father and me from Mr. Kent Rhodes, the owner of the cattle ranch. And—"

Seeing the inward agony Benjamin was feeling, Zack said, "Your parents were on that ship?"

"Yes, sir."

"Where are they?"

"They—they died while we were crossing the ocean, sir."

"Oh, Benjamin!" Catherine said. "How did it happen?"

"It was dysentery, ma'am. Several slaves came down with it. And some—like my parents—died with it. Their bodies were buried at sea."

"Oh, I'm so sorry."

"Thank you, ma'am."

"All of us are sorry about this, Benjamin," Zack said. "If there is anything we can do for you, please let us know."

"Master Johnson, you have already done more for me than anyone on this earth ever did. Thank you for your kind offer, but I will be fine."

Zack nodded. "Dan will pick you up at your boardinghouse in the morning."

The Johnsons walked away, leaving Benjamin standing by the cashiers' booths with the emancipation papers in one hand and the wad of money in the other.

"As soon as I can get to know him better," Dan said, "I want to give him the gospel."

Catherine smiled in approval at her eldest son. "I think he'll be open," she said. "As happy as he is to be free, he will listen to anything you tell him, I'm sure."

The Johnson carriage was the only one left in the plantation owners' parking lot. As they headed for it, Dan said, "Yes, sir . . . I really want to bring Benjamin to the Lord."

At the cashiers' booths, Bryan Arkin observed Benjamin standing there with the papers in his hand, his eyes following the Johnsons as they crossed the parking lot.

"Tell you what, Benjamin," Arkin said, "in all my years of working this booth I have never seen anything like what Zack Johnson did for you today."

Benjamin kept his gaze on his deliverer as he replied, "I have been a slave since I was born, sir. All my life I have lived around slaves. I have seen them bought and sold since I was a small child, but I have never seen anything like this either."

WHEN THE JOHNSON FAMILY REACHED their carriage, Angeline started to climb into the backseat. Instantly, Alexander stepped up and offered his hand, saying, "Here, sweet sister, let me help you."

"What? My little brother is finally going to become a gentleman?"

"I guess my example somehow got through to our little brother's brain," Dan said.

"It wasn't that," Alexander said, as he helped Angeline in. "I just never wanted to infringe on your privilege, Dan."

Angeline gasped. "Privilege! Papa, Mother . . . did you hear that?"

"Yes, we did," Zack said as he helped Catherine into the front seat. "Isn't it nice that your little brother feels it is a privilege to assist his sister into the carriage?"

"Why, yes," said Angeline. "It is very sweet, and I will let him do it half of the time so that Dan still gets the privilege, too—at least until he leaves for Texas."

Dan was at the hitching post untying the reins. "That's right," he said, shooting a grin at his little brother. "Then just think, Alexander . . . it will be your privilege all of the time!"

They heard the pounding of running feet and turned to see Benjamin dashing toward them across the parking lot.

"Master Johnson! Master Johnson!" he called, waving a hand above his head.

Zack waited beside the carriage for him to draw up.

As Benjamin skidded to a halt in front of him, Zack smiled and said, "Yes?" Then he noticed tears streaming down Benjamin's cheeks. "Something wrong, son?"

Dropping to his knees, Benjamin looked up at Zack and said in a choked voice, "Master Johnson, you have so kindly paid the price to purchase me and then set me free. I am a free man, right?"

"Yes. You're as free as any man in the United States and Territories." Zack cocked his head and frowned. "You already know that. What are you leading up to?"

"I have liberty to make my own choices. Right, sir?"

"You do."

"Then as a free man, Master Johnson, and by my own choice, because you set me free, I am offering myself as your slave for the rest of my life."

Zack's face pinched. "You mean, you want to be my slave rather than a free man? Rather than live and work on your own?"

"Yes, sir. No one has ever been so kind and good to me. Please, Master Johnson . . . take me as your slave."

"But, Benjamin, you're free, you—"

"I am free to make my own decisions, sir. And I have decided that I want to serve you and your family as your willing slave for the rest of my life."

Zack reached down, took Benjamin's hand, and raised him to his feet.

"Benjamin, maybe you should think on this for a few days, then see how you feel about it."

"I have already thought about it all that is needed, Master Johnson. You bought me. I am your willing slave. I owe you everything."

"But, Benjamin, I bought you so you could be free."

"Yes. You bought me so that man, Finn Colvin, would not have me, and you gave me freedom. By that same freedom, I choose to be owned by you."

Zack looked at Dan, whose face was wet with tears, and said, "What am I going to do with this guy?"

"Take him up on his offer, Father."

Zack looked down at Benjamin. "You're absolutely sure about this?"

"Absolutely, Master Johnson."

"All right. I gladly accept your offer, Benjamin. But I want to amend it."

"In what way, sir?"

A slow smile worked its way over Zack's face. "Instead of being my slave, you will be my servant, and I will pay you well."

"Your servant?"

"Yes. You will live in the servants' quarters, which are attached to our house."

"And you will pay me, you say?"

"Of course. You will find the wage quite fair."

"I have no doubt of that, Master Johnson." Benjamin's heart was fluttering in his chest.

"One other thing."

"Yes, sir?"

"My slaves call me Master Johnson, but since you are not a slave, you will call me Mr. Johnson."

"Yes, sir, Mr. Johnson!"

Benjamin looked toward the carriage and said to Catherine, "I still cannot believe I am not dreaming, Mrs. Johnson. But if I am, please do not wake me up. I am most happy to be a servant to you, Mr. Johnson, Mr. Dan, Miss Angeline, and Mr. Alexander."

Zack laid a hand on Benjamin's shoulder. "When we work you hard, you might wish you were a slave on another plantation!"

"Never, sir. Never."

"Well, climb in back there with those two young ones, Benjamin."

When Benjamin started to climb in, Angeline scooted across the seat, leaving space between herself and Alexander, and said, "Sit between us, Benjamin."

Zack rounded the carriage and climbed up beside Catherine. He looked past her at Dan, who had the reins in hand and said, "Okay, Daniel Johnson, let's go home!"

As the Moore carriage rolled along the road toward the plantation, the new slave couple, Bartholomew and Hattie, were seated beside Priscilla in the seat that rode backwards. Facing them were Dorena and Evelyn. Lewis drove the carriage with Charles beside him.

"Master Charles and I will take you to your cabin when we get home," Evelyn said to the couple. "We will explain our policies with you at that time and give you opportunity to ask any questions."

Bartholomew smiled. "Mrs. Moore, you people are so kind to us. Our owners in South Africa did not treat us this way. And I can only imagine how we would have been treated by Mr. Colvin, who tried so hard to buy the young man, Benjamin."

Turning in the driver's seat to look back, Charles said, "You can be very thankful Finn Colvin didn't bid for you today, Bartholomew. Except for his defeat in getting his hands on Benjamin, he has never been outbid when he really wanted a particular slave."

Bartholomew set his gaze on Dorena. "Hattie and I were still in the arena when you expressed your appreciation to Mr. Johnson for not allowing Mr. Colvin to get Benjamin. That was a very nice thing to do, Dorena."

"Thank you. My heart went out to Benjamin when I saw him so frightened as he stood on the block. It meant a lot to me that Mr. Johnson would pay such a price for Benjamin to keep that man from getting him."

Priscilla smiled at Dorena. "Of course, Benjamin being so handsome and well built wouldn't have anything to do with your taking such a liking to him, would it?"

"Well . . . ah . . . I will have to say, Miss Priscilla, that I have never seen such a handsome man in all of my life."

Priscilla giggled. "Maybe, since the Johnsons own him, and are such good friends with us, you will get to meet Benjamin sometime. Would you like that?"

Dorena closed her eyes, then looked at her mistress with a shy smile. "Yes. I would like that."

When Dan Johnson guided the carriage onto the winding lane to the mansion, Benjamin was in awe at the beauty of the place. His eyes took in the lovely trees, the well-kept bushes, and the attractive white fence that stretched toward the mansion on both sides of the lane.

By the time Dan pulled rein and halted the carriage at the rear of the house, Benjamin was at a loss for words.

A few slaves were looking on from a distance as the Johnsons led Benjamin toward the mansion. Zack pointed out the section of the magnificent structure that made up the servants' quarters.

"Oh, my!" Benjamin said. "That is really nice."

"Wait till you see the inside of it, Benjamin," Catherine said.

"I am already in the process of anticipation, Mrs. Johnson."

They were almost to the mansion's back porch when Zack said, "Dan, I want you and me to take Benjamin before the slaves at the close of the work day so they can all meet him."

"Sure, Pa."

"And after you've shown him his quarters, bring him to the library. Your mother and I will sit down with him and explain his duties."

Benjamin was overwhelmed when he saw his quarters. Lace curtains adorned the bright windows. The walls were painted a bone white, and the room was comfortably furnished. The small cabin he had grown up in on the South African cattle ranch was nothing like this.

He ran his gaze over the large room that made up most of the apartment and said, "Mr. Dan, I must be dreaming. Such a place as this cannot be real!"

"You are going to be happy here, Benjamin. Your offer to become Pa's slave after he had set you free really touched him. It touched all of us. And as one of the Johnsons, let me say that I am very happy to have you as our servant."

Benjamin shook his head in wonderment. "If only my parents could see me now. They would be so glad to know that I am no longer a slave."

"I'm sure they would," said Dan. "Well, my friend, I guess I'd better take you to the library so my parents can have their little talk with you."

Late that afternoon, when the slaves were coming in from the fields, they found Zack and Dan waiting for them at the usual place where Zack gathered them when he wanted to have a meeting. It was an open area between the two rows of cabins. The mothers and children who did not work in the fields were already there.

When everyone was within the large half-circle, Zack lifted his voice and said, "I want you all to meet the new servant I hired today while at the auction in town. His name is Benjamin. He is from South Africa, and he is nineteen years old. I haven't hired a servant since Reuben died because I just hadn't found the right man. Well, today I found him. Benjamin, say hello to everybody."

"Hello, everybody!" he called out.

Some responded with hellos, while others just looked at him.

"Hey, you can do better than that!" said Zack. "Come on, now. Everybody say hello to Benjamin!"

Zebulun took a step forward and said, "I will help them, Master Johnson."

The old preacher turned to face the crowd of slaves. "All right. Jis' like we was in church a-singin'. All together!"

Following Zebulun's lead, the entire crowd of slaves gave Benjamin a warm "hello" in unison.

"That's better!" said Zack. "Thank you, Zebulun."

The old man nodded and returned to his place.

"Now, what I would like for all of you to do," said Zack, "is come by and speak to Benjamin. Welcome him to the Johnson plantation."

Again, Zebulun took the lead, and as he approached Benjamin to give him a personal welcome, the slaves lined up behind him.

While the welcoming was going on, Zack and Dan stood close by. When about half of the crowd had met him, Benjamin turned and looked at father and son. "Mr. Johnson, Mr. Dan—I am the happiest man in the whole world!"

It was midmorning the next day when Dan returned from town in his own buggy and saw Benjamin working in the huge yard, trimming bushes.

Dan stopped the buggy close by and vaulted the fence.

"Hello, Mr. Dan."

"Hello, Benjamin. So how's it going?"

"Just fine, sir. I like this servant business."

"Good. I have to go to one of the back fields for a while, but I wanted to ask you something before I go."

"Yes, sir?"

"Do you like to fish?"

Benjamin's brow wrinkled. "Do you mean to catch fish?"

"Mm-hmm."

"I have never done that, Mr. Dan. In South Africa, only those who make their living selling fish catch them."

"Oh. Well, in this country we catch fish first of all for the fun of it. Secondly, because we like to eat them."

"Oh. I see."

"I made arrangements with my father for you to have this coming Saturday off so you could go fishing with me. How about it? I'd sure like to have some time with you."

Benjamin felt a warm sensation wash over his heart. "You want this black servant to spend time with you, Mr. Dan?"

"Yes. If you think this white man can teach you how to fish, that is."

Benjamin laughed. "I would love to learn."

"Good! Then we'll go fishing together on Saturday. I have a favorite spot on the Cooper River about ten miles north of town."

A serious look captured Benjamin's eyes. "Mr. Dan, you honor me, sir. I do not understand why you want to spend time with me, but I am very glad."

"I want us to be friends. You are this family's servant, and I'm glad for that. But I want to be more than the son of your employer. I want to be your friend."

"Then we are friends, Mr. Dan."

Dan surprised Benjamin by giving him a manly embrace. When he released him and stepped back, he said, "Friends, Benjamin."

A smile spread over Benjamin's handsome features. "Friends, sir."

On Saturday, Dan and Benjamin sat on the west bank of the Cooper River, their lines dangling in the stream. Benjamin had caught on quickly to the mechanics of baiting a hook and already had three bass lying beside him on the ground.

Dan grinned at his friend. "You've got a natural knack for this, I can see. One of these days you'll catch more than I do."

"Thank you for the compliment, Mr. Dan, but I doubt that I'll ever be able to outdo you."

A soft breeze was blowing across the river. Dan was quiet for a few minutes, then said, "Benjamin, has anyone in our family told you that I might be leaving the plantation soon?"

Benjamin's eyes widened. "No. Why? When?"

"Let me explain. I figured that since we're friends I should let you know what's going on in my life. You see, I've had this dream of going out West and becoming a cattle rancher."

"Out West? I do not know about out West. What is that?"

Dan explained the way the country was divided up, then told him of how people were migrating West and that cattle ranching was becoming a big business out there.

Disappointment cast a shadow over Benjamin's heart, but he disguised it as he said, "I know about cattle ranching, Mr. Dan."

"Yes, I know. You were raised on a cattle ranch."

"Right. And I have a deep love for cattle and horses. I miss being around them."

"From what I've read, they sort of get in your blood."

Benjamin looked at him questioningly. "In your blood?"

Dan chuckled. "Sorry. That's American talk. I mean, when a man has worked with cattle and horses for a while, he gets to where he has a special love for them, for the ranch life, and can't be happy unless he's ranching."

"Oh. Now I understand. When are you going out West?"

"I'm not exactly sure. But it will probably be within a couple of months."

Benjamin nodded, feeling the pricking of disappointment again. "Where in the West are you going?"

"Texas."

"How far is that from here?"

"Well, it depends on where in Texas. It's a huge state. I'll be going near the city of Austin. So from here, it's about thirteen hundred miles or so."

"That is a long way."

"Yes."

"So this is definite?"

"Well, almost. I've been praying about it for some time, but the Lord hasn't given me the 'go' sign, yet."

A blank look captured Benjamin's face.

They discussed ranching in general for a while, during which they each caught another fish.

"Benjamin," Dan said, as he was stringing his latest catch on the line, "you really know a lot about cattle and horses. I envy you."

"You will learn it quickly when you begin ranching in Texas, Mr. Dan. I only know what I do because ranching is all I have known as far back as I can remember."

Dan was quiet as he baited his hook again and tossed it in the water. Suddenly, he said, "Benjamin, how much do you know about the Bible?"

"The Bible? I have heard some of the Britishers talk about it, sir. It is a book from white man's God, right?"

"No. It is the book from the God who created this universe, Benjamin. He is not just white man's God. He created people with black skin, brown skin, yellow skin, and red skin, too."

"Mmm. I have not heard this."

"Do you know who Jesus Christ is?"

Benjamin thought on it a moment, then said, "I was about to say that He was the Son of white man's God. But apparently I should say He was the Son of everybody's God."

"Not was," Dan said. "He *is* the Son of God."

"I do not understand. He died a long time ago, Mr. Dan. My parents only died a few weeks ago, but I have to speak of them in the past now."

"You mean you haven't heard that God's Son died on the cross of Calvary, but He rose from the dead three days later?"

Benjamin frowned thoughtfully. "It . . . it seems that I have heard that, now that you mention it. So if this is true, Jesus Christ is alive today?"

"It is true, Benjamin. And Jesus Christ is alive today."

Benjamin snapped his fingers. "Oh, yes! I do remember hearing some of the British people talk about Him. He is not on earth but is somewhere above the sky, they said."

"Right. In a beautiful and wonderful place called heaven."

"Heaven. This is in the sky, but they said He can see us and hear us here on earth."

"That's right."

"So when you said the Lord hadn't given you the 'go' sign about your move to Texas, you meant Jesus Christ?"

"Right."

"He has some way of talking to you from above the sky?"

Dan smiled. "Yes, Benjamin. He does."

"He shouts down at you?"

"No. He has a way of speaking to you in your heart."

"I do not understand."

"Well, I would like for you to understand. We get our understanding of Him from His Book, the Bible. Since it is all so strange to you, it is best to take it a little at a time. For now, just think about this: The God who made this world loves you, Benjamin. And He wants you to come to know Him through His Son. Will you think about that?"

"Of course."

"Good. Now, let me tell you about a friend of mine who is a cattle rancher in Texas."

Benjamin listened intently as Dan told him about Bill Wickburg, and of Bill's encouraging him to come to Texas and get started in the cattle ranching business. He told Benjamin of the newspaper articles he had read on the subject, and how the desire to become a part of it had grown on him over a period of time.

Benjamin pulled his hook from the water to make sure it still had bait. Satisfied that the worm was still intact, he cast it back in and said, "I can see, Mr. Dan, that you are really intent on going to Texas. I know it will be a wonderful life for you. But when you go, I am going to miss you very much."

"I'll miss you, too, Benjamin. But I'll come back now and then to see my family, of which you have become a part. When I come to see family, I'll see you along with the rest of them."

Dan's words had a powerful effect on the young black man. "Mr. Dan, in my entire life, no friend has ever said anything to me that meant as much as what you just said. You good people look at me as part of your family. What a happy man I am!"

While they were driving home, Dan turned to Benjamin and said, "Has anyone told you about the church services our plantation preacher, Zebulun, holds for the slaves on Sundays?"

"Yes, sir. Preacher Zebulun and some others have asked me to come this Sunday. They were so nice about it. I told them I will come."

"Good. I'd really like to take you to our church in town, but it's nearly all white people. You might feel uncomfortable. A few Negroes attend, but very few. They are free Negroes, of course. Well, except for the personal slave of our neighbors' daughter."

"I understand, Mr. Dan. I know how white people here in the South feel about mixing with black people, even those who are not slaves."

"I'm sorry, Benjamin. I hope someday it will change."

"Don't be sorry. I am a very happy man. It doesn't bother me what other white folks think, as long as the Johnson family wants me as their servant."

Dan chuckled. "And as part of the family, don't forget."

"Oh yes, sir! I won't forget that!"

"Let me tell you, Benjamin, my parents and brother and sister are appreciating you more every day. Especially Mom, I might add. She is thrilled with the way you have made things run smoother than ever in the house. Of course, I agree with the rest of the family."

Benjamin grinned. "That's what a servant is supposed to do, Mr. Dan."

"Well, you're sure doing a good job."

"Thank you. I mean to always do a good job for the people who have given me a new life."

As the days passed, the friendship between Dan and Benjamin grew stronger and deeper. They went fishing together often, and Dan found many other reasons to spend time with his new friend, which pleased Benjamin exceedingly.

One day at midmorning, Zack was in his den doing some paperwork and heard a light tap at his door. "Yes?"

"It is Benjamin, Mr. Johnson."

"Please come in."

Benjamin stepped into the room and closed the door.

"What can I do for you?"

"Sir, I have all the work finished that you and Mrs. Johnson have assigned me for today."

Zack's eyebrows arched. "Already?"

"Yes, sir."

"Hmm. It looks like you can take the rest of the day off. Maybe if Dan isn't too busy, the two of you can go fishing again."

"Well, sir, if you will allow it, there is something else I would like to do."

"Oh? What's that?"

"Sir, I would like your permission to go to the fields and work with the slaves. I . . . . I want them to know that I do not look down on them just because I am your hired servant."

Zack eased back in his chair. "Benjamin, this pleases me very much. I appreciate your attitude toward the slaves. It is very commendable."

"Mr. Johnson, it hasn't been so long since I was a slave. You treat them wonderfully, but they are still slaves. I want to work with them whenever my assignments are caught up, if you will allow it."

"I sure will. This makes me think more of you than ever." Rising to his feet, he said, "Let's go find Dan. I'll let him assign you to the work crew that needs you the most."

A few days later, Dan and Benjamin were riding horses together, heading for town. As they trotted along, Dan said, "I like the way you handle yourself with a horse, Benjamin. You seem so at home in the saddle."

"I should, Mr. Dan. I learned to ride almost before I learned to walk. I can handle a cow pony, too. You know, riding herd at roundup time and having to keep the strays with the herd."

"Oh yes. That's something I'll have to learn when I get to Texas."

"You will learn it real fast once you are herding cattle."

Dan was quiet for a moment, then said, "Benjamin, I want to tell you what an impact your volunteering to work in the fields with the slaves has had on them. You have captured their hearts."

Benjamin smiled. "That makes me very happy, Mr. Dan. I'm really getting to love your slaves. They are fine people."

They rode into Charleston, completed their errands, and headed back toward the plantation. After trotting the horses for a while, they slowed to a walk.

Dan spoke up. "You've been in church services for two Sundays now. What do you think about what you've been hearing?"

"Mr. Dan, Preacher Zebulun is such a loving man. His sermons are very heart touching. He certainly has a deep love for people and a powerful love for Jesus Christ. But there is so much I do not understand yet."

"That's to be expected. It is all so new to you. When a person has been raised without ever hearing the Bible preached and the gospel made plain, it takes time. In the Bible, God likens it to sowing seed, watering it, and finally reaping the harvest. You will keep attending the services, won't you?"

"Oh yes, sir. I will do that."

"And you've been thinking on what I told you before?"

"I sure have. I am glad that God loves me. And I am glad He wants me to come to know Him through His Son."

"Good. Have you come to understand about heaven and hell, and that every human being goes to one of those two places when they die?"

"Yes. That place called hell sounds awful. Preacher Zebulun preached about it last Sunday morning. I am having a hard time believing that when Jesus died on that cross, He did it for me."

Dan took a few minutes to elaborate on the Lord's death at Calvary but found that the light of the gospel still had not broken through Benjamin's darkness. He told him the gospel story from another angle, and it seemed to help, but he could see that Benjamin needed more time.

In the days that followed, whenever they were alone together, Dan lovingly and tactfully witnessed to Benjamin about Jesus Christ and Benjamin's need of salvation. Each time, Benjamin showed more interest and seemed to grasp it better.

Dan kept his family abreast of his progress with Benjamin, and at family altar time they prayed earnestly for Benjamin to be saved.

THE FOLLOWING SATURDAY, DAN AND BENJAMIN were fishing together at Dan's favorite spot. He went over the gospel again, pointing out to Benjamin that when Jesus died on the cross, He was dying for Benjamin personally.

"Mr. Dan, it is not that I do not believe that Jesus Christ died on the cross for all sinners. I do believe that."

"Good. Then are you ready to repent of your sin and put your trust in Jesus to save you?"

"Well, sir, I am still in the dark on something."

"What is that?"

"I cannot quite understand how the Lord Jesus Christ's sacrifice at Calvary could give me salvation. Please . . . I am not trying to be difficult about it. Really I am not. It is just that I cannot see how it works."

Dan nodded. "Let me think about it. I've got to come up with the right way to explain it to you."

Dan prayed silently, asking the Lord for help. Suddenly it came to him.

"Tell you what, Benjamin . . ."

"Yes, sir?"

"I know how to make it clear to you, but we'll need more time than we have left here at the river. I'd like to talk to you in your quarters tonight after supper. Would that be all right?"

"Certainly. I would like that."

When Benjamin answered the knock at his door that evening, he found Dan bearing a beautifully wrapped package in one hand and his Bible in the other.

"Ready?" Dan said.

"Yes, sir. Come in."

When Benjamin closed the door, Dan turned and extended the package. "This is for you from me."

Benjamin took the package and said, "Am I to unwrap it right now?"

"Yes. You're going to need it this evening."

He broke the ribbon on the package and tore away the bright-colored paper to find a new Bible with a black leather cover. "It is beautiful, Mr. Dan. Thank you!"

"My pleasure. Let's sit down at the table. I want to show you some things in Scripture. It will help if you have your own Bible to read as I use mine."

They sat down at the small table, facing each other. "All right," Dan said, "let's read a couple of Scripture passages together. When you've seen them, then I'm going to tell you something that will shed light on them."

Benjamin smiled at him. "Where do we start?"

"In the Gospel of John. Can you find it?"

"Probably, but it will be faster if you show me where it is."

Dan took Benjamin's Bible from him, opened it to John chapter 8, and said, "I would like to have you read a verse to me."

Benjamin nodded as Dan opened his own Bible to the same chapter.

"Okay, Benjamin, what you are about to read came from the lips of the Lord Jesus Christ. I have already shown you that all human beings are born sinners and are held captive by sin and Satan, and that because Satan is going to spend eternity in the lake of fire, he wants company. He wants to keep you his captive and take you to hell with him. Remember?"

"Yes, sir. That is quite clear."

"Good. Then, as a captive of sin and Satan, like all other sinners, you need to be made free, don't you?"

"I do."

"Now read what Jesus said to men who were captives of sin and Satan, in verse 36."

Benjamin dropped his eyes to the page and read, " 'If the Son therefore shall make you free, ye shall be free indeed.' "

"Now, what does that say to you?"

Benjamin looked at it again. "That only God's Son can set me free, and if He does, I am free without a doubt."

Dan smiled. "Do you believe Him?"

"Yes. I am just not quite sure how He does it."

"I'll explain that to you, but first we need to go to the book of 1 Timothy."

A quizzical look framed Benjamin's face. "First Timothy? Is there more than one?"

"These were epistles—letters—written by the apostle Paul to one of his sons in the ministry named Timothy. He wrote two letters to Timothy—both under the guidance and inspiration of the Holy Spirit. Here. Let me get it for you."

When Dan laid the open Bible before Benjamin, he said, "Keep in mind what Jesus said in John 8:36 and read me verses 5 and 6 of chapter 2."

Benjamin found the spot and read: " 'For there is one God, and one mediator between God and men, the man Christ Jesus, who gave himself a ransom for all, to be testified in due time.' "

"Do you know what the word *ransom* means, Benjamin?"

"I am not sure, Mr. Dan. I do not think I have ever heard the word."

"Well, do you know what *redemption* means?"

"I believe so. I remember studying the word in my classes when the British people were teaching my parents and me English. Redemption is the sum paid to set a person free from punishment, slavery, or prison. Right?"

"Exactly. The word *ransom* comes from the same root word as *redemption*. So, when Jesus gave Himself a ransom for all, He was paying the price that God, in His holiness, righteousness, and justice demanded for setting a sinner free from slavery to sin and Satan and the punishment of spending eternity in the prison called hell. Are you following me?"

Benjamin nodded.

"All right. Benjamin, you were brought to this country by Thomas Green as a slave, weren't you?"

"Yes."

"Thomas Green owned you."

"Yes."

"You were to be sold to the highest bidder and become that person's slave, weren't you?"

"I sure was. And if Finn Colvin had bought me, I would be his slave."

Dan smiled. "That is true. Now think about it. You were the slave of Thomas Green and held in his bonds as his captive, weren't you?"

Benjamin thought about his dash for freedom when he jumped from the ship but was caught by the police and delivered back to Thomas Green. "Most certainly."

"But it was established on the auction block that whoever made the highest bid for you would own you when he paid the price."

"Yes."

"My father made the highest bid and paid that price at the cashier's booth. Right?"

Benjamin held Dan's gaze with his own and nodded. "Yes, sir."

"So my father owned you then, didn't he?"

"He did."

"But what did he do, even though he owned you?"

Suddenly Benjamin's eyes lit up. "He set me free!"

"Exactly! And when a lost sinner comes to Jesus, realizing he is a captive of sin and Satan, and calls on Jesus to save him, He does! And because that repentant sinner opens his heart to Jesus, he then belongs to Jesus. So, just like my father paid the price for you, which made you his possession, then he set you free . . . so it is with Jesus. That's why He said, 'If the Son therefore shall make you free, ye shall be free indeed.' Do you see it?"

Benjamin smiled. "It is coming clear."

"While you are thinking on it, let me emphasize something. Look at the verse again. Tell me what price was paid so that lost sinners could be saved and set free, Benjamin. What was the ransom?"

He studied it for a brief moment, then looked up. "Why, it was Himself, Mr. Dan. Jesus gave Himself as the price."

"Hang on to that, Benjamin, and let me show you some other passages that will help you."

With Dan's help, Benjamin followed in his own Bible as Dan read several passages on redemption, showing what Jesus did for sinners when He went to the cross, shed His precious blood, and died, making it possible for them to be set free from sin, Satan, and the damnation of hell.

When Dan finished reading to him, Benjamin was weeping. "Mr. Dan," he said, "I see it! What your father did for me when he ransomed me from earthly slavery is a picture of what Jesus wants to do for me, to ransom me from spiritual slavery!"

"That's it," Dan said. "Do you want to be set free from sin, Satan, and the condemnation that is in you?"

"Yes! Oh yes."

With Dan's guidance, in humble repentance of sin, Benjamin opened his heart to the Saviour.

After calling on the Lord to save him, Benjamin said, "Mr. Dan, when your father ransomed me at the arena, it had to have been because there was love in his heart for this poor slave. He had enough love for me that he paid a high price to set me free. It was a ransom of love."

"I couldn't say it any better than that, Benjamin," Dan said.

Benjamin wiped tears from his cheeks. "And what the Lord Jesus did for me was a ransom of love. But it was a greater ransom, and a greater love."

"Yes, Benjamin. Both were a ransom of love. But of course, the Lord's love is the greatest, and the ransom He paid was the highest—the sacrifice of Himself."

"Mr. Dan, last Sunday morning, when Preacher Zebulun finished his sermon and gave the invitation, one of the slave girls went forward. She had been saved during the week and wanted to tell everybody about it. This is what I should do, shouldn't I?"

"That's right, Benjamin. Jesus said that when we confess Him before men, He will confess us before His Father."

"Then I will do it tomorrow morning."

At the Colvin plantation on Monday morning, Ol' Mose came in the back door of the mansion to start his day's work. He was heavy of heart but did his best not to let it show.

Finn, George, and Edward had just finished breakfast and were about to leave the kitchen. They spoke to Mose, then hurried past him, telling Martha they would see her at noon.

Mose spoke to Mandy, the cook, then said to Martha, "First thing I'll do, Miss Martha, is finish the job in the pantry that I started yesterday."

"All right. How long do you think it will take you to finish firming up the shelves?"

"I'd say 'bout an hour, ma'am."

Martha nodded. "All right. The next thing I need is for you to see if you can get the spots out of the carpet in George's room."

"More whiskey, ma'am?"

Martha bit her lip. "Yes."

"I'll take care of it like I did las' time."

"All right. Then I need you to sweep off the front porch."

Mose's head hung a bit lower than usual. "Yes'm."

"When you get that done, come and see me, and I'll decide what needs attention next."

"Yes, ma'am."

As the morning passed, Martha observed Mose moving about the house, doing his work. She grew more and more concerned as she read his eyes and facial expressions. Something was troubling him deeply.

At noon, Ol' Mose went to his shack to prepare his lunch, as usual. A few minutes later, Finn and his sons came into the kitchen of the mansion, sat down with Martha, and began devouring the food prepared by Mandy.

While they were eating, Martha said, "So, did my men get all their work done this morning?"

"Sure did, Mom," Edward said. "I don't know what Pa's gonna do this afternoon, but George and I are gonna ride our horses out to the back side of the plantation and have us a good race. We haven't raced for over a week."

"As for me," said Finn, "I've got to go into town and do some business at the bank."

When the men had left the kitchen, Martha said to the cook, "Mandy, you'd better put some extra fixin's in the stew for supper. One thing's for sure . . . when George and Edward ride their horses, they always come in for supper extra hungry."

"I will make sho' they have plenty, Miz Colvin."

While George and Edward were changing into their riding clothes, Finn had one of the male slaves hitch his buggy up to one of the buggy horses, then headed for Charleston.

The Colvin brothers stopped by the sewing room to tell their mother they would see her at suppertime, then went to the barn where their saddle horses were kept.

While they were happily saddling and bridling the horses, Edward snickered and said, "I hate to tell you this, big brother, but I'm gonna beat you in every race today. You haven't got a chance."

"Hah!" George retorted. "You're the one who hasn't got a chance! By the time this day is over, you'll have to go home like a whipped dog with your tail tucked in!"

The Colvin brothers continued to banter as they mounted up and trotted their horses past the buildings and across the fields toward the back side of the estate.

Shortly thereafter, Ol' Mose returned to the mansion and took up the tasks assigned to him by Martha.

It was just after two o'clock when Mose carried a bucket of hot soapy water, a brush, and rags onto the back porch and began washing windows. A few minutes later, Martha came out the back door and said, "Mose, I need your help inside the house for a few minutes."

"Yes, ma'am." He laid down the brush and shuffled toward her. "What can I do for you?"

"I need you to move some light things from one place to another in the parlor. Lamps, vases, and that kind of thing. I'll show you."

Mose shuffled beside her as they entered the mansion and headed toward the front.

Martha gave him a sidelong glance. He still looked as if he were carrying the weight of the world on his ancient, stooped shoulders.

By the time they entered the parlor, Martha could no longer hold back. "Mose, before I show you what I want done in here, I need to ask you something."

"Yes, ma'am?"

"All day long I've noticed that you seem troubled about something. Is there anything I can do for you?"

"It is nothin' you can do anythin' about, ma'am. Thank you, though."

Martha shook her head. "I can't let you look so burdened without learning what it is, Mose. Now I insist that you tell me."

He cleared his throat nervously, then said, "Mrs. Colvin, what has me upset is a bad dream I had last night."

Martha's brow furrowed. "A bad dream?"

"Yes, ma'am. I have not been able to shake off its effects since I woke up in the middle of the night and wasn't able to go back to sleep."

"My, oh, my. It must have been some dream."

"It was, ma'am. It was."

"Well, tell me about it."

"Yes, ma'am. Before I do, I want to make sure you understand that as a born-again Christian, I do not put stock in dreams as some kind of message from God. I believe He speaks to His children through His written Word and by the Holy Spirit in their hearts. Often He guides them by circumstances He brings into their lives. Do you understand this, ma'am?"

"I assure you I do," Martha said. "But I want to know about this dream that has so upset you."

Ol' Mose ran a hand over his mouth. "I dreamed las' night that Master George was ridin' his horse at a gallop. The horse stumbled, throwin' him to the ground. His head hit somethin' hard, Miss Martha, and it killed him."

Martha's eyes widened, and her hand went to her mouth.

"Please do not let it bother you, ma'am," Mose said in a comforting tone. "It was only a dream. The reason it upset me so much was because it was so vivid. Like dreams sometimes do, it stayed with me after I got up for the day. I jis' couldn't shake it from my mind, even when I came to work this mornin'. I still can't get it out of my thoughts."

By this time, Martha was trembling, and tears were misting her eyes.

"Miss Martha, please don't let it upset you. It was jis' a dream. I'm sure I will get over it by tomorrow."

"No, Mose. You don't understand."

"Understand what, ma'am?"

"At this very moment, George and Edward are racing each other on horseback at the back side of the plantation." She pulled a hankie from the sleeve of her dress and pressed it to her nose. "I'm frightened, Mose."

Finn came through the doorway of the parlor and heard Martha's words.

Mose was saying, "Please do not let it upset you, Mrs. Colvin. It was only a dream."

Both of them turned toward Finn as he came closer and saw Martha in tears. He looked at Mose and said, "What dream? What's this all about?"

When Mose told Finn, he laughed and laid a hand on Martha's shoulder. "Hey, Martha, calm down! So Mose dreamed that George got killed riding a horse. There's nothing to it. Dreams don't mean anything."

"But those boys are out there riding right now! That's what worries me! They're racing each other."

Finn chuckled. "So? They race each other all the time. Now stop crying. Nothing is going to happen to George."

Finn turned to the old man. "Don't you have some work to do?"

Finn Colvin was sitting on the back porch, reading a newspaper he had picked up in town. Suddenly, the sight of two horses coming at a walk past the slave shacks caught his eye. He squinted, and it took only a few seconds to see that Edward was leading George's limping horse, with George draped over the saddle.

He dropped the paper and bounded off the porch. Slaves looked on wide-eyed as Finn ran up to Edward and saw that he was weeping. He shot a glance at George's lifeless form.

"Wha—what happened?"

His face void of color, Edward slid listlessly from the saddle and said, "We were racing, Pa. George's horse stumbled on a broken tree limb. George was thrown from the saddle as the horse went down. His head struck a rock. He's dead."

Finn examined George's bloody head and ejected a wordless wail, then sobbed, "It's true! It's true! Exactly as Mose dreamed it!"

Edward put an arm around his father's shoulders. "Pa, what're you talkin' about?"

Finn looked at his youngest son. "Ol' Mose had a dream last night. He dreamed that George was riding his horse. The horse stumbled, and George was thrown from the saddle. He hit his head and it killed him! He told this to your mother and me no more than two hours ago!"

Finn worked to get himself under control. "Oh, I hate to have to tell your mother. This will tear her to pieces."

"Pa . . . do you want me to tell her?"

"No, son. I have to do it. I'll let you explain how it happened after I break it to her. Let's take George into the house."

"I'll carry him, Pa."

"No. I'll carry him. Turn the horses over to the slaves and let them remove the saddles and bridles."

As he spoke, Finn planted his feet firmly next to the horse and eased George's body into his arms.

When they moved inside the house, there was no one in sight. Finn carried the body past the kitchen. "I'll put him on the love seat in the sewing room. You stay with him. I'll go find your mother and bring her."

Martha suddenly appeared at the far end of the hall and froze when she saw the body in her husband's arms. She dropped a vase of flowers and cried out in horror.

"Go to her, Edward," Finn said, "while I lay him down."

Edward hadn't taken the first step when Martha bolted toward them, crying, "What happened? What happened?" Her eyes were wide and her face like stone as she said, "Edward! Is he—"

He gripped her shoulders. "Yes, Mom. He's dead."

She shut her eyes tight. "The dream was true, Edward! It was true! Mose's dream was true!"

Finn came from the sewing room and brushed past Edward to fold Martha in his arms. "I don't understand it, Martha," he said. "I don't understand it, but George was killed exactly as Mose dreamed."

"I want to see him," she said, choking on her words.

"I know. But I have to warn you. It's not a pretty sight. His head is caved in where he struck the rock. There's blood . . ."

Martha pushed him aside and ran to the sewing room. At sight of her son, she released a wail and fell across his chest.

Finn stood beside her, his hand on her back. She cried as if her heart would shatter. Edward, who stood next to his father, saw movement at the door and turned to find Ol' Mose.

The old man's wrinkled face twisted as he said, "Master Edward, was he thrown from his horse?"

"Yes. Pa told me about your dream."

Mose seemed unable to say any more. He leaned on the door frame until Martha brought her emotions under control and with Finn's help stood to her feet. She looked at Mose and said, "How? How could you have known?"

"I didn't know, Miss Martha. It jis' happened in my sleep when I dreamed. It . . . has to be only a coincidence."

"Strange coincidence," said Finn. "Last night you dreamed this very thing would happen. And now, here lies George, dead from being thrown from his horse."

Mose met Finn's gaze with tender eyes. "I don't understand it, Master Finn. I am so sorry."

Finn took a deep breath and closed his eyes for a moment, then said, "It's no fault of yours. Go on back to your work."

TWO DAYS LATER, GEORGE COLVIN'S BODY lay inside an expensive coffin in the shade of huge magnolia trees surrounding the family burial plot. The Johnsons and the Moores were there, as well as neighbors from miles around.

Zack and Catherine Johnson, and Charles and Evelyn Moore waited for the graveside service to begin. The minister was from a large church in Charleston. Although Finn would not darken the door of any church, they weren't surprised that he would want some semblance of spirituality connected to George's burial.

There was no singing before the minister approached the coffin and began his short speech. He read one verse from the Psalms, told what a good man George Colvin was and that he had gone to heaven as a result of his good life

When it was over, the Johnsons and the Moores stepped into the line of people waiting to express their condolences.

When it was their turn in front of the Colvins, Catherine and Evelyn spoke kindly to Finn and Edward, then embraced Martha.

"Honey," Catherine said, "Evelyn and I would like to spend some time with you soon."

Finn bristled at their words. "I know what you have in mind, and I'll have none of it! I don't want you talking to Martha about the Bible or anything connected to it!"

He turned to Martha. "Don't you talk to them, do you hear me?"

Charles stepped closer and said in a soft tone, "Finn, our wives only want to help Martha."

"She doesn't need any of your religious fanatic help! Now I'll thank you to leave this property!"

Martha's face pinched as she looked at Catherine and Evelyn through tears.

Zack started to say something, but Finn cut him off. "Now, I said! Leave this property now!"

Benjamin had completed two weeks at the Johnson plantation and thoroughly enjoyed the work assigned to him. He felt a special pleasure in spending time with the slaves and helping them with their work.

On a bright spring day, he left his quarters and entered the Johnson mansion by the rear door. Catherine was in the kitchen with her slave, Daisy, who was in her early twenties. Daisy had lived on the plantation for ten years and was promised to one of the young men who had been the Johnsons' slave for almost as long as she had.

"Good morning, Benjamin," Catherine said. "Did you have a good night's sleep?"

"Yes, ma'am. I never knew what a real bed was until I came here." He glanced at Daisy. "Good morning to you, Miss Daisy."

"And to you, Benjamin."

"And how is Theodore? Is he working in the fields today?"

"He is fine," Daisy said. "And today, Master Zack has him working in the number two barn."

Benjamin smiled. "So how long till you and Theodore become husband and wife?"

" 'Bout three months. Preacher Zebulun is havin' sessions with us, teachin' us about marriage and all."

"Well, that is nice. The two of you make a handsome couple."

"Thank you," Daisy said, a pleased smile creasing her lips.

"Benjamin, I've got some work for you to do right away," Catherine said. "Master Zack said to tell you he will pay you for the past two weeks when he gets back from town."

Benjamin flashed a smile. "I still cannot believe I am actually going to be paid for being your servant, Miss Catherine. The Lord has indeed been good to this South African man. So what do you want done right away?"

"Angeline gets together with Priscilla Moore once a week and they spend the day together."

"Is Priscilla Moore the daughter of some plantation owners, ma'am?"

"Yes. The Moores are neighbors and very good friends. We belong to the same church, so our families visit each other quite often. The girls alternate spending time at one house, then the other. The past couple of weeks, things have been so hectic at both places, they haven't been able to meet. However, Priscilla and her slave are coming here today."

"Yes," said Daisy, "and Dorena always spends some time with me when they are here. We're very close friends."

"So what I need, Benjamin, is for you to make sure the parlor is spic and span. The girls will spend a great deal of time in there and I need you to make sure the back porch is swept and clean, because part of their day will be spent there, too."

"Yes, ma'am. I will take care of it."

Priscilla Moore stood in the vestibule of her home, talking animatedly to her mother about plans for a day with Angeline.

Priscilla's father waited at the open door, watching for the carriage.

"Oh, Mother, I'm so happy for Dorena! She's going to get to meet him today!"

Charles looked over his shoulder. "Who is Dorena going to meet today, honey?"

"Benjamin, Papa!"

Charles gave her a blank look. "I don't understand."

"Charles, dear, you must be getting hard of hearing," Evelyn said.

"What do you mean?"

"All Dorena has talked about around here since the auction a couple of weeks ago is that handsome Benjamin the Johnsons kept Finn Colvin from buying."

"Oh, him! I sure was glad when Zack and Catherine told us about Benjamin being led to the Lord by Dan."

Priscilla nodded. "I think it's so wonderful what Mr. Johnson did by making Benjamin the house servant, rather than a slave. Anyway, Papa, Dorena has had this great big crush on Benjamin ever since that day at the auction, and she's been talking about him nearly all the time. I'm surprised you haven't heard her."

Charles grinned. "I guess I've just been preoccupied. Anyway, from what I know, Benjamin is a fine young man. I hope he and Dorena can become friends. Speaking of Dorena . . . how come she's not down here yet?"

"She'll be here any minute, Papa. She's been fixing herself up very special."

Just then, Dorena appeared at the top of the stairs. "I'm sorry if I'm holding you up, Miss Priscilla," she said.

"You're not. The carriage isn't even here yet."

Charles and Evelyn could not believe their eyes as they watched Dorena descend the stairs.

She had dressed herself with great care, choosing a sky blue calico dress with white and yellow flowers dotting the pastel fabric. The delicate collar accentuated her graceful, slender neck.

Her braided hair was wrapped around her head in coronet fashion. Tendrils of unruly curls framed her lovely face. On her feet were soft black slippers, which she usually wore only on Sundays or in cold weather.

"Will you look at this, Mother!" Charles said. "Dorena, I've never seen you look lovelier!"

The young girl smiled shyly. "Thank you, Master Charles."

The carriage arrived, and moments later Charles was in the driver's seat, putting the horses in motion. The girls waved at Evelyn standing on the porch.

When the carriage came to a halt in front of the Johnson mansion, Angeline was outside, waiting for them. Charles helped both girls to the ground.

"Thank you, Papa," Priscilla said and kissed his cheek.

"Thank you, Master Charles," said Dorena.

Charles smiled, then said to his daughter, "I'll pick you up after supper."

As Charles Moore drove away, Angeline led both girls inside the mansion and took them to the parlor.

Catherine ran her gaze over Dorena and said, "You sure look nice today, honey. I love your hair."

Dorena curtsied. "Thank you, ma'am."

"She's all fixed up for a special reason, Mother," said Angeline. "She's hoping to meet Benjamin."

Dorena lowered her gaze to the floor.

Catherine smiled and laid a hand on her shoulder. "Don't be embarrassed, sweetie. Some of the girls here on the plantation have crushes on him, too. He's a very handsome young man. And a very nice young man, I might add."

"Yes, ma'am. I was glad to learn that he has become a Christian."

"We're all happy about that," Catherine said.

"Is Benjamin in the house now, Mrs. Johnson?" Priscilla asked.

"No, dear. I kept him pretty busy here until about a half hour ago. But when I ran out of work for him, he went to the fields to work with the slaves."

Priscilla's eyebrows raised. "Really? I thought he was a hired servant."

"Oh, he is, dear, but this young man is very special. When his work is caught up around the house and the yard, he chooses to work with the slaves."

"Just shows what kind of person he is," Angeline said. "Mother is right. Benjamin is special."

Dorena sighed. "Yes. That is what I thought when I saw him the day of the auction."

"Well, I'm sure you will get to meet him, dear," said Catherine. "He will come in from the fields with the others. If you want to see Daisy, she's upstairs in my room, doing some work for me."

"All right," Dorena said. "I will go on up. Maybe there's something I can do to help her."

It was late in the afternoon when Angeline and Priscilla were sitting at a table on the back porch of the mansion. The back door opened and Dorena came out with a tray.

"How about some lemonade?" she said. "Daisy and I are going to have some in the kitchen. I thought you might be thirsty."

Priscilla smiled at her. "I am, now that you mention it. Thank you."

Angeline let her gaze trail off toward the barns. As Dorena set the tray on the table, Angeline said, "Here comes Benjamin!"

Dorena's head snapped up. "Oh, it is him!" she gasped, as she set a glass of lemonade in front of Priscilla.

"Relax," Priscilla said, laying a hand on her arm.

"But now that it's about to happen, I'm scared."

"It will be all right," Priscilla said.

Benjamin was veering in the direction of his quarters.

Angeline stood up to get his attention and called to him.

The tall, handsome servant stopped. "Yes, ma'am? Is there something I can do for you?"

"Yes! Please come over here. There is someone I want you to meet."

As he drew up, Benjamin's eyes went to Dorena, who was having a hard time breathing.

"Benjamin," said Angeline, gesturing toward her best friend, "this is Priscilla Moore. Mother told you about our neighbors, the Moores, whose plantation is about three miles down the road."

Benjamin was still looking at Dorena, reliving the moment when she had passed by the auction block and smiled at him. Her striking beauty had captured him then and he had memorized her lovely features. He had thought of her many times since that moment, not knowing who she was or to whom she belonged.

Completely in awe of her, he mentally shook himself. He pulled his eyes from her and looked at Priscilla. Bowing, he said, "It is my pleasure to meet you, Miss Priscilla."

Dorena's dark eyes grew wide and luminous as Benjamin greeted her mistress. She knew it wasn't polite to stare, but at the moment she seemingly had no control of her eyes.

Benjamin's attraction to Dorena did not escape Angeline and Priscilla.

"Benjamin," Angeline said, "this is Priscilla's slave, Dorena."

Again, Benjamin's eyes fastened on the lovely face. For a few seconds he just stared, then blinked and said, "I . . . I am sorry, Miss Dorena. I remember seeing you at the arena when I was on the block two weeks ago."

Dorena felt her heart skip a beat. He remembered her!

"I am delighted to meet you, Miss Dorena. May I say . . . that is a very pretty name."

Benjamin had been working hard in the field and suddenly realized that he showed it. Beads of perspiration glistened on his mahogany skin. Running his eyes down his body, he said, "Ladies, I must apologize for my untidy condition. I just came from the field."

"We understand, Benjamin," said Angeline. "You need not apologize."

Dorena didn't care how untidy he was. In her eyes, he was the handsomest man in the world. She warmed him with a smile like the one she had afforded him at the arena and said, "I recall that at the auction, Benjamin, the slave trader told the audience you are from a cattle ranch in South Africa."

"Yes, ma'am."

156

"Were you born on the ranch?"

"I was."

"I was born in this country, Benjamin, but both sets of my grandparents were brought to America from West Africa . . . the Ivory Coast."

"Were you born on the Moore plantation?" he asked.

"No. It was the Larimore rice plantation north of here some thirty miles. Master Charles did not start his cotton plantation until fifteen years ago. At that time, he bought my parents from Humphrey Larimore, who was planning to sell his land to the family who owned the Desmond plantation on the Santee River."

"Yes," said Priscilla, chuckling. "When Papa bought Caleb and Liza, Dorena was just a year old. Her brother, Matthew, was three. Liza is our house slave, and Caleb is Papa's favorite field slave. Matthew is eighteen now and almost as good a worker as Caleb."

"And your grandparents?" Benjamin asked.

"They are all dead now," she said softly.

"Oh. I am sorry. I would sure like to meet your parents and your brother."

"I'm sure you will have that opportunity, Benjamin," Priscilla said.

"Well, I had better get myself bathed. Miss Dorena, Miss Priscilla, it has been a pleasure meeting you."

As Benjamin headed for his quarters, Dorena said in a low tone, "Miss Priscilla, I am sorry he said my name first."

"Honey, it's all right. His heart is set on you. That is quite obvious."

Dorena's eyes followed the young man until he reached the door of his apartment. As he put his hand on the knob, he turned and looked back. When he saw that she was looking at him, he smiled.

"Angeline," Priscilla said, "have you ever seen a man so enamored over a woman as Benjamin is over Dorena?"

Angeline giggled. "I don't think so. He's fascinated by her, that's for sure."

Dorena smiled at them, then looked back at the door where she had last seen Benjamin. *It would be wonderful if he is the one God has for me.*

After church services the next Sunday, people were standing outside, chatting in small groups.

Angeline leaned close to Priscilla and said, "Can I talk to you alone for a minute?"

"Of course." Turning to Dorena, Priscilla said, "You wait here, okay?"

"Yes, Miss Priscilla."

The two girls went to stand under a magnolia tree. Keeping her voice low, Angeline said, "I have a plan."

"What kind of a plan?"

"It's about Dorena and Benjamin."

"Go ahead."

"Well, for our day together this week, I'm going to ask my father if Benjamin can drive me to your house and pick me up after supper. Since Benjamin is a servant, it should be all right."

"Oh! That will give Dorena and Benjamin a chance to see each other!" Priscilla said.

"That's the point."

"I hope your father will do it."

"You know how fathers are. If I put that 'please, Papa, I really want this' look in my eyes, he will."

Priscilla giggled. "Your father must be a whole lot like mine!"

"Of course. The Lord just fixed it so we females can work on males and they don't even realize it. Especially when it's a daughter who puts that 'please, Papa, I really want this' look in her eyes."

"Okay. Do it! We've got to help this romance along as much as we can."

"That's the way I look at it. Uh-oh. Mother is motioning to me. They're ready to go."

When the Johnson family carriage was rolling through Charleston's streets on the way out of town, Angeline leaned toward the driver's seat and said, "Papa . . ." then stopped speaking.

Zack turned and looked into his daughter's blue eyes. "Yes, honey?"

"I have a real big favor to ask of you."

Zack smiled, loving the girl with all of his father's heart. "Well, what is it, sweetheart?"

"This week, when Priscilla and I have our day together, would you let Benjamin drive me over to the Moores' and also pick me up after supper?"

Still held by the magnetic look in his daughter's eyes, Zack said, "Why would you want Benjamin to drive you instead of one of your brothers or myself?"

"Well, Papa, it's like this. Dorena and Benjamin have developed a powerful attraction for each other, and . . . well, I would like to help it along."

Catherine grinned. "So now you're Cupid?"

"I'm trying to be, Mother."

Dan laughed and without turning around said, "Bless your heart, little sister. I think it would really be nice if Benjamin and Dorena fell head over heels in love. He has had so much sadness in his life. It would be wonderful for him to have some real happiness. Give it all you've got."

"So how do you know about the happiness of being in love, big brother?" Alexander said, reveling in giving Dan a hard time.

"I know because I study our parents and I see the happiness they have."

Angeline giggled and poked her little brother on the chest with a stiff forefinger. He gave her a mock scowl.

Zack looked at Catherine. "What do you think about Benjamin driving our daughter to the Moore plantation, honey?"

"I think it would be fine. Since Benjamin is our servant and not a slave, I see no problem with it."

Zack pondered her words, then looked at Angeline.

"Please, Papa?" she said.

Zack reached back to cup her graceful chin in his hand. "How could I ever turn down such a sweet daughter?"

Alexander guffawed. "You could if you really knew her, Pa!"

The family had a good laugh, and the carriage dropped off the cobblestone streets onto the dusty country road.

On Thursday that week, when Benjamin pulled the Johnson buggy up to the Moore mansion, both Priscilla and Dorena were on the porch. Angeline had shared the plot with Dorena, and both girls were delighted to see Benjamin driving the buggy.

Benjamin's gaze immediately went to Dorena.

As he helped Angeline out of the buggy at the Moores', she thanked him and shot a glance at Priscilla, who smiled and gave a nod.

Angeline turned to Ben. "If you would like to stay a few minutes here at the porch and talk to Dorena, you may. Mrs. Moore has given permission."

Benjamin flicked a glance at Dorena, then looked back at Angeline. "Really?"

"Really."

"It can only be for about ten minutes, Benjamin," said Priscilla.

"That's a whole lot better than nothing!" he said.

The two matchmakers dashed inside the house and went into the parlor. They pressed up close to the lace curtains and remained out of sight from the enchanted couple who stood on the porch looking into each other's eyes as they talked.

THE NEXT WEEK, ANGELINE ASKED HER FATHER to allow Benjamin to drive over to the Moore plantation and pick up Priscilla and Dorena if Priscilla's father was in agreement. This way, she told him, Benjamin and Dorena could be together during the ride. And, of course, if Benjamin were allowed to take them back home, they could be together again.

"I appreciate what you're trying to do, my sweet daughter, but I'd like to talk to Charles Moore about it. And I think Evelyn and your mother should be in on the discussion too."

After Zack talked to Catherine about it, she decided to invite Charles and Evelyn over for dinner so they could talk about it.

Over dinner, the Moores and the Johnsons agreed to let Benjamin drive the girls back and forth. Catherine and Evelyn dubbed their husbands "Cupid."

The girls' little plan was put into effect, and as they observed Benjamin and Dorena together, they could see that it was working.

Some four weeks after Benjamin had become their official driver, Angeline and Priscilla devised a little scheme to leave Dorena and him alone for a little while.

One day, at the Johnson place, the girls were on the back porch of the mansion, teaching Dorena how to knit. It was late afternoon. They were chatting merrily when Angeline noticed Benjamin coming in from the fields. Dorena's back was toward him.

Angeline caught Priscilla's eye. *Shall we disappear?* she mouthed.

Angeline stood up. "Dorena," she said, "Priscilla and I have to go in the house for a few minutes. We'll be back after a while. You go ahead and work on that sweater."

Both girls gave Benjamin a secret little wave as he drew near.

Dorena's head was bent as she concentrated on her knitting. Suddenly she heard a familiar husky voice say, "Hello, lovely lady."

She whipped her head around and quickly stood up. "Hello, Benjamin. How did the work in the field go this afternoon?"

"We got a lot done."

She descended the porch steps until her bare feet touched soft earth. "Miss Priscilla and Miss Angeline are teaching me how to knit."

"That's nice." Benjamin took a step closer to her. "It never hurts for a young lady to know how to knit."

"Especially when she becomes a mother," she said. "There are so many things babies can wear that are knitted."

"Yes, of course."

There was quiet for a few seconds, then Benjamin looked around to see if anyone was in earshot.

"Dorena, I—"

"Yes, Benjamin?"

"I can't go any longer without telling you how I feel about you."

Dorena's heart fluttered. She buried her curled toes in the dust and lifted her big brown eyes to meet his.

"H-how do you feel about me?"

Benjamin took another step and brought himself within arm's reach of her. "I have fallen in love with you, Dorena. You are the most wonderful girl I have ever met. The most beautiful, sweet, and charming girl, too."

Dorena's toes dug a little deeper into the dust. "Benjamin, I have been praying that the Lord would let you fall in love with me. Because I am in love with you, too . . . since the day I saw you on the auction block."

Overwhelmed to hear her words, he said, "I have been praying the same way about you." He took her hands in his and looked into her eyes. "I have never met a young lady like you."

"I have never met a young man like you, either."

Benjamin looked around one more time to make sure they were not being observed, then folded her in his arms. They shared a sweet, tender kiss.

When Benjamin released her, he said, "My heart feels like it is going to jump through my chest."

"Mine, too."

"Dorena, you will be seventeen in another week, you told me."

"Yes. And in just over a month, you will be twenty."

"Yes. I am here and now promising you my love forever."

"And I am here and now promising you the same."

His smile could hardly be contained as he said, "I have never been so happy! Dorena, we have some obstacles to overcome, but in studying my Bible and in hearing Preacher Zebulun preach, I have learned that our God can overcome all kinds of obstacles."

"He sure can."

"The biggest obstacle is that in order for us to marry, you would have to be set free by Master Charles Moore."

Dorena nodded.

"On the surface, this looks impossible. But if this is God's plan for us, He can and will make a way.

"Yes," she whispered, gazing into his eyes.

"We must be patient and let Him reveal His will and His plan for our lives," he said in a low voice.

The following week, the girls had their day together at the Moore plantation.

Benjamin's heart warmed at the prospect of seeing Dorena again as he turned off the road and headed the carriage down the lane toward the mansion. The sky in the west was rosy and slowly darkening. Gray and purple shadows were forming in the wooded areas, and the white fence that surrounded the estate had a pink hue in the light of the setting sun.

Benjamin's pulse quickened as he guided the horse up to the front of the porch and saw Dorena come out the door. She gave him a big smile and crossed the porch.

"Hello, most beautiful woman in all the world."

Dorena giggled. "Hello, most handsome man in all the world."

Benjamin set the brake and hopped down. He rounded the carriage and took both of her hands in his. He looked around to see if anyone was observing them and saw a rider coming down the lane.

"Well, maybe we will have a private moment again one day soon. Is Miss Angeline ready to go?"

"Not quite. Miss Priscilla sent me out to tell you it will be about fifteen or twenty minutes."

Benjamin flashed a smile. "She can take longer if she wants to . . . as long as you can stay here with me."

"I can. In fact, I think my mistress and Miss Angeline planned it so we could have these few moments together."

"Well, God bless them."

The sound of pounding hooves caused Benjamin to turn and look at the rider.

"Oh. It is Lewis Moore," Dorena said in a subdued voice.

"Moore? He is part of the family here?"

"Yes. He is their son. He is not a Christian, Benjamin. He has a mean temper, and he hates black people."

Benjamin nodded, keeping his eyes on Lewis, who was now guiding the horse directly toward them, a deep scowl on his face.

Skidding the horse to a halt, Lewis slid from the saddle and approached them. He glanced at Benjamin with eyes of malice, then set them on Dorena and snapped, "You go in the house right now, girl! You have no business standin' out here alone, talkin' to this slave!"

Dorena stiffened. "Benjamin is not a slave. He is Mr. Zack Johnson's hired servant. He is here to pick up Miss Angeline, and I have Miss Priscilla's permission to stand here and talk to him."

Lewis turned to Benjamin. "You get off the property immediately, black boy!"

Benjamin remained calm and said in a level voice, "I am here by orders of Mr. Zack Johnson and permission of Mr. Charles Moore to pick up Miss Angeline, and she is not ready to go yet."

Lewis's eyes flickered as he said, "Then get off the property till Angeline is ready to go!"

Dorena stepped between them, facing Lewis. "You have no right to order Benjamin off the property when your own father has given him permission to be here!"

Lewis's face darkened. He looked into dark brown eyes that did not flinch under his own cold stare.

"How dare you speak to me in that tone of voice, girl!" As he spoke, he shoved Dorena aside, causing her to stumble.

Benjamin steadied her, then stared at Lewis. His desire was to put the man down with a solid punch, but he remained outwardly calm. "It bothers me when a man treats a lady as you just did Miss Dorena."

"Oh, yeah? Well, just what are you gonna do about it, slave man?"

164

"I will spare you this time. Do not treat her roughly again. Since I have Mr. Charles's permission to be here, and since I have orders from my employer to pick up his daughter, I will stay where I am until Miss Angeline is ready to go."

"Listen, you! Who do you think you're talkin' to? I—"

"Lewis," came Priscilla's voice as she and Angeline walked outside, "what is going on out here?" Moving across the porch, she said, "Did Dorena introduce you to Benjamin?"

Lewis scowled. "Don't patronize me. This slave and I haven't been formally introduced, and I'm not interested in it happenin'."

Priscilla flashed him a look, then turned and hugged Angeline, saying, "It's been a wonderful day."

"Thank you for making it so," Angeline said. She embraced Dorena. "See you at church on Sunday."

"You sure will," Dorena said, smiling at her.

As Benjamin was helping Angeline into the carriage, Lewis stepped up behind him and growled, "I don't want you on this property again, black boy. You're not welcome here."

"Don't pay any attention to him," Priscilla said. "You are very welcome here, Benjamin."

Lewis turned to face his sister. "Now look, Priscilla. Don't you contradict me!"

"Mind your own business, Lewis! Benjamin's coming here is none of your affair. You don't own this plantation. Stay out of it."

"Don't tell me to stay out of it, Priscilla. I'm sick of these lowly slaves tryin' to act like they're as good as white people! They're nothin' more than—"

Priscilla arched her back. "Don't you say it, Lewis Moore!"

Charles Moore bolted through the mansion's front door. "Hey! Stop that arguing right now!"

Priscilla and her brother glared at each other, then looked at their father.

"Your mother and I could hear you two shouting at each other from the back of the house. What are you arguing about?"

"I'll tell you what we're arguin' about, Pa," said Lewis. "It's—"

Charles threw up a palm. "Just a minute! Let your sister tell me."

"He's just acting the fool as usual, Papa. He had the audacity to tell Benjamin to get off the property and not come back. I told him Benjamin's being here is none of his business. He started in again about black people thinking they are as good as white people, and he was about to call them animals again. That's what we were arguing about."

Charles looked at Lewis with disapproval. "Where did you get the idea you can overrule my authority? Benjamin is here because I invited him here. Now, you take your horse to the barn immediately."

Lewis gave his sister a sullen glance and went to his horse and swung aboard, then trotted away.

Charles turned to Benjamin. "I am truly sorry for my son's behavior."

"I am, too," said Priscilla. "Please understand that Lewis is the only one in the family who carries this ill feeling toward Negroes."

Benjamin smiled. "I know that, Miss Priscilla." He turned to Angeline. "Well, Miss Angeline, it is getting dark. I need to get you home."

As Benjamin helped her into the carriage, he gave Dorena a smile that made her heart flutter.

Two weeks later, when Benjamin drove the carriage up to the front porch of the Moore mansion, Angeline and Priscilla were waiting for him. As Benjamin hopped out to help Angeline in, he looked around and said, "Is Dorena where I can see her?"

"She will be here in a minute or two, Benjamin," Priscilla said. "She asked Papa for permission to take you back to her parents' cabin to meet them, along with her brother. Papa said it would be all right."

"Oh, good! I would love to meet them."

Even as he was speaking, Dorena came around the corner of the mansion and hurried toward him.

"I told him," Priscilla said.

Dorena's big brown eyes fastened on Benjamin.

"They are ready," she said, extending her hand toward him. When he took it, she looked at Angeline and said, "I won't keep him long."

Angeline giggled. "I'm sure you would like to."

Dorena blushed and hurried away, holding Benjamin by the hand.

Priscilla watched them go, then sighed. "They are such a handsome couple. It just has to be that the Lord will make a way for them to have a life together."

"I'm sure He will," said Angeline. "A love like theirs came from the Lord. They are His children, and He has a plan for their lives."

166

The two girls talked about the pleasant day they had spent together, and before twenty minutes had passed, they saw the couple come around the corner of the mansion, holding hands.

"So . . . how did it go?" Priscilla called.

"Wonderful!" said Dorena. "Mama and Papa were very warm toward him. They told him that all I talk about is him."

"Well, isn't it?" Priscilla said, laughing.

"Most of the time, anyway. And Matthew really likes him, too. I think they are going to be good friends."

"That's good," said Angeline. "They are only a year apart in age, aren't they?"

Dorena nodded. "Fifteen months, to be exact."

Benjamin looked into Dorena's eyes. "I must take Miss Angeline home now. I will see you again very soon."

"You don't have to make it soon at all!" came Lewis's voice. "In fact, black boy, if you didn't show up around here at all, it would be a good thing!"

"Lewis!" Priscilla said. "Can't you be civil? What did Benjamin ever do to you?"

"He brought his black skin on this plantation! That's what he did!"

Benjamin had a powerful desire to coldcock Priscilla's brash and insolent brother, but he refrained for Dorena's sake.

One hot afternoon in early August, Benjamin was repairing a stretch of white fence where the lane met the road. While hammering nails into a new length of wood, he heard a familiar voice say, "Need some help there, my friend?"

Benjamin looked up and smiled. "I could get it done faster with some help."

"I'm really not looking for work, you understand," Dan Johnson said. "But you and I haven't had much time together the past six or seven weeks. Thought maybe if I volunteered to help, we could at least talk to each other for a while."

"I would like that. You don't have to help. Just stand there and talk to me."

"Couldn't do that," said Dan, moving close to him. "Here, let me hold that board while you finish nailing it."

While they worked together, Benjamin said, "What about your Texas plans?"

"Still in the making. I'm just waiting on the Lord to let me know when it's His time for me to go. I thought I'd be there by now, but I don't want to get ahead of the Lord."

"Well, I will be glad to have you here as long as possible."

Dan gave his friend a wry smile. "Say, I've been hearing things around the house."

"About what?"

"About you."

"Me? What about me?"

"My little sister told me a month or so ago that things were looking pretty serious between you and Dorena. And of late, she said there's no question that you two have fallen for each other."

Benjamin grinned. "Oh, she did, huh?"

"Yeah. Now, come on. Is it so?"

Benjamin hit the last nail, then ran a sleeve across his sweaty brow. "Yes, Mr. Dan. It is so. She is the most wonderful girl I have ever met in my life. She is the most beautiful girl God ever made, and she is a sweet, dedicated Christian. What more could I ask for?"

"I can't think of anything. Sounds like she has really captured your heart."

"Yes, sir."

"Well, I think it's wonderful."

Benjamin looked at the paint bucket sitting on the ground and reached for the brush. While he was opening the lid on the paint can, he said, "Mr. Dan, while we're talking about Dorena and me . . . what about you?"

"What do you mean?"

"I've never heard you say anything about a sweetheart or young lady in your life."

Dan scratched behind his ear. "Well, Benjamin, I date some of the young ladies in the church, but there's no sweetheart . . . no special one. The ones I date are nice girls, but none of them strike me as marriage material. I figure the Lord has the right girl for me out there in Texas."

Benjamin nodded. "Since the Lord seems to be leading you there, Mr. Dan, He no doubt has her waiting for you to walk into her life."

"Sounds good to me."

"I can say that it sure feels good to have found the right girl for me, Mr. Dan, but I have to let the Lord work it out so we can marry one day."

"It will take the Lord to work it out, since you're a free man and Dorena is a slave."

"Yes, sir. I know there are strict rules about that. Slaves have to marry slaves, and they have to marry slaves owned by their masters."

"Mm-hmm. It's been that way since slaves were first brought to this country. And the only way a free man could ever marry a slave girl is to buy her from her owner."

"Yes. I have thought of that. In our case, Mr. Charles Moore would have to be willing to sell Dorena to me . . . if I had that much money. Which I do not. It definitely will take the hand of the Lord to bring it to pass."

Dan nodded. "Especially because Dorena is Priscilla's slave. She will not be for sale."

"I have talked a lot to the Lord about that, Mr. Dan. And in my heart, I know He is going to work it out. Just how and when, I have no idea. Dorena and I will have to wait on Him. Sort of like you are waiting on Him to tell you when it is time to go to Texas."

"Right," said Dan. "But the Lord loves you and Dorena, Benjamin. And in spite of every rule and obstacle, when it is His time for the two of you to marry, He will work it out."

Benjamin smiled at his friend. "Thank you, Mr. Dan. You are a real encouragement to me."

"I sure want to be. The Lord may test your faith and your faithfulness, Benjamin. But just remember . . . with God, all things are possible."

At the Colvin plantation, another slave was dead from a beating.

All the slaves were in attendance at the burial service, as were Finn, Martha, and Edward Colvin. This time, none of the neighbors had been informed.

After Ol' Mose had preached the message at the graveside, and the fragile coffin had been lowered into the ground, he stood alone over the fresh mound, his heart heavy.

Tears rolled down Ol' Mose's cheeks as he thought of Jecholia, whose body now lay six feet in the ground. Jecholia had been nearly seventy years old, and his health had been failing. Slaves who witnessed it said that Jecholia was beaten to death by Edward Colvin.

Raising his tired eyes heavenward, Mose said in his worn and cracked voice, "Heavenly Father, I know You never make a mistake. But in this old man's human heart, it is so hard to understand the hatred of one man fo' another. As You know, I have stood by fo' so many years and watched Master Finn put this unfair and humiliatin' treatment on his slaves. Lord, I don't understand how You can let it go on. It is almost more than this old man can bear."

Almost at once, conviction assailed his heart. He bowed his head low. "Please forgive me, Lord. I don't mean to say that You are wrong because You allow this mistreatment to go on. You are a kind and loving God. It's just that this ol' slave preacher is mortal, and there are things he doesn't grasp.

"Help me to trust You completely and to remember that You have a way of doin' things that Ol' Mose doesn't always understand. Help me to be the witness fo' Jesus I ought to be, and to always remember that Your grace is sufficient. In Your time, all will be made right. I know You are workin' out that which is best fo' Your children here on this plantation."

A quiet peace stole over Mose's heart. He heard footsteps behind him and turned around to see Finn Colvin approaching.

"Don't cry for Jecholia, Mose. He's dead because he disobeyed his overseer, and he disobeyed Edward."

The burden in Mose's heart for Colvin freed his tongue. "Master Finn, you heard me tell in the message that Jecholia was a born-again child of God. And because of that, he is now in heaven."

"Yeah. I heard it."

"You also heard me warn everyone who was gathered around the grave that one day it will be their time to die. And if they aren't saved, they will never see Jecholia again. They will be in hell."

Finn did not reply.

"Master Finn, I have a heavy burden in my heart for you. I want you to be born again so you will go to heaven when you die. I can show you right here in my Bible how to call on Jesus, and—"

"Aw, save your breath, Mose! I'm not afraid to die. I don't need Jesus Christ, and I don't want to hear any more about it, do you understand?"

"But, Master Finn, you—"

"I said I don't want to hear any more about it! Ever! Have you got that?"

Mose looked at him through a fresh wall of tears.

"Ever!" Finn said and stomped away, muttering to himself.

Ol' Mose thumbed away tears as he watched him go, then set his sad eyes on the mound of dirt where Jecholia's body had been buried.

THE NEXT MORNING, MARTHA COLVIN opened the back porch door and looked into the solemn face of her oldest slave.

"Good morning, Mose," she said. "Are you feeling all right?"

Pressing a smile on his lips, he said, "I'm fine, Miz Martha. Where do you want me to work today?"

"In the flower bed on the left side of the front of the house. I'll show you what I want done." Martha led the old man down the porch steps. "Mose, you've got me wondering . . ."

The stoop-shouldered old slave looked at her from the tops of his eyes. "About what, ma'am?"

"You have that look again."

"What do you mean, ma'am?"

"You have the same look on your face and in your eyes that you had after the dream about George. Have you had another dream?"

Mose avoided her penetrating gaze. "I'm sorry I have that look on me, ma'am. Please don't let it worry you. Now, what was it you wanted done here?"

Martha's gaze grew more intense. "Mose, I asked you a question. Have you had another dream?"

He swallowed with difficulty and looked at the ground. "Yes'm."

"When?"

"Last night."

"What was it?"

"Miz Martha, I really should get to work here. I see some weeds, and I have my weed tool in the cabinet on the back porch."

"Mose!"

"Yes'm?"

"What did you dream?"

"You really shouldn't bother yourself about it, ma'am."

"Mose, did you dream that someone else died?"

Mose nodded. "Yes'm."

"Who died in your dream?"

Mose kept his gaze on the ground.

"Tell me!"

Tears coursed down the network of wrinkles on his cheeks. There was anguish in his voice as he said, "The richest man in the county."

For a timeless moment, Martha's heart seemed to stop beating and there was nothing but silence. She studied the old man's weathered face and worked at freeing her tongue from the roof of her mouth. Mose's dream about George and its horrible fulfillment lanced through her like a dagger.

"Mose, you couldn't have dreamed a thing like that! Tell me it isn't so!"

"I'm sorry, Miz Martha. That is what I dreamed last night. I . . . I didn't want to tell you. I knew it would upset you."

Martha put a trembling hand to her mouth. "T-tell me exactly what you dreamed."

"Well, I didn't see any faces, but in the dream I heard a voice say that the richest man in Charleston County was goin' to die before midnight tonight."

Martha's features paled. "Tonight?"

"Yes'm."

"Oh, dear!" Her breath came in short spurts. "Oh, dear! Oh, dear!"

"Please don't be afraid, Miz Martha. Remember, I tol' you I don't believe in dreams as some kind of message from God. He speaks through His Bible, and—"

"I know what you said, Mose, but you had that dream about George, and it happened exactly like you dreamed it!"

"I know. But please don't worry about it."

Martha's entire body was quaking. "I . . . I have to tell my husband!"

As she spoke, she lifted her skirts ankle-high and ran around the front corner of the mansion and toward the barns. She knew Finn was with some of the slaves, getting them ready to put a fresh coat of paint on barn number three.

A tiny squeak came from her throat when she saw her husband standing with his back to her, holding a paint brush as he talked to six male slaves. Two overseers were with him.

As she drew near, one of the slaves pointed toward her, saying something to Finn.

He looked at her over his shoulder then frowned as he saw the look on her face.

"Finn! Oh, Finn! I need to talk to you right now! Alone."

The look in her eyes was enough. Finn spoke to the overseers, telling them to proceed with the paint job, then ushered Martha to a spot out of earshot from anyone else and gripped her shoulders.

"What on earth has happened, Martha?"

"Ol' Mose just told me he had another one of his vivid dreams!"

"You mean about somebody dying?"

"Yes. Like that."

"Was it about someone else in our family?"

"Yes."

"Well, tell me! What was the dream?"

"Mose . . . Mose said he heard a voice in his dream say that the richest man in Charleston County was going to die before midnight tonight."

A feeling like icy water drained into his stomach.

"He . . . he just walked in and told you this, right out of the blue?"

"No," Martha said, shaking her head. "When he came into the house to start his day's work, I saw that same look on his face as when he dreamed about George's death. When I asked him about it, he tried to avoid telling me, but I made him come out with it."

Finn's expression was grim. "I want to talk to Mose. I want to hear this for myself. Come on."

When they rounded the corner of the house, the old man was bent over in the flower garden, digging up weeds with a hand tool. He turned and looked at the approaching pair, then straightened up as much as he was able.

"Mose," Finn said, "I want to hear every detail of this wild dream you had last night."

"There really wasn't much to it, Master Finn. I saw no faces or figures. I was simply standin' out in one of the cotton fields, and a voice came to me and said that the richest man in Charleston County would die before midnight tonight."

175

"Well, that means before midnight last night."

"No, sir. I had the dream 'bout four o'clock this mornin'. Daylight was comin' when the dream woke me up."

When Mose saw the fear in Colvin's eyes, he said, "Master Finn, I know you tol' me never to bring up 'bout bein' saved, but I care 'bout you. The Bible says, 'it is appointed unto men once to die, but after this the judgment.' Every human bein' has an appointment with death, and no one knows when their appointment is set except God Himself. He is the one who set the appointment. People need to face the fact, Master Finn, that their appointment could be today when they awaken and rise from their bed. Or when they pillow their head at night. They must repent and believe the gospel before it is too late."

Finn stared at the old man. Without another word, he turned and dashed up the porch steps and into the house, leaving the door wide open.

Wringing her hands, Martha said. "Mose, I see you're digging out weeds here. Go ahead. I need to be with my husband."

When Martha reached the vestibule, there was no sign of Finn. She heard a door slam down the hall and figured he had gone to his den.

Hastening that direction, she found the door closed when she reached it. Without knocking, she stepped inside to find her husband pacing the floor in front of the fireplace, his features pinched and pallid.

Martha rushed to Finn and took hold of his hands. "Darling, listen," she said, "just because Mose's other dream came true doesn't mean this one will."

"Who are you trying to convince, Martha? Me or yourself?"

"Well, both of us. Maybe it won't happen."

Terror coursed through Finn and he squeezed Martha's hands until she winced with pain. "Martha, I wouldn't be so scared if his dream about George hadn't happened to the letter. Does that old man have some kind of supermental powers?"

"I don't know . . . he claims not. Come, dear, sit down in your chair. I'll send one of the overseers to get Dr. Bosworth. He can come and give you a sedative to settle your nerves."

Finn shook his head. "That isn't necessary. I don't want anyone to know about this. Not in town and not on this plantation. Mose won't tell anyone else, will he?"

"I'm sure he won't," Martha said. "It wouldn't be like him to do that."

"Anyway, Dr. Bosworth couldn't help me."

"But if he was here—"

"No, Martha. Can you imagine what Dr. Bosworth would think of us if we called him out here and told him we wanted him to stay until midnight to keep me alive . . . because of some old slave's dream? He'd think we had lost our minds. We have to face this thing alone."

"When you say alone, you are including Edward, aren't you? He's our son. He has to know."

"Of course. But no one else. Not the house slaves. Nobody."

As he spoke, Finn went to his favorite overstuffed chair and sat down. Martha pulled up a straight-backed wooden chair and sat down facing him.

Edward Colvin climbed from his buggy at the back porch and entered the house. There was no one in the kitchen. Figuring to find his father in the library, he went there but it was unoccupied.

The door to the den was closed. He paused, for he could hear his mother's voice, and she was talking rapidly.

He tapped on the door and called, "Mom . . . Pa . . . can I come in? I need to talk to Pa."

There were light footsteps, then the door opened. Edward saw the distraught look on his mother's face and noted his father sitting in his overstuffed chair, his face buried in his hands. "Mom, what's wrong? You're pale as a ghost."

"Come in, son," Martha said, stepping back to allow his entrance.

Edward moved toward his father, running his gaze between his parents. "What is it?" he asked.

"Mose had another dream, Edward," Martha said.

"S-someone else is going to die? Wh-who—"

"Me!" cut in Finn.

"Oh, no, Pa! This can't be! What did Mose dream?"

When he heard, Edward fell to his knees in front of Finn, crying out that it must not happen. Martha knelt beside him and leaned toward Finn to embrace him.

Ol' Mose finished weeding the flower garden and entered the mansion by the front door. As he shuffled down the hall, he saw Edward coming from the kitchen, carrying a cup of water. Edward gave him a hard look. "Why did you have to tell your dream to my mother?"

"Edward!" Martha called from the doorway. "Don't talk about it out here. One of the house slaves might hear you! Come into the den. You, too, Mose."

When Edward closed the door, Martha said, "I heard what you said to Mose, son. He didn't want to tell me the dream. I saw in his eyes that something was bothering him and made him tell me."

Edward glanced at the silver-haired old Negro. "Okay, Mose. I'm sorry. This whole thing has me very upset."

"I can understand that, Mr. Edward. But it is possible this dream won't come true."

"Your dream about George came true. Why shouldn't this one?"

Mose had no reply. He looked at Martha. "I finished the weedin', ma'am. What else did you want done at the flower garden?"

"I . . . I need to show you. Later. You can go on back to your cabin. If I need you later, I'll send for you."

As Mose closed the door behind him, Edward handed his father a cup of water.

Finn gulped it, spilling much of it on his hands and clothing.

The Colvins stayed in the den through lunchtime and Martha found Mandy in the middle of the afternoon to tell her not to prepare supper.

Finn was numb with fear, and though Martha and Edward were doing all they could to encourage him, the same fear gripped them.

As the sun was setting, there was a knock at the door. Edward opened it to find Ol' Mose standing there with a Bible in his hand.

"Mr. Edward, could I please talk to Master Finn?"

Edward turned and said, "Pa, Mose wants to talk to you. He's got his Bible with him."

Finn leaned close to Martha and whispered, "The old fanatic just wants to preach to me again. I don't want to hear it."

"Tell Mose that your father is not up to talking to him," Martha said.

When night fell, there was another knock at the door. Edward opened it to find Mandy standing there with a worried look on her face.

178

"Mr. Edward," she said, trying to see past him into the room, "if'n you an' Massa Finn and Miss Martha are feelin' hungry, I will be glad to fix somethin' light. Soup or somethin' like that."

"No, Mandy, we're not hungry."

The worry on her face deepened. "Is somethin' bad wrong, Mr. Edward?"

"I appreciate your concern, but it's nothing for you to be concerned about. Good night, Mandy."

When Edward returned to his parents, Martha said, "Son, let's take your father to the library. He can lie down on the sofa."

"That would be good, Mom. Would you like that, Pa?"

Finn nodded. When he stood up, his knees were so weak that Edward had to support him.

When they had made him as comfortable as possible on the sofa in the library, Martha and Edward drew up chairs and sat close to him.

Finn glanced at the old grandfather clock in the corner of the library and noted that it was 7:25. He drew in a shuddering breath.

"Please, dear," Martha said, patting his arm. "Just concentrate on the fact that Edward and I need you. When that old clock strikes twelve, you will still be with us."

Finn closed his eyes and fought the distress welling up within him. It seemed only seconds had passed when the clock began to strike eight times. Its sound caused Finn's body to jerk, and he lifted his head to stare at the clock as if it were the very messenger of death.

His voice rose in panic. "I'm gonna die! I'm gonna die! And there's nothin' I can do about it!"

Several hours had passed, and Martha was patting her husband and speaking in soft, soothing tones when the old grandfather clock began striking the eleventh hour.

"Martha!" Finn cried. "It's my heart! I've got these awful pains in my chest!"

Edward gripped his father's arm. "Hang on, Pa! Hang on!"

Seconds later, the pain eased somewhat.

Martha lifted his head and placed a cup of water to his quivering lips. "Here, darling. Drink."

When he had drained the cup, he said, "What time is it?"

Martha flicked a glance at the clock. "Three minutes after eleven. You just do as Edward said. Hold on."

When it was almost midnight, cold sweat covered Finn Colvin's body as he waited to be snatched through death's door. He glanced at the clock and saw that it was two minutes to midnight, then looked toward the ceiling and cried out, "Please, God! Oh, God in heaven, please don't let me die!"

Martha and Edward looked at each other. This was the first time they had ever heard him talk to God. He had used God's name in vain repeatedly over the years, but he had never prayed for anything.

When the last chime was echoing away, Finn opened his eyes, looked at Martha and Edward, and began to weep with relief. His voice barely more than a squeak, he said, "I made it, Martha! Mose said it was supposed to happen before midnight. I'm not gonna die! You were right, Martha. You said when that old clock struck twelve, I'd still be with you. The dream was wrong!"

Martha wrapped her arms around him, weeping for joy. "Yes! Thank God, it was wrong!"

It took Finn some time to shake off the effects of the ordeal, but after he had pulled himself together, he said, "The pains are gone from my chest."

"Wonderful!" said Martha. "They were probably caused by tension."

Finn glanced at the clock. "It's almost twelve-thirty. I'm so hungry I could eat a horse. Let's go to the kitchen and eat somethin', and get to bed. The richest man in the county is still alive and he has work to do tomorrow!"

The Colvin family embraced each other and headed for the door. Just as they stepped into the hall, there was a loud knock at the back door. Mandy had left lanterns burning in the kitchen.

"Who could be knockin' at this time of night?" Finn muttered. "Edward, go see who it is and what they want."

Finn's knees were still weak and he leaned on Martha as the two of them moved slowly down the hall. When Edward opened the back door, they stopped and looked on as a young slave named James stood there with tears streaming down his face.

"Mr. Edward, I know it's late, but I saw de lights was still on downstairs."

"It's all right, James. What's wrong?"

"I jis' wanted you and Massa Finn and Miss Martha to know 'bout Ol' Mose as soon as possible."

"Ol' Mose? What about him?"

"Well, suh, Ol' Mose was havin' bad pains in his chest late dis evenin', an' he died 'bout ten minutes befo' midnight."

ON SUNDAY MORNING, APRIL 5, 1857, Martha Colvin stood on the wide, sweeping porch of the mansion, holding her Bible in one hand and a parasol in the other. There was a definite feel of spring in the air as she raised her gaze toward the azure sky dotted with puffy clouds.

A small contented smile crossed her lips. It had been over a year and a half since she had opened her heart to Jesus, and the rich joy of her salvation was as fresh in her soul as the day she was saved.

She was wearing a dress almost the color of the sky, and her eyes of the same shade lit up when she saw the Johnson carriage coming down the lane. The Johnsons had been such a blessing to her . . . as had been the Moores. She thought of how Finn had changed to a degree after his scare over Ol' Mose's dream, and now allowed her to go to church. The Johnsons and the Moores alternated picking her up for services.

Martha remembered how going to church before her conversion was an almost painful mixture of Holy Spirit conviction, a desperate desire to be saved, and fear of what Finn's reaction would be if she became a Christian. Now she could hardly wait from service to service. The fellowship of other Christians strengthened her spiritual walk before her unsaved husband and son, and the pastor's messages were always thought provoking as well as uplifting.

She felt a warmth steal over her heart as the carriage drew closer. As usual, Dan Johnson was at the reins, with Alexander sitting between him and their father. Catherine and Angeline were in the back.

As Dan drew the carriage to a halt, Zack jumped out and gave Martha his hand. When she was seated facing Catherine and Angeline, Catherine squeezed Martha's hand. "It is such a joy to see you with so much sparkle in your eyes, Martha, dear."

Martha chuckled gleefully. "Something I didn't have all those times when you and Evelyn were trying to win me to the Lord. Living under the conviction of my lost condition, yet fearing what Finn would do if I got saved . . . I was one miserable person."

"Well, honey, those days of misery are over."

"Mm-hmm. Though Finn still isn't saved, at least he never stands in my way of going to church. Not even on Sunday nights or Wednesday nights. I was thinking just a few minutes ago that it's been over a year and a half since Ol' Mose died and I came to you and Evelyn, and you led me to the Lord."

Catherine smiled. "You've grown so much in your Christian life since then. And you know that our family prays daily that Finn will come to the Lord, as well as Edward and his new wife."

Martha nodded. "I appreciate it more than I can express."

The carriage turned onto the road and headed toward Charleston.

"Mrs. Colvin," Angeline said, "have you heard that Priscilla and Craig are planning to become engaged soon?"

"I knew they were quite serious about each other, but I hadn't heard anything about an engagement. I'm so glad for Priscilla. Craig Hartman is such a fine young man . . . and you can tell he adores her."

"For sure! I know they're going to be very happy. The Hartmans are wonderful Christians and have raised their son to walk with the Lord."

Martha set her soft eyes on Angeline. "What about you, dear? I've seen you talking to several young men at church since I've been going there, but I haven't noticed you with one particular young man. Do you have a special young man in your life?"

"No, ma'am. I haven't found the right one yet."

Alexander turned in the seat and said, "It's too late for my sister now, Mrs. Colvin. She's an old maid at nineteen."

Angeline gave him a mock scowl. "I'm ahead of you, little brother. You're just a year younger than I am, and you've had a grand total of two dates."

"That's because I'm very picky about who I date."

Angeline giggled. "No, what it really means is the girls at church are picky, and they won't go out with you. You didn't tell Mrs. Colvin that the two who did go out with you were both blind."

Martha laughed as Alexander gave his sister a stiff look and turned back forward in the seat.

Dan chuckled. "You'll learn one of these days, Alexander, that you can't get ahead of our sister. Best thing to do is keep quiet."

"I'll get her one of these days," he said with a grin.

Angeline turned to Martha. "Anyway, Mrs. Colvin, as I was saying before we were so rudely interrupted, I haven't found the right young man yet. But I'm willing to wait for the Lord to bring him into my life."

Martha nodded. "That's the wise way to look at it, Angeline. You want to make sure you get the right one." She looked toward the driver and said, "Dan, are your plans for going to Texas coming together?"

"Yes, ma'am. It began to look like the Lord was never going to give me the go sign, and I got pretty impatient. Sometimes the Lord makes us wait a lot longer for the things we want than we think He should. But when we let Him work it out, He always does it above and beyond what we ever imagined. He knew two years ago, when I was wanting to get to Texas so bad, that the perfect ranch for me was going to come up for sale in March of 1857."

"So it's a closed deal?" Martha asked.

"Only by my word and the word of the man who is selling it to me, but we both believe that a man's word is his bond. So in that sense, it's a closed deal. Of course, I sent him an agreed amount of earnest money to hold the ranch for me. But it won't be a legally closed deal until the papers are signed and I pay him the rest of the money. The Lord really worked it out for me in beautiful style. I'm getting the ranch for a very good price."

"I've been to Texas twice to visit my husband's uncle and aunt," Martha said. "Exactly where is this ranch you are buying?"

"Do you know where San Antonio is?"

"Yes. Finn's uncle and aunt live in Round Rock, just north of Austin. Uncle Wes and Aunt Bertha lived near San Antonio back in 1836 when the battle took place at the Alamo. They talk about it a lot."

"Well, that's easy to understand, since it was the turning point in Texas history," Dan said. "I'm looking forward to seeing the Alamo, I'll tell you that. Anyway, ma'am, the ranch I'm buying is about ten miles northwest of San Antonio. Rich grass country. The owner's name is Hollis Jourdan. He's a sixty-nine-year-old widower. He will leave me four cowhands who have been with the ranch for several years. They said they want to stay on with the new owner."

"I'm sure they will be a great help to you," said Martha.

"Oh yes. When the Lord works something out, He does it up right. From what I'm told, the area is all cattle ranches. You remember the Wickburgs, who sold their plantation here and moved to Texas to go into the cattle ranching business?"

"Yes."

"Their ranch is near Austin. Bill is one of my closest friends."

"He's the one I'm going to shoot when I see him!" Angeline said.

Martha laughed. "For taking big brother away from you?"

"That's it."

"But, little sis, you'll still have Alexander!" Dan said.

She let out a big sigh and said, "Oh, joy bells!"

Alexander grinned. "Since only a blind girl would marry me, and there aren't any around Charleston, and since you're going to be an old maid the rest of your life, you'll always have me, Angeline."

She looked skyward and said, "Lord, help me!"

"Dan," Martha said, "you were telling me about Bill Wickburg."

"Oh yes. Bill and his father put me in touch with Hal Robards, who has a huge ranch a few miles due north of San Antonio. And he's a Christian. It was Robards who put me in touch with Hollis Jourdan. The ranch has a little over five thousand acres, and from what Mr. Jourdan told me, it is thick with grass and has a nice creek running through it."

Dan guided the carriage into Charleston and headed down the street toward the church.

"Sounds wonderful, Dan," said Martha. "I'm so glad your big dream is about to come true. I know your family will miss you, but they also want you to be where God wants you."

Zack, who had been content to listen to the conversation up to now, said, "That's for sure!"

"So when do you plan to leave, Dan?" Martha asked.

"I am to meet with Mr. Jourdan and close the deal on April 15, ma'am, so I'll be taking a train from Charleston this coming Friday in order to be there in plenty of time."

"I wish you well, Dan."

"Thank you, ma'am."

"I know a lot of people will miss you."

Alexander chuckled. "I know of eight young women at church who will miss him terribly, Mrs. Colvin. Every one of them has had high hopes of becoming Mrs. Daniel Johnson."

Dan playfully rammed an elbow into his little brother's ribs, and Alexander let out a howl, then burst out laughing as they pulled into the church parking lot.

On Wednesday morning, Dan was saddling his horse when the barn door opened and Benjamin entered. "Morning, Mr. Dan," he said. "Your mother said you wanted to see me."

"That's right. I've got to ride out and check a stretch of fence on the far west side of the estate. One of the slaves told Pa that part of it is in need of repair. I'd like for you to ride out with me."

"Well, of course. That is, if your father or mother don't already have plans for my services."

"I already cleared it with them."

"All right then!"

"Which horse do you want to ride?"

Benjamin ran his eyes to the horses in the stalls. "I'll take the gray roan."

"Okay. Saddle him up."

Moments later, Dan and Benjamin were galloping through the cotton fields. They jumped the horses over irrigation ditches and weaved around trees that stood in clusters, finally arriving at the fence Dan wanted to inspect.

They dismounted and led their horses by the reins, moving slowly as Dan scrutinized the railings.

Benjamin chuckled. "Mr. Dan, you could have made this inspection by yourself, but I'm glad you invited me along. Our days of spending time together will soon be gone."

Dan stopped. "I had an ulterior motive for inviting you along, Benjamin . . . other than wanting to spend time with you, I mean. I want to talk to you about something."

"About what, sir?"

"You and Dorena."

Benjamin's eyebrows arched. "Yes?"

"I am glad to see that you and Dorena are so deeply in love. I know you both desire to marry, but because of the situation, it is impossible."

"We very much want to get married, Mr. Dan, but she is owned by Charles Moore. I have not even considered trying to talk to him about purchasing her. Your father is very kind to pay me for my work here on the plantation, but I will never be able to set aside enough money to make Mr. Moore a reasonable offer for her."

They started walking along the fence again.

"Benjamin, we are not only brothers in the Lord, but we're best friends, aren't we?"

"We sure are."

"Well, I have an offer to make to my very best friend."

"What kind of an offer?"

"Just a minute," Dan said, dropping the reins and moving to the fence. "Here's the place the slave was talking about. Looks like it's about . . . mmm . . . thirty feet or so in length. It'll take new lumber to repair it. I think this stretch of fence must be the oldest on the estate. I'll have to get some men on it right away."

"I will be glad to help, Mr. Dan," Benjamin said.

"I'll tell Pa. Now, about that offer . . ."

"Mm-hmm?"

"Once I have things going good on my Texas ranch, Benjamin, I want you to come and work for me."

Benjamin's eyes widened. "Pardon me?"

"You heard me right. When I know I can pay you a good wage, I'll write and let you know. I want you with me on my ranch."

"B-but, Mr. Dan, you already have four men waiting for you at the ranch. You won't need a fifth man."

"Oh, but I will. I plan to expand the ranch's beef output as soon as I own it, Benjamin. I'll need you. With your experience on the cattle ranch in South Africa, you'll be a valuable asset to me."

"But what about Master Zack? What would he say about this? After all, he is the one who paid the ransom to set me free."

Dan grinned at him. "I have already discussed it with both of my parents. They agreed to let me make the offer to you. Reluctantly, of course, because as Pa put it, you are the best worker they have ever had on the plantation. They said they will miss you, but they know how close you and I have become, and they want to see both of us happy. In fact, Mom said she would be relieved to know I had someone like you with me out there. How about it? Will you plan to come?"

Tears misted Benjamin's eyes. "Mr. Dan, your offer touches me deeply. I am honored that you would want me to come and be one of your ranch hands, but—"

"But what?"

"I couldn't leave Dorena. Even though we cannot become husband and wife, we have promised never to marry anyone else. The Moores are so good to let me spend time with her when I am there. We've prayed all along that the Lord would make a way for us to marry, but so far He hasn't done it. Mr. Dan, I appreciate your offer more than I could ever tell you, but my love for Dorena is too strong. I cannot leave her and go to Texas. I . . . I hope you understand."

Dan grinned. "Benjamin, the Lord can do the impossible. In fact, He has made a way that you and Dorena can become husband and wife."

"Mr. Dan . . . what do you mean?"

"The man who is selling me the ranch sent me his financial records for the past five years so I could see just how well the ranch is doing. The way I see it, I should be sending for you within no more than two months after I move onto the ranch. Because you and I are best friends, and I want to help you to have Dorena for your wife, I plan to pay you double what the ranch hands are being paid. This will only be between you and me."

Benjamin waited for Dan to go on.

"Since the other ranch hands are paid seventy dollars a month, you will make a hundred and forty. I figure to buy your clothes for you as a reward for coming to work on the ranch, so your expenses will be at a minimum. You should be able to put a hundred dollars aside each month. Don't you think so?"

Benjamin swallowed hard and nodded. "Yes, sir."

"As you know, women slaves sell for around three to four hundred dollars. Priscilla and Craig will be getting married in a few months, so Dorena will no longer be her slave. I figure that since Charles Moore is a Christian brother, and he knows about the love you and Dorena have for each other, he will let you pay him the ransom to set her free. At the most, it will be five hundred dollars."

Benjamin's eyes were glittering. "Why, Mr. Dan, that would mean, in four or five months, I would have enough to buy her! I'm looking at seven months, eight at the most, till I could marry Dorena and take her to Texas."

"That's right . . . if Charles doesn't ask for more than five hundred for her. But even if he did, you are still looking at a matter of months until the two of you could get married."

Benjamin swung his fist through the air and shouted, "Praise the Lord! This is the answer to our prayers!"

Dan smiled broadly. "Our God doesn't always get in a hurry like we do, Benjamin, but when He does put the wheels in motion, things work out so wonderfully!"

"They sure do! Ah . . . Mr. Dan?"

"Yes?"

"Do you suppose I should go to Mr. Charles Moore right away and tell him our plan? Ask him if he will sell Dorena to me and how much he will want?"

"The quicker, the better," Dan said.

"All right. When we get back to the house, I will ask Master Zack for time off to go to the Moore plantation."

"And will you let me know how it goes as soon as you get back?" Dan said.

"That I will, my best friend!"

Benjamin was about halfway to the Moore plantation when his attention was drawn to two slaves who were frantically trying to lift the corner of a wagon partially loaded with cotton bales.

He focused on the scene and realized the wagon was tilted to one side.

He dug his heels into the gray roan's sides and put him to a gallop. The roan jumped the fence and raced across the field.

As the horse skidded to a halt, Benjamin slid from the saddle and immediately saw that the weight of the wagon was on a man's chest, crushing the life out of him.

Running his gaze quickly over the wagon and its partial load of cotton bales, Benjamin said to the two panicky slaves, "You two get down there with him so that when I lift the wagon, you can pull him out."

They stared at him in disbelief.

"Hurry! Get down there!"

As they obeyed, Benjamin bent his knees and got a firm grip on the bed. Taking a deep breath, he adjusted the position of his feet, then strained with all his might and lifted the heavy wagon till he knew it was off the man and the slaves had pulled him free.

When Benjamin eased the wagon down, the two slaves were bending over their companion, who was now breathing raggedly but freely.

"I know you," one of the slaves said. "You are the hired servant from the Johnson plantation . . . the one who has a heart for Dorena."

"That's me," Benjamin said.

"You must he very strong! Manfred an' me couldn' lift the wagon together!"

Benjamin put his attention on the injured slave. "Are you hurting bad?"

"You . . . you saved my life," the man replied. "Thank you."

"Are you in pain?"

"My chest . . . yes. But I think it is not serious. My breathin' hurts less with each breath."

Speaking to the others, Benjamin said, "It is best that we take him to Master Charles. He may want to send for a doctor."

"That is best," said Manfred.

Benjamin looked down at the injured slave. "What is your name?"

"Andrew," he replied between ragged breaths.

"All right, Andrew. I will carry you. It may hurt some when I pick you up, but I will try not to hurt you more than is necessary."

The slave closed his eyes and nodded.

Benjamin cradled Andrew in his arms and said to the others, "I will appreciate it if one of you will bring my horse."

Charles Moore was standing at the back porch when he saw the slave named Manfred running toward him, calling, "Massa Charles! Massa Charles!"

"What is it, Manfred?"

"Massa! De wagon fall on Andrew! We was workin' an' de wagon act strange. Andrew crawl underneath to see what wrong. Suddenly it make big crack sound, and de wagon fall on him! Me an' Thomas try to lift wagon, but it too heavy. Benjamin—from Johnson plantation—come along. He lift wagon off Andrew!"

Moments later, Charles was inside Andrew's cabin, asking him questions about his injury.

"Massa Charles, I do not need a doctor. The pain is easin' off."

"All right, Andrew," Charles said. "I will not send for a doctor right

191

now. But if you should experience pain later, I will have a doctor here to examine you."

"Thank you, Massa. I appreciate yo' kindness." Then to Benjamin he said, "I am so glad you came along when you did. Fo' sure, de wagon would have killed me soon if it had not been removed."

Charles set appreciative eyes on Benjamin. "Son, I stand amazed at your strength. How you lifted that wagon, I'll never know. But I sure do thank you."

Benjamin smiled. "I am glad the Lord gave me the strength to do it, Mr. Moore."

Charles looked a bit puzzled and said, "This isn't the girls' visiting day. What was your purpose in riding over here today, Benjamin?"

"I came to have a talk with you, sir."

"Oh? Well, in that case, let's go to the house."

MAIL ORDER BRIDE SERIES
NO. 5
1855
USA
AL & JOANNA LACY

As Charles Moore and Benjamin walked toward the mansion, Lewis came out of one of the barns and headed their way. When they drew abreast, Lewis gave Benjamin a malignant look, then said to his father, "I'm headin' for town to pick up the baling twine we ordered. Just wanted to see if there's anything else you need me to get while I'm there."

"I can't think of anything, son."

Lewis nodded and went his way.

"I must apologize for my son's rudeness," Charles said.

"Why does Mr. Lewis so dislike me, sir?"

"It's not you in particular, Benjamin. Lewis has a dislike for all black people."

Priscilla was in the hall when she heard the back door open and saw Benjamin with her father. She whirled about and dashed to the winding staircase.

"Dorena!" she called to Dorena, who was halfway up the staircase. "Come down, quick! Benjamin is here with Papa!"

Dorena quickly descended the staircase. "What do you suppose Benjamin is doing here today?"

"I have no idea, but I thought you would like to see him." Priscilla gave her a little shove. "Go!"

Dorena scurried to the hall and saw Charles and Benjamin about to enter the library. They stopped as Dorena moved toward them.

"I'll wait for you in the library, Benjamin," Charles said, then went inside and closed the door.

"Hello, beautiful lady."

"Hello, yourself," she said softly.

"I am here to talk with Mr. Charles. My, you certainly look lovely. I like the new way you have styled your hair."

She touched her hair with the tips of her fingers. "Thank you. Actually, it was Miss Priscilla who fixed it this way."

"You tell her she did a wonderful job."

"I will. Well, I must not detain you from your talk. I will see you Thursday, Benjamin, when the girls get together."

"I will look forward to it as always," he said.

When Dorena reached the winding staircase, Priscilla was waiting for her on the bottom step.

"Could we go up to your room?" Dorena asked.

When they entered the room and Priscilla led her toward the sitting area, she noticed a frown on Dorena's flawless brow.

"Whatever is the matter?"

"Did you hear Benjamin say why he is here?" Dorena asked in a low voice.

"No. I couldn't make out what was being said. Why is he here?"

"He said he's here to talk to your father."

"Is that all? I mean, is something wrong? You're upset."

Dorena shook her head. "That's all Benjamin said. He didn't tell me what he was going to talk to Master Charles about."

"What could be wrong?"

"Well, nothing, I hope. But, again, there might be something wrong. I can't help but wonder why Benjamin would want to talk to Master Charles. It worries me."

"Did either of them behave as if something were wrong?"

"No. They both seemed quite relaxed."

"Well then, there isn't anything to worry about."

"All right, son. What did you want to talk to me about?" Charles asked.

Benjamin shifted nervously on his chair. "It's about Dorena, sir, but first I need to tell you what Mr. Dan talked to me about this morning."

"I'm listening. Go right ahead."

"You are aware, sir, that Mr. Dan has put money on a large cattle ranch out in Texas?"

"Yes. He's to leave Friday, if I remember correctly."

"That's right. Well, sir, this morning Mr. Dan talked to me privately and made me an offer concerning his ranch in Texas."

"An offer? You mean he wants you to go with him and work on his ranch?"

"Yes, sir."

Benjamin took several minutes to carefully explain Dan's offer, then told Charles that when he had enough money, he wanted to return to Charleston and pay him the ransom for Dorena and make her his wife.

Charles smiled. "Benjamin, it is quite obvious how you and Dorena feel about each other. I think it would be wonderful if one day you could marry."

"You do, sir?"

"Certainly. I will allow you to pay the ransom for her when you can afford it. But with one stipulation."

"Yes, sir?"

"This can only take place after Priscilla is married."

"Oh yes, sir. I understand. As long as Miss Priscilla is in this house, she will want Dorena at her side. It is my understanding that Miss Priscilla and Mr. Craig Hartman are about to become engaged."

"That's right. Dorena must have told you this."

"Yes, sir, but she doesn't know why I am talking to you right now. Do you have any idea, sir, how long it will be until Miss Priscilla and Mr. Craig plan to be married?"

"No date has been set as yet, but the way they're talking, I'd say it won't be more than a few months."

A smile spread over Benjamin's handsome face. "Good. I want to thank you, sir, for your attitude about Dorena and me. I appreciate it more than I can say."

"I fell in love once, myself, son. And I'm still in love. In fact, more than ever. I understand how you feel."

"I'm glad, sir. My next concern is for Dorena's parents and her brother . . . what they will think of me taking Dorena all the way to Texas to live."

"I don't think they'll be upset about it. I know that Caleb, Liza, and Matthew are fully aware of how much Dorena loves you. I'm sure they will be glad to know she can live her life as a free woman and be married to the man she loves, even if it is in Texas."

"Sir, I would like to talk to them before I tell Dorena. Would it be possible to talk to them today?"

Charles grinned. "I admire your persistence, son. You stay right here. I'll go set it up and come back for you in a little while."

While Charles was gone, Benjamin spent time talking to the Lord, asking Him to work in the hearts of Dorena's family.

In half an hour, Charles reentered the library. "All right, Benjamin. It's all set. I had to bring Caleb in from the fields, but he and Liza are waiting for you to come to their cabin. Matthew is there, too. I didn't tell them anything, except that you wanted to talk to them about something very important."

"Thank you, sir."

"You are welcome. When you're through, come back here to the library."

Priscilla was seated in her bedroom in her favorite overstuffed chair. Dorena stood at the window.

"You're right, Priscilla," Dorena said. "Since neither Benjamin nor Master Charles seemed upset, I think that whatever they are talking about has to be something good."

"I agree. And it has something to do with you."

"Really? Why do you think that?"

"Well, what other connection does Benjamin have with Papa?"

Dorena thought on it. "None that I know of."

As she watched the slaves move about below, Dorena said, "Oh! I'm supposed to tell you that Benjamin really likes the way you styled my hair."

"He's a man of good taste!"

Dorena giggled. "Of course. He picked me, didn't he?"

"That's proof of it," Priscilla said, noting Dorena's sudden concentration on something below. "What are you looking at, honey?"

"Benjamin."

"What?"

"He just came out the back door and is heading toward the cabins."

Priscilla joined her at the window and saw Benjamin walking briskly in the direction of the slave cabins. He spoke to slaves as he went.

"What do you suppose he's up to?" Dorena muttered as she watched him moving down the path.

She admired his straight, broad back and wide shoulders and thought, *Oh, how I love him!* She watched him until the path carried him out of sight. She turned to her mistress and shrugged her shoulders, saying, "Guess I will just have to wait until he's ready to tell me what this is all about. But waiting is not one of the things I do best."

Priscilla put an arm around her shoulders. "Come on, now, worry wart. Whatever is going on has to be something good."

Dorena let out a sigh. "Of course. Well, sweet Priscilla, I'd better get back to work."

Dorena's family was standing on the porch of the small cabin, watching for Benjamin to come around the bend in the path.

"It has to be about Dorena," Caleb said.

"I can't imagine what it could be," said Liza.

"Maybe he wants to become a slave on this plantation so he can marry her," put in Matthew.

Caleb chuckled. "Well, son, to tell you the truth, that wouldn't surprise me. He does love your sister very, very much."

"Here he comes," said Liza.

Benjamin had two slave boys flanking him as he hurried along the path. He had a hand on each boy's shoulder and it was evident they admired him. Presently, Benjamin said something to them and smiled. They nodded and came to a stop, letting him move on.

As Benjamin drew up to the cabin, he said, "How is my favorite family on the whole Moore plantation?"

"We are fine," said Caleb. "Especially me. Your coming to talk to us got me out of working for a while."

Benjamin laughed.

"Please come inside, Benjamin," Liza said.

Benjamin ran his eyes around the sparkling clean room as he stepped inside. The furnishings were sparse and rather crudely made, but Liza had done a wonderful job of making it a home for her family. A sense of abiding love filled the room.

As they sat down at the room's only table, the eyes of Dorena's family were fixed on Benjamin, waiting for him to speak.

Feeling somewhat intimidated by the intensity of their gaze, Benjamin prayed in his heart for just the right words.

"I . . . I . . . have something very important to discuss with you," he began. "You know that I am very much in love with Dorena, and that I adore her with all of my being."

When Benjamin finished telling them about Dan Johnson's offer, and of his plan to purchase Dorena from Charles Moore after Priscilla was married, they sat in stunned silence.

Benjamin waited for their response, but the silence prevailed.

Finally, Matthew said, "Benjamin, this is a bit of a shock, as you might imagine. Texas seems a million miles away. But my parents and I are happy about your good fortune and wish you much happiness and success."

Caleb cleared his throat. "Matthew is right, Benjamin. We do wish you the very best. We will miss our daughter terribly, but we know she loves you very much. How could we ever stand in the way of her freedom and the fulfillment we know she will find as your wife?"

Liza's eyes were swimming in tears. She reached across the table and took hold of Benjamin's hand. "I agree with everything my husband and son have just said. Dorena's freedom will be a wonderful thing. We will be happy knowing she is happy."

Caleb gripped Benjamin's other hand with his work-worn hands and said, "We will be proud to own you as our son-in-law."

Nearly an hour had passed when Charles Moore heard a light tap on the library door.

"Yes?"

The door opened and Evelyn looked in. "Benjamin is here to see you, dear."

"Send him in, honey."

Benjamin thanked her and stepped into the room. Before Evelyn closed the door, she smiled at her husband and said, "You two have my curiosity up. I didn't even know Benjamin was on the place till he passed through the kitchen a while ago. Mind if I ask what's going on?"

"After Benjamin and I talk here for a little while, honey, we'll probably be having a family meeting. I'll let you know shortly."

"Very well, mystery men. See you later."

When the door was closed, Charles invited Benjamin to sit down, then said, "All right. Let's hear it."

"Sir, Dorena's family reacted exactly as you thought they would. They have put their blessing on our plan and our upcoming marriage."

"Wonderful! You look like a very happy man."

"You're right about that, sir. Superbly happy! The Lord is working out what looked to be impossible."

"He is a marvelous and powerful God, Benjamin. His love for His born-again children is so great that He delights in bringing about the impossible in their lives."

"Yes, and I praise Him for it, sir. And I also have warm thoughts toward Mr. Dan, who was willing to be God's vessel to bring all of this to pass."

"You will be very happy working for Dan, Benjamin. The man has a deep love for you."

"And I for him, sir."

Charles left his chair and went to the desk in the corner of the library. He picked up a sheet of paper. "I drew up this written guarantee for you. The only thing I left blank was the amount of ransom to be paid for Dorena."

Benjamin nodded and let his eyes run the lines.

"As you can see, I am guaranteeing that you can purchase Dorena any time after Priscilla gets married."

"Yes, sir."

"When we agree on an amount, I will fill it in and sign the document."

Benjamin handed the paper back.

"The price I have in mind, Benjamin, is four hundred dollars. Does that sound fair to you?"

Benjamin smiled. "Very fair, sir. Dorena is worth more than all the money in the world, but I appreciate the reasonable price. I will plan on paying four hundred dollars for her."

"Good!" Charles sat down behind his desk. "I'll just fill in the amount and sign it. If you should not be able to come up with the money by the time our daughter marries, Dorena will be held here for you until you can. It's all stated here in the agreement, as you've just read."

"Yes, sir."

When Charles had signed the document and blotted it, he put it in an envelope and gave it to Benjamin. "There you are, son."

"Thank you, sir. May God bless you abundantly."

"He has in many ways, Benjamin. One of those is by bringing you into my life. You have been a blessing to me."

"Thank you, sir," Benjamin said, pressing the envelope firmly over his heart.

"You wait here," Charles said. "I want my family to know all about this."

Moments later, the library door opened and Charles came back, leading Evelyn, Priscilla, and Lewis.

When everyone was seated, Charles told them about Benjamin's plan to go to Texas and work on Dan Johnson's cattle ranch. He asked Benjamin for the document and passed it around to his family. When it was handed back to him, he ran his gaze over their faces and said, "I just wanted you to see this agreement I made with Benjamin and make sure you understand it."

"I understand it, Papa," Priscilla said, "and I think it's wonderful. Dorena and Benjamin deserve a life together."

"And I appreciate you being fair with him on the price, dear," Evelyn said. "From what you said about the wages Dan is going to pay him, he should be in a position to ransom Dorena as soon as Priscilla and Craig get married."

Charles turned to his sullen-faced son. "Do you understand the agreement, Lewis?"

"Yeah. I understand it."

"Good. Now, Dorena needs to be told about this. Priscilla, where is she?"

"In her room, Papa."

"Will you go fetch her, please? I want to give her and Benjamin some time together so he can tell her all that has transpired. Then I want all of us to meet with them. Take her to the small parlor. Benjamin will be waiting for her there."

Priscilla hoisted her skirts and ran up the stairs in a very unladylike fashion. She drew up to Dorena's room and knocked loudly.

Seconds later, the door came open.

"Come on!" she said breathlessly and grabbed Dorena's hand. She kept a tight grip and pulled Dorena toward the staircase.

Half-stumbling, Dorena said, "Priscilla, what has taken hold of you?"

"You'll see, honey! You'll see!"

"Has this got to do with Benjamin?"

"Yes! I told you it would have to involve you and that it would be good. It is exceptionally good! Come on! Papa is going to give you and Benjamin some time together so he can tell you about it, then Papa wants the family to talk to both of you."

Benjamin was standing in the center of the room when Priscilla fairly pushed Dorena into the parlor, kissed her cheek, then said to Benjamin, "When you two are ready, come to the library. We'll be waiting for you there."

Nodding, Benjamin said, "We will be along in a little while."

Priscilla backed out and closed the door behind her.

Dorena stood like a statue, hardly daring to breathe.

Seeing her perplexity, Benjamin quickly closed the gap that separated them and took both of her shaking hands in his own strong ones.

"Let's sit down, sweetheart," he said.

He led her to a small settee and sat beside her. Looking into her eyes with adoration, he said, "I have some very good news."

Dorena nodded. "It must be, the way Miss Priscilla was acting."

"It involves our future together, darlin'. You know that Mr. Dan is leaving Friday for Texas to begin his new life as a cattle rancher."

"Yes."

"Well, he talked to me in private this morning, and that's where this story begins . . ."

When Benjamin had brought her up to the moment, Dorena sat with her head bowed.

Myriad thoughts raced through Benjamin's mind while he studied her, waiting for her reaction. Little did he know that Dorena was taking time to thank the Lord that truly "with God, all things are possible." Then he saw tears trickling down her cheeks. They dripped off her chin and splattered on their clasped hands.

Finally, Dorena raised her shining eyes. "Nothing in this world would make me any happier than to spend my life with you, wherever it may take us," she whispered in answer to the question burning in his brown eyes.

Benjamin wrapped his powerful arms around her delicate form and they held on to each other for a long moment.

Then Dorena drew back and looked into his eyes. "I will do everything possible to be the best cowboy's wife there ever was," she said.

Benjamin kissed the tip of her nose. "I have no doubt about that, sweetheart. And you will be the very best because you are the very best, and the most wonderful lady in all the world."

When Benjamin and Dorena walked into the library, the Moores, minus Lewis, stood to their feet.

Priscilla dashed toward Dorena and took her in her arms. "Oh, I'm so happy for you! Of course, when the time comes for us to part, I will miss you something awful!"

Dorena hugged her tight. "And I will miss you in the same way."

She set her teary gaze on the head of the Moore family. "Mr. Charles, how can I ever thank you for being willing to let Benjamin ransom me?"

"You don't have to, dear. Just seeing you with so much joy on your face is thanks enough."

Evelyn went to Dorena and kissed her cheek, saying, "I'm glad we get to keep you a little longer. I'm going to miss you real big myself!"

"I will miss you, too, Miss Evelyn. You and Mr. Charles both. You have been so good to me."

Charles smiled. "Well, I guess we all should get back to what we were doing. I just wanted us to rejoice a little together once Dorena knew the situation."

Priscilla embraced Dorena again. "I know you and Benjamin will have a wonderful life together in Texas." She kept her arm around Dorena's waist as she turned to look at her father. "Papa, you're the best papa on the face of God's green earth."

Charles grinned. "I hope I can always make you believe that, sweet daughter."

The Moores left the library in order to give Benjamin and Dorena a few more minutes together.

When the door closed, Benjamin took her in his arms once more and said, "Truly, the Lord has blessed us, sweetheart."

"Oh yes. Isn't it wonderful when we see His hand working in our lives?"

"It sure is."

"I am so thrilled we can now become husband and wife. Though I will miss my family, I want to live on that ranch in Texas because that's where you will be, my darling."

18

A LARGE CROWD WAS MILLING ABOUT Charleston's railroad terminal as Dan Johnson and his family stood beside the Atlanta bound train. He embraced each member of his family while Benjamin remained a couple of steps away.

When Dan released Alexander from his embrace he turned to Benjamin and said, "As soon as I can see my way clear to meet the salary I have promised you, I'll let you know."

Benjamin nodded, fighting the hot tears. "That will be fine, Mr. Dan."

"In the meantime, you enjoy your times with Dorena."

"I will, sir. She's looking forward to becoming a Texan herself."

"Good." Dan's eyes met Benjamin's misty gaze, then he opened his arms and embraced him.

"Keep me up to date on things, won't you, Benjamin?"

"I will, Mr. Dan. I can hardly wait to be riding the range on the ranch for my best friend."

The conductor was calling for all passengers to board.

"Something else, Benjamin. When you go to work for me on the ranch, you will no longer call me 'Mr. Dan.' It will be just plain Dan."

"That will take some time getting used to, but I like it."

Dan picked up his overnight bag, told his family good-bye, and hurried toward the train.

Dan Johnson's trip had him traveling across South Carolina into Georgia, where he changed trains in Atlanta. From there he traveled to Mobile where he got on a train that would stop in New Orleans, then go on to Houston.

When he boarded the train at Mobile, he had gotten acquainted with Roger and Frances Galloway, who were in their midfifties. Roger was owner of a meat packing plant in Houston, and between Mobile and New Orleans, he showed great interest in Dan's new venture into the cattle business and asked him to contact him once he was marketing his cattle.

No one had been sitting beside Dan on the run between Mobile and New Orleans, but when the train took on passengers, he looked up to see a lovely young woman about his age pause and look down at him. She had a small overnight bag in one hand.

"Pardon me, sir. Is this seat taken?"

Dan was instantly on his feet. "No, ma'am. You are welcome to sit here. I've been riding by the window. Would you like that seat?"

"It really doesn't make any difference."

"Well, you sit there. I'm sure you will enjoy it."

"All right. Thank you, sir."

"May I place your bag in the overhead rack for you?"

"Why, yes. You are very kind."

While Dan was putting the bag overhead, the young woman smiled at the Galloways and sat down facing them.

When Dan was seated beside her, he said, "I'm Dan Johnson, Miss—"

"Stephanie Lanford, Mr. Johnson."

Dan gestured toward the couple across from them. "Miss Stephanie Lanford, meet Roger and Frances Galloway. They're returning home to Houston from Mobile."

Stephanie and the Galloways greeted each other, then she turned to Dan. "Where are you from and where are you going, Mr. Johnson?"

While Dan was explaining his background and his new venture into the cattle business, the train lurched and began to roll out of the station.

Soon they were out of New Orleans, rushing past swampland, misty bayous lined with moss-draped cypress trees, and large patches of magenta flowers.

Frances set kind eyes on Stephanie. "We haven't heard about you, dear. Where are you from, and where are you going?"

"Well, Mrs. Galloway, I am from a little town a few miles north of Mobile called Creola. And I am on my way to Galveston to get married."

"Galveston," Roger said. "Your young man lives there, I presume?"

"Yes, sir. He and his father are in the boat sales and repair business."

"Well, Galveston is a good place to be in that business."

"They are doing well at it, sir."

"How soon are you getting married, ma'am?" Dan asked, thinking of his own intention of finding the right woman and making her his wife.

"Next Saturday afternoon." Excitement showed in her eyes.

"How long have you known the young man, dear?" Frances asked.

Stephanie's cheeks flushed slightly. "Well, ah . . . not very long, actually. We . . . ah . . . have corresponded by mail a lot."

Frances's brows pinched together. "You're not one of those mail order brides, are you?"

"Oh, no! I wouldn't marry a man I had never met. Lloyd and I met several months ago at a social function in Mobile. It's just that . . . well, we were only together a matter of a few hours. But somehow we just knew we were meant for each other. So when Lloyd got home to Galveston, he wrote to me saying that I had captured his heart. He asked if I would write him back and tell him if I felt any special attraction to him. It went from there to a marriage proposal by letter, and so here goes Stephanie to marry Lloyd and live happily ever after."

"I'm sure you will, dear," said Frances. "I'm glad you met Lloyd in person, though. I saw two of these mail order bride situations right in our neighborhood, and neither one worked out."

"Well, now, Fannie," said Roger, "we've seen some others that did work out."

"Well, yes. But I don't know how any of them ever work. Just think of it! Marrying somebody you've only met through the mail."

"I sure wouldn't want to try it," Stephanie said. "Would you, Mr. Johnson?"

"Oh, ah . . . no."

"Are you married?" she asked.

"No, ma'am. But when I do marry, it'll be a young lady I have gotten to know well, I guarantee you. No mail order bride for me."

The conversation went from the subject of Stephanie's wedding to the strain developing in the country between the Southern slave owners and the politicians in the northern states who were trying to pass laws against slavery. Dan and Roger discussed it at length.

At Houston, Dan told the Galloways good-bye and had the pleasure of meeting Stephanie's fiancé before hurrying to another track to catch his train for San Antonio.

As the train moved westward across rolling wooded hills and green fields, Dan saw cattle grazing on the ranches. His heart pounded with excitement at the knowledge of his big dream being realized. He thanked the Lord for the way He had led in his life.

It was almost noon as the train neared San Antonio. Dan ran his eyes over the sun-kissed prairie and thought again of how the town made its indelible mark in America's history. Twenty-one years ago, a small band of men—including Jim Bowie, Davy Crockett, and Colonel William Travis—fought and died at the Alamo in the Texas revolution against Mexico. Such courage had never failed to stir Dan whenever he read about the fierce battle at the Alamo.

Soon the big engine chugged into the depot at San Antonio. Dan leaned close to the window and studied the crowd on the platform.

When he stepped off the train, he waited to be approached. He had given his description by mail to Hal Robards.

Presently, a man wearing a wide-brimmed hat and a woman in a bright-colored sunbonnet detached themselves from the crowd and headed straight for him. "Dan Johnson?" the man asked, smiling.

"Yes, sir."

He grabbed Dan's hand. "Hal Robards, and this is my wife, Ethel."

After greeting Hal's wife, Dan said, "I'll get my trunk from the baggage coach, then I'll buy you folks lunch. After that, you can take me to the hotel."

"I know I told you in the last letter that I'd set you up in one of the hotels," Hal said, "but Ethel and I decided to keep you at the ranch with us until you can settle your purchase of the Circle J and move there."

"Our ranch house has two spare bedrooms, Dan," said Ethel, "so there's room for you. Is that all right?"

"Well, of course! I'm sure the cooking will be much better there than at any café in town."

"I guarantee it!" Hal said.

While they were eating lunch at one of San Antonio's finer cafés, Hal said, "Whenever you want to go, I'll take you to the Wickburg ranch near Austin so you can see your old friends."

"That would be great," Dan said. "As you know, I'm to close on the Circle J tomorrow morning."

"Mm-hmm."

"I'm not sure just how long Mr. Jourdan will need in order to get his belongings out of the house, but I'm sure that until that time I'll need to be at the ranch most of the time every day, learning the ropes. So once I'm all settled in, I'll let you take me to see Bill and his folks."

"You just let me know when you're ready. I'm sure the Wickburgs want to see you as soon as possible."

"And I them. Bill and I are very close friends, and his family has always treated me wonderfully."

The next morning, Hal Robards and Dan Johnson left the Rocking R ranch and headed through cattle country toward the Circle J. As the wagon bumped and rattled along the dusty road, they passed a ranch where Dan's attention was drawn to a patch of black dots near the road.

"Those cattle up there?" he asked.

"Yep. Looks like they're roundin' up a bunch so they can single out the calves born in November and December and brand 'em."

"I see. This is all new to me, as you know."

Hal chuckled. "You'll catch on."

Gradually the black dots assumed the shape of cattle, and cowboys on horses moving in a wide circle around a dusty patch where several small fires sent tendrils of smoke skyward.

Moments later the two men were on the outskirts of the scene of action. There was noise, dust, and ceaseless motion as the cowboys singled out the calves, roped them, and slid from their saddles to wrestle them to the ground. Other cowboys moved among them with smoking branding irons, ready to burn the brand into the calves' hides.

Dan was mesmerized by the bawling and bellowing of the herd, the crackling of horns, and the pounding of hooves. The great mass of cattle seemed to be eddying like a whirlpool amid the shouting cowboys and the shrill whistling sounds they made as they rode about on their horses.

He watched with interest as the cowboys with the branding irons pressed red-hot metal to cowhide. Smoke rose from the touch of the iron, and the calves bawled lustily at the burning sensation on their flanks. The rank odor of burned hide and hair rode the morning breeze.

"I can see I've got a lot to learn, Hal," Dan said.

"Well, I have to say, my friend, if I went to South Carolina to take over a cotton plantation, I'd have a lot to learn too."

Dan kept his eyes on the branding work as the wagon carried him past the scene.

"Herdin' cattle, roundin' 'em up, brandin' 'em, and takin' care of 'em is sometimes dangerous work," Hal said. "Exceedingly toilsome, too. When you're out there workin with 'em, there's little or no rest.

"The danger is that you're continually among wild, vicious, wide-horned bulls. And even though most of the male types are always steers among the herd, even the steers can be dangerous. In many instances—and I've seen this with my own men and cattle—the cowboys owe their lives to their horses."

"How's that?"

"Sometimes when a bull sees a man down on his knees, holdin' a calf he has thrown, he'll charge him. A good cow pony will whistle a warnin' and put himself between the chargin' bull and his rider till the rider can get in the saddle. The horse will then dodge the bull till he gives up on gorin' the cowboy."

"I've never even thought about that kind of danger," Dan said. "A steer won't charge a man, will he?"

"Not like a bull will, but often when the herd's milling, the steer's horns can gore a man's legs while he's in the saddle just because he's in amongst 'em. A good cow pony will keep his rider out of that kind of danger. The Lord has just given 'em a sixth sense about those sharp horns."

"Amazing," said Dan. "You don't suppose the God of creation planned for men to use horses in cattle work and gave them that sixth sense, do you?"

Hal laughed. "You'd have a hard time convincin' a died-in-the-wool evolutionist of that, my friend."

"Well, God said in His Word that a person is a fool who says He doesn't exist, and denying God's existence is the foundation of fools like that fella Jean Lamarck and those upstart pals of his, Charles Darwin and Alfred Russell Wallace."

"Fools, all right," Hal said.

"Anyway, thanks for telling me about the cow ponies. That's interesting and necessary information for this green owner of a cattle ranch."

"Here it is, Dan," Hal said. "The Circle J property starts right here at this fence. We'll get to the gate in about five minutes."

Hal guided the wagon off the road beneath a large wooden arch that bore a four-foot-square frame with a *J* in a circle. "You won't see the ranch house, bunkhouse, barn and outbuildings till we pass through that stand of cottonwoods up ahead."

As Dan ran his gaze over the Circle J property, he could not believe its beauty. The wide creek—often lined by trees of various descriptions—wended its way through the five thousand acres like a golden thread in the Texas sunshine. Among the rolling hills of green pastures dotted with Texas longhorn and white-faced Hereford cattle were huge wooded areas. The slight breeze wafting across the land made the leaves in the tightly packed trees dance and flutter.

Dan could feel it in his bones. He was going to be happy here. "Hal," he said, "I'm looking forward to visiting your church. I appreciate your letters that answered my questions about it."

"You'll love it. Pastor Mike Custer is a powerful preacher. His sermons are filled with the gospel and sound doctrine through and through."

The wagon passed through the stand of cottonwoods and Hal pointed up ahead with his chin. "There's your new home."

Dan immediately loved the log house and log-constructed buildings around it. He could see four men working in the corral next to the barn.

When Hal pulled the wagon to a halt in front of the ranch house, a silver-haired man sitting on the porch rose from his chair and said, "Howdy, Hal, Dan."

Hal wrapped the reins around the brake handle. "Good to see you, Hollis."

"Good morning, sir," Dan said with a smile and hopped out of the wagon. As he headed for the porch, he studied the wizened little man who was ludicrously bowlegged and had a face the color and texture of a burned-out cinder. He was hobbling toward the edge of the porch, and one of his short, crooked legs dragged a bit.

Dan mounted the steps and extended his hand. He towered over Jourdan. As their hands clasped, he said, "So far, what I've seen of the place is magnificent, sir."

"Glad you like it." Jourdan turned to Hal and shook hands, then turned back to Dan. "Do you want to take a ride over the place and look at all of it before we close the deal?"

"That's not necessary, sir. Let's go ahead and close the deal, then I'll take a tour."

"Fine. C'mon into the house. I've got everythin' ready."

They sat down at the kitchen table to finish the paperwork. When the money had exchanged hands and the papers were signed, Dan eased back on his chair and said, "This is like a dream, Mr. Jourdan. I can hardly believe it's really happening."

The old man laughed. "You'll believe it when those hands of yours are blistered good."

"Yes, I'm sure I'll come out of the clouds about then."

"Well, the blisters will soon turn into calluses, son, and by then you'll have this cattle ranchin' in your blood. It's a good life. It's gonna be hard to leave it, but these old bones of mine tell me I have to do it."

Dan nodded. "I'm sure glad both of our last names start with a *J*. The name of the ranch can stay 'Circle J,' and the brands won't have to be changed."

"Yeah, I thought of that 'bout the time I sent my last letter," said Jourdan. "Well, now that the place is yours, I'll need five or six days to vacate the premises. That okay?"

"Certainly." A sly grin curved his lips as he added, "Of course, the rent will be fifty dollars a day."

The three men had a good laugh, then Jourdan said, "All that goes with me is my personal property—clothing, keepsakes, and the like. The furniture in the house, lanterns, and everything here in the kitchen stays."

Shoving his chair back, Jourdan said, "Let's go out to the barn. I want the boys to meet their new boss."

Hal went with them to the barn where Dan met Tim Cook, Chad Underwood, Floyd Shaffer, and Jose Martinez. They were a jolly bunch, and Dan could tell right off that he and his ranch hands were going to get along well. They told him they would help him in every way to learn the cattle business.

"Well, Hal," said Jourdan, "I'll take Dan through the house, barn, and other buildin's, then how about you and me takin' him on a grand tour of the property in your wagon?"

"Sounds good to me," said Robards.

Nearly two hours had passed when the wagon rolled back into the yard after Dan had seen the property lines to every corner.

As Hollis Jourdan climbed out of the wagon, he said, "Dan, I hope you're happy with it."

"I love it more every minute, sir." To himself he thought, *The only thing missing is a wife and children to share it with.*

On Sunday, Dan went to church with Hal and Ethel Robards and loved it at once. He and Pastor Michael Custer felt a kindred spirit between them, and Dan knew he was going to be happy in the church. When he saw Mexicans and Negroes in the congregation, he was thrilled because Benjamin and Dorena would be welcome here.

He moved onto his ranch the following week. Ethel Robards and Grace Custer, the pastor's wife, came to help him with the ranch house by giving it the "woman's touch."

On the first night, Dan wrote letters to his family and to Benjamin to let them know he was now living on the ranch.

Day by day, the ranch hands worked with their new boss, instructing him about raising cattle and operating a ranch. Hal Robards spent half a day with him, teaching him how to structure and handle the financial part of the cattle ranching business.

When Dan had been on the ranch for ten days, he rode to the Rocking R and told Hal he was ready to go visit the Wickburgs. They left early the next morning on horseback and arrived at the Box W ranch just before noon. There was a warm reunion, and Bill proudly introduced Dan to his new bride, Betty.

During lunch, Bill elaborated on how he and Betty got together through a mail order bride advertisement.

Shaking his head, Dan said, "I'm glad for both of you. It's quite obvious you are happy together. But . . ."

"But what, ol' pal?" Bill said.

"I'd be afraid to order a bride by mail."

"Well, I'll tell you, Danny, you'll find that eligible young ladies are scarce as hen's teeth in Texas. The entire West, for that matter. Something like one for every two hundred unmarried men."

"Really? I . . . well, I've known about the mail order bride system since it first hit the papers back in '49 when the gold rush took California. But it seemed scary to me for both the man and the woman to come to a marriage agreement through the mail. I mean, they've never met, yet when she comes west, she's expecting to be carried off to the marriage altar as soon as she gets off the train or the stagecoach."

"No, Danny," Bill said. "It's seldom like that. Most of the couples agree that she will live in a boardinghouse or a hotel until they see if they're really compatible for marriage. And when it comes to Christians using the system, they have tested each other's salvation testimony by mail before she ever comes west. And they put a lot of prayer in it before she arrives; then they pray together while she's living in the boardinghouse or hotel. Betty and I didn't marry until we were absolutely sure the Lord had led us together and we had been counseled over a period of several weeks by our pastor."

Dan sighed. "Well, I feel better about it now."

Bill chuckled. "Christian men here in the West need wives, too."

"How many newspapers did you put ads in?" Dan asked.

"Eight. And, of course, in the ads I made it plain that I am a born-again man and that only born-again women need reply."

"I see," said Dan, smiling.

"And then, when Betty answered, she asked for my testimony, wanting to be sure I was a Christian for real. In her first letter she left no doubt for me that she was really saved. Once that was clear, and we had both received peace from the Lord, I sent her the money to come. She lived in the home of a family in the church for several months while we fell in love. Then we got married. And as you can see, we're happy."

When Dan and Hal climbed into the wagon to head back, Betty invited Dan to come back when he could stay longer. She and Bill lived in their own house on the ranch and it had a guest room.

As the wagon pulled out of the yard, Dan turned and waved. He focused on the happy young couple and once again felt the emptiness in his life and in his heart. *Lord, please bring the right young lady into my life soon.*

Letters from Dan's family and from Benjamin came on Monday, May 4. Benjamin's letter informed him that Priscilla Moore and Craig Hartman had set their wedding date for Saturday, August 8.

Dan immediately wrote back, telling Benjamin that he wanted him to arrive the last day or two of May and begin his job the first of June. This would give him June, July, August, and September to save up the money for Dorena's ransom. He could go back for her the first week of October.

At the Moore plantation, Benjamin helped Angeline out of the carriage. "I hope you have an enjoyable day, Miss Angeline."

Priscilla and Dorena were coming out the door. Glancing at them, she said, "I will, Benjamin. Thank you for bringing me over."

Benjamin's eyes stayed on Dorena, who was warming his heart with a big smile. "Benjamin," Priscilla called, "I'm excusing Dorena for a few minutes so she can stay here and spend them with you."

Benjamin's eyes brightened. "Thank you, Miss Priscilla. Your kindness is very much appreciated. We do need time together."

"I know; I'm in love, too."

When the two young ladies had gone inside, Benjamin and Dorena embraced, then sat down on the porch steps.

"I have something to show you, sweetheart," he said, pulling an envelope from his shirt pocket.

Dorena glanced at it. "A letter from your best friend!"

"Yes! And I want you to read it."

She took the letter from him and read it slowly. When she came to the part with the date Dan Johnson wanted Benjamin to come, and realized that Benjamin would be coming for her the first week of October, she said, "That's not very far away."

"Just a little over five months from now."

"Five months," she said, closing her eyes. She felt overwhelmed at times with all that had happened in her life of late. She couldn't imagine what a life of freedom would be like. The thought of being away from the security of the plantation and the watchcare of Master Charles and Miss Evelyn was a little frightening.

In all of her life, Dorena had never been any farther from home than Charleston and the plantations closest to the Moore estate. She thought of the hustle and bustle of the city . . . the horses and carriages, the crowded boardwalks with people shoving and pushing her, and some even being rude and calling her unkind names.

Benjamin studied her as she sat with her eyes closed. He watched the emotions playing across her face and fear struck his heart. He laid a hand on her shoulder, which caused her to open her eyes.

"Honey," he said in a whisper, "what is it? Do you not want to marry me? Do you not want to be free and no longer subject to a master? Do you not want to make a home with me in Texas?"

Startled, Dorena blinked and looked up into Benjamin's questioning eyes. In that instant she knew she had nothing to fear. He was her world now, and the one with whom she wanted to spend the rest of her life.

"Yes, darling," she said softly. "I do want to marry you. I do want to be free, and wherever you go, I will go with you. Since the Lord wants you in Texas, then He also wants me in Texas."

Benjamin cupped her face in his hand and looked deeply into her eyes. "I am sorry," he said. "Certainly you have had some natural fears about all of this. Now that a date is set, it has made you a bit on edge. I should have thought of this and not come at you so bluntly with it."

"No, no, darling. Do not blame yourself. It's just that it's such a complete change in my life."

He pulled her close. "I understand, my love. I understand. Please know that as this change comes, I will protect you with my very life."

Looking up into his dark eyes, she smiled, then laid her head against his chest and said, "I know you will. Thank you for understanding what was going on inside me . . . and for knowing my need."

Tightening his arms around her, he said, "The Lord has His mighty hand on us, Dorena. Everything is going to be all right. We have a wonderful future ahead of us on the Circle J ranch. Mr. Dan is such a good friend to both of us."

She nodded. "And isn't it wonderful? Now we can actually see our wedding day on the horizon."

"Oh yes. And this makes me so happy!"

"Me too."

Benjamin kissed the top of her head. "It is best that I go now. Miss Priscilla will be needing you."

She smiled up at him. "I will see you when you come back for Miss Angeline this evening."

With that, Dorena turned and mounted the porch steps. Benjamin watched her as she crossed the porch and stopped at the door. She gave a little wave and moved inside.

Dorena stopped in the vestibule after closing the door behind her and took a deep breath. As long as Benjamin was close by, her fears had subsided, but alone again, new fears plagued her mind. She thought of San Antonio and the new life planned for her there. On the plantations, there were many more black people than white people. Whatever would it be like in a world where the opposite was the case?

Sighing deeply, Dorena said, "Dear Lord, I ask You to take these fears from me. You will be with us in Texas. It has to be all right." A deep peace settled over her. She smiled brightly and moved down the hall, humming a nameless tune.

Benjamin was about to climb into the carriage when he saw Lewis Moore come around the corner of the house.

Lewis gave him a malignant stare and said, "I hoped you'd be in Texas by now."

"Not yet," was all Benjamin said.

Drawing up to the spot where Benjamin stood, Lewis sneered, "Well, how long?"

"It will be a while yet," Benjamin said, not willing to give the insolent man any satisfaction.

"Too bad. I was hopin' I wouldn't have to look at your face on this property anymore."

Benjamin felt the muscles in his back stiffen, and his blood seemed to heat up. Without another word, he turned his back on Lewis and climbed onto the carriage seat.

Lewis stared hatefully as Benjamin snapped the reins and put the horse and carriage into motion.

AS THE WEEKS PASSED, DAN JOHNSON was slowly learning cattle ranching from his ranch hands and from Hal Robards, who often came by to help him.

Never far from Dan's thoughts was his longing to find the right girl and get married. He kept a sharp eye for available young women in the San Antonio church, in spite of what he had been told about the woman shortage in the West. He figured the Lord would work it out, and most likely she would be in the church.

He soon learned that every single young woman he met and liked was engaged to be married or was spoken for. In talking to the single men in the church, he learned they also were discouraged over the ratio of men to women.

One day, while in town, Dan bought a copy of the *San Antonio News*. That evening, as he was reading through the newspaper, he found an article about the great number of mail order brides coming West from the eastern states.

He thought about Bill and Betty Wickburg and what they had told him about meeting through the mail order bride system. "It worked for you, Bill," he said aloud, "but I wonder how many times the marriages are successful, even for Christians who take all the necessary precautions."

He pushed the idea out of his mind and read the rest of the paper.

But during the next several days, the idea of advertising for a bride kept driving into his thoughts. Since it seemed he couldn't shake it, he finally began praying about it, asking the Lord to show him if in spite of his aversion to the idea, this was what he should do.

The next Sunday morning after the service, Dan was in line to shake hands with Pastor and Mrs. Custer at the door. Just in front of him were Del and Mary Windham, a young couple he was getting to know. He liked both of them very much.

When the Windhams had spoken to pastor and his wife and moved on, Dan took their place and complimented the pastor on his sermon. Then he noticed that the Windhams had stopped a few feet away and were looking at him.

As he moved away from the pastor, Del motioned to him and smiled, saying, "Mary and I would like you to come to our house one evening this week for dinner."

"Well, as a bachelor whose cooking is not much, I'll take you up on it. Do you have a particular evening in mind?"

"How about Tuesday at six o' clock?" Mary said.

"Sure. Tuesday will be fine."

"Okay," said Del. "We live at 564 San Pedro Avenue, just a few blocks north of here."

At the appointed time on Tuesday evening, Dan arrived at the Windham home. They sat down to a beautiful meal.

While they were eating, Del asked about Dan's background.

After Dan told them about his family and the cotton plantation, Del said, "Mary and I just learned a few days ago that Mary is with child. We're both so excited."

"Well, I'm happy for you," Dan said. "What is it they say . . . the pitter-patter of little feet make a home complete?"

"I've never heard the saying," Del said, "but it makes sense."

Dan chuckled. "Well, they don't really say it. I just made it up."

The Windhams laughed.

"So did you two meet at the church?"

"No," Del said. "I came here to work at the San Antonio Bank and Trust two years ago. It seemed that every young lady in the church who wasn't married was engaged or spoken for. So . . ." Del reached across the corner of the table and took hold of Mary's hand. "I put some ads in eastern newspapers for a mail order bride about fifteen months ago, and look what I got!"

"Well, isn't that something?" Dan said, then told them about Bill and Betty Wickburg.

"I'm glad to hear of another Christian couple who are together because of the United States mail," Mary said with a smile.

Dan shook his head. "I have to confess that I've had an aversion toward the mail order bride idea ever since I learned about it. It just seemed like a way to open yourself up for heartache. I mean, I figured for a couple to meet by letter and then for her to make the trip and both of them find out they were simply not cut out for each other was a waste of time and emotions. It would be especially foolish for Christians. But when Bill and Betty told me their story, and how Bill advertised that only born-again women need reply, I got a new view of it."

"Good," said Del. "Unless by some miracle you should find the right woman right here in the San Antonio area, you'll probably end up being a bachelor for the rest of your life. The Lord can use the U.S. mail to bring two people together."

"I can see that now," said Dan. "I'll soon be twenty-four years old. I need to find the woman God has for me and move into that phase of my life. I really feel that the Lord wants me to do it now."

Mary nodded. "That wonderful young woman is out there somewhere, Dan. The quicker you get the ads put in the papers, the sooner she will be in your arms."

"All right. I'm going to do it. I'll stipulate that I'm only interested in a born-again young woman who wants a husband of like faith, and who wants to raise their children in a Bible believing church and in the nurture and admonition of the Lord."

"That's the way to do it," Del said. "That will narrow down the field, but you sure don't want someone who would pull against you in your Christian life. I received several letters, and most of them were ladies whom I felt really knew the Lord. Then I had to pray for the Lord's leadership, and He put Mary on my heart. She came to San Antonio from a small town in Pennsylvania. After a courtship of three months, we found ourselves deeply in love and we got married."

"I'm sure glad you invited me for this meal," Dan said. "Your story has convinced me this is the way the Lord would have me go."

When he got home that evening, Dan sat down and wrote his newspaper ad. The next day he went to the office of the *San Antonio News* and had them send ads to several major newspapers in the East.

In Madison, Wisconsin, Pastor Glenn Pryor and his wife, Nora, left the parsonage together late one afternoon and walked across the lawn to the church building. They had just entered the pastor's office when they heard footsteps in the hall, followed by a knock on the door.

"Tracie's right on time," said Nora, and opened the door.

She greeted Tracie McLeod and said, "I'm glad you were able to get off work on time."

Tracie stepped into the room. "Me too. Hello, Pastor."

"Hello, Tracie. Come on over here and sit down."

The two women took chairs in front of the desk, and the pastor eased into the chair behind it. "Tracie, you said Sunday that you needed to talk to us about a problem. Tell us about it."

She brought up the subject of Harold Liston, to whom she had been engaged for almost three months when he was killed in a work accident. This had happened nearly a year ago. Both the pastor and his wife were aware of the situation, for Harold had been a member of the church, and the pastor had conducted the funeral service.

"Pastor, Mrs. Pryor, I have grieved all this time and haven't even dated another man. I know the Lord took Harold to heaven because He had a good and proper reason, but I'm having such a hard time letting go of him."

"That isn't unusual, Tracie," said the pastor.

"But am I doomed to a lonely life without marriage because I can't bring myself to let go of Harold? I feel guilty and disloyal to him whenever I've considered accepting dates from the young men in the church. I've turned them all down."

Nora took hold of her hand. "Tracie, you mustn't feel guilty. You are not being disloyal to Harold by letting another man into your life, even though it appeared that the Lord had chosen Harold as your mate for life. It was the Lord who took him. This means that He has someone else for you."

"I agree," said the pastor. "I feel sure the Lord will send His chosen young man into your life once you realize you're not wrong to want to marry. You deserve to have a life of love and happiness."

Tracie's eyes filmed with tears. "Thank you, Pastor and Mrs. Pryor. This relieves me greatly. Both of you have been a tremendous help. I kept telling myself I shouldn't feel guilty to be a wife and mother . . . but hearing you say it seals it for me."

—∽∽—   —∽∽—   —∽∽—

The next morning Tracie awakened with a new lease on life, and when she left the boardinghouse where she lived, there was a spring in her step. As she headed downtown to her job, she said, "Thank You, Lord, for using Pastor and Mrs. Pryor to help me. It's such a relief to have that awful guilt off my heart."

The walk from the boardinghouse took Tracie past the cemetery where Harold was buried. The sight of the grave had always added to the heaviness of her heart.

On this bright, sunny day, as she came abreast of the cemetery, the euphoria she was feeling seemed suddenly smothered when Harold's tombstone came into view.

She passed through the iron gates and followed the gravel path to the stone that marked the grave. Unmindful of the dew on the grass, Tracie knelt down and caressed the cold headstone. Tears misted her eyes as once again she thought of the man to whom she had given her heart, and of all the dreams and plans they had made for their future.

She thought of yesterday's talk with the Pryors, and the pastor's words reverberated through her mind. Suddenly there were other words coming into her mind from a voice she would never forget. Harold seemed to be saying that he was releasing her. He was letting her go so she could fulfill God's purpose for her life.

A fragile peace stole over Tracie's heart. The months of agony were over. Bowing her head, she thanked the Lord for His matchless grace and tender care, and prayed for guidance.

She leaned close to the headstone and planted a kiss where Harold's name was engraved, then whispered, "There will always be a special place in my heart for you. Thank you for releasing me so I can go on with whatever God has for me in life."

She rose to her feet and touched the top curve of the stone. Giving it a light pat, she murmured, "Good-bye, my love."

Tracie walked the gravel path to the board sidewalk without looking back. By the time she had walked a block, the euphoria had returned. All was well. The Lord was in control of her life and He would direct her path.

As she moved down the street, her eyes took in places that reminded her of sweet times she and Harold had shared together. Maybe she should move elsewhere and start over.

Soon she arrived at the office building where she worked as a secretary.

Upon entering the office of the Madison Land Management Company, Tracie took one look at her coworker, Leah Desmond, and saw a turned-down mouth and eyes that revealed agitation.

Tracie's desk was next to Leah's, and as she passed between the desks to sit down, she said, "You look very unhappy, dear. What's wrong?"

Leah shook her head. "I'm sorry, Tracie. I shouldn't let my troubles get to me like this. Good morning."

Tracie leaned toward her. "I'm your friend, aren't I?"

"Yes."

"Well, come on, now. What's wrong?"

Leah sighed. "You know that I've been wanting to get away from Madison since Frank broke off our engagement and left me for that other woman three months ago."

"Mm-hmm. You've brought it up at least once a day since then. And honey, I can't blame you. So what's this got to do with being upset today?"

"Well, I haven't told you about it, but a couple of weeks ago, I answered an ad in the *Madison Chronicle.*"

"You answered an ad?"

"Yes. A mail order bride ad."

Tracie's eyebrows arched. "You mean you wrote to a man and offered to be his mail order bride?"

"Exactly. I want out of here, Tracie."

"So tell me about it. Who's the man?"

"His name is Dan Johnson. He's twenty-three years old, the same as me."

Tracie smiled. "Well, I'm glad I'm not that old."

Leah was able to manage a slight grin. "You will be on your next birthday."

"Don't remind me. Anyway, tell me more."

"Dan Johnson owns a cattle ranch near San Antonio, Texas."

"I see. Well, he's probably well-off then."

"Probably. But in his ad he said he wanted a born-again woman for his bride."

"Oh, really?"

"Yes. He asked that any young woman who replied please enclose the testimony of her salvation. So I did. I told him I was born again when I got baptized and joined the church." As she spoke, Leah opened her purse and pulled out an envelope. Shaking it angrily, she said, "He had the audacity to tell me that baptism doesn't give the new birth. That it only takes place when a person receives Jesus Christ into his or her heart in repentance of sin, trusting Him alone to save them. He said it's not Jesus plus religious rites or deeds or church membership."

"Haven't I told you the same thing, Leah?"

"Huh?"

"We've talked about this, and I told you the same thing. Don't you remember? I showed you in the Bible that to become a child of God—to be born again—you must receive Christ into your heart: John 1:12 and Ephesians 3:17, among other Scriptures."

Leah shook her head. "Tracie, I talked to my minister about that and he said you are misinterpreting it. Our church teaches that a person becomes a child of God when he or she is baptized, whether the person is an infant or an adult." Tossing Dan Johnson's letter in her waste basket, she said, "You and this Johnson guy are both wrong. I don't want to hear any more about it."

Tracie began her work, her heart burdened for Leah. But something else bothered her. She couldn't get the Texas rancher's letter off her mind. At closing time, Leah left the office, bidding Tracie good night and saying she would see her in the morning.

Tracie finished a letter she was writing for one of the officers of the company, sealed it in an envelope, and laid it in the mail basket to go out the next day. Rising from her desk, she sat down in Leah's chair and foraged through the papers in the waste basket until she found the envelope postmarked San Antonio, Texas, with the name Dan Johnson in the upper left-hand corner.

Tracie sat with the other boarders at the supper table, attempting to eat her meal, but her mind was on the letter in her purse, which she had not yet read.

While conversation at the table went on around her, Tracie thought about Dan Johnson and his desire for a mail order bride. The marvelous thing was that the prospective bride had to be a young woman who was truly born again.

". . . don't you think so, Tracie?" a female voice said.

Tracie looked up to see everyone looking at her and realized it was the landlady, Maude Foster, who had addressed her.

223

"What was that, Maude?" she asked.

"We were discussing Madison's new mayor. I said he's doing a good job, don't you think so?"

"Oh. Ah . . . yes. I'm sorry. I had my mind on something."

As soon as dessert was over, Tracie excused herself and hurried from the dining room.

The others at the table looked at each other with raised eyebrows.

"You need to remember that Tracie is still grieving over the loss of the young man she was to marry," Maude said in a low voice. "He's been dead for almost a year, but she must have loved him dearly. Maybe she's had a hard day, too, in addition to her grief."

When Tracie had entered her room and closed the door, she took the envelope from her purse and sat down in a chair close to the open window. While the breeze did its best to cool her hot cheeks, she took out the letter and read it.

A smile curved her lips. She found this Dan Johnson quite interesting, noting that he was very kind and tactful in his reply to Leah, and explained to her from the Word of God how to be saved. Not only was he a Christian gentleman, but his handwriting captivated her. She could tell he was totally masculine but different from most rugged men. He wrote quite clearly, and his signature was intriguing.

Shaking her head in wonderment, she said, "Mr. Dan Johnson, I like you."

By the light of the setting sun, she read the letter twice more, then left the chair and placed the letter on the small round table in the center of the room.

Questions plagued her mind as she paced the floor, stopping at the window periodically to stare at the gorgeous colors on the long-fingered clouds floating on the horizon.

When darkness prevailed over Madison, and it was almost time for bed, Tracie went to the closet, took out a well-worn cotton gown, and laid it on the bed. Moments later, after hanging up her dress and donning the gown, she stepped in front of the dresser mirror and loosened the tight coil of long blond hair at the nape of her neck and let it fall in soft waves down her back.

She went to the washstand and poured water into a flowered basin from a pitcher of the same design and washed her face. After drying, she picked up a hairbrush and went back to the chair by the window to sit on the edge of the seat.

She glanced at the lanterns in the street below and gave her hair several quick strokes with the hairbrush. All the while, she couldn't get Dan Johnson's letter to Leah Desmond out of her mind.

She rose from the chair and walked to the dresser, saying aloud, "Oh, well, I'll sleep on it," then picked up her Bible. She sat on the edge of the bed to read a chapter from the Gospel of John.

Finally, she doused the two lanterns in the room and crawled into bed, fluffing the pillow, but she couldn't seem to get comfortable. With each change of position, the letter kept invading her thoughts. Try as she might to fall asleep, she could not.

"Lord is this You keeping me from going to sleep?" she said aloud. "Has this letter come into my hands because You engineered it?"

She rose from the bed and flared the lantern on the small round table, then read the letter one more time. When she put the lantern out again, she slipped between the sheets and said, "Tracie McCleod, Dan Johnson may already have his mail order bride by now." A few seconds passed. "But, Tracie, you're not going to have any peace until you write him, are you?"

"Lord Jesus," she said, "I can only do what I feel You are pressing my heart to do. I must write to him. Tomorrow."

Once again, as Tracie tried to fall asleep, she lay awake with one thing on her mind. Sitting up, she said, "Oh, all right. There's no time like the present."

She left the bed and fired the lantern on the small round table and took out pen, paper, and ink from the table's single drawer. Before she began, she bowed her head and entreated her heavenly Father for wisdom, asking that every word she wrote would be the word He would have her use, and that His will would be accomplished.

After several attempts and many sheets of wadded-up paper, Tracie managed to write a complete letter, making sure her salvation testimony was as clear as possible. She read it over, folded it, and quickly sealed it in the envelope addressed to Dan Johnson.

As though Tracie had been holding her breath all the time she was writing, she gave a big sigh of relief, blew out the lantern, and returned to

bed. Still her mind was wound tight as she tried to recall everything she
had said in the letter.

It was a restless night for Tracie McCleod, but sometime in the wee
hours, sheer exhaustion drove her to sleep.

It was the third week in May when Dan Johnson walked out of the San
Antonio post office carrying his mail. There was a letter from his mother
and one from Benjamin, plus four more letters from prospective mail order
brides.

Dan smiled to himself. He had just posted a letter to the young woman
he felt was to be his bride. He stuffed the mail into his saddlebag and rode
home.

After supper that evening, Dan read the letter from his mother and
thanked the Lord that all was well with his family. Benjamin's letter advised him that his train would arrive in San Antonio on Friday, May 29 at
4:00 P.M. A thrill shot through Dan's heart at the thought of Benjamin
actually coming to the ranch and working with him.

Finally, he picked up the four letters from young women back East who
had written in response to his ads. Since they had taken the time to write,
he figured it was only right that he at least read the letters.

The first three were laid aside one by one, each time with Dan thinking
how glad he was that the matter was settled. The letter was already on its
way to Sally June Bender in St. Louis, Missouri. Then he read the fourth
letter and something about it touched his heart. Tracie McCleod of Madison, Wisconsin, was no doubt a born-again child of God. The testimony of
her salvation was clear and biblical. Her vibrant personality came through,
and she made sure he knew that she had a heart full of love to give the man
God had chosen for her.

Telling himself this was some fine young lady, he inserted the letter
back in the envelope, read his Bible and prayed, then climbed into bed. As
he tried to drift off to sleep, Tracie's letter kept going through his mind.
The obvious sweetness of her had captivated him.

After tossing and turning for at least an hour, Dan felt impressed to
read her letter again. When he had done so he said, "Dear Holy Spirit, it is
almost as if You are shouting at me in my heart. You want me to write
Tracie McCleod, I know it. But Lord, I was sure it was Sally June that I was

supposed to write to and offer to pay her way to San Antonio. What's happening here?"

Dan mildly argued with the Lord about the situation. But the longer he argued, the more he knew he should write to Tracie and establish with her that she was the one he felt God was telling him should be his mail order bride.

"But Lord," he said, looking heavenward in the darkness, "this means I have to get to the post office first thing in the morning and ask them to give me back the letter I mailed to Sally June."

The Lord seemed to say, "Yes, son. You must do that."

Dan sat down at his desk and prayed, asking for wisdom, then started the letter. As he wrote, he asked some things about Tracie, telling her that she very much interested him. One question was about the feeling he had in reading her letter that she had been through some heavy heartache. He wanted to know if he was right, and if so, could she share it with him.

With a prayer of thanks to the Lord for speaking to him so plainly in his heart, Dan sealed the letter.

The next morning, he was at the post office before opening time, tapping on the door and waving at the clerk who was almost ready to open for business. He was able to get the letter back that he had posted to Sally June Bender, and with peace flowing like a river through his heart, he posted his letter to Tracie McCleod.

20

ON SATURDAY, MAY 23, CHARLES AND EVELYN MOORE were in the library when Priscilla entered the room. "Benjamin is here to see Papa," she said. "May I bring him in?"

"Certainly," Charles said.

Priscilla disappeared for a few seconds, then returned with Benjamin at her side. Evelyn stood up and greeted him, then said, "I'll leave you two men to your business. Are you still leaving on Tuesday, Benjamin?"

"Yes, ma'am."

"Dorena has been counting the days, Priscilla tells me. She's having a powerful case of mixed emotions. She knows she's going to miss you terribly when you leave, but she also knows that in order for the two of you to have your life together, you have to go to work for Dan Johnson."

"It's very hard for me, too, Mrs. Moore," Benjamin said. "But I know I have to keep focused on the day Dorena and I can be married."

"That's right." Evelyn headed for the door. "And you just stay focused."

"I will, ma'am."

Joining Priscilla at the door, Evelyn turned and said, "I assume you and the Johnsons will want to take Dorena with you to the depot on Tuesday?"

"Yes, ma'am, if that is all right with you and Mr. Charles."

"Of course," said Charles.

Evelyn smiled. "We'll tell you good-bye on Tuesday when you come to pick her up, then."

"Yes, ma'am."

Charles closed the door behind the ladies and led Benjamin to an overstuffed chair that faced his. When they were seated, he said, "All right, son, what did you need to see me about?"

"I just wanted to make sure that you will stand by your written guarantee, sir."

Charles grinned. "I most certainly will. My word is my bond, Benjamin, and I would stand by it even if I hadn't given it to you in writing. Dorena will become yours the minute you can lay four hundred dollars in my hand."

"Please do not think I have any distrust by asking, sir. I . . . I just had to make sure."

"I understand, son. This is a big undertaking on your part. It never hurts to make sure everything is in place."

"Thank you, Mr. Charles. My plan is to return in October. I'll have the four hundred dollars by then."

"Sounds like a solid deal," Charles said.

Benjamin rose to his feet. "Thank you for giving me your time, sir. I will be going now."

"Did you want to see Dorena while you're here?" Charles asked, standing up.

"I would like that, sir."

"Well, you wait here, and I'll find her. You can have a few private moments right here in the library."

When Charles opened the door, Priscilla and Dorena were standing in the hall.

"I knew Benjamin would want to see her, Papa," Priscilla said.

Charles let out a chuckle. "You were ahead of me, weren't you, daughter?" Then to Benjamin and Dorena, "You two take your time."

When the door was closed, Benjamin folded Dorena's small frame into his arms and held her tight.

Clinging to him, she said, "The days have passed by so quickly since you told me you will be leaving on Tuesday."

"Let us hope they will pass by as quickly while we are apart," he said. "Five months sounds like such a long time."

"The only thing that will help me to endure it, my love, is that I know at the end of the five months you will come for me and we will be together from then on."

She laid her head against Benjamin's chest. Deep inside she had been carrying a profound fear that something would happen and she would never see him again. She turned a luminous face up to him.

"Oh, Benjamin, I love you so much."

Looking down on her precious, beautiful features, he said, "I love you so much, too, sweet Dorena. Do I see worry in your eyes?"

She forced a smile. "Well . . . five months is a long time, and—"

"Everything is going to be fine, sweetheart. We will both be very busy and the time will hurry by."

Thinking on his words, Dorena knew she would be enmeshed in Priscilla's wedding preparations with hardly any time for herself, for which she was grateful.

"Yes," she said, "we will both be very busy. October will be here before we know it."

The couple spent a few more minutes in the library, then Benjamin told her he needed to go. He and the Johnsons would pick her up Tuesday morning at about 7:30.

Dorena closed the door to her room and sat down on the featherbed, pressing her hands to her face. She broke into sobs, giving way to copious tears, all the while trying to convince herself that her fears were unfounded. When her well of tears finally ran dry, she was exhausted but felt a sense of relief from her pent-up anxieties.

Bowing her head and closing her eyes, she said, "Dear Father, please give me grace to endure whatever might lie ahead. I want Your will to be done in Benjamin's life and in mine. I am trusting You to let our dreams come true."

On Tuesday morning, the Johnson carriage pulled away from the Moore mansion.

Zack Johnson was at the reins with Catherine beside him. On the seat behind the driver, facing backward, Alexander sat beside Angeline. Benjamin and Dorena sat together facing them. They rode quietly, each lost in their own thoughts.

On one hand, Benjamin was very excited about his journey to Texas and the prospect of a bountiful future. On the other hand, leaving Dorena would be the most difficult thing he had ever done. But knowing he could never have her without earning the ransom money made his departure more palatable.

Dorena reminded herself that she would never be free to marry Benjamin unless he had the money to purchase her from Master Charles. Their being apart until October just had to be.

After telling Benjamin good-bye on the train station platform, Zack, Catherine, Alexander, and Angeline stepped away, allowing the heavy-hearted couple a few private moments.

Benjamin held both of Dorena's hands as they looked deeply into each other's eyes and pledged their love and faithfulness, agreeing they would live for that happy day when they would be reunited. Each promised the other they would keep letters going between them.

When the conductor's voice called for all passengers to board, Benjamin cupped Dorena's face in his hands and said in a low voice, "Sweetheart, in your darkest hours, always remember that with God, all things are possible."

Tears brimmed her eyes. "I will not forget, darling. I will keep my heart fixed on the day when I look up the lane in front of the Moore house and see you driving in to pay my ransom and claim me."

Moments later, the Johnsons stood beside Dorena as she stared after the diminishing train. She covered her mouth to smother the sobs trying to escape.

On the afternoon of Friday, May 29, Dan Johnson drove the Circle J wagon into the parking lot at the San Antonio depot. He had allowed more than enough time to buy groceries and supplies at the general store and was a bit early.

As he hopped out of the wagon and headed toward the terminal building, the sun peeped under its porch roof and painted the log walls a golden hue.

He stopped at the tracks beside the platform and glanced eastward, focusing on the distant prairie where the tracks seemed to meet. As yet, there was no sign of billowing smoke from the engine's smokestack.

A few railroad workers were milling about, and he noticed some people coming from the direction of the parking lot.

Dan began to pace slowly up and down the length of the platform, glancing eastward from time to time. When he saw more people coming from the parking lot, he recognized neighboring rancher Jules Crain and his only son, twenty-two-year-old Wyatt. They spotted him and moved his direction.

Dan smiled as they drew near. "Good afternoon, Jules, Wyatt. You fellas here to meet someone?"

"Yep," Jules said, lifting his hat and setting it on the back of his head. "My nephew, Nat Crain. He lives in Galveston. He and Wyatt are about the same age and have long been close cousins."

"He's comin' to spend a few weeks with us at the ranch," Wyatt said.

"So, who are you meetin', Dan?" Jules asked.

"Friend of mine who's coming from South Carolina to become one of my ranch hands."

"Hey, that's good. I'm glad to know the Circle J is doin' well enough that you need to hire a fifth man."

They heard the shrill sound of the train's whistle and turned to see it rolling down the tracks and sending billows of black smoke toward the sky.

Soon the train rolled to a halt in the depot, and passengers began alighting from the coaches. Dan and his neighbors were still standing together, all three watching the coach platforms as passengers descended the steps.

"Hey, Dad!" said Wyatt, pointing at car number one. "There he is!"

Nat Crain saw his uncle and cousin and walked toward them. After both Jules and Wyatt had shaken hands with Nat, Jules introduced him to Dan.

Even as Dan was shaking hands with the young man, he looked up and saw Benjamin coming out of car number three.

"There's my friend now!" he said. "Excuse me!"

The trio watched as Dan hurried across the platform toward a tall, muscular young Negro.

Jules swore. "Will you look at that! That is his new ranch hand?"

"Must be, Dad," said Wyatt.

All three looked on, stunned. Their astonishment intensified when they saw the two men hug each other and pound each other on the back.

Jules swore again. "Will you look at that!"

"Uncle Jules," Nat said, "how far is this guy's ranch from yours?"

" 'Bout three miles."

"Well, you can be glad it ain't any closer. Not with that black dude livin' there."

"Uh-oh," said Wyatt. "He's bringin' him over here."

"Well, I ain't shakin' hands with him," Jules said.

As Dan and Benjamin drew up, Dan said, "Gentlemen, I'd like for you to meet my best friend, Benjamin."

Jules's face twisted into a mask of repugnance. "You just ruined what kind of neighbors we might have been, Johnson," he said.

Dan's head bobbed in disbelief.

Open contempt showed in Wyatt's eyes as he looked at Benjamin and said, "Don't be comin' around our place. We shoot blackies."

"Let's get outta here, boys," Jules said and led his son and nephew away.

Dan drew in a long breath. "Benjamin, I'm sorry."

"Don't let it bother you, Mr. Dan. I'm used to it."

Moments later, they reached the Circle J wagon in the parking lot, and Dan said, "Just drop your knapsack in the bed, alongside the groceries and supplies, Benjamin."

"All right, Mr. Dan."

When they climbed up in the seat and sat down, Dan said, "That's twice."

"Pardon me?"

"I told you when you came here you would no longer call me 'Mr. Dan.' From now on, it's just plain Dan. Okay?"

Benjamin chuckled. "Yes, sir. And I told you it would take me a while to get used to it."

"Well, you work on it, my friend. The other four ranch hands just call me Dan. Since you're not only a Circle J cowboy, but my very best friend, you address me without the mister."

Benjamin laughed. "I'll sure try!"

When they were out of town and driving through cattle country, Benjamin kept saying how good it was to see herds of beef cattle again.

Soon they turned onto Johnson property and Benjamin got more excited when he saw cattle with the Circle J brand. He marveled at the beauty of the ranch.

As they were approaching the thick stand of cottonwoods, Dan said, "So, is everything still on schedule for Priscilla's wedding?"

"Sure is. Still August 8. And Dorena's expecting me to get her shortly thereafter."

"Good. Guess I might as well show you the surprise I have for you."

Benjamin chortled. "You didn't go and get married and not tell me, did you?"

"No!" said Dan, laughing. His mind went to Tracie McCleod, but no one on the ranch knew about her or about the fact that he had placed mail order bride ads in eastern papers.

As the wagon passed through the cottonwoods, Dan's thoughts stayed on Tracie for a moment. He was eagerly waiting to hear back from her.

As they neared the clearing, he pointed with his chin toward the ranch house, barn, and outbuildings. "Here's home, Benjamin! What do you think of it?"

Benjamin could not find enough adjectives to express his pleasure. As they came nearer, he glanced past the ranch house and pointed at a long, low-roofed structure with several windows. "Is that the bunkhouse?"

"Sure is."

"My new home!"

"For a while. You know, we haven't discussed where you and Dorena are going to live when she gets here."

"You're right, Mr.—I mean, Dan. I knew I would be living in the bunkhouse with the other ranch hands, but I hadn't given any thought to what I would do when I brought my bride here."

"Well, I did. Remember I said I had a surprise for you?"

"Yes, sir."

"A simple yes is good enough, Benjamin. None of the cowboys on this ranch call me sir."

Benjamin chuckled. "Yes, sir!"

As the wagon came near the house, Dan kept the horses at the same pace and drove past the barn, sheds, and bunkhouse. It was then that Benjamin saw four men working on a new structure at the edge of a stand of trees. As they got closer, he could tell that it was a log cabin. The roof was on and the log walls were going up on the framework.

As Dan drew rein in front of the cabin, the four men laid down their tools and headed toward them.

Dan introduced Benjamin to Jose Martinez, Tim Cook, Chad Underwood, and Floyd Shaffer, who gave him a warm welcome.

"Now, Benjamin," Dan said, gesturing toward the cabin, "here's the surprise I had for you. This is the house where you will carry your bride over the threshold when she comes."

Benjamin's eyes widened and his jaw dropped.

"Like it?"

Benjamin finally was able to say, "I love it! Dorena will love it!" With that, he pounded Dan on the back and said, "Thank you! Thank you! Thank you!"

"These fellas and I have been working on it a little at a time," Dan said. "We figure to have it done and furnished by late July. In the meantime, you can live in the bunkhouse."

"Sounds great to me. I will tell Dorena about the cabin in my first letter. It will encourage her to know she will have her own house to live in."

"You tell her, my friend," Dan said. "And tell her we're looking forward to the time when she lives here on the ranch."

"I will, M—ah . . . I will, Dan!"

It was on Wednesday, June 3, that Dan received a letter postmarked from Madison, Wisconsin, and with the name Tracie McCleod beautifully written in the upper left-hand corner. Unable to wait till he got home to read the letter, he jumped in the wagon, dropped the other mail on the seat beside him, and ripped open the envelope.

When he unfolded the letter, his eyes fell on a photograph that showed him a beautiful young blond with a sweet smile and very expressive eyes. "Oh, Tracie," he said, "you are a sight to behold!"

While carefully holding the picture, Dan's gaze hungrily took in the words of her letter. When he came to the explanation of her great heartache, and he read of Harold Liston's death, he said aloud, "Bless your heart, Tracie. That had to be rough."

When Tracie told him how she had gotten peace from the Lord through her pastor and his wife, and they helped her to realize she must not feel guilty for wanting to find the man of God's choice and marry, he said, "Bless your sweet heart again, little lady."

When he finished reading the letter, he looked at the picture again, holding it as if it were some great treasure. Waving the letter toward heaven, he said, "Thank You, Lord! Thank You!"

People walking past the wagon stared at him, but he was oblivious as he slipped the letter and photograph back in the envelope, put the horses in motion, and drove down the wide, dusty street. Moments later, he hauled up in front of the town photographer's studio.

On June 9, Tracie McCleod arrived at the boardinghouse late in the afternoon and looked in the cubbyhole that held her mail. When she saw the letter from Dan Johnson, her pulse quickened. She snatched up the letter and hurriedly made her way down the hall to her room. When she had closed the door behind her, she opened the letter with trembling fingers.

Inside the folded letter was a photograph of a handsome, dark-haired man wearing a big smile. Tracie smiled back at him and said, "Well, Mr. Dan Johnson, aren't you the rugged good-looker!" Folded next to the photograph were several fifty-dollar bills.

Her hand still shook as she held the letter and read it. Dan told her that after much prayer and seeking the Lord's guidance, he felt perfect peace about asking her to come to San Antonio with the prospect of becoming his bride. He would provide her a place to live until they married. He thanked her for the photograph, telling her she looked a great deal like he had pictured her in his mind, but that she was more beautiful than he could have imagined.

Tracie felt a swelling in her throat as she read the words, *Tracie, somehow I love you already, even though we haven't yet met face-to-face.*

He went on to explain that the money with the letter was for her travel expenses, and he asked her to come as soon as possible.

Tears spilled down Tracie's cheeks. As she wiped them away, she said, "Dear Lord, You have worked in my life in a marvelous way. I know in my heart this is the man You have chosen for me. It's a little frightening, Lord. You understand. Just help me to be the wife Dan deserves."

The next morning, when Tracie entered the office building and headed down the hall, her heart was fluttering with joy. She would talk to the office manager and give her two-week notice. With that done, she would go to the railroad depot after work and buy the tickets for her trip to Texas. That evening she would write to Dan and give him her train schedule.

Inside the office of the Madison Land Management Company, Tracie saw no sign of Leah Desmond yet.

Glancing toward the rear of the large room, she saw that the office manager's door was open. Bill Campbell was always at work ahead of the rest of the employees.

Tracie opened a bottom drawer in her desk and dropped her purse in, then closed it and moved toward Bill Campbell's office.

Her movement in the doorway caused Campbell to look up. "Oh! Good morning, Tracie."

She noted a dismal look in his eyes that was not ordinarily there.

"Good morning, sir, I—"

"Come on in," said Campbell. "I need to talk to you."

"I need to talk to you, too, sir."

When Tracie was seated, Campbell said, "Ladies first."

"Mr. Campbell, you don't look like you feel well. I can talk to you later."

"Oh, no. I'm not sick, Tracie. Just a bit upset. But go ahead."

Tracie told her boss that she was going to San Antonio, Texas, to get married.

"I'm so happy for you, Tracie! But . . ." Frowning, Campbell said, "How . . . ah . . . how soon are you planning to leave?"

"I thought I would give you the usual two-week notice, sir."

Campbell shook his head and looked down.

"Is two weeks not enough, Mr. Campbell?"

"Well, let me tell you what I needed to talk to you about."

"Yes, sir."

"Yesterday, after you left the office, Leah quit her job."

"What? You mean she's gone?"

"Yes. She cleaned out her desk immediately after quitting."

"Did she say why she was leaving so suddenly?"

"No. Just that she had to get out of Madison right now and that she was leaving on a train last night."

Tracie's heart sank. "So, my giving notice just now has your back against the wall?"

"It sure does. Tracie, I hate to ask you this, but I need you to stay until I can find someone to take Leah's place. Then I'll need you here long enough to train her. And in the meantime, I'll have to find another secretary to take your place. Could—will you do this for me? I know it's asking a lot, since you've no doubt set a date for your wedding."

Tracie thought of Dan's message to come to San Antonio as soon as possible. But she did owe a lot to this company. She had been there for almost four years and they had been good to her . . . especially Bill Campbell.

"Well, sir," she said, her throat dry. "I feel I owe you this. I'll do it."

Campbell wiped a palm over his brow. "Oh, thank you, Tracie! Thank you! I'll get busy right away and advertise for someone to take Leah's place."

On Monday, June 15, Dan Johnson sat in his wagon in front of the post office, reading Tracie's long letter. She had started the letter by telling him she felt it was God's will for her to come to San Antonio with the prospect of becoming his bride. She added that just as he was finding that he loved her already, she was feeling the same toward him. This had put Dan's heart to pounding with elation.

Tracie went on to explain that she had gone into her boss's office on June 10 to give her two-week notice and then planned to go to the railroad depot after work and purchase her tickets. When Dan read that her coming would be delayed, and why, disappointment washed over him. However, he could see what she was up against and appreciated her loyalty to the Madison Land Management Company.

On Tuesday, June 16, Tracie was at her desk when a Western Union messenger came into the office and said, "Ma'am, I have a telegram for Miss Tracie McCleod. Where might I find her?"

"You're looking at her," Tracie said with a smile.

As soon as the messenger was out the door, she opened the yellow envelope and took out the telegram. Tears filled her eyes as she read it. Pressing it to her heart, she said, "Thank You, Lord. Dan is such an understanding person."

After work that afternoon, she went to the Western Union office and sent a wire to Dan. She told him that two women had applied for the job Leah had vacated. She would keep him posted by mail how it was going and when to expect her. She closed off the telegram: "Love, Tracie."

As the weeks passed and Benjamin learned about Texas cattle ranching, he wrote to Dorena every week, letting her know of his progress and of the growing success of the ranch.

Dorena wrote back each time, saying how much she missed him and how much she was looking forward to the day when Benjamin came to get her. In each letter, she asked questions about the cabin and how it was coming along.

21

DAN KEPT HIMSELF QUITE BUSY at the ranch to help the time pass quickly. He prayed many times a day, asking the Lord to give the Madison Land Management Company a new secretary so Tracie would soon be free to come to Texas. He was tempted to tell Benjamin about her so that he could pray about it, too, but his desire to surprise Benjamin was too strong. He would just pray twice as much.

Benjamin loved the church and was becoming friends with many people. He and Pastor Mike Custer were growing closer as Benjamin shared his plans to ransom Dorena, marry her, and bring her to San Antonio, and they spent time praying about it together.

On June 23, Dan received a letter from Tracie, telling him that the two applicants had not worked out.

Dan stayed awake that night into the wee hours, praying that the Lord would take control of the situation and let Bill Campbell find the right woman to take Leah's job. He sent a letter to Tracie the next day, telling her how much he wanted her to be there with him, and that he was praying extra hard and long about the situation.

Letters were exchanged twice more, with no change at the Madison Land Management Company.

On Tuesday, July 7, Dan left his five cowhands at the corral, where Chad Underwood was breaking a newly purchased horse to the saddle. As Dan neared the ranch house, he saw a rider galloping across the prairie toward him. When the rider skidded his mount to a stop, he recognized Bobby Finch, one of the Western Union messengers.

"I've got a telegram for you, Mr. Johnson," said Bobby.

"Would it be from Madison, Wisconsin?"

"Sure is," said the young man as he took a yellow envelope from his saddlebag. "Here you go."

Dan's pulse quickened as he signed for the envelope.

As Bobby galloped away, Dan hurried into the house, saying, "Oh, Lord, is this going to tell me my prayers are answered?"

His eyes scanned the lines. "Yes!" he exclaimed. "Thank You, Lord!"

Bill Campbell had hired two women on the same day to take the places of Leah Desmond and Tracie McCleod. Tracie explained that she would train them through Friday, July 17. She would board a train for Chicago on Saturday and be in Houston on Monday, then arrive in San Antonio at 2:00 P.M. on Tuesday.

Dan went to his bedroom and fell on his knees for a private praise service. When he returned to the corral, it was all he could do to keep from telling his men that his prospective bride was coming. But he wanted to surprise them—especially Benjamin.

Chad Underwood was now trotting the stallion around the corral to the cheers of his fellow cowboys when Dan approached and told them he was going into town.

As he headed into the barn to saddle his horse, Benjamin called to him.

Dan turned and smiled. "Yes?"

"Bring me a letter from Dorena. It has been eight days since I received her last one."

"I'll do my best," said Dan, and hurried into the barn.

The sun was lowering in the sky when Dan stepped into the bunkhouse where the men had their supper on the stove. Benjamin's eyes lit up when he saw Dorena's letter.

Later in the evening, when a full moon was rising over the Texas prairie, there was a knock at the back door of the ranch house. Benjamin stood there, and Dan invited him in.

When they sat down in the den, Benjamin said, "Just thought I would tell you that Dorena says everything is still on schedule. Craig and Priscilla will be married on August 8. Mr. Charles told Dorena she would remain in the mansion, keeping her own room, until I come to get her. Since I will have the four hundred dollars after I get my pay on September 30, will it be all right if I leave the next day?"

"Of course," said Dan. "I want that young lady here as soon as you can get her here."

Benjamin smiled. "Me, too." Then a serious look came into his eyes. "Dorena told me something else in her letter."

"Yes?"

"Finn Colvin and his son, Edward, are dead."

"What happened?"

"Dorena said Finn and Edward were beating on a slave in the barn when some sixty slaves broke the door down, charged in, and beat both men to death. The overseers were frightened and did nothing to interfere."

"Hmm," said Dan, shaking his head. "I guess they finally had enough brutality from those two. God's wheels grind slowly sometimes, but they do grind."

"So I've heard," said Benjamin.

"Did Dorena say what Martha is doing with the plantation?"

"She has it up for sale. She's going to move elsewhere, but Dorena doesn't know where it will be."

"I see. Martha is a sweet lady. I hope the Lord will give her a happy life."

"Me too," said Benjamin.

Tracie McCleod had enjoyed every minute of her trip to Houston. When the train carried her across Illinois, Missouri, Arkansas, and the northwest corner of Louisiana, she watched the changing landscape with great interest during the daylight hours. Even at night, when sleep was elusive in the uncomfortable coach seat, she marveled at the bright stars in the great black canopy overhead.

Soon she was headed west toward San Antonio. Not knowing what to expect in south Texas, she stared with wide-eyed wonder at the sun-kissed prairie with its grassy fields, huge patches of forest, sparkling streams, and countless herds of cattle.

When the conductor passed through the coach, calling out, "San Antonio . . . fifteen minutes!" her heart began to pump harder. She framed Dan's picture in her mind—his kind eyes, dark hair, square jaw, and manly ruggedness. She felt a thrill go through her, and when the train did a slight turn and she saw the town, her excitement increased.

Soon the train ground to a halt in the San Antonio depot and Tracie found herself stepping down from the coach with overnight bag in hand. Her eyes roamed the crowd of people on the platform and she saw him threading his way toward her through the throng, his eyes bright and shining.

Dan was taller than she had imagined. In the photograph, he was seated. In less than a heartbeat, Tracie knew for sure that she was in love with him. This was, indeed, the man the Lord had planned for her all along.

Dan's chest felt like it was on fire as he threaded his way toward the lovely, petite blond. The tug he was feeling at his heartstrings gave him absolute assurance that he was in love with her. Strange as it might seem to someone else, he knew Tracie was God's choice for him.

When they were but a few steps apart, a huge smile lit up Dan's deeply tanned face, and a beaming Tracie returned the smile.

Drawing up face-to-face, they stood looking into each other's eyes.

"Tracie?" he said, breathlessly.

"That's me," she replied, her cheeks a bit flushed. "Dan?"

"That's me."

Every inch the Southern gentleman, Dan gave her his arm and said, "Let's get away from the crowd."

When he found a less public spot, he looked into her eyes and said, "The camera simply didn't catch it all. No camera could."

Her cheeks flushed a deeper red. "Thank you."

A bit off balance with the moment upon him, Dan said, "Tracie, I . . . I don't know whether to hug you, then go get your luggage, or just go get your luggage."

"Well, my mother used to say that first impressions are generally the correct ones."

Chuckling, he replied, "Your mother was a wise woman," then took her in his arms.

Looking down into her big blue eyes, Dan said, "I'll go get the luggage now. I'll put it in my wagon in the parking lot, then come back and get you." A sly grin curved his mouth. "You won't go away, will you?"

"Not to worry," she said with a giggle. "I'll wait right here."

Dan hurried off toward the baggage coach, looking back over his shoulder once. She smiled and gave him a wave to assure him she was not going to move.

As he weaved his way among the crowd, Dan said to himself, "You are one fortunate man, Daniel Johnson."

On the ride to the ranch, Dan and Tracie asked questions of each other. As answers flew between them, they got better acquainted. Between asking and answering questions, Tracie's head turned from side to side as she tried to take in everything all at once. Her mind and her vision were so occupied that the time sped by.

Soon they turned off the road and headed for the arch bearing the big Circle J.

Tracie's eyes widened. "I like that, Dan."

He grinned at her as they passed under the arch and followed the rutted lane that lost itself ahead of them in the huge stand of cottonwoods.

Tracie suddenly spotted several cattle grazing in the rich grass a few yards from the lane.

"Oh! Those are your cattle! I see the brand."

Dan chuckled. "Soon they will be our cattle, little lady."

Their eyes met as she said, "That sounds wonderful to me."

Dan's heart felt like it was going to explode.

As they neared the cottonwood forest, Dan purposely slowed the team to a mild walk and said, "Tracie, when we get to the house I'll explain the arrangements I've made for you until . . . well, until we get married."

"All right."

"Right now, I need to explain about my ranch hands."

"Yes? You said you have five of them."

"Mm-hmm." Dan told her he had not let any of his men know about her; he wanted to surprise them. He then brought up Benjamin, explaining in brief about his background as a slave in South Africa, and how his father had ransomed Benjamin at the slave auction in Charleston and set him free.

Tracie was deeply touched when she learned how Benjamin had offered himself to Zack Johnson as a slave and was hired as a servant. Dan told her that by using Benjamin's own ransom as an example, he had had the privilege of leading Benjamin to the Lord after explaining to him how Jesus had paid the ultimate ransom for him at Calvary.

He told her that now he and Benjamin were best friends. Then he told her about Dorena, and how Benjamin was saving the bulk of his pay to go back to Charleston and ransom her so they could get married and he could bring her to the ranch to live.

"That is so beautiful, Dan!" Tracie said. "I can't wait to meet Benjamin."

"You'll get to meet him real soon," Dan said, as they neared the clearing. "I purposely put all five men to work on a stretch of fence out of sight from the house and buildings. I want to get you inside the house before they come back. I'll bring Benjamin in so you can meet him first."

"This sounds fun!" she said, clapping her hands together.

Dan grinned as the wagon came clear of the trees. Nodding straight ahead, he said, "There's the house and the rest of the buildings."

Tracie leaned forward and strained to take in the placid scene before her. The house, barn, bunkhouse, and sheds offered a pleasant scene. She stared long and hard at it, shielding her eyes against the bright rays of the sun.

The many-windowed ranch house was spread out and inviting. After living in a boardinghouse for quite some time with very little to call her own, she could hardly wait to make this her home.

She could see a roofed porch wrapped around the front and sides with welcoming chairs placed in strategic spots all around. A person was sure to find shade somewhere, no matter what time of day they sought it.

The windows were not large, but they were numerous, and she could glimpse the patterned tie-back curtains at each window. Wildflowers grew all around in abundance, and shade trees dotted the yard.

A multicolored dog came out to greet them, which delighted Tracie.

"Is he yours?" she asked.

"No. He belongs to Tim Cook. He stays with the men in the bunkhouse."

"What kind is he?"

"He's half and half."

"Half and half?"

"Mm-hmm. Half mutt and half hound."

Tracie laughed. "What's his name?"

"Mutt."

"Really?"

"That's what Tim calls him, so we all do."

Mutt raised up on his hind legs and put his forepaws on Tracie's side of the wagon. She was sure he was smiling at her as he puffed and wagged his tail. "Look, Dan! He's welcoming me to my new home!"

"Well, good for you, Mutt!" Dan said.

Dan moved around the rear of the wagon and took a few seconds to pet the friendly dog, then gave Tracie his hand and helped her down. He kept hold of her hand while she spoke to Mutt and patted his head. When she turned to him, he took her other hand and looked into her eyes, saying, "Let me be the second, then, to welcome you to your new home."

Tracie could hardly catch her breath. She gave him a sweet smile and said, "Thank you, Dan," then turned and let her eyes take in the house and surrounding lush prairie.

"I hope this all meets with your approval," he said, still holding her hand.

"Oh yes. You have no idea how happy I will be to have a home of my own. This is perfect."

"I'm glad you like it. Before we go inside, I want you to get a glimpse of the back side."

As Dan led her, Tracie spoke to Mutt, who walked beside her. She told him what a nice doggie he was, and Mutt wagged his tail vigorously as if he understood what she was saying.

When they reached the side of the house, Dan stopped. "I don't want you too much in view from back there in case the guys might have come back for some reason."

Tracie's eyes took in the barn, corral, bunkhouse, and other outbuildings. Shading her eyes against the brilliance of the sun, she said, "Oh, Dan, it's such a nice place. I love it!"

"Good. I want you love it." He led her back to the front porch and up the steps. Telling Mutt to stay outside, Dan opened the screen door. The other door was already standing open because of the day's heat. Letting go of her hand, he gestured toward the inside and said, "Ladies first."

The interior of the house was dim compared to the brilliance outside, and much cooler. It was a very pleasant sensation after being in the heat of the Texas summer sun.

Tracie stood still for a moment, waiting for her eyes to adjust. Finally, she stepped further into the cozy parlor and turned slowly in a circle, trying to take in everything at a glance.

Dan stood watching her, a grin on his lips.

The furniture was rustic, but colorful throws and pillows, along with a bright rug and the beautifully patterned tieback curtains made it a pleasant, comfortable room. A gentle breeze came through the open windows and toyed with the curtains.

Tracie recalled that in one of Dan's letters he had told her that Hollis Jourdan—from whom he had bought the ranch—had been a widower for several years. The rug, pillows, and curtains were quite obviously new, and they definitely had a woman's touch.

There was a huge fireplace on the north wall; empty now, but she could picture a fire blazing in it on a chilly winter's day. Again, the small figurines that sat on fancy doilies atop the mantel made her think it was not a man who put them there.

Dan stood quietly, waiting for her reaction.

Tracie turned to him, her face beaming. "I love it, Dan! It's quite different from anything I have ever seen before, but I love it."

The man let out a pent-up breath. "I'm so glad. I want your happiness above all else."

Her flawless brow puckered and a tender look captured her eyes. "That means more to me than I can ever tell you," she said.

She grabbed his hand. "Come on! I can hardly wait to see the rest of the house!"

When she had explored the bedrooms and inspected the closets, they entered the large, homey kitchen.

"Oh, this is beautiful!" she exclaimed, then checked out the cookstove, cupboards, table, chairs, and pantry. The room had a definite feminine touch, as did the rest of the house. Smiling at Dan with her eyes shining, she said, "I love the whole house! It's perfect!"

Dan's face was beaming. "I'm so glad you're happy with it."

"It couldn't be better," she said, glancing over the kitchen again. "Ah . . . Dan . . . ?"

"Mm-hmm?"

"Correct me if I'm wrong, but it's hard for me to believe a man decorated the interior of this house."

"Pretty observant, aren't you?"

Stepping close to him, she said, "Okay, who did it?"

"Remember I told you in one of my letters about Hal Robards being my contact to Hollis Jourdan, from whom I bought the ranch?"

"Yes."

"And I told you the Robardses are Christian neighbors?"

"Yes. Her name is Ethel."

"Right. Shortly after I bought the ranch, Ethel Robards and Grace Custer, my pastor's wife, came in voluntarily and decorated it up like you see it. I paid for it all, of course, but they did the shopping and decorating."

Tracie giggled. "I knew it! I just knew it! No offense, Mr. Johnson, but I knew it had a woman's touch."

Dan laughed again and took her hand. "I want you to feel free to change or add anything you want. I'm sure with a little closer inspection, once you live here, you will want to add your own personal touch to our home."

Our home," she echoed softly. "What a blessed sound that has to it."

"We both know, don't we?" Dan said.

"Yes," she replied in a whisper. "We both know."

There was a sweet silence between them for a moment. Then Dan said, "Now, as to your place to stay until we're married . . ."

"Yes?"

"Other than Pastor and Mrs. Custer, the only other people I told about your coming were Hal and Ethel Robards. They promised to keep it a secret. You have been invited to stay at the Robards's ranch until we marry. We're supposed to eat supper there tonight. They have a large house and plenty of room, so you won't be in the way one bit."

"I appreciate this."

"You'll love them," Dan said.

At that instant, they heard Mutt bark as he ran past the side of the house.

"I think the boys are coming in," Dan said. He peeked through the curtain. "Sure enough. Mutt is meeting them at the bunkhouse."

He guided Tracie back to the parlor and sat her down, telling her to stay right there. He was going to bring Benjamin in first. After that, he would have the other four men come in and meet her.

Tracie sat quietly on the couch and waited. Only a few minutes had passed when she heard the screen door open and a voice deeper than Dan's say something she couldn't distinguish. As their footsteps grew louder, so did their voices.

She heard the deep-voiced man say, "What kind of a surprise, Dan? Can't you tell me anything till I actually see it?"

"Nope. Come on. The surprise is in the parlor."

Seconds later, Dan entered the room and winked at Tracie, waiting for Benjamin to see her.

She was smiling as Benjamin drew up beside Dan and stopped short. His eyes widened and he quickly removed his dusty hat. "Hello, ma'am," he said.

Dan laid a hand on his best friend's muscular shoulder. "Benjamin, I want you to meet Miss Tracie McCleod, who will soon become Mrs. Daniel Johnson."

Tracie thought she saw the black man's face lose half its color as he stammered, "I . . . I am v-very g-glad to m-meet, you m-ma'am."

"And I am very glad to meet you, Benjamin," she said rising from the couch. "Dan has told me a lot about you."

Benjamin looked at Dan, a huge question mark showing in his eyes.

"I told you I had a surprise for you," Dan said, chuckling. "You see, Tracie is going to be my mail order bride."

"B-but, you never—"

"I wanted to surprise you!"

Benjamin swallowed hard. "Well, you did!"

"Come on. Let's sit down and we'll tell you how all of this came about."

Benjamin listened intently as Dan told him about placing the ads in the eastern newspapers, and how Tracie had dug his letter out of Leah Desmond's waste basket and written to him. The Lord had brought them together.

Astounded by it all, Benjamin told Tracie how happy he was to see what a wonderful young lady the Lord had given Dan.

"Thank you, Benjamin," she said. "And I'm happy that Dan has such a good friend in this world." With that, she surprised Benjamin by leaving her seat and leaning over to give him a sisterly embrace.

As Tracie sat down again, Dan said, "I've told her all about Dorena and that she'll be here in October."

"Yes," said Tracie, "and I think it's wonderful. I can't wait to meet her."

"You will love her, Miss Tracie. And I know she will love you."

"Well!" said Dan. "Benjamin, will you go out and tell the other guys I have someone I want them to meet, please? And don't tell them. Just bring them in and let me take it from there."

Benjamin grinned. "I will be back shortly, boss."

Dan's other ranch hands were as surprised as Benjamin when they were brought in and introduced to the young woman who would become their boss's mail order bride. Each one made Tracie feel welcome.

When the ranch hands filed out of the parlor, Benjamin told Dan and Tracie he was going to write a letter right after supper and tell Dorena all about Tracie and the upcoming wedding. Tracie said she would like to write a note to Dorena to send along with his letter. This pleased Benjamin, and he thanked her for it. Dan gave her pen, paper, and ink, and she wrote it while Benjamin waited.

When the sun was lowering in the sky, Dan drove Tracie to the Robards's ranch where she was warmly welcomed.

Tracie told Hal and Ethel how deeply she appreciated them opening their home to her, but they must allow her to do her share of work around the place. They agreed, and the two couples sat down for a hearty meal.

That evening, Benjamin wrote the letter to Dorena and told her about the lady who had come from Wisconsin to become Dan's mail order bride. He added that the way it looked, it would not be long until the wedding took place. Before sealing the envelope, he inserted Tracie's note, in which she had told Dorena how excited she was that she would be coming to the ranch in October, and that she knew the two of them would become good friends.

For the same mailing, Dan wrote to his parents and siblings in South Carolina, breaking the news to them about Tracie and telling them all about her and what a wonderful Christian she was. He told them he and Tracie already knew the Lord had definitely led them together, and the wedding wasn't very far away.

Several days later, Dorena's return letter came to Benjamin, and with it was a note for Tracie. The note was so sweet it brought tears to Tracie's eyes when she read it.

On the following day, a letter came from Dan's family. They were rejoicing over God's leadership in his life. Also in the envelope were four letters to Tracie, one from each member of the Johnson family.

Tracie immediately wrote letters to Dan's parents, as well as one to Angeline and one to Alexander. In each letter she told them she loved them and looked forward to the day she could meet them.

The next few evenings, as Dan and Tracie spent time alone in the ranch house, they told each other details about their lives. Dan found out that Tracie's parents had died when she was in her teens, and she had supported herself from that time on. She expressed her desire to meet Dan's family as soon as possible.

Tracie loved the church. The people were kind and loving to her, and the Custers were especially warm. Tracie and Grace Custer struck up a quick friendship.

Evening after evening, Dan and Tracie found that they had much in common as to their likes and dislikes. Each time they were together, they prayed together and asked the Lord to guide them concerning the wedding and their future.

One night, they were talking about their past lives when Tracie alluded to Harold Liston. She put her hand to her mouth and said, "I'm sorry, Dan."

He smiled and took her hand. "You don't have to be sorry, Tracie. I know Harold was once a vital part of your life. I understand. Please don't be afraid to mention him."

Tears filmed her eyes as she reached up and touched his face. "Dan," she said softly, "you are so tender and understanding toward me. I love you. I love you with all of my heart."

Dan folded her in his arms. "I love you with all of my heart, too." He kissed her sweetly and tenderly, then looked into her eyes and said, "You are the most wonderful woman in all the world. I am so grateful to the Lord for picking you out just for me."

A thrill passed through Tracie's heart. She laid her head on his chest and held him tight.

One day, when Dan and Tracie were alone in the ranch house, he said, "Sweetheart, I'm concerned about Benjamin. He is so lonely for Dorena."

"Yes, that's quite evident. I'll be glad when October comes and he can go get her."

"I'm thinking that since next Saturday is August 8, and Priscilla's wedding will take place, maybe I should go ahead and give Benjamin the hundred dollars he's lacking so he can go on to South Carolina and bring her back here."

Tracie thought a moment. "Darling, may I give you my opinion about that?"

"Of course."

"Please remember that he used to be a slave. Then he became a servant. Now he is a hired hand on this ranch."

"Yes?"

"I'm afraid that if you give him the hundred dollars, you could damage his self-assurance. He needs to know he has earned the money so when he uses it to pay for Dorena, he will have paid the ransom money himself."

Dan was silent for a moment, then nodded. "I hadn't thought about it in that light. I'll loan him the money and let him pay me back later."

Tracie said, "But that might very well hurt Benjamin's pride. It will mean more to him if he has actually earned the money, then takes it and makes his purchase. This will make it fully a ransom of love."

Dan pondered her words, then folded her in his arms and said, "No wonder the Lord made women. We men would be lost without you. You're right, sweetheart. That never crossed my mind. I wouldn't want to hurt his pride. And what's more, I must allow it to be absolutely a ransom of love. I guess I'll just have to stand back and let this happen between Benjamin and Dorena in God's own time."

Tracie kissed his cheek. "Honey, you're the smartest man in the world."

"I am?"

"Why, yes. You're going to marry me, aren't you?"

"I sure am."

"Then that proves you're smart!"

They had a good laugh together and shared a sweet kiss.

Benjamin and Dorena continued to write to each other every week.

During this time, Jules and Wyatt Crain showed their resentment toward Dan Johnson on every occasion afforded them. They resented having a black man employed at his ranch.

The Crains had affected some of the other ranchers in the area, too, causing them to show both Dan and Benjamin their indignation. Even Tracie was treated rudely by Mrs. Crain and other ranch women when shopping in town with Ethel Robards.

When Benjamin was in town from time to time and Wyatt Crain saw him, he went out of his way to come face-to-face with Benjamin so he could be rude to him.

This treatment hurt Benjamin, but not once did he retaliate by word or deed.

22

BY THE TIME AUGUST ARRIVED, Dan and Tracie had fallen deeply in love.

One night, during the third week of August, they took a moonlight walk along the creek that rambled across Circle J land. They were in a wooded area when they stopped and sat down on an old fallen tree.

The forest of cedar and cottonwood around them was a haze of shadows and half-images where the moon shone its thin beams of silver through the dense trees. The dappled moonlight danced on rippling water.

"Honey, I think it's time to set the wedding date," Dan said.

"Me too."

"I have a date in mind, Tracie . . ."

"Mm-hmm?"

"How about Saturday evening, September 19? That will make it almost two months since you came here. Even though we've known we're made for each other ever since the first day we met, we can show ourselves and everybody else that we didn't rush into the marriage."

"Sounds perfect to me," Tracie said, the moonlight reflecting from her eyes.

"Good. Then let's seal it the proper way."

Dan kissed her soundly, then held her close and said, "We'll go into town and talk to Pastor Custer tomorrow."

"Oh, darling," Tracie said on a sigh. "I'm so happy. The Lord is so good!"

Dawn came to the Texas prairie with a clear sky on Saturday, September 19, 1857, promising a beautiful fall day.

Tracie awakened moments after gray light touched her window. Although the days were still quite warm, the nights had a decided chill to them. She had left her window open several inches and the cool air invaded her room.

Turning on her back, she pulled the covers up to her chin. Her first thought was that this was her long-awaited wedding day. She lay in bed, daydreaming about her future.

Soon the sky took on a pink color and began to brighten. Tracie closed her eyes and spent a few minutes talking to the Lord, praising Him for His blessings in her life, then she went back to daydreaming about her future as Mrs. Daniel Johnson.

She sat up with a start when she suddenly realized how much work there was to do this day. She bounced out of the bed, ready to face the most exciting day of her life.

Early in the afternoon, Tracie went out into the fields on the Robards's ranch and picked a myriad of wildflowers of every hue and color imaginable. She and Ethel filled every vase and container they could find and placed them in the wagon for the drive to town.

At the church, they adorned the altar with the gorgeous flowers. The wedding would be a simple one, and the wildflower arrangements made it perfect.

That evening, the church auditorium was filled with well-wishers who watched the groom, his best man, and the pastor come from a side room as the pump organ played the beginnings of "The Wedding March."

Dan smiled nervously at Benjamin, who stood next to him as best man.

The church was aglow with lantern and candlelight. Finally, the organ signaled that the bride was coming, and everyone rose to their feet. Dan's heart swelled with joy and love when he saw Tracie coming down the aisle on the arm of Hal Robards. Ethel Robards, Tracie's matron of honor, walked in front of them.

As Tracie moved sedately down the aisle, Dan had never seen such a beautiful bride in all his life. Her dress was a deep lavender cotton broadcloth, and with the light from lanterns and candles shining on it, it resembled shimmering silk. Wildflowers were tucked in her hair, and she carried a small bouquet in trembling hands.

Moments later, the happy couple stood before Pastor Mike Custer and never took their bright eyes from each other's faces as they took their vows, hiding them deep in their hearts to always be remembered.

Life on the Circle J ranch was a happy one for the newlyweds. Tracie and Dan were both busy from morning till night on weekdays, seeing each other only at meal times.

Tracie was enthralled with a house of her very own to tend and to make comfortable for her husband. She spent hours in the kitchen. Since she had never had much cooking experience, her new role as a cook was a challenge. She loved Dan even more because he was always willing to try whatever she prepared, and each time, he praised her for the good meal.

Mutt had taken a liking to Tracie and came around quite often. When she was cooking, she always shared some with him. More and more, Mutt was seen laying near the back door of the house. Tim Cook knew why and didn't interfere.

Dan and Tracie's quiet evenings were spent reading or just basking in each other's company. Sometimes there was a third party on the floor nearby, panting and wagging his tail.

On Wednesday, September 23, Dan Johnson and Floyd Shaffer were on a hay wagon in front of the barn, loading the hayloft. Dan saw one of the Circle J wagons emerge from the cottonwood forest and head for the house. It was Benjamin and Jose Martinez, whom Dan had sent into town to purchase some supplies and pick up the mail from the post office.

He watched the wagon pull up beside the house and saw Benjamin hurry to the back door and hand Tracie the mail, then he and Jose unloaded the supplies at one of the sheds. When they were finished, Jose took the wagon to the corral to unhitch the team and Benjamin headed toward the hay wagon.

Dan pitched the last forkful of hay up to Floyd in the loft, then smiled down at Benjamin. "Anything come from my family?"

"Sure did," said Benjamin. "There was a letter for you and Miss Tracie from your mother."

"Good."

"What do you want me to do next, Dan?" Benjamin asked.

Something in Benjamin's tone made Dan look at him closely, and when he looked into Benjamin's eyes, he saw a hint of worry. "Something's wrong, Benjamin," he said. "What is it?"

"It's Dorena."

"What do you mean?"

"Well, I didn't say anything to you last week when there was no letter from her. But there was no letter in today's mail, either. This makes two weeks in a row."

"That's odd," Dan said. "She's never gone this long before, I know."

"I'm concerned," Benjamin said. "I think something is wrong. She has now left two of my letters unanswered."

"Sometimes the mail does get delayed. You'll probably get both letters at the same time tomorrow."

Benjamin managed a weak smile. "Yes, you're probably right."

"It's just a week from tomorrow that you leave for South Carolina. There are a couple of things I need to talk to you about before you go, and the sooner the better."

"Certainly," said Benjamin. "We could talk now. . . ."

Dan nodded and told Floyd to put the hay wagon away when he was done in the loft. Then he and Benjamin went to where the windmill and stock tank stood behind the split-rail fence in the corral.

As they leaned against the fence, Dan said, "First thing I want to talk to you about is this: Since we're out of the South and you are no longer a slave, or even a servant, you need a last name. All of Dorena's letters have had to be addressed to you in care of Dan Johnson. People in Texas and the West need a last name."

Benjamin grinned. "I see your point, Dan. Can this be any name I want?"

"Of course."

"All right, I will think about it and let you know when I come up with the name I want."

A sly grin bent Dan's lips upward at the corners. "I have a suggestion."

"Oh? And what name would that be?"

"How about Johnson?"

Benjamin's eyebrows raised in surprise. "Really? You want me to have the same last name as you?"

"Sure."

"Dan . . . I would be very proud to carry your name."

"Good. We'll go into town tomorrow and talk to Judge Carstairs and make it legal."

"Wow! Wait till I tell Dorena about this!"

Dan grinned. "Now that we've settled that, there's something else I need to discuss with you."

"Yes?"

"Since the ranch has done so well, and we're adding to our herd because of the demand for beef . . . I want to make you my partner."

Benjamin's mouth fell open. "Your partner! Dan, I don't know what to say!"

"Well, just say yes. As my partner, you will reap the financial benefits. Your cabin is all finished and ready for you and Dorena to move in. You will receive a fair percentage of the ranch's profits and will make a good living far beyond what you have been earning on a cowhand's salary. How about it?"

Tears spilled down the black man's cheeks. He shook his head in amazement and said, "Truly, the Lord has blessed me, Dan. Beyond my wildest dreams. Of course I will accept your offer."

"Okay, partner!"

"I'm going to write a letter to Dorena and tell her about all this. If I mail it in town tomorrow, it should reach her a day or two before I get there. And you know what?"

"What?"

"I'm going to tell her that since we've been corresponding by mail ever since I came here, she will be my mail order bride, just like Miss Tracie is yours!"

When Benjamin Johnson boarded the train in San Antonio on Thursday, October 1, he was deeply concerned about Dorena. No letter had come in answer to his latest one. It was now more than three weeks since he had received her last letter. As the train rushed down the tracks toward Houston, he prayed fervently, just as he had repeatedly for the past week, asking the Lord to keep His hand on Dorena and to correct whatever problem she was facing.

When Benjamin arrived in Charleston, he rented a horse and buggy with the spare money he had saved up in addition to the 400 dollars ransom money.

When he drove onto the Moore plantation, his heart quickened. There was no one in sight at the front of the mansion, so he drove around back and parked at the porch. He saw a few slaves who waved at him then quickly moved away.

He mounted the steps and crossed the porch to knock on the back door. His knock was answered almost immediately by Lewis Moore, who snarled the words, "What do you want?"

"I want to see Master Charles," Benjamin said, knowing full well that Lewis knew why he was there.

Lewis came out the back door, causing Benjamin to step back. He walked past Benjamin, and went down the steps to stand by the buggy. Benjamin followed him.

"And what did you want to see my father about?" Lewis said, fixing the black man with eyes of malice.

"You know what I want to see him about. You were there when Master Charles gave me the written guarantee that I could ransom Dorena for 400 dollars whenever I could pay it."

"Well, that guarantee doesn't count anymore."

Benjamin stiffened. "What are you talking about? I have it right here in my shirt pocket." As he spoke, he drew the folded paper out and put it in front of Lewis's eyes.

Lewis laughed. "Like I said, it doesn't count anymore."

"Why? Your father is a man of his word."

"My father *was* a man of his word. He's dead."

Benjamin's chest tightened. "Dead?"

"Yes. He died a month ago. Upon his death, I became master of the plantation. The day after Pa's funeral, I sold Dorena."

Panic beat through Benjamin like the frantic wings of a frightened bird. "Sold her! To whom?"

"A slave trader named Jock Webster in Charleston. I saw Webster that next week, and he told me he had sold her to some plantation owner in the western part of the state."

Benjamin blinked angrily. "Why did you sell her? You had no right to do that!"

An expression of amusement tilted the corners of Lewis's mouth. "Sure I did. Like I told you, I'm master here now."

"I want to talk to Miss Evelyn."

Lewis eyed him with hostility. "Wouldn't do you any good. She has no say about what goes on with the slaves. Besides, there's nothin' to talk about. Dorena's gone. She belongs to someone else now."

"What about her family?"

"They're still here, but you can't see them. Get in that buggy and go. I want you off this property right now."

Benjamin squared his shoulders, anger alive in his eyes.

"If you don't go immediately," Lewis said, "I'll call for the overseers. They'll escort you off. But they might break a few bones before you reach the road."

"What plantation owner has her?"

Lewis broke into an evil laugh. "I have no idea. You'll have to find her yourself. And I hope you don't."

With lightning speed, a rock-hard fist lashed out and slammed Lewis's jaw. He hit the ground six feet away and lay flat on his back, unconscious, while Benjamin climbed in the rented buggy and drove away.

At the kitchen window, Evelyn Moore—who had seen and heard it all—looked at her son lying in the dirt and said, "Good for you, Benjamin!"

Two hours later, Benjamin drove westward out of Charleston. He had learned from Jock Webster that the plantation owner who bought Dorena was Russell Cobb. His plantation was near the Georgia–South Carolina line. Benjamin had gone to the man who rented him the buggy, asking for permission to drive it to Barton. The man refused, saying that he would sell him the horse and buggy. Benjamin had no choice but to buy them, which cost him 150 dollars of his ransom money. Praying for help from the Lord, he headed for Barton.

Russell Cobb sat Benjamin down on the porch of the mansion after hearing his story. Asking for his manumission papers to make sure he was a free man, Cobb said, "Young man, I'm sorry to tell you this, but I don't have Dorena any more."

"Where is she?"

"I sold her to a plantation owner friend of mine over in Louisiana. Name's Laird Milburn."

Benjamin shook his head in frustration. "Why?"

261

"Well, let me explain. I had sent a letter to Jock Webster, telling him I needed a new house slave for my wife. When he brought Dorena to us, my wife and I were taken with her beauty and sweet countenance. We were both concerned about the sadness we saw in her eyes, but we bought her anyhow, figuring we could make her happy.

"Dorena did an excellent job for us, but she never cheered up. My wife tried to find out what was bothering her, but she wouldn't say. As far as her work, there was nothing to complain about, but her sadness was hard to live with day after day. This went on for two full weeks. We knew it wasn't going to work out. Then one day Laird Milburn was in the area and dropped by to see us. I told him about Dorena. He asked to see her and bought her immediately, saying she was perfect."

"Perfect for what?" Benjamin asked.

"Well, it just so happened that Laird had been looking for just the right wife for his prize slave, Zanu, who is the son of an African tribal chief. When Laird laid eyes on Dorena's beauty, he knew he had found the right one."

Benjamin's stomach turned sour.

"I felt good about selling her, because I figured this might be exactly what Dorena needed to erase the sadness in her eyes. You know . . . having this prime slave for her husband. I'm sorry, but I knew nothing about you. She must have given up that you would ever be able to find her."

"Mr. Cobb," Benjamin said with shaking voice, "where is Mr. Milburn's plantation?"

"It's near the town of Bogalusa, in eastern Louisiana. But you're probably too late. They might already be married."

Benjamin thanked Cobb and left in the buggy as twilight closed in around him.

At the Milburn plantation, three miles south of Bogalusa, Dorena lay on her cot in the small cabin she shared with three other young women. Moonlight flowed through the windows while her companions slept. For Dorena, sleep had come with difficulty ever since she had been sold by Lewis Moore to slave trader Jock Webster. She hadn't even been able to tell her family good-bye.

And now, here she was on the Milburn plantation with a wedding staring her in the face. Her skin crawled at the thought of the times she had been brought face-to-face with Zanu, in Master Laird's presence, so they could get acquainted. Her heart belonged to Benjamin. It made her sick to think of being some other man's wife. Her new owner had not set the day that she and Zanu were to wed, but she knew it would be soon.

Dorena wiped tears as she thought of Benjamin, wondering what he had done when he arrived at the Moore plantation and learned that she had been sold.

"Dear Lord," she whispered, "I know that You are the great God of the universe. There is nothing You cannot do. I am begging You to please deliver me from this terrible situation and bring Benjamin and me back together. Please, dear Jesus. Please let Benjamin find me and take me with him before this horrible wedding takes place."

It was midmorning when Benjamin careened his buggy off the road and headed down the lane toward the Milburn plantation. As he drew near the mansion, he looked for slaves working about, but no one was in sight. He wondered where they had Dorena.

Suddenly, a man with a revolver on his hip was hurrying down the steps of the mansion's porch, waving his hands and shouting for Benjamin to stop.

Benjamin drew rein and said, "Sir, my name is Benjamin Johnson. I have come to talk to Mr. Laird Milburn. Will you take me to him, please?"

The overseer frowned. "What's a slave doing with a horse and buggy?"

Benjamin handed the man his papers.

When the overseer handed them back, asking what Benjamin wanted to see Mr. Milburn about, he explained briefly about Charles Moore's guarantee that he could purchase Dorena so he could marry her and showed the man the written document.

As the overseer was digesting this information, Benjamin said, "Has the wedding taken place yet?"

"No, not yet."

"May I see Mr. Milburn, please?"

"He's not here. And even if he was, you couldn't see him. He has no time for this kind of thing. He bought Dorena to make her Zanu's bride. That's that. Now, you turn around and see how fast you can get off the property."

"Sir, I only ask for a bit of human kindness here, and—"

The overseer drew his revolver, cocked it, and lined the muzzle on Benjamin's face. "I said get off the property, and I mean it. Turn that buggy around right now and go! Or I'll shoot you!"

Despair washed over Benjamin as he looked down the black muzzle of the gun. In his heart he asked the Lord to do something for him quickly. He could not give up.

Immediately, they heard the pounding of hooves and the rattle of a carriage. Benjamin looked behind him and saw a distinguished-looking man with silver hair sitting in the driver's seat. Seconds later, the man drew the carriage to a halt, looked at Benjamin, then at the overseer, and said, "Mack, what's going on here? Why are you pointing your gun at this man?"

"He's a free Negro, Mr. Milburn," said Mack. "He came here to talk to you, and I told him you don't have time. He got stubborn about it, so I put the gun on him and told him to leave. He'll only be trouble."

"So what did he want to see me about, Mack?"

When the overseer told his employer the story, Milburn looked at Benjamin and said, "I'm sorry about what happened at the Moore plantation, young man, but I have already told Zanu that Dorena will be his wife."

"Please, sir. Dorena loves me. She would not willingly marry another man."

Milburn smiled. "You're right about that, son. She has been protesting vehemently about the wedding, saying she was promised to a free Negro man."

"Mr. Milburn," Benjamin said, "I am asking for some human compassion. I am asking you to allow me to purchase Dorena so she can become my wife."

Chuckling, Milburn said, "Mack said you were going to pay Charles Moore 400 dollars for her. I paid Russell Cobb 500 dollars."

"Well, sir, I—"

"She's not for sale! She is to be Zanu's bride."

Praying in his heart for God's help, Benjamin said, "Sir, I am asking you to reconsider forcing her to marry Zanu. She is a slave. But as a human being, doesn't she deserve some happiness?"

Milburn studied him. "Tell you what. If you can cross my palm with 1,000 dollars right now, I'll consider selling her to you."

Benjamin showed him the 250 dollars he had left, explaining about having to buy the horse and buggy. He knew he could get the other 750 dollars from his partner in Texas if Milburn would give him the time to get it. He was offering to give Milburn the 250 dollars as earnest money when they heard a loud roar of excited voices coming from behind the mansion.

"The contest is already in progress, Mr. Milburn," Mack Ottwell said.

Looking that direction, Milburn grinned. "So how's it going?"

"Well, before I came out front to spell Luke Braden a few minutes ago, Zanu, Leonard, Cecil, and Bernard had eliminated eight other slaves. Cecil and Leonard are about to compete right now. Zanu will compete with the winner of that match, and then the champion will be declared."

Milburn grinned. "Mack, you and I both know Zanu is going to win." Then turning to Benjamin, he said, "I like you, young man. Come with me."

Benjamin hopped out of the buggy and Mack Ottwell holstered his gun. Leaving Ottwell behind, Milburn ushered Benjamin toward the rear of the mansion. As they walked, Milburn explained that periodically the male slaves had a contest to see who could lift the heaviest load of cotton bales onto a flatbed wagon. The winner got bragging rights until the next contest. Zanu had only been there for one previous contest and won it hands down. The other strong men had determined to beat him this time.

"The reason I do this," said Milburn, "is that the contest gives some excitement to the slaves and a little break from their work. They're easier to handle for some time after a contest."

When they reached the back, Benjamin saw a crowd comprised of overseers and slaves of all ages gathered in a circle near one of the barns. His eyes searched for Dorena, but he couldn't find her.

"Well," said Milburn as they drew near the wagon where two muscular slaves stood ready, "it looks like Cecil and Leonard are about to begin."

Benjamin saw that four large cotton bales had been tied together with ropes. The bales lay at the feet of the two contestants.

For a moment, all eyes turned to the plantation owner and the husky black man at his side.

Dorena was in the laundry room near the kitchen. She had been given the job as laundress for the Milburn family and was too busy to join the other slaves who were gathered outside, watching the contest.

As she scrubbed sheets and bedding in a large galvanized tub, she wept, begging the Lord to deliver her from marrying Zanu. Salty tears dripped off her chin into the soapy water as she mindlessly scrubbed the bedding and listened to the roar of the crowd outside as they cheered the contestants.

Soon she had the bedding in a tub of clear water and rinsed it out. Deciding to take a little break before she started washing clothing, she left the laundry room and stepped out on the back porch. Her line of sight went to Cecil and Leonard, who were about to vie with each other. The crowd was waiting with bated breath.

Dorena's gaze slowly left the two competitors and drifted to Laird Milburn. It was then her eyes settled on the tall, broad-shouldered man who stood beside Milburn. Even with his back toward her, she knew that form. An involuntary gasp escaped her lips. For a fraction of a second she was afraid she was hallucinating, then he turned his head a bit and Dorena saw his unmistakable profile.

It was Benjamin in the flesh! He had come for her!

Cecil bent over to grasp the bundle when suddenly a feminine squeal cut through the air, followed by the cry, "Benjami-i-in!"

His head whipped around to see his beloved Dorena racing toward him from the rear of the mansion. She ran with open arms, and tears glistened on her cheeks as she repeated his name.

Zanu stood with Bernard a few feet from where Cecil was about to lift the bales. His gaze flashed to Dorena, then to the stranger, and his eyes widened.

Benjamin started toward Dorena, but Laird Milburn made a quick move, stepping in front of him. Immediately, two overseers were at Benjamin's side, eyeing him warily.

Milburn turned and pointed a stiff finger at Dorena. "Stop right there, girl!"

When Dorena stopped, she was no more than ten feet from Benjamin. "Dorena," said Milburn, "move back with the others."

Benjamin and Dorena stood spellbound for a few seconds, looking hungrily into each other's eyes. Benjamin gave her a smile that warmed her all the way to her bare toes. Flicking a glance at Laird Milburn, she turned and walked to the edge of the crowd, wiping tears and silently sending a prayer of gratitude heavenward.

From where he stood, Zanu—who was taller and heavier than Benjamin—scowled at him. Benjamin met his hard gaze but showed no emotion.

Cecil still stood over the bundle, which lay some twelve feet from the flatbed wagon. Bare from the waist up, he flexed his muscles. They rippled and corded under his shiny black skin. Benjamin heard one of the overseers tell Milburn that the last contestants to be eliminated had tried to pick up three bales per bundle.

Every eye was on Cecil as he hoisted the bundle waist-high and staggered toward the wagon, every muscle straining. When he started to lift it onto the bed, it fell short, and he dropped it.

While moans of disappointment swept through the crowd, Cecil walked away, his head lowered in shame.

Two slaves picked the bundle up and carried it back to the starting point. Leonard then hoisted it, staggering a little, but was able to put the bundle on the wagon bed to the cheers of the crowd.

While the bundle was being placed at its original spot again, Zanu stood over it, flexing his muscles. He glanced at Benjamin and scowled again. Quickly, Zanu picked up the bundle and with seemingly little effort carried it to the wagon and laid it gently on the bed. The crowd cheered him.

Bernard got the bundle about as far as Cecil had. It was now down to Leonard and Zanu. Another cotton bale was added to the bundle. Zanu flexed his up, carried it confidently to the wagon, and this time dropped it on the bed with a thud. The crowd cheered him.

While the cheering was going on, Laird Milburn turned to Benjamin and said in a voice that only Benjamin could hear, "You look pretty strong to me. Do you think you can out-lift our champion?"

"Possibly," said Benjamin, wondering what the man had in mind.

"Tell you what. I want you to compete with Zanu. Another bale will be added to the bundle. More bales will be added, if need be, until one of you loses. If you can out-lift Zanu, and will pay me 1,000 dollars for Dorena, you can have her. I'll give you the time to go to Texas for the money."

The proposition momentarily stunned Benjamin. As he thought it over, Milburn studied the emotions crossing the young man's face.

267

"I'm a man of my word, Benjamin. You can count on me to uphold my end of the bargain."

Benjamin prayed in his heart for God's help, then said to Milburn, "We have a deal."

"Okay. Warm up a little while I talk to Zanu."

Dorena watched as Milburn stepped to Zanu and Benjamin began working his arms, shoulders, and back to loosen them. A frown of puzzlement lined her brow.

Standing close to Zanu, Milburn kept his voice low and told him the husky man was the one to whom Dorena was promised, and he had come to purchase her from him.

Milburn then explained the contest he had set up, and told Zanu if he let the smaller man out-lift him, he would lose Dorena. She would be purchased by Benjamin Johnson.

Zanu turned and looked at Benjamin. He gave him a mean look and from the side of his mouth said to Milburn, "He looks strong, but he cannot out-lift Zanu."

Milburn grinned and walked to the center of the circle of slaves and overseers to explain the contest between Zanu and Benjamin. A low murmur traveled through the crowd.

"One more thing," said Milburn so that all could hear. "If Zanu wins, there will be no recourse. The wedding between Zanu and Dorena will take place this evening!".

Milburn's words cut into Dorena's heart. Zanu was so much bigger than Benjamin. Their entire future lay in the balance. She began praying, asking the all-powerful God to give Benjamin the strength to beat Zanu in the contest.

The heavier bundle was now ready.

Milburn told Benjamin to go first.

Benjamin stepped to the bundle and worked his arms once more, sent a glance toward the one and only woman he would ever love, then spread his feet apart for the lift.

23

DORENA WAS PARALYZED WITH FEAR as Benjamin grasped the bundle and lifted it waist-high. His legs remained perfectly steady as he carried the bales to the wagon, raised them above the level of the bed, and set them down softly.

The slaves seemed hesitant to raise a cheer for Benjamin. Dorena knew why. Zanu had used his size and strength more than once to bully the other slaves.

She breathed a tiny bit easier, then tensed up when Zanu matched Benjamin's lift. She found her fingernails digging into her palms as another bale was added to the bundle, which not only added to its weight but made it more cumbersome.

Both men were given a few minutes to rest, then Laird Milburn told Zanu to go first.

Zanu leered at Benjamin, flexed his muscles once again, and picked up the bundle. This time he staggered beneath the weight and had a hard time controlling it. The crowd looked on apprehensively as he reached the wagon, breathing hard, and strained to lift it high enough to place it on the bed. It only bumped the side of the wagon, and an oooh swept over the crowd.

The veins in Zanu's neck, shoulders, and biceps stood out like ropes as he tried again, straining every muscle in his body. But still he could not clear the wagon's edge. In frustration, he dropped the bundle at his feet.

There was dead silence from the crowd.

Laird Milburn set eyes on Benjamin as two slaves grunted and pulled the bundle back to its starting point.

Zanu stepped close to Benjamin and gave him the evil eye for a full five seconds, then turned away, still puffing from exertion.

Benjamin prepared to make his lift.

Dorena's hands went to her mouth. *Please, God, give him strength in great measure.* Holding her breath, and willing strength into him, she watched as he closed his eyes. She knew he was praying. Then Benjamin took hold of the bundle and hoisted it, and headed for the wagon.

When he reached it, he had the same problem Zanu had experienced. The bundle bumped the side of the wagon but it seemed impossible to get it high enough to place it on the bed.

The crowd was hardly breathing as they waited.

Benjamin's mind went to Dorena. The love he had for her was strong. He could not let Zanu have her. With a prayer in his heart, he reached down inside himself to depths yet untouched and gave an upward jerk.

The bundle landed on the wagon bed with a solid thump.

Dorena's knees went weak and she exhaled her pent-up breath.

Breathing hard, Benjamin turned and gave her a loving, triumphant grin.

A wide smile suddenly graced Dorena's lips and her eyes lit up with love for him.

No one cheered for Benjamin, but the crowd stood in awe. While the defeated Zanu looked on, Milburn took Benjamin and Dorena into a nearby tool shed.

Dorena, who thought she would then be turned over to Benjamin, was shocked when Milburn said, "I'll take the 250 dollars now as earnest money. When you return with the 750, Dorena will be yours."

"Master Laird," said Dorena, "I do not understand."

Milburn explained the agreement between himself and Benjamin.

Batting her eyes, she said, "Benjamin! You are going to pay 1000 dollars for me?"

"Yes," he said, looking at her with eyes of love.

Her lips trembled. "And I love you for it . . . and for winning the contest so you could ransom me. And I praise the Lord for giving you the strength."

Benjamin handed Milburn the 250 dollars.

Milburn nodded. "I'll go to the house and make out a receipt for this. In the meantime, I want you two to have a few minutes together."

When they were alone, they embraced and kissed. While he held her,

Benjamin explained that since he was this close to Texas, he would drive the horse and buggy to the ranch. He was now in partnership with Dan and he was sure Dan would advance him the 750 dollars. He would come back for her as soon as he had the money in hand.

Dorena clung to him and said, "I love you so much! How can I ever thank you for not only winning the contest, but for being willing to pay such a sum for my ransom?"

Benjamin kissed the tip of her nose. "May I remind you of the ransom our Lord Jesus paid for both of us? Dorena, sweetheart, what Jesus did was a ransom of love . . . and in a small way, but just as sincerely, what I am doing now is a ransom of love."

They were sharing another tender kiss when they heard Laird Milburn's footsteps approaching the shed. They broke apart just as he opened the door.

"Here's the receipt, Benjamin," said Milburn, placing it in his hand. "And congratulations on winning her fair and square."

"Thank you, Master Laird," said Dorena, "for allowing Benjamin the opportunity to compete for me."

"You're quite welcome, dear. I know true love when I see it." Then he said to Benjamin, "Time for Dorena to get back to work."

Benjamin allowed Dorena to move outside ahead of them, but Dorena refrained from overstepping her bounds with her owner by stopping in front of the shed and letting them walk ahead of her toward Benjamin's buggy. Benjamin looked over his shoulder and gave her a loving glance and a wave of his hand.

"Hurry back, darling!" she called. "Please hurry back!" A sudden dread seized her and she prayed, "Father, please forgive my doubts and fears. Help me to trust and not be afraid." As always when she prayed, peace settled over her heart.

She watched until the buggy was out of sight, then wiped the tears from her cheeks. With confidence that this time would be different, she made her way toward the house to do the rest of her wash, humming a happy tune.

Benjamin Johnson drove across Louisiana into Texas, sleeping in the buggy at night and purchasing food along the way with the money earmarked for train fare to get him and Dorena to San Antonio.

Dan and Tracie happened to be on the wraparound porch at the front of the house when Dan pointed across the fields. "We've got company, honey."

Tracie squinted to bring the driver of the buggy into focus. "Dan . . . that's Benjamin!"

"Sure enough! But he was supposed to bring Dorena on the train."

"I don't see her. She's not with him, Dan."

When Benjamin stepped out of the buggy, he said, "I have a long story to tell you. First, let me get myself a couple of hugs."

After embracing both Tracie and Dan, Benjamin sat down on the porch and told them about Charles Moore's death, Lewis having sold Dorena, how he had to use 150 dollars of the ransom money to buy the horse and buggy . . . then go from place to place to finally locate her.

He explained what happened at the Milburn plantation with Zanu and the cotton bale contest, and asked Dan if he would advance him the 750 dollars needed to purchase Dorena.

"Now, Dan," Benjamin concluded, "I don't want the 750 dollars as a gift . . . just an advance on money I will earn as your partner."

"I understand," said Dan. "The advance is yours. I'll go into town right now and get the cash from the bank."

"Thank you, Dan. I appreciate it so very much."

"Hey, pal, we're partners. I'm just thrilled to know that after all that hassle you can finally go back and ransom that sweet girl."

"Me too," said Tracie, patting Mutt's head as he sat beside her chair.

"Bless you both," said Benjamin. "Now, I have one problem to solve. I would like to have the wedding at our church. I want you to be my best man, Dan. And I know Dorena will want Miss Tracie to be her matron of honor. But since Dorena and I will be traveling together alone from Louisiana, to be proper we will have to get married in Bogalusa before we leave."

"No you won't," Dan said quickly. "I want that wedding to take place in our church. I'll go with you so I can be the chaperone on the return trip. Then when we get back, you and Dorena can go to Pastor Custer and make arrangements for the wedding."

Benjamin frowned. "But you have your hands full here on the ranch. It would cause problems for you to be gone that long."

Dan shook his head. "The ranch hands can take care of things while I'm gone. I'll get one of the ladies from the church to come and stay with Tracie at night."

"That's fine with me," Tracie said. "You take Dan up on his offer, Benjamin. Let's get that girl here to her new home. It's only right that you get married in the church where you're a member, and she soon will be."

Dan rose from his chair. "You get some rest, my friend, and I'll dash into town and get the cash."

At the Milburn plantation, Dorena worked long hours doing the laundry and working in the fields. She was glad to stay busy, which helped the time to pass more quickly.

Her nights were filled with dreams of Benjamin, and she awakened in the mornings telling herself she was one day closer to his return. She kept her carpetbag under the bed and partially packed, so when he came it would take only minutes to be ready to go.

Eight days after Benjamin left the Milburn plantation, he and Dan turned off the road and headed down the lane toward the mansion. Benjamin was at the reins.

As they neared the mansion, an overseer moved in front of them, holding up his hands for them to stop. His face was not familiar to Benjamin.

The overseer stepped up on Dan's side and said, "What can I do for you, gentlemen?"

"I am Benjamin Johnson," said the man who held the reins. "Do you remember me? I was here several days ago."

"You're not familiar to me," said the overseer, "but I've only been working here a week. Name's Cameron Derks."

Benjamin explained to Derks that he was a free Negro. He introduced Dan, saying they were partners on a cattle ranch near San Antonio. "I have come, Mr. Derks, to close a deal I have with Mr. Milburn. I am purchasing a slave girl named Dorena from him."

Derks's face blanched. "Mr. Johnson," he said, "I'm afraid I have bad news for you."

"What do you mean?"

"Well, just two days before I came to work here, a slave girl named Dorena was killed back there between the barns."

Benjamin's eyes bulged and the veins in his neck stood out. "Wh-what happened?"

"A team of horses had just been hitched up to a wagon. Nobody was in the seat yet when something spooked them. They bolted, and this Dorena was in front of them, crossing from one barn to another. From what I was told, she tried to get out of the way, but both the team and the wagon struck her. She was killed instantly."

Benjamin's heart pounded wildly as if it were trying to tear itself out of his body. *How can this be? Dorena dead? No! No! It can't be!*

A numb Dan Johnson laid a firm hand on Benjamin's shoulder.

"I'm sorry," said Derks. "The day I started to work here, they buried her in the slave cemetery."

"May I see Mr. Milburn?" Benjamin said, his voice breaking.

"I'm afraid not. Mr. and Mrs. Milburn are on an emergency business trip to New Orleans and won't be back for several days."

Benjamin thumbed away the tears that filled his eyes. "Could I see Mack Ottwell then? He knows I was here to purchase Dorena. I . . . I would like to have what possessions were hers."

"Mr. Ottwell isn't here anymore, Mr. Johnson. I am his replacement. He quit his job quite suddenly, I understand, and went elsewhere."

A devastated Benjamin said, "I would like to see her grave, Mr. Derks. Where will I find it?"

"It's at the extreme northeastern corner of the estate. I was out there near it a couple of days ago. There's a small wooden marker at each grave. Dorena's grave will be the freshest one, and the marker will bear her name."

Benjamin released a tremulous sigh and handed Dan the reins, saying he didn't feel like driving.

Dan headed the buggy across the fields in a northeast direction, trying to think of something to say to his best friend. Slaves by the dozens were working in the fields. Some paused in their labor to look at the buggy. Benjamin saw some of them pointing at him.

Soon they were at the cemetery, which was surrounded by oak and cypress trees. As Dan brought the buggy to a halt, Benjamin pointed to the fresh grave with its swollen mound of dirt. It was several yards from the cemetery's edge.

They climbed out of the buggy and Dan laid a hand once more on Benjamin's shoulder.

"I don't know what to say, my friend. This is such a shock. Do you want me to come along, or would you rather be alone?"

"You're my best friend on earth, Dan. I would like you by my side."

As they started into the cemetery together, Benjamin said, "I just don't understand. Why would the Lord take her from me?"

"I can't answer that, but God doesn't make mistakes."

Benjamin could hardly see for the tears that flooded his eyes.

Dan read the markers as they threaded their way toward the new grave. He noted that all the markers bore single names and only gave the age of the person at the time of death.

When they reached the grave, Benjamin wept uncontrollably. While he sobbed, Dan lowered his eyes to the marker. He frowned and said, "Wait a minute, Benjamin. Something's wrong here."

"What do you mean?"

"This girl's name was not Dorena! It's Lorena! And she was fourteen years old!"

Benjamin looked at the marker for a second, then said, "Let's go!"

The two men dashed to the buggy and Benjamin took the reins, putting the horses to a gallop. They raced to the mansion, found Cameron Derks, and told him about the name on the marker. Derks apologized and immediately took them to the head overseer, Wiley Chance, who recognized Benjamin on sight.

Benjamin introduced Dan to the head overseer, then Chance said, "Benjamin, that little gal of yours has been so excited. Just this morning I heard her tell some of the other women that you would be here in another day or two, she was sure."

Benjamin smiled. "She couldn't be any more excited than I am, sir."

"Mr. Milburn left me with instructions. You are to pay me 750 dollars to finish the deal on Dorena. He said to tell you he's sorry he had to be gone when you came back."

"I am too," said Benjamin, taking a small leather pouch from his pocket. "I have the money right here."

"Fine. I'll send one of the slaves to get Dorena. She's working in a field on the west side of the estate."

With the financial transaction done and Dorena's emancipation papers in his pocket, Benjamin stood at the rear of the mansion, gazing westward. As they waited, Wiley Chance gave Dan a detailed description of Benjamin's victory over Zanu in the lifting contest.

Suddenly Benjamin saw his bride-to-be running toward him as fast as she could. Dan and Wiley smiled at each other as they watched Benjamin bolt toward her.

When Dorena ran into his open arms, he picked her up, laughing heartily, and swung her around several times, then planted her feet on the ground and told her the money had been paid. She was his! Dorena swayed, a bit dizzy from being swung in circles, and both of them were giddy with happiness.

"Well," he said, holding her in his arms, "let's go home."

Dorena looked deeply into his eyes. "Darling, is something wrong?"

"What do you mean?"

"Call it woman's intuition, but I see something in your eyes. What is it?"

"Nothing is wrong now, sweetheart. But something happened when we first got here. I'll tell you about it on the way home. Now that you're mine, everything is perfect. Come on. Dan is eager to see you."

Tracie Johnson had been keyed up for the last two days awaiting the imminent arrival of her husband and the happy couple. She had fixed up the cabin where the newlyweds would live and had it ready for them to move in.

She was in the kitchen, baking bread, when she heard the front door of the ranch house open, followed by the sound of Dan's voice. Darting to the front of the house, she set eyes on Dorena and said to Dan, "I'll hug you in a minute." Then she pulled Dorena close and kissed her cheek. "Welcome home, honey."

Dorena was overwhelmed with Tracie's display of kindness and affection. She kissed her cheek in return, saying, "Thank you, Miss Tracie. It really feels like home."

Tracie held her for a long moment, telling her they were going to be good friends, then she went to Dan and embraced him.

Turning back toward Dorena, Tracie said, "I feel like I've known you all of my life. You're not only my sister in the Lord, but we will soon be related in another way. After all, my last name is Johnson, and yours will be shortly!"

Everybody laughed, then Tracie went to the kitchen to take her bread out of the oven. When that was done, Dan and Tracie took Benjamin and

Dorena to the cabin so Dorena could see her new home. She was thrilled with it and thanked Dan and Tracie for how good they were to Benjamin and her.

When they returned to the ranch house, Tracie took Dorena to her room to help her get settled.

Dorena stopped at the open door and ran her gaze over the room. "This is really nice, Miss Tracie; just like you have decorated our new house. Thank you for allowing me to stay here till Benjamin and I get married."

"We're happy to have you, honey. And . . . would you do me a favor?"

"Of course."

"Since we're practically sisters, how about you drop the 'miss' and just call me Tracie?"

Dorena thought of the time Priscilla had told her she could drop the 'miss' when they were alone. Smiling at Dan's wife, she said, "Thank you. From now on, it will be Tracie. This is just all so new and different for me. I was born a slave, and until Benjamin set me free a few days ago, it is all I have ever known."

Tracie looked into Dorena's dark brown eyes and said, "I can't imagine what you've been through, but from now on, you're a free woman. I'm here for you, and as you adjust to your new life, please know that I will help in any way I can."

When Dorena had unpacked her carpetbag and put her things away, Tracie took her back to the parlor, where the men sat talking. They jumped to their feet when the ladies entered, then sat down with them.

Dorena held Benjamin's hand and said, "Darling, you should tell M—ah . . . Tracie about what happened when you and Dan arrived at the Milburn plantation. You know . . . Lorena."

Tracie's eyes were wide as Benjamin told her of the horrible scare when overseer Cameron Derks told him Dorena had been killed.

Tracie shook her head. "I feel bad for that little fourteen-year-old girl, but I'm so glad it wasn't you, Dorena."

After more conversation about their trip, Tracie told the group she needed to get back to her kitchen and start supper. She had a nice meal planned.

During supper that evening, Benjamin and Dorena tried valiantly to stay in the conversation with Dan and Tracie, but from time to time they found they couldn't take their eyes off each other.

Finally, Dan said, "Benjamin, I assume you'll be taking Dorena into town tomorrow to meet Pastor and Mrs. Custer, and to talk to him about setting up the wedding?"

"You assume correctly," said Benjamin, flashing a smile. "Now that my sweetheart is a free woman, I want to marry her in a hurry so she won't be free any more!"

Dorena laughed. "I won't mind at all being enslaved to you, my darling."

Benjamin smiled at her. "There is something I need to tell you."

"Yes?"

"You know, of course, that I was very concerned when your letters stopped coming."

"Mm-hmm."

"Well, not knowing as yet that you had been sold by Lewis Moore, I kept writing to you. In one letter, I told you that you would be my mail order bride, like Miss Tracie is Dan's."

Dorena laughed. "I think that's wonderful!"

The next day, after meeting with Pastor and Mrs. Custer, and setting the wedding date for Saturday, November 14, Benjamin and Dorena went to a jewelry store where they picked out Dorena's wedding ring. After looking at several rings, Dorena picked a plain gold band.

As they walked out of the jewelry store, Dorena said, "All my life I have seen white women wearing wedding rings. But as a slave, I knew I would never have one, even when I got married. Oh, Benjamin, the Lord is so good!"

"That He is," said Benjamin, taking her by the arm to escort her around the end of the hitching rail to board the buggy.

Suddenly, Dorena felt his body stiffen. She looked up to find him staring at two white men who glared at him with naked hatred in their eyes.

"Who are they?" she whispered.

"Jules Crain and his son, Wyatt. They don't like black folk."

People on the street paused to look on as they saw Jules and Wyatt draw up and heard Jules say, "Well, if it isn't Dan Johnson's full-fledged partner! I told him what I thought of that stupid move. It was bad enough, hirin' you as a cowhand, but makin' you his partner! That was more than I could stomach!"

"Yeah, me too!" said Wyatt. "Imagine that! White cowboys on the Circle J takin' orders from a blackie!"

Benjamin felt Dorena's fingernails digging into the sleeve of his light jacket.

Focusing on the older man, Benjamin said softly, "Mr. Crain, I have never done anything to you and your son. Why do you dislike me so?"

"Because you're a blackie, that's why. And it's more like hatred than mere dislike, boy."

"Yeah," said Wyatt. " 'Hatred' is the best word. And that goes for your girlfriend too."

An intense fear spread up Dorena's back and down her arms and tears filmed her eyes.

"I don't hate you," Benjamin said. "I love you in spite of how you feel about us."

Jules laughed. "You what? You *love* us? How could you love somebody who can't stand the sight of you?"

"You are my enemies, right?" Benjamin said.

"We sure are!" said Wyatt.

"Then I love you, because my Lord Jesus Christ tells me in His Word that I am to love my enemies. He loved me when I was His enemy. So by His grace, I can love my enemies. I love both of you."

Father and son were stunned to hear Benjamin's words. As long as he had their attention, he took advantage of it to tell them the story of Calvary, giving them the gospel and quoting 1 Timothy 2:5 and 6 to show them the ransom of love Jesus paid on the cross to deliver them from the bondage of sin and an eternity in hell.

The crowd gathered around the foursome stood spellbound at Benjamin's tenderness toward men who had shown him nothing but hatred.

Wyatt said, "I don't care about this ransom of love, blackie! That's ancient history, and I ain't religious anyway!"

"Me, neither!" said Jules. "Don't give me no 'ransom of love' stuff!"

"But without that ransom, you will face God in your sins when you die," said Benjamin. "You *will* die, you know."

"Shut up!" Jules said. "I don't want to hear about it!"

"The thing for you and your girlfriend to do, boy," Wyatt said, "is to climb in your buggy and get clear out of Bexar County!"

"We have as much right here as you do," Benjamin said softly. "We are free people, just like you are."

Wyatt took a step closer, his face beet red. "But you ain't white like we are, black boy! And let me tell you somethin'. If you don't leave this county, I'll find a way to drive you out!"

"We both will!" warned Jules. "Come on, son. We've got things to do."

Benjamin felt a powerful grip on his arm as the Crains stomped down the street.

As he helped Dorena into the buggy, she said, "What could they do to run us out of the county, Benjamin?"

"Nothing, honey. Don't worry about it. They can't do a thing to run us out."

There was a chill in the late fall air as the beautiful wedding took place on November 14 as planned.

The people of the church had become as attached to Dorena as they were to Benjamin, and almost all the members were in attendance to witness the ceremony.

Benjamin's dark, handsome face was wreathed in smiles as Dorena met him at the altar, with Dan and Tracie flanking them. When Dorena smiled at him, he thought it seemed bright enough to light up the whole building.

They took their vows with hearts full of love and a deep gratitude to the God who had removed all obstacles preventing them from being together. When the ceremony was over, the happy couple stood at the door holding hands as the people passed by, wishing them every happiness.

In the days that followed, both Johnson couples were extremely happy. The only dark cloud on the horizon was the vicious treatment both partners and their wives received from the Jules Crain family and their friends.

In the second week of December, Dorena had prepared breakfast one morning, and the two couples enjoyed the time together in the log cabin.

When the meal was almost over, Dan looked at his partner across the table and said, "Benjamin, I have an appointment in town at nine o'clock this morning. I need you to ride over to the Box D ranch and take a message to Duane Davis for me."

"Sure," said Benjamin.

Dan took a small envelope from his shirt pocket and handed it to his partner. "Just give him this. He's expecting it."

"Will do."

Ten minutes later, Benjamin kissed Dorena good-bye, telling her he would be back in a couple of hours.

After delivering the written message to Duane Davis, Benjamin rode away from the ranch house. He had enjoyed the half hour he spent with the Davises, who had treated him kindly ever since he had come to the Circle J.

Eager to get back to the ranch, Benjamin put the horse to a gallop. Moments later, he was drawing near the Crain ranch. The road led him around a large stand of cottonwoods. As he skirted the trees, he heard gunshots crack the air and echo across the prairie.

Was someone hunting game? On the other side of the trees he saw a man lying in the road. Two riders were racing away as fast as they could go. A riderless horse stood by the fence.

Benjamin pulled rein and skidded to a stop. He slid from the saddle and knelt down to turn the man over.

It was Wyatt Crain!

There were two bloody holes where the bullets had plowed through his coat and hit him in the chest.

Wyatt opened his eyes, gritting his teeth in pain. When he focused on Benjamin, he swallowed hard and said in a strained voice, "I'm . . . hit bad, Benjamin."

"I can see that. I will put you on my horse and take you to the doctor in town."

"Y-you will?"

"Yes. Neither slug looks to be near your heart. Who were those men who shot you?"

Wyatt closed his eyes and licked his lips. "Enemies."

"What kind of enemies?"

"Just . . . enemies."

"Black enemies? Somebody else you have told to get out of the county?"

Wyatt's silence was enough. Benjamin had thought the riders were possibly black when he saw them riding away. Running his hands under the wounded man's body, he said, "All right, Wyatt, let's get you to the doctor."

MAIL ORDER BRIDE SERIES
NO. 5
1855
USA
AL & DANN LACY

24

IT WAS AN HOUR PAST NOON—more than time enough for Benjamin to return from his errand at Duane Davis's ranch.

While Dorena sat at the kitchen table, wringing her hands, Tracie squeezed her shoulder and said, "Honey, Benjamin probably just got to talking to Duane and lost track of the time. Duane is a very friendly person, and I know he likes Benjamin."

"But Benjamin would know being this late would worry me," said Dorena. "He told me he would be back in a couple of hours. It has been almost five hours. I'm afraid something is wrong. You know what those Crain men said they would do. Maybe they decided to kill my husband to get him out of the county for good."

"Now, sweetie, you mustn't think the worst."

"How can I help it? I live in constant dread whenever Benjamin leaves the ranch. Back on the plantation there was protection for Negroes. But here in the West, there is no one to protect us. I thought everyone was free no matter what color of skin they had. I just wasn't prepared for the prejudice we've been shown by white people. On the plantation I felt secure, knowing that Master Charles would keep us safe. Out here, there is no master to protect us."

"Sweetie," said Tracie, "let me help you with that. You say you have no master here to protect you. Listen to me. You are God's child, aren't you?"

"Yes."

"Then you have the Master of the universe to protect you. And so does Benjamin, who is also His child. No man on earth can give you the protection and care that your own Lord and Master can. No harm can ever come to a Christian without first getting past the Master. If it gets past Him, then it is His will, and it is right."

Dorena's eyes grew large as the wisdom of Tracie's words penetrated her heart and mind. "Oh, Tracie," she said in a tear-clogged voice, "how could I have such little faith? I've let the fear of the Crains and their friends cloud my mind, when all the time my Master was wanting me to trust His care and protection."

"That's right," said Tracie. "Years ago I memorized Psalm 118:6, and it has been so precious to me. 'The LORD is on my side; I will not fear: what can man do unto me?' The Crains and their friends are only men, honey. You need not fear them."

"Oh, thank you, Tracie, for giving me that verse. I must ask my only Lord and Master to increase my faith and help me to trust both Benjamin and myself to His care."

The sound of a horse trotting into the yard met their ears. The women hurried through the house and moved out onto the front porch.

Dan saw them and guided his horse toward them. He brought the horse to a stop and swung from the saddle. "Sorry I didn't make it back for lunch, honey."

"You didn't miss a thing," Tracie said. "We haven't had lunch. We've been preoccupied with the fact that Benjamin hasn't returned from the Box D yet."

Lines creased Dan's brow. "That's strange. He should've been back a couple of hours ago."

"So we've been discussing. Dorena's been worried that the Crains might have done something to him."

Dan's features lost color. "I'm going over to the Davis place right now and see if Benjamin got there this morning."

Just as Dan put his foot in the stirrup, Dorena's attention was drawn to two riders who had emerged from the forest of cottonwoods. "Look!" she said. "One of them is Benjamin!"

Dan and Tracie swung their eyes that way, and as Dorena lifted her skirt ankle-high and bounded off the porch, Dan said, "The other one is Jules Crain!"

Dan and Tracie joined hands and ran after her.

Benjamin urged the horse forward, then slipped from the saddle and wrapped Dorena in his arms. Crain drew rein and stopped beside Benjamin's horse.

"Oh, darling," Dorena babbled through tears of relief, "I've been so worried!"

"It's all right, sweetheart. I'm home safe and sound. Everything is all right."

With an arm around Dorena's shoulders, Benjamin said, "Could we sit down and talk? I want to explain what happened."

With a sheepish look on his face, Jules said to Benjamin, "Would it be all right if I tell the story?"

Benjamin nodded, and Dan said, "Let's go inside."

When they were seated in the parlor, Jules told them about Benjamin riding toward home from the Box D ranch and finding Wyatt lying on the ground with two bullets in his chest. He choked up and blinked at the tears filling his eyes as he told how Benjamin had picked Wyatt up and taken him into town to Dr. James Madson.

"Doc says Wyatt will live. Neither bullet was near his heart. One lung was punctured, and the other slug was high enough to miss the lung, though it did damage the clavicle on his right side. Wyatt will be several months recovering, but he will live!"

"We're glad for that," Dan said.

Jules sleeved tears from his cheeks. "I couldn't have blamed Benjamin at all if he had just ridden away and let Wyatt bleed to death. Not after the way we've treated him and his dear wife here."

Benjamin squeezed Dorena's hand and sent a glance to Dan and Tracie.

"Benjamin," Jules said, "if it hadn't been for you, my son would be dead now. You have shown me what you're really made of."

Benjamin nodded and smiled.

"Do you know who shot him?" Dan asked.

"Yes," Jules said. "Two black men from the Bar-X ranch. Wyatt told me who they were before he went into surgery. But I'm not gonna press charges. Wyatt and I had threatened to run them out of the county, just like we did Benjamin and Dorena. We were the ones who were wrong, Dan, but it took Benjamin's kindness and compassion to show us that."

He looked at the black couple and said, "Benjamin, Dorena, I am asking you to forgive me for the way I've treated you and for the threats I made."

"You are forgiven, Mr. Crain," said Benjamin.

"Yes," said Dorena.

Jules's lips quivered as he nodded his head to them. Then he set his tear-filled gaze on Dan and Tracie. "I am asking you to forgive me, too, for making it so hard on you for hiring Benjamin and then making him your partner."

When they both told him he was forgiven, Jules said, "I'm gonna go to all of my friends whom I've influenced against you and tell them how wrong my family and I have been. They won't be lookin' at you with scorn anymore."

The next words that came from Jules Crain's mouth made them even happier.

"Benjamin, that day on the street when Wyatt and I were givin' you and Dorena such a hard time, you warned us about dyin' and facin' God in our sins."

Benjamin nodded.

"Well, I haven't been able to get it out of my mind. You told us about the ransom of love that Jesus Christ paid on the cross to deliver us from the bondage of sin and an eternity in hell."

Benjamin's heart was swelling up inside him as he nodded again.

"I would like to know more about this ransom of love."